COME, FOLLOW ME

'I Have Walked through the Ages . . .

'I am immortal, time itself. I was in the darkness when the first man-creatures squatted around their fires. I watched the pyramids rise and the Temple of Jerusalem destroyed. I drifted on the wind of the Black Death in Europe and watched as the crematoria consumed the children of Abraham . . .

'As long as people will do evil to exist and perpetuate themselves, I shall live.'

He snatched up the violin, placed it under his chin and suddenly his fingers danced over the strings. The children stirred. He played a little more, and one by one the children sat up, zombies.

'They are hungry, Sheridan, from their sleep,' he crooned. 'They want to feed. Shall I give you to them?' The laughter was inhuman. 'Yes, I believe I shall!'

And as he played, the children got off the cots . . .

Come, Follow Me

Philip Michaels

CORONET BOOKS
Hodder and Stoughton

Copyright © 1983 by Isis Literary Productions

First published in the United States of America 1983 by
Avon Books

Coronet edition 1984

British Library C.I.P.

Michaels, Philip
    Come, follow me.
    I. Title
    823'.914[F]   PR6063.I/

    ISBN 0–340–36380–0

Printed and bound in Great Britain for
Hodder and Stoughton Paperbacks, a
division of Hodder and Stoughton Ltd.,
Mill Road, Dunton Green, Sevenoaks,
Kent (Editorial Office: 47 Bedford
Square, London, WC1 3DP) by
Richard Clay (The Chaucer Press) Ltd,
Bungay, Suffolk

ACKNOWLEDGMENTS

The author wishes to thank the following people, who gave generously of their time and professional expertise in assisting him with specific details found in this book:

Staff Inspector William Kerr, Information Services, Toronto Metropolitan Police Department
Allan Hirsh, MA, psychologist
David Ryan, PhD, psychologist, and Sherida Ryan, occupational therapist, neurology
Paul Zurin, composer and musician

Part I

Prologue

On Tuesday the 22nd of July in the year 1376 the town of Hamelin in the province of Brunswick, Germany, celebrated the feast day of Saint Simon. The revelries had begun at dusk and continued throughout the night. As the first glimmer of dawn shimmered across the waters of the river Weser a weary and sated silence lay upon the town.

In his small dwelling on Sirens' Hill the scholar Gotha came away from the windows overlooking the river. He moved through the room replenishing the oil lamps that had burned during the night and filled the ornate brass urns with incense. To those who could not smell, the tranquillity of the morning was complete. Such a person could imagine the delicate odor of hyacinth and cornflower coursing through the air, feel the sharp tang of the mulberry bush and the ripening apple groves. Gotha harbored no such illusion. Even though his oil and incense had smoldered all night, the stench of cold roasted meats, wine turned rancid, and human excrement pervaded the air he breathed. The feast of Saint Simon, celebrated with honeyed venison, sweetcakes, fruits, and drink, had become cold and sour like dragon's breath. No sooner had he opened his door than he flinched and drew a wet handkerchief laden with spices over his nose and mouth.

Gotha could have endured it if this were all. But it was not all. Over the remnants of the feasting was another, horribly repugnant odor: that of the infestation. As Gotha walked down the hill into the dry, mud-caked street in this hamlet of four hundred souls he wondered if Hamelin would ever truly rid itself of the plague's stench. On either side of the narrow lane he saw the source: whole carcasses, maggot-ridden and green, still showing evidence of a vicious gnawing, waiting to be buried; cheeses with their centers bored through; heaps of baked loaves, dry and hard like bricks, half eaten, long dark hairs clinging to the crusts.

The rats . . . Gotha remembered they had first erupted upon the town almost six months ago to the day. He had noted the exact time in his journal. They had invaded the town by night, a silent carnivorous army that had waited until all were asleep before launching its assault. No one knew where they had come from. Yet by morning they had laid seige to Hamelin.

Gotha had heard of similar infestations in other communities to the north and west, but what overtook his town was beyond comprehension, even imagination. The rats were monsters, the largest the size of cats. Bold and cunning, they struck the granaries first, contaminating the wheat. While a frightened citizenry took up spikes, hoes, and axes the rats made for the animal pens, aiming at lambs and calves, flinging themselves upon the milk cows, burying their teeth in pigs' necks. Their poison spread quickly, and the animals died one after another. People who roasted such flesh, believing fire cured all evil, fell sick and also perished.

Having weakened the town, the rats struck. In time it was not safe to walk the street for fear of gray-black shadows that would leap out and tear at one's legs. Even by day the scraping of claws could be heard on wooden staircases. The rats invited themselves into the homes and dwelt side by side with the people. By the end of the second month it wasn't unusual to hear the scream of an infant whose mother had turned her back only to look over and discover a rat feeding in the cradle.

As Gotha passed the church he recalled the fervent Masses the priest had led. The holy man had begged God to end the pestilence with fire. When the Lord appeared not to have heard him, he extolled the faithful to confession so that their sins might be cleansed and this punishment ended. The priest had not survived the sickness that visited itself from one door to the next. Even his church proved no sanctuary as the vermin invaded it, teeming

4

across the sacristy, whittling away the wooden crucifixes, polluting the Communion wine, contaminating the Host.

Gotha walked across the cobblestone square where the ghost of yesterday's fire still weaved in the air. In the orgy of celebration the townspeople had created a mammoth inferno, feeding it with anything they believed to be contaminated. Straw-filled mattresses, linens, clothing, even furniture that had suffered claw marks were all consigned to the flames. The few remaining dogs pawed through the warm ashes at the edge of the charred ruins, jumping back when their noses touched ember.

Gotha ducked under the archway leading to the council room. It would be here, not at their homes, that he would find the mayor and the six members of the corporation which ruled Hamelin.

The scene was much as he expected. The mayor, a grossly pitiful figure, was stretched out on a couch, one leg sprawled across the floor, his belly heaving as snores erupted. The rest of the corporation was scattered about the council room, most of them curled on the floor with woolen blankets over their shuddering bodies. One lay on the banquet table, bile crusted on his mouth and chin. Another was dozing on the mayoral throne.

The scene disgusted Gotha, yet he asked himself why these men should appear or behave any differently than those over whom they ruled. At this hour Hamelin, which should have stirred with morning life, lay silent, because in each house, each room the sight Gotha beheld here was repeated. It reflected the ecstasy of relief, the venting of a terrible joy because the infestation had been destroyed.

All the same Gotha remained uneasy. He had carefully scrutinized the reasons for his misgiving, but its cause defied even his prodigious intellect. After all, had he not been present in this very room when a mob of townspeople had broken in and demanded that the mayor, upon pain of death, do *something* to rid Hamelin of its plague? Had he not spent long hours studying the accounts of other infestations that had come upon the territory of Brunswick in a futile attempt to solve the riddle of this one? And had he not been present when, in the last desperate hours before the townspeople returned to extract their vengeance, the

5

mayor had introduced a beguiling stranger to the corporation, feverishly promising deliverance?

This was what Gotha knew for certain: It was the stranger who troubled him.

He was an unusual creature, this man, tall but very thin, almost skeletal. Ragtag clothing, a patchwork of gaily colored fabrics, hung on his frame as it would on a scarecrow. The face was lean, the nose long and sharp, the lips thin and twisted into an ever present smile that could not help but be a leer. Under a thick patch of long, oily black hair, lice-infested, were arched eyebrows, hooded agate eyes.

The stranger did not speak but deferred to the mayor, who extolled his virtues. From the official's stream of babble Gotha discerned that the stranger had already rid other communities of similar infestations. But how or why he had come to Hamelin was never mentioned. When presented with their savior the townspeople jeered at this pitiful jester and laughed when he told them, in a shallow, solemn voice, that by dusk Hamelin would have no more rats.

"It was the strangest sight I had ever witnessed," Gotha had written in his journal later that night. "The Piper, for that was the only name by which he called himself, abruptly descended the staircase from the council room, pushing his way through the ridiculing throngs into the street. From under one arm he brought out a long flute, the measure of a man's arm, delicately cupped at one end. Without further ado he raised the instrument to his lips. . . ."

Never before had Gotha heard such music. Sweetly cloying yet at the same time pernicious, it wended its way above the square. Instantly the laughter ceased. People drew back into their doorways, recoiling on some base, primeval instinct.

But not so the rats. The silence of the town was shattered by their squealing as they tumbled out of the houses. Within minutes the earth of the street had disappeared, replaced by a swarming brown mass that heaved of its own accord, bodies churning over bodies, a trail of slippery blood being left behind.

6

At their head walked the Piper, his eyes lightly closed, the flute held high as though his song was addressed to the heavens. He must have been aware of the horror rolling behind him but paid no heed, not until he had reached the bank of the Weser. Only then did he turn around and, standing to one side, move his flute in a half-circle motion, his head and arms rocking in time with the instrument, coaxing the vermin from the water's edge into the current. The squealing rose to a whinelike pitch as the drowning began.

Gotha tried to reach the Piper, but by the time the last of the rats was gone, so was the Piper. Dumbfounded, the scholar ran back to the town to seek out the mayor, but in the square the celebrations were already under way. Gotha succeeded in finding one of the corporation members, who, while he knew nothing of the Piper (no one did), took him to the council room and showed him the Piper's reward: half of all Hamelin's gold, set in a silver chalice. That was the price agreed upon. The townspeople would have given triple that, given anything, the man said, to have the plague destroyed. He exulted over the bargain but fell silent when Gotha looked at him and said: "You are lying."

That was why the scholar was here this morning, to discover what lay beneath the lie.

The mayor was a man of gross habits, given to lechery, drink, and violence. Yet seldom if ever was he not cognizant of what was happening around him. No matter how much he imbibed, his sense of suspicion and survival remained unaffected. It was this sense which now roused him and made him open his eyes to see Gotha. For a moment he did not move, his ears straining to listen for any activity. There was none. Last night he had distributed untainted foodstuffs from his own vaults and barrels of wine from his cellars. He had watched as his townspeople gorged themselves. Only when he was satisfied that they would not wake until late the next morning did he partake. God alone knew that he needed the wine more than any other man present, not to enjoy but as a narcotic so that he would not have to remember what seemed impossible to forget. He knew too that if anyone stirred early the following morning, it would be Gotha. He was prepared.

Grunting, the mayor heaved himself to his feet and, leaning on the table for support, plodded to where Gotha stood.

"You are up with the sun, scholar," the mayor rasped. He coughed and spat the phlegm out the window.

"Have you paid the Piper yet?" Gotha asked. "Has he departed?"

"To be sure." The mayor stretched and yawned. "He was paid last night."

Without comment Gotha went over to the far wall and tapped lightly on the timber beam. A false panel dropped. The scholar was not surprised by what it revealed.

"What did you pay him with?" Gotha demanded, turning, his back to the silver chalice laden with gold coin. "This should have been his, or so I was told. Tell me, Worship, did you cheat the creature, or are you waiting to do so? Perhaps murder him and keep the booty for yourself."

The mayor did not look back at his accuser. He remained at the window staring out into the square.

"Neither," he said at last.

The answer angered Gotha, and he strode over to the mayor.

"In God's name, who is he? Where did you find him, and what unholy power has he at his command?"

The mayor passed his hands over his face as though trying to cleanse himself.

"Does it matter?" he asked wearily, more of himself than of Gotha. "Look out there. Listen. What do you see, hear?" He paused, then: "Nothing. Utter, blessed silence. How long has it been, Gotha, since you had heard no infant's scream, no mother's wail, no death rattle from the mouths of our elders? The terror is finished. The vermin are gone. We can begin to build again, to live like humans and not some animals always on guard for the pair of red eyes, the click of claws. . . ." The mayor thrust his arm out the window. "They are sleeping, Gotha! For the first time in months they are sleeping without fear, without nightmare. Do you think they *care* with what or how much the Piper was paid?"

8

Gotha was puzzled by the last words. There was a sorrow to them, a strange, deep regret for something that had been done and now could never be undone.

"What did you pay?" he asked once again.

Before the mayor could answer, if he was ever to answer, Gotha heard the music, that odd lilting melody coming from deep within the town. It was at once merry and sad, enticing and fearful. The scholar leaned out the window and peered across the square. Because the sun was shining almost directly into his eyes, he could only discern the gently rocking flute and a pair of legs clad in tattered dyed skins. Behind the music he heard the delicious laughter of children.

"No!" Gotha whispered. "No . . ."

He whirled around, but the mayor's back was to him, head bowed.

Chapter One

Puerto Plata, the Dominican Republic, present day

Thane Sheridan was awake even before his eyelids snapped open. The sunlight in his dream gave way to that which was filtering through the bamboo curtains. The sound of the flute and childrens' laughter dissolved into the raucous backfire of a small car and the faint buzz of a power mower somewhere on the seventeenth green. Cautiously he began pulling himself away from the town of Hamelin in the year 1376, focusing all his senses on the present.

The bedroom was swathed in a woman's scent. In one corner, strewn across a rattan chair, were his clothes. Directly before the bed was the vanity with its triple mirrors, the two on either side angled slightly. In the right-hand reflection Sheridan saw his bathing suit hanging side by side with Gwen's bikini. His peripheral vision recorded the bulbous ceramic lamp on the night table. By its base rested his diver's Eagle Star watch and his glasses, specially tinted to adjust to sunlight intensity. The time was five thirty-seven, February 2. A slow shudder passed through Sheridan's body as tensed muscles quivered, relaxed. The motion caused the woman beside him to stir. Gwen rolled over, her long sun- and sea-bleached blond hair cascading across his shoulder. Sheridan gently brushed the strands away from her face, pressing his lips to her cheek. Still asleep, Gwen smiled and returned the kiss before snuggling back into the pillow. Sheridan waited another minute to make certain she was asleep and then, in one motion, cantilevered himself out of the bed.

The tiles felt cool to the soles of his feet. There was a slight breeze moving through the room, raising the hairs on his forearms. Sheridan looped the belt of his terry cloth robe and, closing the bedroom door, descended the circular staircase to the bungalow's living room.

Dory and Bill McBride looked up as Sheridan came toward them. Without a word Bill went into the kitchen for another cup. Dory McBride fixed a faltering smile on Sheridan.

He dreamed again, she thought. *God help him, but the dreams have come back. He's trying to hide them, but they're forcing their way out.*

Yet to look at Sheridan she would have thought nothing was amiss. He was not a tall man, five ten, with a strong, heavy build, equally proportioned between wide shoulders and a well developed chest, and thick muscular thighs and calves. The sandy brown hair was thinning rapidly at the temples. The nose with its prominent nostrils descended toward a soft mustache, which in turn tapered along the edges of his mouth to a short curly beard. The eyes were widely spaced, their soft hazel color conveying the impression that he was a sensitive man. Yet he could not be called handsome except perhaps in profile. Arresting, disturbing, a man one remembered. He wasn't vulnerable as handsome men were. As he brushed past, not breaking stride to kiss her on the forehead, Dory smelled cold sweat mingled with Gwen's jasmine perfume.

When Sheridan emerged from the bathroom, coffee was waiting for him on a table beside his favorite chair, an old heavy wing chair with faded floral print.

"So much for sleep," Bill McBride said, stretching back into the sofa, one arm thrown behind Dory. "I'd say good morning but . . ."

Thane Sheridan said nothing. He drank a tall glass of juice, then took his first sip of coffee. It was not unusual for the McBrides to be up at this hour: Bill was generally at the embassy by half past six to go through the overnight reports and cables. Dory, a tours operator representative, liked to be at the resort as the first golfers trudged off to the links.

"What say, amigo?" Bill queried.

"Can you get me the overnight East Coast papers?"

McBride noticed his friend gently massaging his right wrist with his thumb. Five years ago a killer who had taken down three out-of-town families in San Francisco had gone for Sheridan. The Exacto knife, modified to hold a six-inch retractable blade, had sliced Sheridan's median and ulnar nerves, severing the minor artery, moving cleanly through the tendon. Six hours of microsurgery and two years of therapy had given back Sheridan 90 percent of the use of his hand. But the habit of kneading the scar when he was tense remained.

"I can get you the papers," McBride said. He kept his voice light but knew all the same where Sheridan was headed. "Which ones do you want?"

"Boston, New York . . . and Philadelphia."

Chicago was the last place the Rambler had visited. Sheridan had gotten close to him there. The scent had been very strong. Unless he backtracked, it seemed likely the Rambler would keep on moving east. It was part of the pattern.

"Why, Thane?" Dory asked sharply. A thin film of hysteria coated her words. "Why do you want the papers?"

"Because I can feel him," he said almost inaudibly, as though he were speaking to himself and not to her. "He's surfacing. He's coming out again."

Sheridan replaced the lighter on the coffee table and sat back in the chair, his gaze fixed on the geometric design of the coffee cup. He realized Dory couldn't understand what he meant. How did you explain the intangible yet undeniably real bond that grew between the hunter and the quarry? How could you tell someone that after having lived so long with a man who still had no face, no name, you felt as though you knew him as intimately as you did a lover, able to predict his movements, his reactions, even glimpse his thought processes? Except that you could do all this not out of love but out of unfathomable hate—and fear.

Dory McBride disregarded her husband's warning squeeze on her forearm.

"He's not back, Thane!" she cried. "There hasn't been a report of . . . of anything like he's done for over three

13

months! The dreams aren't premonitions. It's just your subconscious working out what you've put yourself through. For God's sake, Thane, please, let it alone."

Sheridan's gaze softened. Dory had been Anne's best friend. She had come out and stayed with him after the funeral. She knew all about the dreams, had seen their ferocity firsthand when they had threatened to sweep him into their madness. But what she did not understand, what had taken Sheridan two painful years to recognize was that the dreams were his stepping stones. Through them he had followed the Rambler. They would cease only when the hunt was finished.

He looked past Dory to McBride. "I want to send a flyer to the Bureau in Washington. I could be wrong about the East Coast. The scanners should send *anything* resembling the Rambler's work in the next pouch . . ."

His voice trailed off, and he turned to Dory.

"I'm sorry. I can't tell you how good it's been here. With you and Bill . . . and Gwen."

"Then don't end it," Dory said fiercely. "You promised us a month. It's only been a couple of weeks. If nothing else, you owe it to *yourself.*"

She was right. After Chicago he had been a wreck. For three weeks he had tracked the Rambler, moving from abduction to abduction, desperately searching for that one clue he could use as a springboard which would vault him over his quarry, put him in a position from which he could watch the Rambler approach instead of always having to follow. But time had run out on him. The Rambler took down his quota, and the children stopped disappearing. Sheridan knew as much when a taxi driver delivered a cassette recording to his office. By then he had become familiar with the horrible rasping voice that spoke to him, gloating over victory, all too aware of the rage that was building within the heart of the listener.

An hour later, following the instructions on the tape, Sheridan found the children. They were dead, as he knew they would be. Drowned, as he had expected. And then Sheridan cracked. Chicago was the sixth city the Rambler had visited. Sheridan had believed, really believed, that he would take the killer there. Thirty children had paid with their lives so that he could reach out and touch the Rambler. Now six more had perished, and he had missed him again.

So close . . . another few days, one more move by the Rambler toward the trap Sheridan had set. That's all it would have taken. But it was the Rambler who was one step ahead, not he. Sheridan played and replayed that cassette until he had memorized the words—so that he could flay himself with them, punish himself for his failure. Finally, at the end of a two-day drunk, he took a flight out of O'Hare for Santo Domingo, running from the frustration and rage, running from his own fears. . . .

"We'd rather you stayed, Thane," McBride said, breaking Sheridan's reverie. "You're not ready to go back, not yet."

That was the truth. Even Sheridan could admit as much. Bill and Dory's friendship was the best balm he could have asked for. The sun, clear waters, and the McBrides' Dominican friends were an unexpected bonus. As was Gwen, who had been staying with them when he arrived. . . .

"I know I'm not ready," Sheridan said. "But it's not up to me. It never is. When I finish with him, I can change that. I want so badly to change that, believe me."

A miniature lizard darted across the balcony railing. Beyond, above the carefully manicured and continuously watered lawns, snow-white gulls hovered, then swung down for a graceful landing, long beaks picking even before the webbed feet touched ground. The laughter of day-shift workers coming in on open trucks and ancient Blue Bird buses rose over the morning.

"I better warm up the chopper," McBride said.

As Santo Domingo, CIA station chief, McBride ferried between the capital and Puerto Plata, some two hundred kilometers to the south, twice each day. Those who didn't know, believed McBride played on his rank to use the Ranger III as an expensive convenience. But in fact every time he flew, even at night, McBride patrolled a wide area of mountain and jungle that lay between Puerto Plata and Haiti to the west. There were three hundred thousand Haitians cutting sugar cane in the Dominican Republic. Each one had a machete. In the west the regime of Baby Doc

15

Duvalier was making invasion threats under the guise of socialist rhetoric. McBride's machine was equipped with concealed machine guns and the latest in Langley photo equipment.

"Give me ten minutes," Sheridan said.

"What should I tell Gwen?" Dory asked him.

What should you tell her? That a former CIA Vietnam vet, a former chief inspector of San Francisco Homicide, a former father and husband has once more become the tracker, the hunter?

Sheridan said absently, "Tell her I'll take the hotel shuttle back. We'll be out on the reef by noon."

Chapter Two

Monday, the 6th of February, had been drecky for Edna Rosenberg. So when a small panel truck suddenly backed out into the Eighth Avenue traffic, leaving an empty parking space, she considered it a small deliverance. This minuscule action disappeared into the stark horror of the events that followed. Edna Rosenberg scarcely remembered the incident. It never came up in her questioning by the police. The few seconds were nothing more than a fragmentary explosion of aurora borealis over the eternal Arctic night. . . .

Edna Rosenberg maneuvered her K-car station wagon into the opening. She felt the front wheels bump against the curb, shifted into park, pressed on the accelerator as her husband had so often instructed her to do, and immediately shut off the engine. She sat back, listening to the rain drumming on the roof, cascading across the windshield.

"Gott in himmel, I'm already *in yennervelt!"*

That morning Sol Stein—*Doctor* Stein, excuse me—had called to say that her husband Abraham's varicose veins would have to be stripped. Two weeks off his feet. What does a butcher do who can't walk? Next the travel agent had very nicely informed her that the trip to Israel would be an extra three hundred dollars. Passover, you know. The shopping had tired her, the people upstairs were late with the rent again, the bank had called about a check. . . . The drive from Brooklyn to Steuben Town in Lower Manhattan had unnerved her. The return trip in the rain and dark seemed threatening. Edna Rosenberg sighed. Still there had been no choice. Rachel was waiting.

The image of her daughter brought a smile to the creased, worn features of Edna Rosenberg. She had had Rachel late in life, after several miscarriages and a difficult labor. The birth had been a triumph. It completed her, gave her existence magic and delight. She would have been perfectly satisfied if Rachel had developed into an ordinary child. But to have discovered that she was the mother of a child prodigy, a little girl of ten whose hands and fingers were magic with the violin, this was truly a windfall.

That was why Edna Rosenberg had driven into Steuben Town this evening. Sparing no effort, she had made sure that Rachel had the very best teachers, those who taught in the building directly ahead of her. The New School of Drama and Music. Usually Abraham picked up their daughter after his shift at Zabar's. But all last week Rachel had been staying late, taking extra classes to prepare for a special course. Edna could scarcely believe it: Her daughter had been chosen to play for, be tutored by the great Leopold Ulric!

"All this too shall pass. . . ." Edna Rosenberg stated firmly, speaking to the foul weather. When she got out of the car, she seemed to care less about the deluge, carefully locking the door and walking, not running, toward the front steps of the school.

Four stories above Eighth Avenue, from one of the half dozen dormer windows, a man was watching Edna Rosenberg mount the steps. When she disappeared from sight, he moved away from the window toward the partially open door of the music room. The sound of a slamming door traveled up the eight staircases. The man smiled. He remembered passing the building cornerstone on his way in. The date chiseled into the now weathered granite was 1923. Constructed of solid red brick, the edifice had originally been designed as a private boys' school. During the Depression it had served as a soup kitchen-infirmary. For almost thirty years after the war its high-ceilinged classrooms and long narrow corridors once again rang with the noise of children. When the Ryerson Memorial had been constructed on the East Side, the children had moved away. For five years, until the creation of the New School

18

of Drama and Music, the building had stood empty. The man, who had taken pains to learn the history of the building, was very glad to hear the sound of children. It was as though the building absorbed some of their youth and came back to life once more. Yes, he was very glad to hear the sound of children.

The man pictured Edna Rosenberg downstairs. She came here often, so she wouldn't be waiting in the antechamber, beneath the vaulted ceiling with its large and unbearably ugly cut-glass chandelier. The chandelier offended him. Its design lacked grace, an ethereal quality he believed essential to light. It would have given him great satisfaction to wrench it from its ceiling mooring and watch it disintegrate on the weathered hardwood floor.

But Edna Rosenberg would not be under it. She would pause in the antechamber just long enough to remove her raincoat, give it a few judicious shakes over the runner carpet, and put it back on before entering the lobby. In the large rectangular room, with its fading oak panels and dormant fireplace, she would take a seat in any of the dozen armchairs. Perhaps she would peruse the magazine selection on the sideboard. Either way, her behavior would be calm and patient, reflecting her certainty that at seven o'clock, three minutes from now, her daughter would be putting away her violin and preparing to come downstairs.

Good, let her believe that.

The man left the music room, using the back staircase. As he passed the third floor he heard the final strains of Mendelssohn's Violin Concerto. Rachel Rosenberg was very, very good. She and her contribution would be missed.

The second floor, used exclusively by drama students, was silent. Classes had finished at five. No extra sessions had been scheduled. The dance arena and stage on the ground floor were also deserted. Counting himself, Mrs. Rosenberg, her daughter, and the instructor, there were only four people in the building. Seeing the ease with which Mrs. Rosenberg entered the New School of Drama and Music, one might have thought the school open, its entries vulnerable. That was not the case. Over each of the four doors, including the twin emergency exits, cameras were mounted. The photos of both parents of each student

19

were on record. If there was no guard in the lobby, none of the electronically operated doors would open until security had visually confirmed the caller's identity. There had been cases where brothers or sisters, relatives or close friends had been denied entry because visual identity could not be confirmed. The parents had never protested. On the contrary they had telephoned apologies to the principal the following morning. Although the New School of Drama and Music was an open school, accepting students on the basis of talent and merit rather than background, over half of the four hundred students came from well-to-do families. In addition the school's reputation for excellence drew a number of offspring whose parents were on diplomatic assignment in New York. The customized security arrangements had been provided by such people, to whom caution and precaution were a way of life.

The man walked through the corridors bordering the dance arena, making his way from the west side of the building along the south wall and slipping into the instructors' lounge adjacent to the reception area. There were cameras in the central corridor, to the left of the chandelier, but they could not see into the recessed area of the lobby, by the front windows, where Edna Rosenberg sat.

The music stopped, the ensuing silence abrupt, unnatural. The man checked his watch. By one minute past seven Rachel Rosenberg would have cleared her music stand and neatly tucked the sheets into the space at the bottom of her violin case. She would slide the bow between the leather straps on the upper side of the case. The violin itself, an expensive Fernac, would be placed in the plush green felt cradle and the case locked.

The man soundlessly opened the door between the lounge and the lobby. Two floors above, Rachel was talking to her instructor, who was reassuring her about their choice of a presentation piece for Leopold Ulric. The girl would have much preferred one of the more soulful Vaughan Williams melodies. The instructor was tugging on his heavy leather trench coat, gently leading his pupil. He allowed her to pass through the door first, then reached back and turned out the lights. A faint echo, a violin case

20

bumping against the banister pursued by girlish laughter, traveled down the flight of stairs.

Edna Rosenberg looked up, her expression one of anticipation as she strained to hear more. That motion brought her forward in the chair, about three inches from the worn headrest. She was listening for the wrong sound. She never heard the man come up at all, not even after he had stepped off the carpet and onto the bare floorboards. She only felt the fingers around her throat.

The man could have killed Edna Rosenberg in seconds. He was strong enough to snap her neck in a vicious cross motion or smash her Adam's apple against the back of her throat. Instead he completely encircled her neck with the wide fingers of both hands. If he had missed the central nerve behind her left ear, Edna Rosenberg would have had time to struggle, thrash, perhaps beat the heels of her shoes against the floor. Instead she collapsed, head lolling to one side.

Quickly the man came around and grasped her under the arms. He dragged the inert form past the coffee table to a wing chair that faced the front windows, obscured by heavy beige curtains. He propped her up and bent both knees so that the boot-encased shoes were parallel and firmly on the ground. He stationed himself beside her, his back to the antechamber, taking care not to obscure her legs and the hem of her coat. He wanted the child to recognize these.

The instructor was saying good-bye, hurrying to the front door. The man knew that the instructor's girl friend was waiting for him at the Chunking Restaurant two blocks north on Eighth Avenue. The instructor's rudeness served him well that evening. If he had had the courtesy to come over to Mrs. Rosenberg, he would have had to die. And still the child would have been his.

Rachel Rosenberg was walking quickly over the carpet, skipping across the threadbare floral pattern. The man heard none of what she said, not the greeting to her mother, not the question directed to him. He waited until he felt her directly behind him and then brought his hand out from his coat pocket. Rachel Rosenberg's face disappeared into a blurry hydrocarbon cloud of chloroform gas as the man whirled around while simultaneously bending to be at her level. The cannister was slipped back into the pocket, and his other arm encircled the girl, pressing both her and the violin case that was slipping out of lifeless fingers against his chest. When he was sure of his grip, the man removed the case from between Rachel's body and his own and placed it in Edna Rosenberg's lap. The girl weighed next to nothing. He carried her as he would a sleeping child, supporting her under the buttocks with her arms draped over his shoulders, her face buried in his neck. Quickly he retraced his steps to the rear of the building. He knew that security had logged Edna Rosenberg's entry. They were waiting for her to leave. When she failed to do so, an officer would come up from the basement to investigate. All attention would be on the front camera screens, interior and exterior.

The man took no chances. He opened the rear door, which looked out onto a long, wide alley. To the left were the loading bays, large enough to accommodate the grand pianos, stage sets, and lighting and acoustical equipment that passed through. On the right was a metal stairwell, eight steps descending to the ground. Above him, fixed into a recess in the brick wall, was another camera. The poncho raincoat he had jammed into one of the garbage bins was also there. He squatted and reached out, tugging at the thick army-style cover. It came loose, bringing up an empty Polaroid carton with it. The man shook it open, stooped down, and wriggled his head and neck through the opening. The poncho fell into place, draping his body to the knees. From the back the child was invisible. The rain and gloom afforded him cover. The high-intensity lights would show a hunched-over figure making for the small panel truck parked in the alley, its grill pointed toward the street. The security monitoring this camera would think that the man was carrying a package, or else that the shape on his left shoulder was only a shadow, an aberration of light. No alarm would be raised until security could not account for the man. By the time they discovered the mother, Rachel Rosenberg would be only a memory.

Chapter Three

William C. Rodgers, director of Special Investigations, New York City Police Department, was affectionately known to his staff, but never addressed by them, as Mr. Bill. The sobriquet had been bestowed upon him by Thane Sheridan.

Mr. Bill was a tall, rangy man, his face slashed by deep creases, the skin perpetually tanned, somehow too weather-beaten for the city. Yet his trademark was a three-piece Brooks Brothers suit, a firm that measured his family's business in generations. The swept-back pure silver hair gave him the look of a riverboat gambler. When he adjusted his bifocals, the effect was Lincolnesque. Mr. Bill had been, some said still was, one of the best trackers in the history of the department. He had the chameleon's ability to blend in with any terrain.

His bureau was on the seventeenth floor of 1 Police Plaza, the office itself done in elegant New England style: lined bookcases of warm, oiled wood, a large globe in the far corner by the sofa, a sideboard for pewter bric-a-brac. Along the right-hand wall a refectory table stretched from the window almost to the convenience door. On it painstakingly painted miniature lead soldiers representing the Continental and British armies were arranged meticulously, their deployment duplicating the Battle of Yorktown.

Mr. Bill replaced the figure of General Cornwallis, warm from his touch, and moved back behind his barrister's desk. The top was brilliantly clean except for a dozen five-by-eight black and white photographs. The dates across the top ranged from October 17, two years ago—the

San Francisco killings—to coroner shots taken in Chicago three months ago. These were photos whose circulation was restricted to the commissioners of police in the cities of San Francisco, Denver, Las Vegas, Tallahassee, St. Louis, and Chicago. In each instance the officers involved, from the patrolmen who took the initial call to the forensic photographers, had been explicitly warned not to mention the details they had chanced to look upon. The penalty for a leak to the media was immediate expulsion. Likewise, when the coroners' inquests were completed, the victims' remains were shipped to the next-of-kin in sealed coffins. Each of the thirty-six funerals had been a closed-casket affair.

There had been those who had wanted at least some public disclosure, but they had been overruled. The victims, Mr. Bill had pointed out, were children. A community's psyche could somehow absorb the butchery of adults by adults, or even attacks on the elderly. But to show people what had really happened to their children, what could happen to *other* children, was to invite an ancient madness to return: vigilantism, persecution by race or creed, the victimization of former mental patients and those with criminal records, sex offenders in particular.

Mr. Bill looked down at the photograph lying dead in the center of the desk. What had once been Rachel Rosenberg, New York City. It made him want to throw his reasoned arguments against vigilantism out the window. Instead he had called Thane Sheridan.

The intercom on the communications console by his desk sounded. His car was ready. Mr. Bill placed two thick rubber bands around the photos and deposited the packet in the bottom drawer, locking it. Sheridan hadn't been at Puerto Plata when he had called yesterday. McBride said he was already in Santo Domingo, making reservations for New York. Sheridan had read the Rachel Rosenberg account in the overnight *Times*.

"You've gained weight. Looks good on you. Your color's not bad either."

Beyond the limousine windows New York lay in profile under a gray, listless sky. The weather was unseasonably warm, in the low forties with a pervasive wind humming through the girders of the Triborough Bridge. Thane Sheridan unbuttoned his thick sheepskin jacket. He was looking upon the city as he once had the Central Highlands of Vietnam. Then too he had not known the terrain intimately. He was suspicious of it, a little afraid, his movements uncomfortable. That would change. Mr. Bill recognized the expression. He had been operations director for the Highlands. Sheridan and McBride had been part of his team.

"You should have called me as soon as the body was found," Sheridan said absently.

"Not before the coroner finished with her. Even so, I'm not certain it's him."

Sheridan glanced across at his former chief. Mr. Bill knew about the dreams. He knew they had brought Sheridan to New York.

"Then why did you call me?"

"Because I wanted you to have a look at her. Nothing more. Just look at her and tell me what you think. You're the only one who's seen the other thirty-six firsthand. If there's no connection, I'm sending you back to McBride. There's nothing here for you."

But I can't go back, Sheridan thought. *Bill and Dory gave me what I needed—the quiet solace of friendship—without asking for anything in return. But Gwen will still be there. She deserves more, wants more than just a man who buries his terrors in her lovemaking.* He hesitated. *And if there is a connection . . .*

The driver turned off the FDR Drive at the UN complex. A light greasy rain started to fall as he swung the long car onto Second Avenue and headed for Greenwich Village. Sheridan knew their destination. He had been to New York a half dozen times. On four occasions he had gone straight from the airport to Thompson Street in the Village. The official coroner's building was right around the corner from Police Plaza. The laboratories and cutting rooms in the Village belonged to an earlier time. They hadn't been used since the new complex had opened. When Mr. Bill formed Special Investigations, he had had the facilities on Thompson Street reopened. For his use only.

"Do you have the complete on-site reports?" asked Sheridan as they stepped from the sidewalk into a small door cut into the much larger warehouse-style sliding doors. Even though it was midafternoon, this section of Thompson Street, in the rain, was quiet.

"They're coming down." Mr. Bill led the way, stooping slightly to pass under the wire nests of high-intensity bulbs.

The corridor opened up on a series of glass-walled units behind which white-clad figures moved past lab tables laden with scientific equipment. Forensic medicine never ceased to amaze Sheridan. The men and women working on Thompson Street had been recruited from the best university departments in the land, wooed from the drug industries by salaries which reflected an open-ended budget. All the members of Mr. Bill's scientific force had also signed an oath preventing them from discussing any of their work or revealing anything about the material which came in to be examined. The precaution was eminently justified: The scientists in the glass cubicles were prepared for it when a slice of internal organ revealed the existence of plague or an entire body had to be reconstructed from a single finger. Their training inured them to the horrific or gruesome. Not so the public.

Mr. Bill signed them in with security and clattered down the metal stairs to the morgue. The white antiseptic tile shimmered from the reflection of overhead fluorescent. A dozen cutting tables, their veined marble surfaces dulled by countless scrubbings, were unburdened, the stainless steel troughs which caught the blood gleaming. A Fuomi surgical lamp hung over each table like some carnivorous plant. There was no attendant in sight. Sheridan recalled that Thompson Street did not employ regular morgue personnel. The corpses were handled by in-house coroners whose security could be assured.

Mr. Bill picked up two pairs of surgical gloves, handed one to Sheridan, and opened the top center drawer of the refrigeration cabinet. Sheridan felt the dry icy air on his face as the drawer slid forward. His mouth tightened, teeth clamping together, when he saw that what Mr. Bill

26

was taking out was not a body but a green bag of heavy polyurethane.

"Let me take it."

Sheridan picked up the bag. Whatever it held had the general shape of a human figure. Sheridan set the bag on the nearest table and in one motion brought down the zipper.

Only the genitals indicated that the remains were those of a female. The scalp had been sheared away, leaving only tufts of hair around the ears. There was almost nothing left of the face itself: The lips and nose had been cut off, the eyes gouged out. Sheridan noticed that the bone of the sockets was almost perfectly smooth with only a few telltale nicks to indicate where the killer's knife had strayed. The arms and legs were the only parts left intact. The torso bore a ragged-edged hole over the left breast.

"Was she raped?"

"No."

Small mercies.

"You should have called me," Sheridan said again softly. "You've given him extra time."

"You're sure?" the director asked.

Yes, I'm sure! Christ, I can feel him laying her out, looking down at her, smiling as he reaches for the knife. There is no struggle, because Rachel Rosenberg is unconscious. He doesn't like them to struggle. Others do, but not him. He can't be neat that way. He's whispering something, to her, to himself. . . or to his dark gods. She isn't a human being to him anymore. If she ever was. She's a sacrifice.

"She was Jewish," Mr. Bill said. "The district commander has been getting calls from the family rabbi. He's managed to put on some muscle through the mayor's Brooklyn liaison office."

"That she was Jewish has nothing to do with the killing," Sheridan said abruptly.

"To you, no. To us it's a potential complication."

"If the rabbi doesn't back down, bring him in. You'll get his cooperation on nondisclosure. He won't want the family to see her like that."

The odor of formaldehyde was burning the tissue on the inside of Sheridan's nostrils.

"You knew," he said, peeling off the gloves. "You knew the minute you saw her that it was him. He's back. The Midnight Rambler has come to town."

"How can you be certain?"

This was not Mr. Bill speaking. Slowly Sheridan turned in the direction of the voice and saw a woman standing by the morgue door. He glanced back at the director.

"Who is she?"

"NYPD, Homicide. She was first on site." Mr. Bill paused. "I've given her the initial briefing," he said carefully so that Sheridan wouldn't misconstrue his meaning. "She'll be your liaison."

Sheridan nodded but said nothing. He hadn't wanted anyone to interrupt him now. He wanted time alone with Rachel Rosenberg. He wanted to examine the wounds because these might tell him how she had drawn the Rambler to her. He wanted to talk to people who knew her, her friends, teachers . . . and the parents. But now his communion had been intruded upon.

Sheridan slowly drew himself away from the dead child and turned to the policewoman. As in all other cases he would be working with a local liaison. Mr. Bill never gave away much in the briefing even though the officer had already been sworn to secrecy. Sheridan could understand their frustration: first their case was taken away from them, then they were subjected to an oath for reasons that were never explained. The final insult was having to work under an outsider. Sometimes what Mr. Bill told them, that this was not an isolated killing but one more in a much larger pattern, was not compensation enough.

The policewoman approached the refrigeration cabinet, the echo of heels against asphalt tile shimmering off the stainless steel equipment. Sheridan caught the rapid flutter of her eyelids, the involuntary intake of breath as she looked down at Rachel Rosenberg. But her control held, and she took a full sixty seconds to examine the cadaver.

"How can you be certain it's the same killer?" the policewoman repeated, turning to face him.

"Because the heart was cut out," Sheridan said. "Just as it has been in the first of his victims in each city. The son of a bitch carved right through the ribs to get at it. If he was fast enough, he could have scooped it out while it was still beating."

"What else?" the woman challenged him.

"In all other cases scalping also occurred. And there was facial disfigurement, like this, to a greater or lesser degree."

"Jesus Christ!" The woman shook her head and slowly approached Sheridan. "Sabina Morell, detective sergeant, Second Precinct."

Although of slender build Sabina Morell had very long legs and a generous bosom. She was almost as tall as Sheridan. Her fine blue-black hair was cut simply, shoulder length. Small shell-like ears gave way to flaring cheekbones, a sloping, slightly turned up nose. Beneath full lips was an aggressive jaw. The eyes were a spectacular turquoise. Although there were no rings on her fingers, Sheridan noted that the second knuckle on the middle finger of her left hand was pronounced. Usually that meant it had been broken in hand to hand combat.

"Sheridan," he said softly. "Thane Sheridan."

Sabina Morell appraised him coolly, but obviously the name meant nothing to her. She turned to Mr. Bill.

"The district commander told me you wanted to see me right away, sir?"

Sheridan noticed the eyes were wary, as though she were anticipating conflict.

"Sheridan is in charge of the case," Mr. Bill said tonelessly. "He'll hold the rank of inspector. You will—"

"I'll be his liaison," Sabina Morell said, cutting him off sarcastically. "Sheridan isn't a member of the department. He doesn't have jurisdiction—"

This time it was Mr. Bill who interrupted.

"I'm afraid he does. He doesn't want it, but it's his all the same."

"I can't see—" Sabina Morell started to say.

"He's not a member of the NYPD," the director continued, "but neither was he on the force in San Francisco, Vegas, St. Louis, or any of the other places where the Rambler did his work. Here, as in the other cases, Sheridan will be working in a special investigator's capacity, his author-

29

ity coming from my office." Mr. Bill tightened the screws just a little. "Which is all the authority he needs."

"So I answer to him directly and not to the district commander?" Sabina Morell demanded.

"Precisely," Mr. Bill answered. "In every city where he's worked, Sheridan has been paired with a local homicide detective as liaison. At best the men have been of real value to him, a stranger in their environment. Only twice has he had to ask for new partners because of professional incompatibility, jealousy, or outright incompetence. I trust that that won't be the case here. Even though he's never worked with a woman . . ." Mr. Bill let the words hang.

Sheridan's eyes flickered over the policewoman's set expression. He had to give her kudos for restraint. But he had run into similar reactions up front only to discover hidden recriminations later on. Indignation, justified though it might be, still had no place in this case. That was why her question impressed him.

"Does that worry you—my being a woman?"

She was sharp, very quick, picking up on a doubt he wasn't aware of showing.

"No reason it should," Sheridan said quietly. "I'll need all the help you have to offer. I take it you brought the investigation report with you?"

She patted her briefcase. "Right here."

"You can have an office on my floor at the Plaza," Mr. Bill said to Sheridan.

"If it's all the same to you, I'd rather have one here, space permitting."

"Why?" Sabina Morell asked.

"I try to stay out of departmental traffic. There are too many bodies downtown. Too many secretaries who want to take notes, receptionists who answer a dozen lines. Reporters wandering about. This is the first time I'm in on the ground floor. I'll set up my command post here. By midnight I want it functional."

"You think the Rambler will hit once more before we reach him?" she asked.

Sheridan looked from her to the director. "He killed Rachel Rosenberg four days ago. In Chicago and St. Louis there were eight and ten days respectively between the
30

first and second killings. The interval is becoming shorter."

"What do you need?" Mr. Bill asked.

"Seven telephone lines: two outside, one to your office and one to your car, both with scramblers, one to the Bureau in Washington, one to the field office here, as well as a channel with Langley. A computer terminal with links into the main police computers of all the cities the Rambler's visited. A Teledon hook-up with Hirsh in Langley and a six-zero technical clearance from the Agency. One car, equipped, with a similar unit for Sergeant Morell as well as a back-up standing by."

"Armament?" Mr. Bill asked quietly.

"Hanyatti .38 as escort weapon. A Venus with shoulder straps for the finale."

"What the hell are you going after?" Sabina Morell exclaimed. She had seen a demonstration of the Venus once, in Quantico during advanced training. The weapon was about the size of an Uzi, but it differed from the Israeli submachine gun in two crucial aspects: the Venus had *three* barrels, rotating like the old Gatling guns but with blinding speed, literally spitting the bullets out. The weapon also carried two ammunition clips, fed into the chambers simultaneously with two more levered up against the bottom of the barrel waiting to be snapped into place. The weapon's killing power was devastating. After a specialist had emptied both clips into a dozen hanging beef carcasses, there wasn't a chunk of meat bigger than a fist left.

"If you want the same, I'll be happy to oblige," Sheridan said quietly.

"I'll pass, thanks," the policewoman retorted. "But maybe you can tell me what authority the CIA has in all this. As far as I know we're running a *domestic* investigation here."

"That it is, Sergeant," Sheridan agreed. "And the Agency isn't *actively* involved nor does it have any authority. However nowhere is it written that domestic law enforcement can't call upon Langley for certain resources and information. Which is exactly what I intend to do if necessary."

31

"No, wait a minute. It seems that you're moving hot off the mark before you've even read my report!"

Sheridan shook his head. "I'm sorry if it appears that way," he said sincerely. "But what you must understand, *never forget,* is that four days ago the clock began running for us. The Rambler is going to take down five more children. In every city he's taken six. Rachel Rosenberg was New York's first."

"But does that automatically mean he'll kill again before we reach him?" Sabina Morell stopped short. "Oh, my God!" she whispered. "That's why you want to set up shop *here.* You *expect* him to kill again. You *know* you won't get him before he takes a second . . . or even a third!"

"I pray to God we do," Sheridan said softly. "You don't know how I pray. But we have so little to help us. And it's been four days . . ."

The high-pitched screech of wood being twisted into wood pierced the stillness of the workshop. Gently the E-string peg was tightened. An ancient finger, the nail cut parallel with the tip, plucked the string. The sympathetic vibration between the instrument's belly and back gave out a clear resonance. The master, his head cocked, eyes lightly closed, smiled to himself. The pitch was perfect.

Otto Morell held the violin, at arm's length, up to the light which swam in from the skylight. The soft hazel swirls of the fruitwood took on a golden hue. His eye traveled from the ornately sculpted scroll down the polished fingerboard, across the purfling of the belly, across the bridge boarded by twin f-holes to the concave chin rest. Flawless. Holding it at a different angle, he peered through the f-hole and saw his signature affixed in indelible ink. The name and instrument were worthy of each other.

Otto Morell was a master craftsman who had reached the biblical age of seventy-two. A short spry gentleman with plump cheeks settled over a long, nicotine-stained mustache, a thick potatolike nose, and bushy white eyebrows that accented ice-blue, alert eyes, he was regarded by most concert violinists as the premier creator of their instruments. Some clients—Yehudi Menuhin and Itzhak

Perlman—felt he was greater than any of his formidable predecessors: Guarneri "del Gesù," the Amatis, or even Stradivari. It was as though he infused his creations with a magic that rose from the instrument itself, lifting the talent or genius of the performer to unanticipated levels.

To Otto Morell this was so much nonsense. He placed the violin in its case, custom designed by his friend the Calabrian, Gerussi of Boston. He picked up the bow, ran his fingertips across the sheen of horsehair, then slid that in between the leather loops. As at the conclusion of every act of creation, a sad feeling came over the craftsman. He knew this would be the last instrument he would ever build. In his eyes that made it special. He hoped that the player he had designed it for, the virtuoso Leopold Ulric, would also recognize the exceptional within it. Morell thought he would. As a violinist, Ulric had no peers among his contemporaries. Critics, aficionados, and other players shared that opinion. If this had to be his last creation, Otto Morell was satisfied to have made it for such hands.

Otto Morell sidestepped to the end of the worktable. Carefully he knelt down, his finger searching for the catch in the boards. When he found it, a square yard of wood flooring sprang up at a 10 degree angle. He levered it up on almost invisible hinges and fixed the catch. The safe, built into the thick concrete support floor, was the most modern piece of equipment in the workshop, constructed to his specifications by the Moro brothers of Detroit ten years ago. It was fireproof up to 3000 degrees. Otto Morell pulled back the door and lowered the case with its instrument into the cavity. Come what may, the creation was now safe. No thief, no disaster would penetrate the triple steel-lined, asbestos-sheathed safe. He lowered the door and locked it, pulling out the catch and letting the wooden floor fall into place.

Now he was truly finished. The musician for whom he had fashioned this creation would come for it only after Morell had departed. A tic, brought on by fear, tugged at Otto Morell's left eyelid as he stepped back from the small, all but invisible oubliette. Such an arrangement was more than satisfactory. He had no wish to look upon this musician ever again.

Otto Morell removed his glasses and absently began to polish them with a patch of chamois. He vowed that this time he would turn a deaf ear on all requests to make yet another instrument. He anticipated a dozen serious queries, two or three of which he would truly regret declining. But he had no choice. Morell reached for his cane and hobbled away from the worktable, dragging his cast-enclosed left foot behind him. An accident that once might have left him with only a twisted ankle had instead resulted in splintered bones. Even after three months the healing was incomplete. Nor did the degeneration stop there. His eyesight, always a worry, was failing markedly. Thus far his hands and fingers had held their own, but after a half century in this climate rheumatism and arthritis were reaching out to claim their due.

Otto Morell stopped suddenly and looked around himself. The loft workshop was spotlessly clean in spite of the wood particles that danced in the shaft of light. There, beneath the skylight, was the workbench with its vises and grips, the pegboard behind it covered with awls, lathes, chisels, hammers, and screwdrivers. In the cabinets below were his resins and epoxies, the lacquers, glosses, and enamels, waxes and preservatives he patiently applied coat after coat. Off to the right was the ancient jigsaw he had purchased secondhand in 1940 and which had carved out the initial designs of over fifty masterpieces. Across the room, behind the gleaming doors of a floor to ceiling cabinet, were his woods—the burled walnut, ash, blood-stained mahogany, and radiant cherry, the rich fruitwood and gnarled beech.

The instruments and elements of his creations. Perhaps he might still work with them, for his own pleasure, as long as time permitted. Otto Morell smiled. Fancy had never been an indulgence of his. What was finished was finished. He had made the decision, irrevocably.

The master wiped his hands on the chocolate-brown leather apron which came down to his knees. It was worn to a shiny beige across the chest and at the large pockets. Making sure he was leaning on his good leg, Otto Morell swung the apron over his head, folded it neatly, and placed it on top of the worktable. He struggled into a long black coat, taking care to wrap the gaily colored scarf, a Christmas gift from Sabina, twice around his neck. At the thought of his niece Otto Morell smiled. It was the custom in his house that upon completion of a work Augusta would make a special dinner of venison. All his friends would come. He hoped very much Sabina would be there. Only twice in twenty years had she missed the ritual and both times only because she had been out of the country. But earlier in the day Augusta had called him to say Sabina was working on a new case, one that had to do with the murder of the little girl, and might not be able to come. Otto Morell was prepared to forgive his niece for her absence.

Taking a final look around, he turned out the lights and descended the staircase cautiously, one step at a time. Outside, the rain continued to fall in a fine mist. Otto Morell forced a hat on top of his shock of frizzy hair and double-locked the front door.

The street was empty. A long rolling wind came out of the darkness, nipping at his coattails. Otto Morell did not fear the night. He had lived in the neighborhood too long, from a time when dawn was ushered in by the clatter of the milk wagon and the air was pungent with the smell of baking bread. It had been, he reflected, a gentler time, when Steuben Town's boundaries had extended all the way to the river, through what was now Tribeca. The German and Austrian immigrants had arrived first, followed by Italians and Spanish. At the beginning the prejudice among the nationalities had remained, a throwback to the Old World mentality. But as the years went by and the second migration arrived and intermarriage worked its compromises Steuben Town left the petty tensions of Europe behind. The community became aware of America, aware that it was part of America. Finally that it *was* America.

As Otto Morell walked he could see in his mind's eye the soup kitchens of the thirties, the blanket of despair that obliterated national differences. He remembered Rumanian Jews who carved hot spiced meats for hungry Germans, and Spaniards who shared their paellas with Italians. He could still hear the streets ringing with the cries and laughter of children who were the first generation of Americans, who caused their parents sorrow because they were the end of a continuity the parents could not bear to surrender. Yet in the children Otto Morell saw the hope of the community, the promise of its fruition and the beginning of a new continuity. He despaired when they returned to the Old World to fight a war not of their making and rejoiced when they came home proud, flushed with victory, their muscles flexed, eager to build.

God, how he loved these streets! Every corner, every building was like a book, the chapters containing the stories of those who had passed through here, sometimes leaving, but more often staying. Staying to contribute, to build, to provide for their children.

Otto Morell adjusted the scarf so that it covered a little of his nose and warmed the air he was breathing. To contribute and build. He had done that for over fifty years. Now he had to fight, to protect what once he had believed to be inviolate.

The two men knew the route the old man would take. He would walk down Broome Street, then turn right on Varick, and walk north until he reached Vandam. Instead of following Vandam all the way west he would turn right into a lane used by tractor trailers which serviced the twin Cunard Lines container depots on either side. The old man would walk slowly in between the great concrete bays, feeling safe because of the lights strung out over the ramps, because the area was patrolled by a private security force. He would reemerge below Clarkson Street, heading north.

The two men had taken the precaution of dressing like laborers: woolen caps, heavy cheap parkas, Kodiak work boots with the jean cuffs stuffed into the ankle pads. Each wore heavy but supple leather gloves. The parkas gave them a bulk neither actually possessed. These were slender, lithe men, of medium height, their tawny high-cheeked faces betraying an Indian ancestry. But they had adjusted to the clothing as much as to the weather. Neither diminished the intrinsic skills or interfered with the predator's instincts honed to such a fine degree in the hills of Bolivia and Peru. The one called Santiago spoke softly to his cousin, Roncaron. He spoke in English, although it still twisted the tongue. But Letelier had counseled them always to speak in English, never in Spanish.

"He approaches."

The cousins did not like the old man. If the truth be known, they were afraid of him. The old man was *malas noticias*—bad news. To others he appeared harmless, a relic hobbling to his death. To them he possessed great spiritual strength they felt keenly. But the old man had to die. Letelier had so decreed, and the cousins were his servants. But although their fear of Letelier was great, as such was his due, it had not been strong enough to compel them to kill the old man on the first night. Twice before he had passed between them, unaware of the death that lay only a few feet away. He had shamed them with his serene indifference. Tonight they could not hesitate. Letelier was impatient. In a way, they reasoned, the old man was fortunate. Because of their fear of touching him unnecessarily his death would be mercifully quick. Letelier would be told the master had suffered, for he wished it so. But the cousins knew the old man's heart would burst quickly.

Otto Morell was halfway down the lane when he heard the hollow clatter of a rolling, empty can. He stopped and slowly pivoted, leaning heavily on his cane. The lane was empty save for the trucks lined up along its length—the blue and white Peterbilts, Macks, black Reos, and White Stars standing in a row like some awesome Praetorian Guard, their exhaust stacks rigidly fixed spears. He observed the lane for a full minute before starting to turn around. He heard another sound, the sole of a shoe or boot grating on loose asphalt.

"Who is there?"

As though his question had been a command, two figures disengaged themselves from the sides of trucks on either side of the lane. It wasn't until they were a few feet away that Otto Morell recognized them. His uneasiness was mirrored in their eyes.

"What do you want?" he demanded.

"Mr. Letelier is not pleased," one of them said. "He does not like lies being told about him."

"Letelier is a criminal!" Otto Morell said softly. The disgust in his voice was tempered by the pity he felt for the two men before him. "He is a destroyer of children and women. His drugs and whores—"

"Shut up, old man!" Santiago hissed. "Shut up now or I'll cut you."

"No, not you." Otto Morell shook his head. "You're too much of a coward. You did not touch me before, you will not do so now." He smiled as the cousins glanced at one another. He had walked between them twice. Now they knew the third time would be no different.

"Mr. Letelier does not like your committee," Santiago continued. He hadn't moved in any closer but remained three or four feet from the master. "He does not enjoy being hounded in his neighborhood, where he lives and contributes—"

"Letelier is filth!" Morell silenced him. "He is a corrupter who knows only how to maim and destroy. Tell him we will be rid of him and his kind very soon. Soon he will not be able to prey upon anyone!"

Suddenly Otto Morell realized he had erred in not keeping both men in sight. While Santiago was speaking Roncaron had moved around to the side. The master heard the sound of compressed air. All at once his trouser leg was wet. He felt liquid seep through the fabric and trickle into his cast. The smell of gasoline wafted into the rain-laden air.

"Don't do this," Otto Morell said calmly. "Don't bring more tragedy upon yourselves. Letelier is a coward. He refuses to confront me directly. Don't let him use you to hide his cowardice."

Roncaron did not reply. In his hand was a tank the size of a small fire extinguisher, with a short rubber hose and plastic-tipped nozzle. Deliberately he aimed at Otto Morell's cast and sprayed.

"If you do anything more, your lives will have been forfeited."

Roncaron hissed something in Spanish to his cousin, averting his eyes from the cold, pitiless gaze the old man held him with. The fool was crazy. His eyes reflected the madness within him. The cousins suddenly felt an oppressive air building around them, as though the wind were swirling about them, binding them in a shrinking tunnel.

Otto Morell turned around, so that his back was to them. Slowly he took up the pace again, his cane leaving its mark in the patches of dirt. He had taken three steps before he heard the sigh of escaping air. Instantly he felt the gasoline trickle through his scarf and onto the back of his neck.

Roncaron moved around him now, spraying his coat. Just before the film of gasoline coated his face, Otto Morell saw the terror in the young Colombian's eyes.

"You are dead now," he said softly, his words rich with certainty, a pitiless contentment. They were the last Otto Morell uttered. Santiago threw a flaming rag that fell upon the cast with a sodden slap.

The cousins ran. They expected the old man to start screaming. The security patrol might hear him but not in time. So they ran until they could see the flickering neon sign at the end of the lane, the smoke shop on the corner of Clarkson Street. Something was wrong. Santiago reached out and grabbed his cousin by the shoulder, slowing him down. Panting, they staggered around to see something that cut them to the marrow: In the middle of the lane Otto Morell was burning, twitching and shaking like some marionette whose strings are controlled by a demented puppeteer. It was a macabre dance of death that paralyzed the cousins. Instinctively Santiago reached inside his parka and fingered the smooth blue oval that hung at his breastbone. The stone was protection against the evil eye. He clutched it tightly as both backed away, and was still holding it when the gas cylinder he had thrown at the old man's feet exploded, the flames consuming whatever was left of Otto Morell.

George Morenno's steak and seafood house was on the fringe of the neighborhood, up on West Twenty-fifth, a half block west of Eighth Avenue. It was one of two restaurants Sabina frequented on a regular basis. She loved the paneled walls, warm and soft from the glow of candles on the tables, the raised dining area which overlooked the bar, and the bustle around the espresso machine. Sometimes she ate upstairs, in the gallery overlooking the main dining area. But more than the decor it was the people who at-

tracted her. She was on a first-name basis with the
waiters—Joe from Venezuela, dour Alex, the more formal
Roberto, and Spanish Raymond. Heading them was
George, an irrepressible showman from Parma who
clowned with his guests, joking with the women at the gentle expense of their escorts.

Sabina also knew when to come: By eight o'clock the
place was usually in a din. If there was a sports event on
somewhere, the line of those with reservations overflowed
the small foyer onto the street. But now, at six o'clock, she
and Thane Sheridan were the only diners. Joe had seen to
it that they had the corner table and left them to themselves.

For the umpteenth time Sabina wondered why she had
blurted out the offer of dinner. She had still been furious at
Mr. Bill's high-handedness when the director of Special Investigations left. There had been an awkward pause before
Sheridan had said, "They'll be working on the office upstairs. Can we sit down and review what you know in the
commissary?"

"Why not? You're the boss."

The commissary turned out to be nothing more than a
tiny hole-in-the-wall at the very end of the building. A Mr.
Coffee machine, two Formica tables, half a dozen orange
plastic chairs.

"Black?" he had asked.

"Cream and sugar."

By the time Sheridan brought the coffees over, she had
her notes out. He stopped her from shuffling the papers by
covering her hand, as though it were the most natural
thing in the world.

"I'd rather hear it in your own words."

It took her a few seconds to regain her composure.

"There's not a hell of a lot," Sabina Morell said, lighting
a cigarette. She pursed her lips, sending the smoke to the
perforated tiles.

"I wasn't supposed to be in that day, Monday, the 6th,
but my partner's transfer to Narcotics had come in. There
was paperwork to finish up. I was passing the front desk
when the duty sergeant called me. There was a messenger

beside him, a young black kid, who had delivered the package."

"Addressed to you specifically?"

"There was no name on it." She shook her head. "The driver had been told to drop it off with anyone at Homicide."

"It was a tape recording, a cassette."

Her eyes snapped up.

"I'm sorry," he said quickly. "I didn't mean to get ahead of you."

"Yes, it was a tape," she said carefully, wondering why Mr. Bill hadn't mentioned that he had already briefed Sheridan. "I took it into the office, played it. . . ."

She could still hear that sickening nasal voice drifting up at her, rich with hatred and triumph.

"Where did you find Rachel?"

"Look, if you've been through this with Rodgers, then what's the point?" she demanded, anger spilling over.

"Mr. Bill hasn't told me anything," Sheridan said quietly. "Go on."

The anger turned to astonishment.

"What's going on here?"

"Please, Sabina, just continue. I need to hear it, everything."

She gave a sigh of exasperation.

"The tape was about a minute long. The instructions as to where to find the body were specific." Sabina hesitated. "I don't know why, but I got out of the station like a bat out of hell."

"Did anyone else hear the tape?"

"No, I took that with me. I remember yelling at the desk sergeant to hold the delivery kid until I called in."

Sabina's narrative came to an abrupt stop. Sheridan knew why.

"And the instructions were accurate," he coaxed her. "You found Rachel exactly where the tape said she'd be."

"Yes. I found her . . . what was left of her . . . at the old incinerator on Houston Street and FDR Drive wrapped in newspaper. The killer had placed her in one of the furnaces. I guess he knew the city doesn't use the facilities anymore."

"Then what?"

Sabina looked up at him. "I called in. But instead of a full homicide team only Rodgers arrived, along with a wagon from this place. Since then I haven't been allowed to return to the site. Rodgers's department took over the investigation."

"What about the delivery boy?"

"Clean. Rodgers had me run the initial interrogation. Then a couple of heavies I'd never seen before took over. The kid should have screamed about habeas corpus—they kept him incommunicado overnight. When I came back, he was gone."

And he'll stay gone until we're finished, Sheridan thought to himself.

"How come Rodgers didn't tell you any of this?" Sabina demanded suddenly.

"Because he knows I'd rather hear it from you," Sheridan murmured. She noticed the scars on his wrist and hand at the same instant as he began massaging them.

"The autopsy," Sabina started to say.

"She died quickly," Sheridan lied. "The rest was done when she was dead."

"Christ . . ."

"Sabina, I want you to listen to me now," he said softly. "You're in on this thing, and you have to know what I know. After, if you'd rather opt out, that can be arranged."

She hesitated. "All right. I don't think it can get any worse."

How wrong she was. . . .

Sheridan spoke without pause for almost an hour, sitting in profile in the harsh glare of overhead fluorescence. Quietly, without drama, he sketched out the investigations he had conducted in the other cities, how the first murder was always ritualistic, in that way different from the ones that inevitably followed. He explained how, after the second set of killings, he had become certain the murderer was one and the same man. All the while he spoke in the manner of a narrator recounting a story that had nothing to do with himself but was someone else's nightmare. He explained the necessity for secrecy, of preventing the media from linking the killings. He told her about the resources they would have at their disposal and which she would have to learn to use—quickly.

When he was finished, Sabina felt weak, as though someone had physically beaten her. Yet something was missing. Now she knew the scope of the case and the desperate need to move on it quickly. The details on the other killings were en route. But the man . . . She had no handle on Sheridan, no understanding of how he was related to all this.

And there was the sorrow within him. A deep underlying sadness which, for all his detachment, still made him appear vulnerable. Perhaps that was why, when he gently dismissed her, she had mentioned—no, insisted on—dinner.

Sabina took another sip of wine, her fingers straying to the hot cheese-garlic bread that one day would be her downfall. Sheridan was drinking mineral water. He had buttoned up his jacket, but from where she sat, Sabina could see the dull sheen of the holster which kept his Hanyatti .38 in place. His face seemed somewhat softer in the subdued light, the candle diminishing the creases across his forehead and cheeks. Yet every so often she would watch his gaze wander over to the bar or the magnificent antique vanity George had smuggled in after his last trip to the Continent, and she knew he was thinking of the Rambler.

"I'm sorry," Thane Sheridan said.

"For what?"

"For taking the case away from you, for being a poor dinner companion." He looked up, managing a smile. "But the food is great."

"Don't worry about my professional pride," she said, hoping he recognized her earnestness. "There's more than enough here for both of us."

She speared a slice of tomato. "When will your files arrive from Chicago?"

"They'll be in by the time the communications are in place. Mr. Bill told Chicago to get them to a special courier."

He watched her eat, silently sipping the water. He hoped very much she would work out. He had to get the Rambler this time. Somehow he knew there wouldn't be another chance. At least not for him.

"Do you have children?" he asked, surprising even himself.

Her fork, laden with tomato, stopped halfway to her mouth.

"Yes, one. A boy."

She put the fork back on the plate. "You guessed, right?"

He shook his head, smiling shyly. "You look like a mother."

Their eyes met, the double entendre clear to both at the same time, and the laughter erupted.

"Jesus, I'm sorry," Sheridan muttered. "I didn't mean it—"

"It's okay, really." She was still unable to stop laughing.

"My son's name is Toby," she said at last. "He's ten."

"Your husband—"

"We're separated," she broke in quickly.

"I'm sorry, I was intruding."

Sabina was silent for a moment, then said, "That's what my husband kept telling me, that he was sorry for intruding on my career, anytime my job got in the way of domesticity."

"It's not easy," Sheridan commented.

"I learned that the hard way," Sabina said. "After I had Toby, I went back to school, finished up my bachelor's degree. Richard—my husband's name is Richard Dwyer—thought it would stop there. Actually he had thought the pregnancy would finish me off."

"But it didn't."

"Hell, no. I didn't spend four years getting a degree in criminal sociology to become a *hausfrau*. I knew that from the beginning, but I gave it two years."

Her voice fell. "I tried. I really did. But as much as I love my child, he wasn't enough. I had to go back."

"To police work?"

"Crazy, isn't it?" She grinned. "I suppose I could have done law, but one attorney in the household was enough. Besides, I needed action, a direct, daily challenge. I love this city, for all its bitchiness. I love Steuben Town even

44

more. That's where my contribution was to be: to help roll back this tide of shit we're drowning in."

She sipped her wine. "Sometimes it's difficult, too damn difficult to know if you're any good, or *doing* any good."

"You're good," Sheridan said quietly.

"Thanks for the vote of confidence." Her tone was wry, but she sounded pleased. "My husband told me that at first too. Then I realized it was only tolerance on his part. I couldn't live with that. Almost anything else, but not condescension—no respect, as Rodney Dangerfield would say."

"Is your boy with you?"

"Richard has him. We agreed that if I took the detective's exam, Toby would live with him." She ran a finger along the stem of the wineglass. "I almost didn't go for it at that point. It was one of life's unfair choices: be untrue to yourself and live in Traffic all your career, or give up your child and take on something which will make you grow, be a better human being, a better parent . . . maybe."

"You're probably not a better mother now," Sheridan said. "Just different, working under new circumstances."

"I've been in Homicide for two years."

"Old circumstances. But you know what I mean."

Sabina lowered her eyes. "I think I do . . . and I'm grateful for it."

Joe came by with their entrees. The aroma of grilled marinated lamb enveloped the table. Sabina waited until they had been served and the wine poured before she asked, "And you? You seem to understand where I'm coming from. You must have been there yourself."

He knew the question he had asked about her personal life would boomerang back at him. He wished he hadn't said anything. But now he couldn't put her off. It wouldn't be fair. Maybe too he wanted the hatred to flow again, not too much, not yet, but enough to keep him keen.

"I did two tours of duty with the CIA station Saigon," Sheridan said, slowly cutting into the meat. "That's where I met Mr. Bill. We were one of the first teams in the Highlands, running networks that stretched out into Hanoi. We did better in the early days of the war—sixty-six, sixty-seven—than anytime later. Of course later the whole conflict went to hell in a handbasket. . . .

"After Vietnam I returned to San Francisco, completed a degree in criminal psychology, and went to work for SFPD. That's where I met my wife."

"Children?" Sabina Morell asked.

"One. Andrew. He would have been nine next month."

She put her fork down. "I'm sorry. I shouldn't have—"

"Anne and I had been married eight years," Sheridan continued, ignoring the interruption. Absently he began to massage the underside of his wrist. "Andrew was seven when the first children began to disappear. He wasn't called the Rambler then. After he killed the first child, we had him pegged for a psycho—nothing more. That was our first mistake. Four other children disappeared. Andrew was his last one. I pried my son's body loose from a stack of others when we found out where he had been keeping them."

"Thane, please—"

"My wife went insane after that. She was a criminal psychologist liaisoned to SFPD from Berkeley. Somehow she saw the on-site photographs. For two years she wasted away in a sanitorium. Finally she found a way to kill herself."

Thane Sheridan began to eat once more, chewing the meat slowly, thoroughly. They did not speak until he finished. Sabina left her plate untouched.

"When I heard about the initial killing in Vegas, I flew down to view the body. The boy looked pretty much as Rachel Rosenberg must have when you found her. After hightailing it back to San Francisco and arranging for an indefinite leave of absence I came back to Vegas. The police there weren't really equipped to handle something like this, so they let me in on the case. Not that I was of any help. The Rambler took his quota and disappeared."

"Denver, Tallahassee, St. Louis—all the same?"

"Exactly. After Vegas I got in touch with Mr. Bill and convinced him that we had a mass murderer on our hands, someone who had mobility, a pattern to his killings—someone who wouldn't stop until we took him down. Mr. Bill had the necessary leverage to set up, very quietly, mind you, a special task force for the Rambler. He opened the doors at the FBI and Langley, arranged for the funds, my accreditation. . . ."

Sabina noticed the pained look on Joe's face as he removed her plate, and she expressed her regrets to the chef. Her lack of appetite had nothing to do with the food. Sheridan ordered cappuccinos for both of them.

"You mentioned that the press hasn't connected the killings," Sabina said. "They're usually the first to see a pattern even if you try to run them in the opposite direction."

"Even so, it's been our deliberate policy to do just that," Sheridan told her. "After Denver Mr. Bill was convinced that the Rambler was weaving his way across the country. But when he showed up in Tallahassee, we realized we couldn't predict his next target city. And even though I spent months going over the details of the killings in the other cities, I couldn't come up with any common elements."

That wasn't exactly the truth, but Detective Sergeant Morell did not have to be apprised of everything. Not yet and hopefully never.

"Because there wasn't any common ground, we could honestly disclaim any connection if we had to. Believe me, the panic that would erupt if people believed the Rambler was on his way to their town would be monstrous."

"Who is 'we'?" Sabina asked.

"Officially every investigation was run by the individual city's homicide division. The Bureau in Washington was kept abreast only because the murderer had crossed state lines to get into and out of the killing ground. Unofficially each incident was relayed to Mr. Bill here in New York, where he set up task force headquarters. He would then arrange to parachute me into the investigation as FBI liaison."

"But that's not the case here," Sabina protested. "No one's mentioned any FBI involvement. As far as the precinct is concerned, it's my case and I'm handling it."

"That's the way we're going to keep it," Sheridan told her. He leaned forward to light a cigarette for her, then one for himself. "You're the front person, I'm riding shotgun. You've questioned Rachel's teachers at the NSDM, run a background check on them. Tonight I'll read the reports on that and the assault on Edna Rosenberg. Tomorrow we'll go over the evidence found at NSDM as well as whatever you picked up at the incinerator plant. That should bring me right up to date."

Sabina finished her coffee, smoking in silence.

"You said you were in on the ground floor," she murmured. "What did you mean?"

"Every other time I arrived too late. Even in Chicago the Rambler had taken down a second child before I was integrated into the investigation. But his scent was very strong there. I really believed I could get to him. I would walk around the city and I could feel his presence, like a sour odor, or a shadow you glimpse out of the corner of your eye."

"The sixty-four-dollar question," Sabina said, brushing a stray wisp of hair behind her ear. "You're a hunter. From what I can gather from Mr. Bill, you're the best he's ever had. Your SFPD commendation list is almost embarrassing. So why is the Rambler still walking around?"

Sheridan ground out his cigarette and signaled to Joe for the check. Every other liaison he had been given had asked the same question. Until Tallahassee Sheridan hadn't had an answer. The conclusion he had arrived at after Florida terrified him.

"We'll talk about that tomorrow," he said. "Let me get my papers, and we'll go over everything in one shot."

"I want you to take him, Thane," Sabina Morell said suddenly. "He can't do here what he's done before. It has to end here!"

The fury in her voice shocked him. "Why?"

"Because my son is a student at the New School of Drama and Music. As was Rachel Rosenberg. If anything were to happen to Toby . . ."

He was helping her with her coat when Sabina said: "Look, there's a party at my uncle's place this evening. I promised to stop by, and I'd really like you to come. We'll only stay a few minutes."

"I'd like that very much," Sheridan said. Another little lie. His family had been destroyed years ago. He avoided the pain and envy other people's happiness brought out in

48

him. But he saw how much it meant to her. A little warmth and laughter would go a long way in supporting her through what they had to do.

Two minutes later, as she was starting the engine, Sabina Morell's world fell apart.

The squad car, siren screaming, twisted to the side of the street, swerving in front of their vehicle. A uniformed patrolman leaped out and ran to the driver's side. Sabina recognized him from the Second Precinct.

"What is it, Marty?" she asked, window rolled down.

The young officer swallowed hard, his eyes straying to Sheridan.

"Your uncle . . ."

"What is it?"

"We found him in the Cunard compound. He's . . . he's dead."

"Oh, Jesus, his heart!"

"No, it wasn't an accident," the officer cried. "Someone murdered him. Christ, Sergeant, I'm sorry."

"Get back in your vehicle and give us an escort," Sheridan ordered. "Now! Move!"

As soon as the officer ran back to his car, Sheridan unlocked the panel between his seat and the driver's. From within the recess he pulled out the Venus. Quickly he struggled out of his coat, unstrapped the revolver holster, and slid the special lightweight webbing over his shoulders. Within seconds the Venus was tucked away, the grip protruding, instantly at hand. Up ahead the patrol car was fishtailing along West Twenty-fifth Street.

"Sabina, keep up with him."

She remained frozen at the wheel, her fingers like talons around the rim, eyes staring ahead, seeing nothing, the motor running. Sheridan leaned across and rammed the gearshift into drive.

"Let's go!"

Sabina Morell remembered nothing of how she got them to the Cunard depot. Training and instinct took over as she followed the lead car. When she turned into the lane, blazing with light from the head lamps of the tractor trailers, she saw the morgue vehicle, a distinctive black with frosted rear window, begin to pull away. She accelerated, swinging the sedan in its path. Sabina jumped out from behind the wheel and ran around to the tailgate, wrenching it open. Before anyone could stop her, she had pulled out the stretcher. Instead of a body with a sheet over it there was only the green zippered corpse bag.

"No!"

She began tugging at the zipper, her eyes stinging from tears. A pair of hands came around her shoulders, the grip strong, pulling her back.

"Let go, Sabina, please. You don't want to see him that way."

William Rodgers came around her and gently pried her fingers off the zipper tab.

"Take her to the car," he told a patrolman. "And get a paramedic."

"Has my aunt been notified?" Sabina asked, voice dead, stone cold.

"I sent a car to the house when one was dispatched to find you."

"I should go home. They'll be waiting for me."

"We'll get you home, Sabina," Mr. Bill said.

"How . . . how did he die?"

"Sabina—"

"Tell me—*how did he die?*"

"They set him on fire. The coroner thinks his heart gave out before he could suffer." Mr. Bill turned on the patrolman. "Get her into the car and keep her there!"

The attendant pushed the stretcher back inside the car and slammed the gate. Rear tires spun, and the morgue wagon moved off.

"Who did it?" Sheridan asked softly. A few feet away the search was on for evidence. At both ends of the lane, cordoned off by sawhorses and motorcycle units, the crowds were gathering.

"Not the Rambler."

"I didn't see the body," Sheridan reminded him.

"But I did," Mr. Bill said pointedly. "Otto Morell was set on fire. We've found a gasoline cylinder and a piece of the hose and nozzle. Someone sprayed him, then flamed him."

He paused and looked at Sheridan. "I'm sorry for her,

Thane. I really am. She's a hell of an officer, but under the circumstances I'll get you a new assignee."

"Maybe that won't be necessary," Sheridan murmured. "Hold off until I have a chance to speak with her."

Mr. Bill shrugged.

"Who did it? You know more than you're telling me. It might help me with her."

"It's a feud. Would you believe it? A goddamn feud over territory. Something straight out of *Pogo.*"

Mr. Bill cupped his hands to light a cigarette.

"For three years now the Dominicans and Colombians have been making inroads into this neighborhood. Between the two groups they control eighty percent of the city's cocaine and pharmaceutical traffic. You know how they work: find a nice but on-the-way-down neighborhood, buy a little real estate on the periphery, and get down to business. If the locals start a fuss, the muscle moves in."

"Against a seventy-year-old man?"

"Morell was special. He'd lived here longer than anybody. He was the district elder. He carried a lot of respect."

"What was the Second Precinct doing? Or downtown?"

"You've heard of the Favereau Commission? No? I'm not surprised. They've been investigating the 'special relationship' between the Dominicans and Colombians and our people."

Thane Sheridan turned away. That was not what he had wanted to hear.

"Otto Morell was not only organizing the neighborhood against this scum, he was putting pressure on Albany. Not directly, but he knew a good many influential people. Given what he did, he moved, on occasion, among those who count."

"What *did* he do?" Sheridan asked.

"He was a craftsman. A violin maker for the best in the world. He also lent his name to charity and fund-raising numbers."

"Somebody has taken a big, big risk," Sheridan observed.

"The stakes are that high," Mr. Bill said. "The South Americans carve out their turf and guard it violently. One look at the Miami murder sheets will tell you that. I think

51

something has them worried. Either that or else Morell came across something he wasn't supposed to find out."

"A City Hall connection. Or Albany?"

"Could be," Mr. Bill murmured.

The two men were silent for a moment; then Sheridan asked, "What about my communications?"

"They'll be ready in an hour."

"I'll see you back at Thompson Street. I'm going to take her home now."

"Let me know what you think," Mr. Bill called after him. "We don't have all that much to choose from by way of a replacement."

Sheridan waved his hand but did not look back. He returned to the car, motioned the patrol officer away, and took one of the paramedics aside.

"How is she?"

"Could be a lot worse." The paramedic was young, no more than twenty-three or twenty-four, but his face was drawn, worn smooth by horror. "If she had seen what was left of her relative, I would have put her under. As it is, she's handling the shock. Someone should stay with her though."

"Thanks," Sheridan said.

"You with the cops?" the paramedic called to him.

Sheridan turned around.

"Get them, will you? I knew the old man. He was a decent guy." He paused. "I live in the neighborhood too."

Sheridan went back to the car. Sabina Morell was sitting behind the wheel, her head on the rest, a cigarette smoking in her right hand. He reached down, removed the burning filter, and threw it away.

"I'm taking you home," he said. "There's nothing we can do here. Would you move over a bit?"

"If you don't mind, I'll drive," she said at once, sitting up. The red eyes, still brimming, reached out to him. "I'll take it easy, I promise. It's just that I don't think I can sit and do nothing."

He knew the feeling and went around to the passenger side. As soon as he got in, she moved off.

"Sabina . . . I'm sorry. Really. I only just met you, and now this. . . ."

52

"Please don't say anything. I appreciate what you're trying to do, but I can't accept it now. There's so much that has to be done. I have to help Augusta. . . ."

Her voice dried in her throat.

"Would you light me a cigarette, please?"

He did, passed it to her. She accepted silently. Her fingers were like dry ice to his touch.

"I'll take you to Thompson Street—"

"No, it's all right. We'll go to wherever it is you have to go, then I'll take the car."

"Thane, the Rambler—"

"Don't even think about him," he interrupted.

"I don't want to be taken off the case! I know Mr. Bill's going to scout for a replacement."

"I promise you nothing will be done for at least another twenty-four hours," Sheridan assured her. "Call me tomorrow morning and let me know what's happening, all right?"

She nodded, tight-lipped. Sheridan could feel her composure loosening, cracking. As she turned onto Hudson the car suddenly swerved. The right wheel climbed the curb, shackled garbage bins teetering and falling toward the steps of the basement entrance. The screech of metal tearing metal ripped through the car as one of the cans lodged itself under the front end. Sabina pressed on the accelerator, her arms working furiously, the car plowing sideways until the tail of the rear bumper was lodged in between the spikes of a short iron gate. She was out of the car before he could stop her.

"Sabina!"

"They're in there!" she screamed back. "I saw them—" The rest of the words were lost as the door slammed behind her.

The Casa Mendoza was done up to resemble, allegedly, a South American coastal tavern. Fishnets with cork bobbers hung from a weathered timber ceiling. Clusters of green, yellow, and red lights were suspended at intervals, complementing the track lights over the bar. There were half a dozen tables up front, a series of blue-black vinyl booths stretching the length of the bar. The bodega was about half filled, the clientele almost all male, young, and South American.

Sabina Morell did not pause to take in the startled faces that greeted her entry. She ignored the hoots of "Puerco!" that were flung at her. A hand slapped her on the buttocks as she passed by, but she paid no attention. The cousins, who had just perched themselves on the barstools, saw her, and, grinning, turned away. But there was fear shimmering from within the gold-toothed grins.

In one motion Sabina kicked the legs out from under the first stool, tumbling Roncaron against his neighbor. There was the sound of breaking glass, as drinks spilled, and mother oaths. As Sabina had anticipated, Santiago came to the rescue of his cousin's bruised macho. His hand coming at her was all the excuse Sabina needed. She whipped her gun out of the belly holster, raking the barrel across Santiago's face. Blood erupted from his nose as he screamed. A piece of tooth danced across the Formica bar. Instantly Sabina dropped, her knee making contact with Roncaron's forehead, smashing his skull against the length of iron pipe that served as a footrail.

"Listen to me, asshole!" She grabbed him by the hair, shaking him. "You paying attention?" She jammed the gun barrel into his groin. Roncaron groaned.

"Good boy. Now listen. You are a murderer of old defenseless men. You with your balls like peas can only kill the helpless. Isn't that right, turd? I'm going to take you down. You, your faggot cousin, and the pimp Letelier. You understand me, don't you, slug?"

Roncaron's eyes were glazed with terror. Sabina jammed the barrel harder into his groin and thumbed back the hammer. Roncaron's bowels voided.

"You disgusting pig!" she whispered to him.

"You gonna die here, woman. You know you aren't leaving here alive."

They had crowded around her in a semicircle. Under the track lighting she saw knives and razors.

"No one dies."

Sheridan was standing in the doorway, the Venus cradled in his hands.

"Move away," he ordered gently. "Very slowly, back off."

Two came at him, and the Venus spoke. One clip was emptied and a jagged line of torn up linoleum was stitched into the floor.

"The next time it's up the middle."

The crowd parted, eyes on the weapon, mesmerized by it, hungry to snatch it away and use it on him who shamed them with it. But they parted. Sheridan came over to where Sabina was, still clutching Roncaron's hair.

"Get up!" he said harshly.

She rose slowly, faltering. The crowd sensed the vulnerability that was coming off her in waves. Only the triple barrels with their deadly promise kept them back.

"Get me out of here, Thane," she whispered.

"Frisk them!" he ordered.

"You ain't taking nobody, man!"

He knew they might still rush him. They smelled her weakness and were drawn to it in spite of themselves. There was no reason, only the lust for the kill. Very soon they would lose their respect for the gun. Sheridan reached down and hauled Roncaron to his feet, using him as a shield. Sabina did the same with Santiago. The crowd inched forward.

"Take out the bartender and whoever else is behind us." Sheridan murmured.

Death was only seconds away, the vicious, senseless slaughter the Venus would inflict. Then—the sound of a siren. And another. Sheridan did not take his eyes off the crowd. He was furious with Sabina for what she had just done. But inadvertantly she had given him something. Thane Sheridan's eyes traveled from one face to the next. The smell of the Midnight Rambler was very strong, his presence overwhelming, almost sickening Sheridan. The Rambler had been here, maybe still was. He was very close. . . .

Part II

Chapter Four

The next day was February 11, Vietnam Memorial Day. For Thane Sheridan it was something else: day five since the Rambler had killed. He had at best forty-eight hours before the next child was taken.

At midmorning he drove out to Brooklyn, passing a parade forming on Lafayette Avenue. The cadet marching band was struggling to get its instruments off the school bus. Along the sidewalk men in their fifties and sixties were huddled together under the cold sun, which had already climbed high in the sky. Sheridan didn't see many young faces in their ranks. He wondered why, even after the agony, shame, and anger, the veterans of his war to whom this day had been dedicated still stayed away.

Slowly he drove to Cumberland Street. He stopped at the corner, reading the headlines off morning papers plastered along the side of a vendor's booth. The Brooklyn daily was still running the Rosenberg killing as a lead. But no connection had been made between this slaying and the ones in Chicago. Otherwise the typeface would have screamed out a different message. Sheridan wheeled the car onto Cumberland.

The district was residential, the duplexes each with their hundred square feet of tended lawn. Most had hedges or shrubbery and a short chain-link fence. The paint was new, the sidewalks and gutters clean. The Rosenbergs, as owners, lived on the ground floor of number 274.

"What you want?"

The elderly woman who had come down to answer the door did not disguise her hostility. The sharp black eyes summed up Sheridan as an outsider.

"I have to see Edna Rosenberg," Sheridan said, offering his Special Investigations ID.

"We are sitting *shiva* here, mister. Please, go away."

She started to close the door on him.

"I'm sorry," he said. "I didn't know. But it's very important."

"It's always very *important*," the old woman said bitterly, "and everyone is very *sorry*. But have you caught him yet?"

"No."

The old woman clicked her dentures in disgust.

"Rose, who is it?" The voice was male, subdued but authoritative.

"A *paskudnyak* from the police department who has no respect for *shiva*."

Sheridan heard the slap of leather against terrazzo. The rabbi was younger than he had expected, with a face that reflected patience reinforced by fortitude. He had left the door to the apartment open. Low voices, the tinkle of china filtered into the hallway.

"I am Rabbi Schecter. May I see your identification?"

He read it through and said, "Rose, would you go upstairs, please."

The old woman sighed heavily, nostrils quivering like a mare's, and began to mount the steps.

"And please, close the door." He turned back to Sheridan. "How can I assist you, Inspector?"

"I need to speak to Mrs. Rosenberg. Her husband as well. I'll also need a very recent photograph of their child."

"Nothing else?" The question was rich with irony.

"I'm sorry to have to ask for even this," Sheridan murmured.

"They've been questioned by the police already," Rabbi Schecter said. "To go over the details again—"

"You've seen the body, Rabbi."

The eyes snapped up, growing in pain behind the black frame glasses.

"I did."

Rabbi Schecter had *insisted* on viewing the corpse. He had gone so far as to ask for and receive an audience with the rebbe of the Luvaritchers of Brooklyn, before whom he pleaded for support. The rebbe had intervened, and a day later Schecter gazed down upon the remains of Rachel Rosenberg. He vowed the family would never see her like this.

"He's going to kill again," Sheridan told him, breaking the silence. "He's going to go after another child, and another after that unless I stop him."

The rabbi looked at Sheridan very carefully.

"You are different from the others," he said finally. "I know they weren't going through the motions, that they were sincere as far as it was possible for them to be so. But you are different. You know the killer."

"If I did, Rabbi, I would have brought you his head. But I can find him. With help I can find him."

"Go downstairs. I'll bring the Rosenbergs to you."

It was the kind of rec room he had once finished for his son: knotty pine paneling, perforated tile ceiling, smooth linoleum on the floor. The only difference was in decor. This was a girl's room with soft pastel curtains, a flower-print divan, the closet open to reveal baby strollers and dolls. The atmosphere created by these girlish touches jarred with the professionalism of the far corner: gleaming music and instrument stands, an expensive tape recording unit with matching amplifiers and speakers, a high-gloss enamel bookcase for sheet music, and an entire wall unit given over to records. Rachel Rosenberg had wanted for nothing.

Thane Sheridan looked at each piece carefully, touching some. He ejected the cassette in the machine: Schubert's "Trout" Quintet. He glanced through a sheaf of sheet music and cocked his head to read the titles of the albums. He was seeking to reach out and touch Rachel Rosenberg. He wanted to know why the Rambler had done so.

In one respect it was a futile effort. There was no pattern to be discerned among the Rambler's thirty-seven victims, other than their age bracket. The killer made no distinctions based on racial origin: He took whites, blacks, Orientals, and in two instances American Indian boys. Sex was not a factor either: twenty males, seventeen females. Social position of the parents appeared irrelevant. The Rambler selected from all strata, from the upper middle class right down to the most recent immigrant. Of thirty-six victims sixteen had been Catholic, fourteen Protestant, one, a Japanese, Shinto, the remainder Jewish.

"She was an exceptional child, Mr. Sheridan. Perhaps you will want to borrow a tape recording of one of her performances."

Sheridan had been so intent on his thoughts he hadn't heard them come down. Rabbi Schecter was in the lead. Behind him followed a tall, big-boned man, with stooped shoulders but head held high, pale gray eyes staring straight ahead. Had he not been holding his wife's arm, Sheridan might have thought him blind. He moved in shuffling footsteps, slippers dragging along the floor.

"This is Abraham Rosenberg," Rabbi Schecter said by way of introduction, "and his wife, Edna. I've told them who you are."

Sheridan came forward and held out his hand. "I'm very sorry," he said. "Condolences are poor enough, but I ask you to accept mine. Also my thanks for seeing me."

"Do you have news for us, Mr. Sheridan?" Edna Rosenberg asked. Her voice was brittle, like autumn leaves.

"No, I'm afraid not."

"But you have more questions."

"Yes. Most of them have already been asked, but I have to put them to you once more."

Silence. Sheridan glanced at the rabbi, who nodded.

"Mrs. Rosenberg, you were in the lounge area, waiting for your daughter, when you were attacked. You don't remember hearing or seeing anyone until he had his hands on you?"

"That is correct," the woman answered woodenly. "I have said that already."

"Did you feel his breath on you?"

Edna Rosenberg's eyes narrowed. "What are you saying?"

"Did you feel his breathing? Was it heavy, like that of a man who has just run a great distance or climbed a staircase? Was there any wheezing or a hacking cough?"

Rachel Rosenberg's mother considered the questions. "No."

"Was there any scent to his breath? A peppermint flavor or a distinctive odor that you remember?"

"Strega," she said instantly.

"Strega?"

"Yes, the Italian liqueur. His breath was like Strega. Resiny."

"What about the grip? Soft fingers or rough, calloused?"

"Callouses. He was very strong. A workman's hands."

Edna Rosenberg gripped her husband's right hand and showed it to Sheridan.

"Like these."

The butcher's fingers were blunt, powerful, scrupulously clean but weathered from the cold, rough texture of the meat he handled.

"How did your attacker approach you, Mrs. Rosenberg?" Sheridan asked quietly. The question was sudden, designed to prompt a hidden memory. Perhaps the answer would add to what he already knew from police on-site reports.

"I don't remember. I would never have believed such a thing possible."

"I know the incident happened very quickly," Sheridan persisted. "But even for a split second did you have any idea, any sixth sense or intuition of who was attacking you?"

"In my whole life I have never been touched by anyone other than my husband, Mr. Sheridan," Edna Rosenberg said with dignity. "No one we know, have known for thirty years—no one at the school would have presumed to touch me like that. So no, I *don't* know."

"It was raining the night you came to pick up your daughter. You didn't see anyone who looked out of place?"

"I was lucky to find a parking space right away. I sat in the car for a moment, then went directly into the building."

For a moment Sheridan said nothing. He turned away, toward the music corner, and closed his eyes.

"Mrs. Rosenberg," he asked softly, "at seven o'clock Eighth Avenue is a busy street. How did you manage to find a spot so easily?"

"Because a truck was backing away just as I drove up—"

"Just as you drove up, or was it waiting for you?"

"I don't understand," she stammered.

63

Sheridan turned around and approached her slowly. He had to be very careful now.

"Did the truck pull out a few seconds *before* you were in a position to take its place, or did you wait behind, off to one side, leaving it enough room to back out?"

Edna Rosenberg hesitated. "I waited. It was only a few seconds, but yes, I waited for it to move."

"Can you give me a description of the truck?" Sheridan asked gently.

A few minutes later, after he had coaxed the details from her, Sheridan said, "Now that you're thinking about the vehicle, something else might come back. Please, no matter how small or insignificant the observation, write it down—immediately. Then call me at a number I'll leave with you. It's a confidential line, manned twenty-four hours a day."

"Is there anything more, Mr. Sheridan?" the rabbi broke in. Sheridan appreciated his concern. He was pushing the woman hard and wondered why her husband didn't volunteer at least some background information.

"A couple more points. Please, it won't take long." He paused. "Did your daughter mention seeing anyone suspicious around the school during the past week? Someone watching. Or perhaps other students might have said something to her?"

"If they did, Mr. Sheridan, Rachel said nothing to me. You must understand, she was practicing very hard—" The voice began to crack.

"I realize that," Sheridan said quickly. "But she was an exceptional girl. If anyone had noticed anything out of the ordinary, she would have."

"There was nothing," the mother said helplessly. "I have tried to think, but nothing . . ."

"And it wasn't unusual for you to be picking Rachel up. You had been doing so all the past week. It was common knowledge."

"Of course. Our friends knew. Abraham was so proud. He talked of nothing else at work. . . ."

Her voice trailed off as the idea dawned on her.

"No, Mrs. Rosenberg, don't even think that," Sheridan said firmly. "I want you to believe me: Nothing you or your husband did or said drew the killer to Rachel."

"We are Jewish, Mr. Sheridan. Rachel was mutilated. We know she was. That was why we were not permitted to see her."

It was as though a cold hand had clamped itself over his heart and squeezed. The words almost tumbled out of his mouth. They seemed so little to offer, yet they would still an ancient fear. But he dared not say them. He could not tell the Rosenbergs about the other killings, point out conclusively that their being a Jewish family had nothing to do with Rachel's death. He understood that if he made such a connection for them, they would use it to reassure friends who shared their fears. The secret would be out.

"Not that she was Jewish, or a girl ten years old," Sheridan whispered. "None of these things had any bearing on what happened. You have a right to the truth. As does the rabbi and your community. If there was any evidence of anti-Semitism, *any at all*, I would tell you."

"Mr. Sheridan, I think it's time," Rabbi Schecter intervened.

"Just the photograph."

The Rosenbergs had already begun to walk away from him, the wife leading her husband. The rabbi handed Sheridan an eight-by-ten glossy.

"They had this in their silver frame in the living room. Abraham himself took it out and gave it to me."

"Why didn't he say anything?" Sheridan demanded. "He could have helped her."

The rabbi sighed. "Mr. Sheridan, Abe Rosenberg has vowed not to speak a single word voluntarily until his child's killer is dealt with. Can you imagine that? Not a word. And I assure you he has kept his promise. I have already intervened for him at work. They moved him from the front counter to the back lockers . . . where he doesn't have to deal with customers."

"Why?"

"Because he believes God is punishing him. Rachel was delivered unto Him for his sins. Atonement, Mr. Sheridan, atonement. The only place he breaks his vow is in his sleep. Even the people upstairs can hear him screaming. . . ."

* * *

Before he pulled away from 274 Cumberland, Thane Sheridan telephoned Mr. Bill on the scrambler line. The two men met an hour later in the Main Bar of the Harvard Club on West Forty-fourth, a small area under the rafters members could reserve for private use. William Rodgers was sitting in a green leather club chair, absently looking out the window. Prints of game and hunting dogs shimmered in the indirect lighting. The mocha walnut paneling further depressed an already low ceiling.

"I brought you two club sodas, with lime," Mr. Bill said.

"I spoke with Mrs. Rosenberg," Sheridan said. "I'll need a printout on a white panel truck, Dodge or Plymouth, New York plates, commercial. The call letters are RRN."

"Where in hell did she get that?" Mr. Bill demanded.

"Someone was waiting for her. He had a space right outside the school. He knew she would be coming to pick up her daughter. He watched her approach on Eighth Avenue, moving slowly. The rain was heavy, she was peering through it for an empty space. He turned the ignition, the reverse light went on. He made sure she was close enough so that no one else would get the space, then pulled out. He probably watched her park and walk inside. There was enough time. All he had to do was go around the corner and back into the lane."

Mr. Bill picked up the electronic remote phone and dialed his office. In clipped phrases he relayed Sheridan's details about the vehicle to his people at Police Plaza. The results of the computer search were to be top secret, his eyes only, until he issued orders to the contrary.

"How did she remember this?" he asked quietly.

"No one picked it up," Sheridan said. "No one bothered to ask her about the parking. So the first mention we had of the truck was from the New School of Drama and Music internal security, which saw the vehicle leave the NSDM drive. Now we know where it came from."

"And the license plate?" Mr. Bill sighed.

"We lucked out. It was a mnemonic trick: The first two letters were her daughter's initials; the *N* she simply remembered."

"And the make?"

"The dealer from whom she and her husband bought

their wagon had Plymouth and Dodge panels. The Rosenbergs are conscientious consumers. They visited dealers all over, even in Jersey. They saw a lot of trucks."

"How do you feel about the truck?"

Sheridan drained his glass of soda and refilled it, the bubbles moistening his fingertips.

"I don't know," he said finally. "I can't integrate it into the picture. Can't make the connection between it and Rachel Rosenberg. Don't get me wrong; when we find the truck we'll find traces of her and maybe something of the Rambler. But I can't feel him. Not the same way."

"The same as yesterday?" Mr. Bill asked quietly. "In the Casa Mendoza?"

Sheridan looked up at him, a tight, surprised smile on his lips.

"I don't really care that an officer temporarily assigned to my office went berserk after seeing how her relative died," Mr. Bill continued, the sarcasm finely honed. "I'm not even faulting you for not stopping her. Not being *able* to stop her. Even the little scene in the bodega could be forgiven, lack of warrant, brutality, threats, intimidation, firepower."

"There was just cause," Sheridan said. "She saw suspects, went in, was threatened. Force had to be used."

"That's not the way Letelier's lawyers say it happened."

"The Colombians are out?"

"Early this morning. Homicide hasn't got anything to link them with Morell's killing." He paused. "Neither do you."

"The Rambler was in there, or around there," Sheridan murmured. "Take it on faith."

"I don't have to. I have the reports of the patrolmen who arrived on the scene. What they wrote in their best grammar-school English reads like a treatment for one of your novels. They say you were standing by the bar with that goddamn Venus weaving from side to side like a three-headed cobra. They'd never seen eyes like yours, not even on Manson or Son of Sam. You looked like a troglodyte watching some creature coming at you out of the night. The *cops* were terrified to walk up to you, lest you pull the trigger."

Sheridan drank the rest of his water. He reached inside his glass, plucked out the lime, and in one bite tore away the bitter flesh.

"Thane, if you said you smelled the Rambler, I believe you. But think! For Christ's sake, think if he's gotten himself into Letelier's crowd! If the Rambler intends to operate using it as a screen, that means you'll have to infiltrate the number-one dope organization in the city to get at him. The tong wars of Chinatown will seem mild by comparison to the bodies we'll be left with."

"We won't have to go that route," Sheridan said. He deposited the rind back in his glass. "Not if you get Nevada for me."

"Jesus Christ on a sidecar, you don't want Nevada, do you?" Mr. Bill exploded.

Sheridan nodded.

"Why? Bringing that crazy son of a bitch in is like letting the proverbial bull into a china shop!"

"I won't be able to cover all the bases," Sheridan said quietly. "And believe me, this game's going to expand. I *need* Nevada. He's the only one who can walk in the territory that's been targeted . . . that I *think* has been targeted."

He paused. "He's the only one who knows how I think, who won't have to second-guess me. I need him."

Mr. Bill grimaced. "I'll get him for you. I just hope he's not on some kamikaze assignment."

"Where is Detective Sergeant Morell?"

"Not at home, or in the office."

"I'd prefer to keep her, if it's all the same to you," said Sheridan. "I need someone who can use brutality, threats, intimidation, and firepower."

By the time Sheridan returned to the lab on Thompson Street, Mr. Bill's cleaning lady, a force veteran's widow, had come and gone. As a result of her patient labor the large loft-style suite sparkled. A fresh coat of wax had been laid down on the wide, pegged floorboards, reflecting the subdued track lighting against the creamy, rough-finished plaster walls. The furniture was old but of exceptional quality, as befitted Mr. Bill's castoffs: One area of the main floor was closed off by old Chinese lacquered partitions, behind which were a desk, a separate switchboard wall panel for a battery of phones, and a Telex. On another table was a 16 millimeter projector. Across from that, on the opposite wall, was a screen, already mounted, and to one side a Zenith console television. On the other side of the screen were the living quarters: the bed, closest to the screen, with a seven-channel phone, then a dresser and armoire. A partition and door concealed the bathroom and shower, whose plumbing connected with the kitchen unit that stretched out along the remainder of the wall. A Finnish dining suite gave way to a mahogany leather sofa with matching overstuffed chairs, which were clustered around a copper coffee table. Modern accents included a chrome pedestal lamp. Along the far wall was a small Mediterranean-style fireplace. Sheridan shook his head at the hodge-podge design. Somehow it worked. He walked over to the picture window in the living room and looked outside. He tapped on the glass. The people passing below could neither hear nor see him. The glass was one way, bulletproof. He came around the corner and mounted the first three steps of the ladder leading to the loft. A reading area: one chair, footstool, lamp, and horizontal filing cabinet. On the floor were three sealed cartons, bonded by an FBI courier. What Sheridan referred to as his Chicago notes.

Sheridan swung off his coat and jacket and went into the bathroom. After splashing cold water on his face he went over to the armoire. His clothing, what there was of it, had been neatly laid out. He took an old camel's hair sweater with elbow patches off the hanger, slipped it on, and went back to the loft ladder. Now, as at the beginning of every other investigation, was the time he had to immerse himself in his private nightmare.

"Sabina . . . I'm sorry about your uncle."

Dr. John Davey, chief of Forensic Science, borough of Manhattan, draped his arm about her shoulder and led her to the glass cubicle which served as a mini-lounge.

"Thank you, John."

Sabina Morell accepted the Londoner's cup of coffee and sat back in one of the red plastic chairs. Fatigue was catching up with her. Her body ached as though every limb had been systematically beaten. She marveled at the way the agony of the soul could be transmitted to bone and muscle. She remembered last night, beginning with her arrival at her aunt's house, as a dreamer might recall fragments of a nightmare. Otto Morell's closest friends were already there. His wife, now a widow, had almost run to her when Sabina had come through the door. The two women flung their arms around and held each other tightly, tears spilling and mingling. Here, in the privacy of his home, among friends, composure wasn't necessary. Only when their silent embrace broke did Sabina say anything to the others. Behind their sincere and profound regret she saw the unmistakable reproach that was one of the reasons Sabina hadn't slept last night. She could not close her eyes without those accusatory expressions swimming before her vision.

Davey passed a hand through slicked-back thinning hair and perched himself on the edge of the counter.

"There's not much to add to the initial report," he said apologetically. "A couple more fragments of the gas cylinder were brought in, a piece of the cane . . ."

"No fibers off his clothing that we can connect to what the cousins were wearing?"

Davey shook his head. "I'm sorry. The fire effectively destroyed any link."

"It doesn't matter," Sabina said. "We know who killed him."

The British scientist reached out and squeezed her shoulder with his smooth hand. He had heard about the incident at the bodega. He also knew that Sabina had been down at the criminal courts first thing this morning. Apparently the cousins had smiled at her on their way out after the hearing which established the lack of evidence against them. Letelier's lawyer had spoken to the press, talking about high-handed police methods, staring openly at Sabina as he did so.

"Unless you get a witness—" Davey started to say.

"I know, John. I didn't come here for that. I want to have another look at what you picked up at the New School of Drama and Music."

70

Davey slid off the counter and went into his adjoining office. A minute later he reappeared with a single-spaced typewritten sheet and handed it to Sabina.

Sabina looked slowly down the list. The floor, rug, and seats in the lobby had all been vacuumed, the dirt and dust sifted for possible clues. A button, threads, a piece of leather or rubber from a shoe sole. Traces of mud led Davey and his forensic investigators into the instructors' lounge. On the edges of the door handle they found traces of wool from the gloves the killer had worn. These matched the fibers taken from Edna Rosenberg's coat, left there when the killer dragged her to the other chair. From the lounge the trail of still-wet markings, parts of a footprint, led the investigators along the corridor that ran along the side of the building. This area too was swept. The forensic team's efforts stopped at the rear exit door. The rain would have washed away whatever minute clues the killer might have left. Nonetheless a team went through the garbage and debris in the alley.

Sabina Morell put the list aside. Perhaps it hadn't been such a good idea to come in. Maybe she should have stayed with Augusta, helped her see to the arrangements that had to be made. But no, she and her aunt were very much alike in temperament and personality. Each needed privacy in order to regroup, reorganize after the tragedy. Looking after the funeral arrangements, cleaning out Otto's clothing, calling the lawyers about the will, informing the bank, these were all things Augusta would use to absorb her grief. But above all there would be the few precious hours of solitude before she was forced to deal with the outside world. That would be the only time left to her in which to somehow understand, if such a thing was possible, what it was that had happened to her husband.

"Nothing we can really deal with, is there?" Sabina said listlessly.

"There's no follow-up," Davey replied, taking out a pipe. He blew through the stem, producing a low whistle. "We can't match what we found with anything . . ."

Sabina knew why he didn't finish the sentence. Only if the killer struck again, leaving behind something else, could the cross-checks begin. Too often the links in an investigation were more expensive than those on the most precious bracelets.

"John, let me see again what you have."

Davey shrugged. He knew the syndrome. Investigating officers often walked around and around their evidence like spectators in an art gallery viewing a painting or sculpture from every conceivable angle. There was always the possibility of discovering something, not new, but hitherto unseen, a detail hidden in the overall composition, a clue which, when standing alone, was meaningless, but which, when added to something one had just learned, was suddenly illuminating. Always the possibility, seldom the consummation.

Davey led Sabina into the lab proper. Along one wall were horizontal shelves, twice the length of the kind found in offices. He ran his fingers along the plastic-sheathed cards until he found the right one. When he pulled the drawer out and up, Sabina's heart sank. Ten plastic containers the size of sandwich bags but made of heavy polyurethane with a special zip lock. That was all the police had on Rachel Rosenberg's killer. Most of the material, fragments of wool, a scrap of cotton, mud samples taken off the carpet, any other foreign fibers not related to lounge carpeting or drapes, could not be linked to anything. Not one piece was unique or distinctive.

"What's this?" She reached for a bag containing a single white hair.

Davey took the bag from her and read his shorthand on the attached tag.

"A strand of horsehair."

"Correct me if I'm wrong, John," Sabina said, frowning. "Wasn't this brown when you found it, as if it had come from the stuffing of one of those old chairs?"

"We found moisture on it when we tested it."

"John, pass me the Black Book," Sabina said at once, her voice low, urgent.

He handed her a ledger from the top of the cabinet. "What did you see?"

"I'm not sure yet. There's something I have to check."

The skylight in the loft had been sealed. For security a

steel shutter had been bolted to the roof and, a secondary precaution, almost invisible lines of filament wire placed beneath the glass. Even if someone managed to get through the shutters, the breaking or lifting of the glass would set off the silent alarms. Thus having only the lamplight to read by, Thane Sheridan had lost all track of time. He closed the last file and placed it on top of all the rest. A stack of multicolored folders which held details of untold brutality, spawned by a faceless horror, a horror he knew only by smell. Thane Sheridan rose and stretched. He climbed down the loft ladder and saw that the afternoon had disappeared. He checked the refrigerator, ground some coffee, filled the automatic drip maker with water, and went back into the living room. He decided he would build a fire while he waited for the water to seep through the filter. He had lit the kindling and was pouring his coffee when the telephone sounded—the blue line, internal security.

"Detective Sergeant Morell, Second Precinct, to see you."

"Send her up."

Sheridan was annoyed by the intrusion. Throughout an investigation, but especially at the beginning, he absented himself from the field, taking stretches of time to go over and over the material gleaned from the other cities. Such a procedure might have appeared a waste of valuable time and mental energy, but Thane Sheridan could not go by standard homicide rules, which governed procedure for many *different* cases, not one whose parameters had been established, whose traits surfaced to repeat themselves time and time again. The Midnight Rambler was one long open file stretching across a continent from the Golden Gate to Manhattan. The usual rules did not apply. Sheridan knew that the homicide chiefs in every city the Rambler had visited understood what the former CIA Vietnam vet, widower and victim, was doing. But they were the only ones who did. Their men often regarded Sheridan as a nuisance, an outsider not to be taken seriously, tolerated but never confided in. His methods had only added to their contempt. Sometimes Sheridan wondered if they didn't have more than a shred of justification for their opinion.

"Come in."

The knocking died away, and Sabina Morell entered.

"Hello," Sheridan said softly. Suddenly he was ashamed of his irritation at her arrival.

"Hi." She came forward hesitantly, not sure of her status much less his welcome.

"I've just made some coffee. Want a cup?"

"Please."

She removed her beret and shook her hair free. He was struck by her porcelain beauty, made more fragile now by the startling discrepancy between white skin and the enormous turquoise eyes. Then he remembered Casa Mendoza. He brought their cups over to the coffee table. Sabina had pulled one of the chairs closer to the fire and was holding her palms out to the flames.

"Nasty out there?"

"It feels as though the rain will continue forever," she said. "You look up and you can't even see the sky, just the constant rain. And the wind, cold and awfully damp. An evil wind."

"There are other winds like that. On the Coast, off the desert, we have the Santa Ana. In North Africa it's the sirocco, in Switzerland the foehn, and France has its mistral."

"I read somewhere that in Switzerland, when the wind blows, people come unhinged. Crimes of passion double, triple. The Swiss criminal courts take the foehn into account when handing down sentences, don't they?"

"It's true, they do," Sheridan agreed.

"Do you believe climate can madden people?" she asked.

"Yes, I do."

"I have the awful feeling I'm intruding," Sabina said, smiling tentatively. "There's an explosive air in here, as though you've been working very hard."

"You're not intruding," Sheridan told her. "You're my partner."

"Still?"

"Still." He paused. "How is it for you now?"

"Hanging in. We're cut from a pretty tough cloth, Augusta and I. We'll survive."

"Who's in charge of the case?"

"Donnellan. He's very good. Used to work up in Boston."

74

"The IRA stalker."

"That's him. I imagine he's quite a bit like you."

Sheridan said nothing. He had heard of Donnellan. Not only because of his IRA hunts but in connection with an affair concerning a Vatican chalice. They were kindred spirits, he and Francis Xavier Donnellan.

"Except he doesn't write books."

"Pardon?"

Sabina put her coffee aside and reached down for her purse.

"He doesn't write books the way you do." She found her cigarettes, offered one to Sheridan, who accepted and lit both.

"Detective Sergeant Morell, only my agent and publisher know my real identity." Sheridan laughed. "Someone's been talking out of class."

"Not at all." Sabina smiled. "My ex-husband is a fan of 'Douglas Ryan.' He was reading an interview done by the *Times Book Review*. I happened to see it—and your picture, mostly the back of your head, but enough profile for me to put the rest together when I saw you."

"That interview was done over a year and a half ago," Sheridan murmured.

"I have a hell of a memory."

"Indeed."

"Why writing, Thane? Especially the occult? It seems so far removed from your experiences."

She was dead wrong. Sheridan hoped she would never have to find that out firsthand.

He rose and went up into the loft. He called her over and began handing down stacks of files. When these were all downstairs, forming a pile level with the ottoman Sabina Morell was sitting on, Sheridan said, "Let me tell you about the Midnight Rambler.

"Mass murders have always tended to take place in a given locale. The Atlanta killings are a good example; also the Ridgewald case in Texas—the mass killings of immigrant workers outside of San Antonio. The Pulman homosexual murders in the Chicago suburbs, the girl scout atrocity in Colorado. In each instance the killers worked a definite territory. They did not venture beyond certain parameters."

"In two of those cases, Pulman and Colorado, there was uncertainty that the right man had been caught," Sabina reminded him. "The guilty verdict was challenged by many. It was believed the jury handed it down because someone had to be put away. It was as though the community demanded an end to the affair, right or wrong."

"True," Sheridan agreed. "It's conceivable that even though the killings stopped, the wrong man was convicted. However, in the Rambler's case, the killer moves around."

"That's assuming he is one and the same man," Sabina interjected.

"He is the same," Sheridan said quietly. "From methodology alone I can prove that. But what we have here is someone who enters a community and savages it within a short period of time. By the time public panic peaks, the Rambler has finished. Nothing more is heard from him. In the aftermath the public slowly begins to unwind. The children are buried, the horror is shunted to the back of the mind. Self-preservation takes over. Now, if the Rambler was to return to that same community a few months later, all hell would break loose. But he doesn't. He surfaces elsewhere."

"One man or several?"

"One," Sheridan said firmly. "Psychopaths are solitary by nature. They can recognize their own kind, but they couldn't work together. Their impulses to kill would have to correlate exactly. The likelihood is a million to one against that. If they tried to collaborate and the impulse of one lagged behind that of the other, one of them would die."

"Given, then, that this is one man and the *same* man, could we be dealing with a *physically* sick individual?" Sabina asked. "If I remember correctly, Charles Whitman, the mass murderer of the University of Texas tower, had a malignant brain tumor, a glioblastoma multiform. I don't think that the true size was ever established because of gunshot wounds to Whitman's head. But the neuropathologist thinks it lay in the medial part of the temporal lobe . . . and was about the size of a walnut."

76

"You've done your homework," Sheridan said. "The Rambler might be suffering from a similar condition, but either way it's of little value to us. Contrary to popular belief, killers with such afflictions do not kill from sudden, episodic attacks of violence. Remember that Whitman kept a diary. He detailed exactly what clothing he would wear, how he would defend his position in the tower, and he had outlined an escape route. He also killed his mother and wife *the night before* he climbed into the tower. The planning and premeditation, the attention to detail and ability to complete the act after having already started it the previous evening all point to a psychopath."

"Given that he's a planner, have you come across any characteristics or behavior patterns which would give him away?" asked Sabina.

Sheridan gestured at the window. "Take a look outside. *Anyone* passing in the street could be a psychopath. You'd never know it. About twenty years ago Cleckley wrote a book which I think still presents the best overall view of the psychopath. He described the condition—to summarize briefly—as a mask of sanity. The psychopath literally indulges in his crime, wallows in it. It matters not at all to him that the risks he takes are enormous, the consequences, if he's caught, swift and certain. Very often the magnitude of the crime isn't commensurate with its ultimate gain. Yet the act is repeated and repeated until from the pattern we can get to him. But except when he is actually committing the crime, the mask of sanity drops over our man. He goes to the office, attends to his wife and children or friends, dabbles in his hobbies, follows a definite and often socially acceptable life-style until the next time."

"What you're really saying is that we can't get to him until he kills again," Sabina said softly. "If after all the investigations you've done, you haven't been able to put together a composite, even a discernable personality profile, much less any identity . . ."

"I'm not saying that at all," Sheridan broke in gently. "There is one pattern he's never wavered from: He never kills the last five victims immediately."

"I don't understand," Sabina protested. "*All* the children were found murdered."

"Yes, but we've held back the crucial detail: The five were murdered *together*, all at once. You see, it's as though the first child is killed to terrorize, to infect the community with fear. The murder is obscene, ritualistic. The first child is a sacrifice, Sabina, to himself, the powers that guide him . . . whatever. From autopsy reports we've kept secret we know that the five others were killed at the same time, just before the Rambler was ready to move on."

"What kind of sick son of a bitch is he?" Sabina breathed. "He keeps children for three or four weeks. . . . Does he abuse them?"

"There has never, not in one case, been any sexual molestation," said Sheridan. "But with every child we found pinpricks in the forearms. They were fed intravenously, a carefully measured protein-vitamin diet. There was also evidence of substantial amounts of phenobarbital in their systems to indicate he kept them sleeping for long periods of time."

"Like a spider, wrapping its food in a web," Sabina said.

"There were no bedsores on their bodies," Sheridan continued. "No bruises or welts on their wrists or ankles to indicate they had been tied up."

"And he murdered all of them by water," Sabina said dully. "They were found drowned, one way or another."

Sheridan nodded but said nothing. He remembered how he had found his own son, stacked in a shower stall with four other corpses. The stall had been water sealed along the sides and base, the children packed inside, standing up, their bodies jammed one up against the other so they wouldn't fall. The stall door had been sealed closed. Then he had turned the water on, let the six-foot stall fill to within an inch of the top. The tallest of the children had been Andrew, only three feet eight inches. . . .

"The location of the bodies was the worst thing of all," Sheridan whispered, his voice becoming disembodied, his eyes glazing over in memory.

"Thane, don't!"

"Always a midtown location, sometimes literally under our noses. That's what I really can't forgive myself for. That in spite of the manpower we still missed his nests . . ."

"Why the writing, Thane?" Sabina asked quickly, wanting to break away from the subject.

Sheridan drained his coffee and leaned forward, elbows on knees, fingers intertwined.

"When the Rambler had finished with San Francisco, I knew that wasn't to be the end of it. I picked up his scent and I was terrified. I knew he would kill again. It was just a matter of when and where. I began to study evil, Sabina. Evil as a vibrant, real force that compels people to actions as surely as love, charity, jealousy, or lust. I had smelled such evil in Vietnam. It was rawer there, in the Highlands, where the mountain people still believed in the powers of magic. They carried M-16 equipment, but they respected the powers of the forests and jungles. They used it to slay their enemies. . . .

"I read so much, asked so many questions of priests, psychiatrists, doctors, psychics, that eventually I was filled with information I really couldn't use or apply. Writing was a safety valve. It allowed me the luxury of speculation. For the first time I let my imagination loose, using what I had learned as a very rough terrain contour map."

That too was a lie. He had asked the questions because they were the only ones left. He never truly believed they would lead him into worlds so far removed from his own, worlds he had come to respect . . . out of terror.

Sheridan paused. "The curious thing is that this process allowed me to get closer to the Rambler than would otherwise have been possible. I was looking for a man who didn't give shit for the homicide rule book. He had an enormous ego. Every killing he committed that I couldn't solve swelled his vanity. He had imagination and cunning. Through the writing I wandered into the labyrinth of his evil, and I have come to believe, as I'm sure the Rambler already knows, that some people are inherently evil. He accepts his condition, and so must I. There is no social or physical or psychological excuse for him. He operates in an inverse universe, where evil is good, sickness is health, torture is pleasure. That's why the Venus. Because when I find the Rambler, I'm going to take him down. And when he's dead, I'll torch his body and watch until even the bones are reduced to ashes."

"Is that what's in the file—your odyssey in search of the Rambler?" she asked softly.

"All of it."

The phone rang, breaking the silence between them.

"It might be for me," Sabina said.

It was. Sheridan handed her the receiver and moved away. When Sabina returned, her expression was one of resignation.

"There was a horsehair found on the chair where Mrs. Rosenberg was assaulted," she said. "The lab downstairs has identified it as being different from the stuffing in the cushions, but that's it."

"I don't follow."

"Horsehair, when wet, changes color. This strand got wet somehow, so it was the color of the cushion stuffing when it was found. But I'm almost positive the strand did not belong in any furniture, that it came off something else."

"Like?"

"A violin, viola, or bass bow."

"What did you want the lab to find out?"

"Where the horsehair had been treated. Their computer doesn't have the information. It's a long shot. But it bothers me. If we knew where the hair had been treated, then we'd know who had it sent here to be made into a bow—"

Sheridan was already moving. "Call the lab on the other line," he said over his shoulder. "Tell them to have the sample packaged and ready for pick-up."

Sheridan went over to the bank of telephones and lifted the green receiver. There was no dial tone. He waited fifteen seconds, then said, "This is New York, Orion One."

"Orion One, this is Langley. What can we do for you, Thane?"

"I'm leaving La Guardia within the hour with a sample. We may have something."

"Acknowledged, Orion One. We'll get Hirsh out of bed."

The line went dead. He reached for the red receiver. The call was automatically routed through Mr. Bill's office to his limousine mired on Fifth Avenue.

"I need a jet with fuel for Washington, return. A car and driver to meet me at Dulles."

"It's yours. What's doing?"

"Morell found something that ties in with Chicago," Sheridan said.

"Oh, shit!"

"I'm on my way to the lab to pick it up now. I'll be back by morning. Langley is standing by."

"Call from there if anything develops."

The line went dead.

"I'll come with you," Sabina said instantly.

"I want you to stay here and read through that," Sheridan told her. "By the time I get back, I want you to know those details, *understand* them, as well as I do."

"All right," she said softly.

Sheridan glanced at his watch. Eight fifteen. Less than four hours remained in day six. He had thirty to forty hours left before the Rambler moved. He wondered if he finally had something with which to bait the trap.

Chapter Five

Thane Sheridan was mentally noting the features that had changed in and around Langley since his last visit. Only eighteen months had elapsed, but things never stood still.

The road leading off the Virginia interstate had been given a fresh coat of blacktop. The light suspension of the medium-size sedan, a departure from the Agency's big Oldsmobiles and Cadillacs, handled the two-lane highway smoothly. At the main gate visual identification had been replaced by an electronic scan: Sheridan and his escort were invited to alight from the car and under the unblinking scrutiny of the evening detail pressed their palms against the cool glass plate. Their skin patterns were electronically reproduced, the patterns fed into the security computer, and the appropriate authorization flashed on the adjoining screen.

Sheridan's driver circled around the statue of Nathan Hale, illuminated by floodlights, and stopped before the main doors. An internal escort materialized to open the door and led Sheridan into the mammoth foyer, where an identity tag the size of a large file card was looped around his neck with a thin chain. Sheridan examined the color photograph of himself. It was exceptionally sharp, and his features were definitely tanned. He thought of Bill McBride. The memory slipped across to Gwen, then, for some reason, to Sabina Morell.

"Believe me, Sheridan, we'd *all* rather be in our beds humping Vegas show girls, real or imagined."

Al Hirsh, chief of what the Agency obliquely termed its Discovery Section, half-walked, half-skated across the marble in slippers. Over a stained but starched lab coat he wore a cardigan, whose front was generously sprinkled with ash from the ever present cigar. The Semitic features thrust out at Sheridan: a long slightly curved nose, tall fleshy lips, a high dome forehead, and thinning wiry hair which no longer hid a freckled scalp.

"I'll take his leash now, sonny," Hirsh blithely informed the security man and slapped a thick, heavy arm around Sheridan's shoulders. Hirsh was in his late fifties, but his enormous physique and strength hadn't diminished for all that.

"You're looking better, *boychik*," Hirsh informed him. "Getting some rays, nookie too probably. Not like me, whom you have to wake up at night."

"Al, you're an insomniac. You stink worse than your cigar, and the only place you'd get laid is in a goat herd. But thanks for seeing me anyway."

Hirsh's booming laughter echoed through the foyer long after the two men had disappeared into the elevator.

The color coding had changed: Blue stripes along the floor, not orange, now delineated a maximum security area. Not that this really mattered. In Hirsh's subterranean empire there were no glass panels. All laboratories and technical facilities were stored away behind the seemingly endless white corridor walls. Soundproof, immune to microwave transmissions, secure from electronic eavesdropping.

"So how many pounds of my flesh do you want this time, Sheridan?" growled Hirsh.

"I don't want any. She does."

Sheridan passed him the sample. Hirsh accepted the polyurethane bag without breaking stride. He read the label, which detailed the contents and the sample's original.

"Right," he barked grimly, and suddenly veered to the left. "This *momzer* again."

"Again."

"I read about the killing. Nasty son of a bitch."

Hirsh pushed an almost invisible panel in the wall and plowed on inside. He hadn't wanted locks on the doors. If an intruder got past the security upstairs into this level, the actual equipment would snare him. All computer consoles were booby-trapped. Unless the inertia alarms were bypassed by special code, Hirsh would bring down Armageddon on the illegal entrant.

"I don't believe you've seen the new Thinking Room. I finally got the morons upstairs to put the crowbar to their wallets!"

The room was roughly twenty-four hundred square feet. Along the walls were the latest generation of supercomputers, some of which Thane Sheridan knew had been designed by Hirsh. Like the old space in the north part of the building, this room was Hirsh's exclusive terrain. This was where he did what he got paid to do: think. With the help of two terminals which sat squarely between the hardware, side by side in a futuristic imitation of a barrister's desk, Dr. Allan Hirsh, formerly of Princeton, Brookings, and Hoover Institute, was the right side of the Central Intelligence Agency brain. He was a virtuoso with the terminals, able to coax out the full text of a Politburo speech on the basis of an obscure reference or reconstruct a Soviet space station design from a single blueprint smuggled out of Novosibirsk. He had predicted the bloody end of the Vietnam War by means of a precise model, which, it was said, McNamara had personally burned in the fireplace of the Oval Office. He was also fond of Thane Sheridan, whom he affectionately referred to as "that anti-Semitic Irish poet."

"What do you want to know?" asked Hirsh, lowering himself gingerly onto the chair before the console. Sheridan sat opposite him, arms folded across its sister's top.

"Horsehair."

"Horsehair?"

"That's the sample."

Hirsh's fingers flew across the keyboard, stubbing with absolute precision. The inertia alarms were bypassed.

"I've learned to read, thank you."

"Where it came from—"

"The ass end."

"Where it came from," Sheridan continued patiently. "Domestic or foreign sources, importer—if applicable, wholesaler, distributor, the major buyers."

"Is that all?" Hirsh demanded.

"I'll give you a clue—the hair is from a violin bow."

"Son of a bitch!" Hirsh muttered. "And here I thought I'd have to reconstruct the whole fucking animal. Okay. Park your butt. I'll give you simultaneous readouts on the twin, there."

"How long, Al?" Sheridan asked quietly.

"Had a piece of gold from a tooth," Hirsh answered, not looking up. "Came off a badly decomposed body. Took me most of the night to piece that Chinese sucker together." He looked up, grinning. "But the mystery of Marshal Lin Piao and his flight to Moscow was solved."

Somewhere in the nether world of light impulses, silicon chips, and microcircuitry a life began forming. If Sheridan had been able to see it, he would have described it as a flickering, tentative probe, skimming across unimaginable time and terrain. Hirsh had taken the first step: His probe was now connecting to the first of what would probably be the many data bases he would tap. It was a one way street: From his terminal Hirsh could go across the country or around the globe. But nothing traveled back, got onto an electronic highway that led to the Thinking Room.

"Okay, we'll let this stew awhile," said Hirsh, leaning over and snatching the sample bag. He unsealed the lock and with a pair of tweezers extracted the horsehair. With one shove of his legs he and his chair were propelled toward the scanning electron micrograph some ten feet away.

Sheridan watched silently as Hirsh inserted the hair into the unit; the photographing began. As high-intensity magnification lenses revealed the very essence of the hair, disclosing its every characteristic, the data would flow into the computer's memory, ready for correlation.

The chair shot across the rich cream-colored linoleum.

"Take five. It'll be a few minutes before we get our Polaroids."

Hirsh pulled out a cigar for himself, tossed a pack of cigarettes to Sheridan, and depressed a button on the floor next to the console stand. At once a heavy suction fan began to draw air.

"I can't stand namby-pamby smoke-allergic hardware."
He lit up and regarded Sheridan.

"Think you're on to something?" he asked seriously.

"I hope to Christ so. It's been a long road."

"Don't bullshit a bullshitter." Hirsh laughed. "You wouldn't be here unless that mental divining rod of yours was twitching."

"I've got him in the city," Sheridan said softly. "He's arrived, and he has his nest."

"You want a probability study done of the Big Apple, where this mother's likely to be holed up?"

"No disrespect, Al, but your stuff can't function without data."

Hirsh shrugged. "Built Lin Piao out of a smidgeon of gold."

"If the hair is what I think it is, I'll want a cross-check with the evidence from the other killings."

"Oh, ho! He's repeating himself."

"Let's hope so," Sheridan said cautiously.

"Where is the previous stuff?"

"Across the river and into the trees. The Hoover building."

"A cakewalk," Hirsh chortled, jabbing fiercely. "I can turn those turkeys inside out, six ways to hell and back, before they notice 'anything suspicious.' "

"You're mad." Sheridan shook his head.

"And you're not?"

Hirsh had scarcely paved the way for his needlessly surreptitious entry into FBI data banks when the alert on his terminal chimed.

"Well, lookee here, we have us some hard info."

"What's the cross-reference?" asked Sheridan.

"The Smithsonian. They're generally pretty decent about animals, bones and shit."

Sheridan stared at his screen, intent on the lines that started to appear. Although the screen filled up quickly, he kept up with the pace. Beside him a silent teleprinter was recording.

"A Chinese horse . . . What the Christ?" Hirsh muttered.

"Wait, there's the cross-reference." Sheridan stopped him. "English or domestic . . . No, it's Chinese."

"Great, a Chinese horse which died five hundred and seven days ago, was seven years old, stood sixteen hands high—Next!"

Sheridan continued to read. The animal had been male. Cross-reference: The urine of mares was very acidic and so damaged the tail hair.

Cross-reference: The horse had been white. Preferred colored because of bleaching process.

Cross-reference: bleaching process. Definitely the Chinese technique. Further reference related to actual chemical ingredients.

Full stop.

Hirsh rerouted the probe into the National Arts Archives, subheading, instrument manufacture, sub-subheading, violin bows. A graphic depiction of a single horsehair appeared on the screen, magnified a thousand times.

"They look like serrated edges," Sheridan said.

"I never knew horsehair had fish scales," muttered Hirsh. There was a pause as he maneuvered the probe into another line of questioning.

"Okay, here we go." Hirsh nodded. "What you have is *real* horsehair with the serrated edges. The cheapies use nylon strings, but they aren't as good, don't give off the same resonance because they *don't* have the edges. Apparently it's the application of the edges against the string that gives the violin its particular tone quality. And if the Smithsonian knows its business, almost eighty percent of violinists use horsehair bows. Everybody wants to be a star," Hirsh said darkly.

"Let's plug into Trade and Commerce," suggested Sheridan.

"Way ahead of you."

Hirsh sat back, fingers intertwined across his generous belly, watching as the probe skirted into the Commerce Department computers located in the basement of the Flagship Building on C Street.

"You don't have to blow him away, you know," he said abruptly, his gaze shifting over the twin consoles to Sheridan. "I know a good number of our members of the Hippocratic faith would be very interested to have a look at the Rambler. How they love to poke and probe . . ."

Sheridan said nothing. He was aware that Hirsh had read his Chicago notes, committed to computers for safekeeping. He wondered how much Hirsh actually believed in his thesis.

"First I have to get to him," he said quietly.

"Actually *I* wouldn't mind having a crack at him myself," admitted Hirsh. "My instruments would take him apart like a stalk of celery."

You don't want to know what makes him move, Sheridan thought. *Really, you don't.*

Green lettering started coming through on the console. In the last fiscal year a shade over three tons of processed horsehair had been imported into the United States from the People's Republic of China. All of it had come through West Coast ports. The median price had been six hundred dollars per pound.

"Pricey stuff, isn't it?" Hirsh mused.

Three importers-distributors were listed who sold the material piecemeal to instruments manufacturers, all two thousand of them. . . . Except for the import points the distribution was strictly by mail or courier.

"Shit!" Sheridan breathed.

"And you thought there was something special about your sample," Hirsh said sympathetically.

"Can you do a match-up between the sample and one from a six-hundred-dollar-a-pound load?"

Hirsh instructed the Commerce computer to furnish him with the description of a horsehair as well as a 3-D picture. When it came up on the screen, he correlated it with Sheridan's sample.

"They're different!" Sheridan murmured.

"That they are," agreed Hirsh. He looked at Sheridan. "Somewhere along the line your particular hair was given more treatment. That could have been done at the distribution point or at one of the outlets. Maybe even the retailer himself added a final touch."

"I have to know, Al."

"If it's the last option, we don't stand a snowball's

chance in hell of pinpointing the manufacturer," Hirsh warned him.

"Let's play it out," said Sheridan. "It's the only thing I have, Al. I'm clutching because time is running out."

Hirsh nodded. "Go get us some coffee. We're going to be here most of the night. My office is out to the left. Can't miss it—the one with the Adrienne Barbeau pinup."

"Thank you, Al."

Hirsh waved him away. He was already calling up a backtracking program.

Chapter Six

The rain had died away sometime in the late afternoon.
But the wind persisted, freezing the water on the street
and sidewalks into treacherous icy stretches. Overhead a
weak sun was giving up the struggle against the gray
mass of clouds that passed for a sky.

Earlier in the day, at midmorning, Otto Morell had been
buried. By prior arrangement with the Lutheran pastor
the graveside service at Springside Heights Cemetery in
Brooklyn had been brief. Only the immediate family and
closest friends had attended. A memorial Mass, with luminaries from the music world, the performers, patrons, and
civic politicians, would be held in St. Bartholomew's in the
evening.

No sooner had Sabina returned with Augusta Morell to
her house than the first visitors appeared. The older people
of the neighborhood were the first to pay their respects—
the tradesmen, the grocery- and fruit-store owners, the cab
drivers, and the women who worked in the garment factories. These were followed by the younger generation, the
café and boutique owners, storefront lawyers and their
staff, the street musicians for whom her uncle had always
had a special affection. They had all known Otto Morell.
Most had been to his home, had partaken of his generous
table, confided their troubles and fears to him, shared
their joys and triumphs with him. Each wore a black
armband.

Although they were solicitous and their condolences
heartfelt, Sabina felt something cold and alien come into
their eyes when they looked at her, into their hands when

they offered sympathy. If Augusta Morell sensed the same, she didn't show it.

At half past one, seeing that the parade through the door would not abate, Sabina left, promising to return before it was time to go to the church. Augusta accepted her departure without question. To Sabina *Tante*'s thoughts seemed very far away from what was going on around her. Equally strange was the sensation she felt walking down to Houston Street. In every storefront window or door was draped a piece of black cloth, sometimes no larger than a handkerchief, in other cases obscuring almost all the plate glass. The community of Steuben Town was mourning one of its own. From the glances and nods Sabina received she knew that beneath the grief there simmered anger. But also something else. It was as though those who acknowledged her were privy to a secret from which she was excluded, that beneath even the anger some kind of terrible resolution had been forged, kept secret, awaiting the proper moment to be unveiled.

Two messages from Thane Sheridan awaited her in Thompson Street. Neither had been flagged urgent and so had not been relayed to her car. The first, logged at seven that morning, read that Langley's test results on the horsehair strand would be completed shortly. The second, sent ninety minutes later, stated that a computer analysis was being done on the results. Sabina frowned. The message was deliberately cryptic, yet she sensed excitement.

There was nothing to do but wait. Sabina went into Sheridan's quarters and sat down at the desk. The pile of dossiers that had been on the left side had, in the course of the previous night, moved over to the right. The files represented the sort of investigation Sabina had never before encountered. Thane Sheridan was a man possessed. In his search for the killer of his child he had strayed into areas which were completely foreign to a rational, procedural inquiry.

Even before she had sat down with the files, Sabina had had a clue as to Sheridan's thinking. It lay in the sobriquet he had given the killer—the Midnight Rambler. He'd taken the tag from the Rolling Stones' song "Sympathy for the Devil." As Sabina read through the discovery reports, the on-site evidence files, and the follow-up investigations she came to appreciate Sheridan's frustration. There wasn't one tangible thread in the lot, no single piece of evidence that could break the mask behind which the Rambler hid.

Sabina traced Sheridan's attempts to conduct the investigation by the rules, coming to the point where he had given up. There was a personal note in the files in which he stated that he would no longer try to piece together the Rambler's portrait from *what* he was doing but would seek, instead, to try to figure out the *why* of his behavior. The result astonished Sabina. Sheridan had returned to the beginning, concentrating on the first murder in each group. The details of the bodies' condition were matched with references to the arcane arts—black magic, voodoo, satanism, sorcery. The position of the bodies, the date and time of day they were found, the age and sex of the victims were related not to forensic science but to the occult. The result was the portrait of a killer who was intimate with the finest details of witchcraft, a murderer who seemed to possess infinite knowledge of the occult, who served not the light but the darkness of the fallen angels.

Sabina understood why these files were never included in the formal investigation reports: The man who had written them would be judged insane, his mind atrophying because of personal grief. Such an evaluation would effectively exclude him from any future involvement in Rambler killings. Yet William Rodgers, Mr. Bill, was privy to the contents. It was he who had insured Sheridan's participation in the investigations that ranged from Vegas to Chicago. Mr. Bill *believed* Sheridan, even though he must have known no one else would.

Who in hell is the Midnight Rambler?

Sheridan's mass of material, both concrete and speculative, had riveted Sabina. She had gone through it all in one sitting and upon finishing, had experienced something she had never felt before; her skin began to crawl, and the shadows of the room deepened as though being pushed back to unveil another, horrible universe. At that instant she understood why Sheridan carried the Venus, why he wanted to witness the Rambler burn. . . .

93

It was a repellant fascination that bade Sabina sit and reach for the first dossier once more. She had the better part of the afternoon to spend going over parts of the information again. Sheridan had been deadly serious when he had said she must know the Rambler as well as he did. Sabina understood why. The Rambler had to be stopped in New York, stopped before he murdered another child. Somewhere in the city he had already made his nest. Sheridan knew him but not the city. It was up to her to know the Rambler so intimately that with that knowledge she could lead them to the nest, help Sheridan destroy him.

Three hours later her concentration was shattered by the ringing telephone. The local line. It wouldn't be Sheridan unless he had already touched down at La Guardia.

"Sabina? It's Antonopulous."

The gravelly tone was as familiar to her as her own. George Antonopulous was captain of the Second Precinct.

"Captain—"

"Get over to George Brown Polytechnic Institute right away," Antonopulous cut her off. "I'll relay further instructions to you in the car."

Sabina's mouth went dry. "What's happened?"

Sheridan had said that the killer was compressing the time between the initial murder and first kidnapping. But yesterday he had estimated they had thirty to forty hours left.

Christ, if he was wrong!

"You'll see when you get here—if you can get through at all! Try for the roof."

The connection was broken. On her way out Sabina told internal security where she was going. Any call from Sheridan should be patched through to the precinct station house. Six minutes later she understood what Antonopulous had meant about her being able to get through at all.

The station house was located in the northern sector of Steuben Town, in a small square half a block west of Eighth Avenue. The cut stone building, square and squat, had been designed as a precinct station house forty years ago. As such it had little architectural grace. It stood dead in the center of the square, the surrounding area taken up by a police garage, parking space, and a pound. Sabina

94

made it as far as Eighth Avenue. She took one look at the situation and took a right, then a left one block north of the station house. She parked in the George Brown Polytechnic Institute yard and ran inside. Two minutes later Sabina was on the roof, looking down four stories at an unbelievable spectacle.

The station house was under seige. The crowd began at the corner of Eighth Avenue and inundated the small square. It had been pushed so far forward that those in front were actually standing on the station house steps. Sabina estimated no less than a thousand people were jammed into the small area, blocking the parking lot and pound, cutting off access to the street. The station house was sealed off from the outside. There was no question of anyone or anything penetrating the dense crowd.

The slamming of the metal fire door made her head snap. Six officers in paramilitary dress burst onto the roof, running in a low crouch. Two of them were carrying a weapons crate held between them. Another gripped a portable generator in one hand, a brace of aluminum stands for spotlights in the other. The last man through the door was Jacobson, who headed up the Emergency Task Force Unit.

"What's going on?" Sabina shouted at him, stumbling as a pebble twisted under her heel.

"Christ if I know!" Jacobson yelled back, his hands working rapidly to screw the two-thousand-watt lamps into the sockets.

"I was down by the freight yards when the call came in," Jacobson said, staring directly at Sabina's knees. "Apparently the whole thing took the station house by surprise. People just appeared out of nowhere, in groups of thirty or forty, coming in from the north and south. What I got from Antonopulous is that no one on the inside heard anything. It was change of shift. Briefings were going on in the basement; the units to be relieved were inside making out reports. Then someone decided to look outside. I'd like to have seen the expression on his face when he opened the fucking door."

Sabina looked sharply at Jacobson. Something he had said . . . She looked over the parapet at the crowd. That was it! The people were silent. There wasn't a single voice to be heard. The sound coming up from the square was that of a thousand feet pounding on asphalt, a slow rumbling thunder that was more unnerving than demonstrators' chanting.

"Give me your glasses!" Sabina snapped at an ETF man. She grabbed the Zeiss Ikon lens and adjusted the focus. Immediately she spotted a common element in the crowd: Everybody was wearing a black armband . . . the kind she had seen on those visiting her aunt that morning, the kind the people in the street had had around their upper arms. And the age of the crowd . . . They were predominantly, but not exclusively, older people. She readjusted the focus, zeroing in on specific faces. Out of twenty she instantly recognized six.

"Jesus, I think I know what they're doing!" Sabina whispered.

"What they're doing, Sergeant, is creating one hell of a mess!" Jacobson retorted. "We've nothing but a token force on the streets right now. How long do you figure news like that will take to spread? If we don't get our people and cars out there, we're going to have a little Watts all our own!"

As Sabina looked down to answer him she saw the stenciling on the crate he was opening.

"What are you thinking of doing with that?" she demanded.

The crate was the size of an army issue locker, five feet by eighteen inches. The first tray was stuffed with flare guns and rockets, concussion, smoke, and CS grenades. The bottom half held automatic rifles and appropriate ammunition.

Jacobson steered her aside. "We don't want to use the stuff, Sabina. But if these people don't disperse—"

"Have you tried talking to them? Do you know what they want?"

"Antonopulous has." Jacobson nodded. "He went outside with a bullhorn and asked what they wanted. No one answered him, Sabina. They just pressed a little closer." He paused. "That's why Antonopulous sent us up here. If he can't get them to move peacefully, we'll have to give them some encouragement."

96

"And *start* a full-scale riot?" Sabina demanded. "The crowd down there can tear the station apart with its bare hands if it wants to! They're *our* people, for God's sake! We can't do this to them."

"They're doing it to themselves." Jacobson shook his head. "It'll be *their* homes, *their* shops and businesses that will be robbed and vandalized unless we get units out on the streets."

"Antonopulous must have asked for temporary help from other precincts!"

"Sure, but you know who can spare what."

Sabina turned away and trained the lens on the first few rows of demonstrators.

"Let me talk to Antonopulous."

"He's one step ahead of you, on the line now," Jacobson said, handing her the communicator.

"Captain?"

"Sabina . . . are you on the roof?"

She didn't bother with the obvious reply. "Captain, I've seen what Jacobson has up here. We don't need it!"

"That's why I called you," Antonopulous said calmly. "They're your people, Sabina. You talk them down, get them to move."

"Our people, Captain!" Sabina corrected him angrily. "And we, the police department, are the reason they're out there!"

Sabina broke transmission. "Give me the goddamn bullhorn!"

She focused on the people in the front ranks, holding the field glasses in her right hand, the bullhorn in her left.

"Tell them to give me spots, both here and from the roof of the station," she called out to Jacobson.

Jacobson issued crisp instructions, and within seconds Nassau Street was bathed in the searing white glow of ten thousand candlepower. Like an ungainly, startled animal the crowd stirred. A few cries were heard, but they kept their composure. Sabina pressed the trigger on the bullhorn. A high-pitched feedback came out, sound waves bouncing off the stone of the station house. She adjusted the volume and spoke, the words metallic, disembodied.

The glasses were trained on the people she was addressing, all of them on the front steps.

"Esther Levine!"

The woman stared up directly at her, her palm shielding her eyes.

"Esther, it's Sabina Morell. I'm up here on the roof of George Brown. You may not be able to see me clearly because of the lights. But I'm here."

Sabina paused. "I can see your husband, Abner, standing beside you. There is George Percy and Jim Hansen . . . Andreas Marcovici, you're standing beside my aunt . . . Aunt Augusta—*Tante* . . ."

A voice wafted up into the harsh glow. She moved the glasses and saw Abner Levine's lips moving. Sabina held the bullhorn away from her mouth.

"Get Antonopulous to give them a horn," she said. "Abner's trying to say something."

"Wouldn't it be easier for you to go down?" Jacobson suggested.

"Let's open up the dialogue and see what happens," Sabina said savagely. "I won't say anything to him down there that I can't say from up here."

She raised the horn. "Abner, Captain Antonopulous is going to bring out a megaphone to you. That's all he's going to do. That way I'll be able to hear you."

No sooner had the echo died away than the station house door opened. Antonopulous, readily identifiable by his usual loud sports coat, came out, walking slowly down the steps, one hand holding the megaphone, the other arm held away from his body to indicate he had nothing to hide. Sabina watched him hand the megaphone to Abner Levine, who had stepped forward. Antonopulous said something to Levine, who shook his head. The captain nodded, held out both hands palms up, and sidestepped back into the station.

"Sabina . . ."

"Turn the volume down a little," she instructed him. "There's too much feedback."

"Sabina . . ."

"That's much better, Abner." She paused to see if more

would be forthcoming. There wasn't, so she took the initiative.

"Abner, what's happening? What are all these people doing here?"

"I think you should know, Sabina."

Even after forty years Abner Levine's voice retained its guttural South German accent. And yes, she knew very well what he was referring to. She had known as soon as she had seen the armbands.

"Abner, this is no way for us to talk. You're only hurting yourselves. The police can't get out to do their jobs—"

"Are the police doing their job for Rachel Rosenberg?"

The crowd thundered its approval, a mixture of applause, shouts of encouragement, and catcalls.

"Are they doing their job for Otto Morell, *your uncle?*"

Sabina closed her eyes. Abner Levine was one of the gentlest, kindest people she knew. Until now she had not thought him capable of malice. But he had also been Otto Morell's closest friend.

"Sabina, why do you not answer me?" Levine demanded once the crowd had quieted. "Do you think we wish to be here? Have we, all of us who live in this community, *your community,* not respected the police, helped them where we could?"

"You have, Abner," she said quickly. "And that's what I'm asking you to do now. Help us."

Abner Levine ignored the plea, his voice rising in pitch. With his great head thrown back, his jaw thrust forward, he stood in the spotlight like some Old Testament prophet. But with the help of the spotlights and binoculars Sabina saw something else: the trembling of his lips, the way in which his body lurched against the cane as though the words were an unbearable burden, carried too long, too far. He was a portrait of despair.

"We have told you over and over what is happening to us. The rot has come into our neighborhood, Sabina. The slime and infestation. We were a peaceful community, but we were not left in peace. The streets and parks were ours once. Now they belong to the drug addicts and criminals and pimps.

"Where have you been, Sabina, that you could not hear

us? Time after time we have appealed to the police. We have volunteered our help, our time, our combined experience—anything we had to offer—in order to come up with some solution. We were listened to and politely acknowledged, but in the end always silently refused.

"Now the infestation has taken a young girl, an innocent. Next, your uncle, who dared to organize us without your help, who took on the burden of proving what the infestation was . . ."

The old man's voice broke. Sabina saw a movement at the corner of the lens. Andreas Marcovici, the young Italian who owned a barber shop, lunged into view, seizing the megaphone from Abner Levine's hands.

"We can't wait anymore!" he screamed. Marcovici was holding the megaphone at such an angle that his cries carried well over Sabina's head. For an instant it seemed as though his anguish was directed not at her but at the heavens themselves. "We were tired, desperate, and afraid. Now we are beyond that. We cannot go back. We know who the killers are. Their punishment has been ordained. They shall not escape!"

If you are beyond desperation, then where are you?

The silent question did not breach Sabina's lips.

What punishment has been ordained? By whom?

"Is this what you've come here for—to threaten us?" Sabina asked. She was banking on Marcovici's volatile personality to lead him into indiscretion. Someone else was thinking the same thing.

"We have come to show you, Sabina, that things may no longer continue as they have in the past."

The speaker was Augusta Morell. Somehow she had slipped the megaphone from Marcovici's grip. In spite of her sixty-five years Augusta Morell was a very beautiful woman. The high cheekbones, aquiline nose, and enormous hazel eyes were set off by thick auburn hair accented by gray. The beauty that had made her Vienna's most desirable debutante had never faltered throughout the years. And now she stood amidst the crowd, her beauty enhanced by her unfathomable will, her pride and determination.

"We have come," Augusta Morell said, standing tall,

100

erect, speaking only, it seemed, to Sabina, "to say that we can no longer accept excuses. We are fully aware of the accommodations the police have with the South Americans. We know the identities of the people who have been bought, for how much and by whom. All this was Otto's work, Sabina. Work of which you know nothing but because of which he was murdered. In time he would have destroyed these accommodations. I tell you, and all your colleagues: *All* of Steuben Town knows. The hoodlums will have to kill every one of us to keep the silence. Soon we will speak. We expect no protection from you; we have our own. We expect no help. We look only to ourselves. Nevertheless, we *shall* triumph, Sabina. We will *not* forfeit our lives, our work, the future we have built here. Not for any accommodation!"

Slowly Sabina lowered the bullhorn. Her senses were numbed by the words she had listened to. Her uncle was murdered because he knew too much. But what had he discovered? Sabina had been aware of Otto Morell's leadership at the Steuben Town Citizens' Coalition. She knew he was forever writing to city and state officials about the criminal element that had invaded his home. But accommodations between the police and South Americans! Where had *Onkel*'s investigations led him? Whom had he inadvertently touched that the reaction was so vicious?

At last Sabina understood the real meaning, the mystery behind Augusta's silence. It wasn't all caused by her grief. Thinking back, Sabina wondered if grief was even a major factor. There had been something else in her aunt's quietude, something she had felt but could not define. She should have recognized the strength behind the silence, the resolve . . . the brittleness of cold vengefulness.

"They're breaking up!" Jacobson called out.

Sabina looked out over the parapet. Like a piece of old wool fraying at the edges the crowd was beginning to come apart. Abner Levine and his wife, Esther, had gone down the steps, followed by George Percy and Jim Hansen. People on either side moved back, forming a thin corridor. Andreas Marcovici followed, then Augusta Morell. And beside her a man, tall, very thin, dressed in a long black coat with a white scarf. Augusta had taken his arm. Sabina moved quickly, trying to get a better angle on the man's face. She saw him briefly before the wind billowed the white scarf across his features. Leopold Ulric, the greatest violinist of his day. Where had he come from? And how? Sabina was certain she hadn't seen him on the steps when she had first scanned those standing by her aunt.

But she knew why he was here. Sabina looked down Nassau Street, then south, following the crowd. The spotlights around St. Bartholomew's pierced the moisture-laden evening sky, the blue, white, and green lamps reflecting off the granite. The church appeared to shimmer as though covered in ice crystals.

That's where they're all going, Sabina thought. *To Onkel's memorial Mass. And how can I go when I wasn't even aware of what was happening to him? How dare I walk among them and take my place beside Augusta, my Tante who shamed me before all of them?*

"It's going to be rough, isn't it?"

Sabina whirled around, startled. She hadn't heard Richard Dwyer walk up behind her.

"Hello, Richard," she said dully. "What brings you up here?"

He stuffed his hands deep into the pockets of the beaver-collared cashmere coat and placed his weight firmly on both feet in what Sabina remembered as his fighting stance.

"Not tonight, Richard. Too much has happened."

His gray eyes regarded her coldly. She thought she saw more broken veins across the top of his nose. The cheeks were becoming jowls. Richard and his bottle had always gotten along too well.

"I spoke to Augusta earlier on. She expects you at the Mass."

Her ex-husband still carried a lot of weight in the community even though he and her son, Toby, now lived on the Upper East Side. Her son and God knew what fresh young thing Richard was bedding these days. But then again, that was all right. It was all part of the profile: chief assistant DA for Manhattan, the police commissioner's prime gunslinger, the DA's point man. Ruthless, calculating, a

102

streetwise fighter. Richard's profile was very high, just the way he liked it.

"I plan to go to the Mass," Sabina said, finding her voice. "Where is Toby?"

"He's waiting in the car, with a patrolman. The PC asked me to come by in case the situation worsened."

"It didn't."

"No thanks to you, my love. Old Levine had a point: Where is the killer?"

Sabina bundled her arms about herself as though suddenly very cold and moved away from him. It wasn't fair, she thought. The police did give a damn. She gave a damn! Yet suddenly everyone was making it seem that law enforcement had its collective hands under its ass, that no one cared about what was happening in Steuben Town.

"It's not only the neighborhood I'm concerned about," said Richard, his somber voice breaking the silence. "It's Toby. Rachel Rosenberg was kidnapped at the New School of Drama and Music. Your uncle was killed a couple blocks from his home. I wouldn't want to think that this sick son of a bitch has decided to work Steuben Town for a while, taking a particular interest in the NSDM." He paused. "Not while Toby's there, at any rate."

"Don't fuck with me like that, Richard!" Sabina turned on him, raw hatred in her voice. "What do you think went through my mind when I found the Rosenberg girl? I saw Toby lying there!"

"Well, nothing more will happen at the school," Richard Dwyer said firmly. "I've seen to that. I met with most of the parents a few days ago. All I was going to ask for was five thousand, combined contribution, for extra security until this is over with. You know what I walked away with?" He shook his head. "Twenty-five big ones. Christ, I could have hired the Lawless brothers for months, not weeks, if I had to."

Sabina was aware of the Lawlesses' reputation. They were brothers, black and really called Lawless. Theirs was the premier private security firm in the city, consisting of specially selected ex-FBI, SAS, and Israeli commando personnel. The rate was five hundred a day per man. Custom-built vehicles were included. Spent ammunition was extra. Although knowing that Lawless was looking after the New School of Drama and Music made Sabina feel better as far as Toby was concerned, that same knowledge left a bitter taste in her mouth. It was a put down, a vote of nonconfidence in her and the Force.

"But I won't have to, will I?" Richard asked softly. "I mean, you *will* find him, Sabina . . . You and that mysterious partner of yours, Sheridan." He paused. "I'd like to meet him sometime, see what he's like."

"He's a professional," Sabina replied. "The best we could have."

"But his status—"

"Obviously the commissioner doesn't see fit to tell you everything," Sabina cut him off.

"Oh, yes, he does, my love," Richard shot back. "But even the PC seems to be left out of this one. Bill Rodgers doesn't deign to answer his calls . . ."

He was fishing, and Sabina wouldn't play.

"The two cases aren't connected," she said slowly. "What happened to Rachel Rosenberg has nothing to do with my uncle's murder."

She turned on him, eyes blazing.

"And you, Richard! What did you know of what Otto was doing? What the hell did you let him get into that it cost him his life? And don't tell me you didn't know!"

"Only as much as you," Dwyer answered harshly. "Sure, I advised Otto and the Citizens' Coalition. I even opened a few doors for them. But I *didn't* tell him to take on the Letelier mob. Christ, if anything, I kept steering him away from them!"

"So what happened?" Sabina cried.

He held out his hands. "I don't know, babe. I swear to God I don't."

She hung her head and felt the hot tears on her cheek. But she recoiled when Richard stepped forward and touched her.

"It's time for me to go."

"You will call me, won't you?" Richard said. "When you bag him, you'll call me first."

You prick! Sabina thought. A juicy, publicity-ridden

104

prosecution is all you want. Something to really put you over the top. She started walking, oblivious to his shouts.

"I'll put him away, Sabina!" he called after her. "I don't care if he gets F. Lee Bailey—"

Chapter Seven

Leopold Ulric was holding Augusta Morell's elbow as delicately as he would the neck of his instrument. With subtle pressure he guided her through the throngs that had gathered before St. Bartholomew's.

Ulric was aware that people were staring at him. Not those from the neighborhood, the widow's friends. They undoubtedly recognized him, but he was respected by them because of his place of honor next to the widow. No, it was the others—the mayor, who, with hand in pocket, was scratching the inside of his thigh, the governor, his sickly face swollen like rising dough, being propped up by his wife, a black-haired bitch with evil, opaque eyes—these and a host of lesser luminaries watched his every move. Yet Ulric would not favor them with a single glance. He didn't have to. His peripheral vision was extraordinary, almost like that of a bird or chameleon. He saw everything.

Leopold Ulric knew they were fascinated by his appearance. He knew others saw him as he did himself: an ugly man who, in a certain light or streak of temper, could look repulsive. Yet their fascination was obvious. He was not as tall as people presumed, just over medium height. But his frame, almost painfully thin, added to his stature, as did the smooth, almost fluid way in which he walked. The long black hair curled about the neck and, with its middle part, gave him the appearance of an eighteenth-century court musician. This made his long, lean face startling: Ulric's complexion was almost Kabuki white, the starchy hue broken by the long, slightly disfigured nose and the eyes, two agate pits. The rail-thin arms ended in the most remarkable hands: not long and dexterous as one might have expected of a virtuoso but small, the fingers short, thick, and callous, as though the muscles had been overly developed. They were very powerful hands.

Leopold Ulric guided the widow between cool cream and blue plaster pillars, the long hewn oak pews lined up on either side. Overhead, magnificent chandeliers illuminated the gold-plated paintings of the sacristy, turning the cover of the Bible resting on the altar into burning gold. Ulric walked with Augusta Morell to the front pew and waited, standing very still, while behind them the church filled. Without looking back he leaned across and whispered a few words to her. The widow nodded and immediately Ulric left, walking quickly along the far side of the cathedral, disappearing through a door which opened to a staircase leading down to the church hall. Bootheels clicked on parquet flooring as he crossed the deserted hall, moving swiftly past the small kitchen, the catering tables folded and lined up on their sides, the stacked chairs, and the small stage, curtain drawn. He made his way up two more flights of stairs and pushed open the door leading outside to the rear of the church. Glancing around, Ulric saw a few late arrivals locking their cars and hurrying across the lawn. He went down the cement walk to the side street, turned left at the pastor's modest house, and continued down the street. Only when he was behind the wheel of his car, the door locked, did his motion stop.

In the darkness Leopold Ulric heard the bells of St. Bartholomew's toll out into the night. Aside from the streetlamps and cathedral floodlights there was no other light. The sky was low and dark, the moon nowhere to be seen. Ulric turned the ignition key, and the heavy Aston-Martin engine rumbled to life. In two and a half hours he was scheduled to appear on the stage at Lincoln Center. He knew that many of the "celebrities" at the funeral would be there. He had insisted—and of course his wish had immediately been granted—that the concert be performed as a memorial concert for Otto Morell. But before homage could be paid, there was work to be done. Leopold Ulric's eyes gleamed in the dark. His soft laugh was lost in the engine roar as he depressed the clutch and spun the car away from the curb.

The Aston-Martin rested in the alley, its silver gray lacquer gleaming under the weak bulbs that purported to light the delivery entrances of the Portuguese fish market and grocery store. The only sound in the alley was that of the rats rooting in the flimsy wooden crates for fish heads and entrails. Their scurrying was punctuated by the soft cracks of the aluminum engine block cooling. It was this sound that drew the boys into the alley.

They were all Dominicans, thirteen, fifteen, and sixteen. Each wore a ragged leather jacket emblazoned with a grinning death's head, a forked tongue quivering from its mouth, and lettered across the top in luminous green: THE TRIBE.

"What the fuck is that, man?"

The Aston-Martin was a big heavy machine, with its engine mounted far forward, its design unique but understated. Unlike its exotic counterparts the Ferrari and Lamborghini, the DBS V8 turned only the heads of aficionados.

"Trans Am."

"No way, asshole. Maybe a Z-28."

One of the boys stepped on a rotten lettuce and almost lost his balance. The others laughed. But all fell silent as they approached the vehicle. The extra wide tires, shining exhaust, and almost opaque rear window exuded a feeling of wealth.

"Fucking look at that, man!"

They walked around the car slowly, not touching, like primitive hunters warily approaching an unknown beast, not yet sure if it is dead or merely sleeping. Two peered in through the driver's window. Even in the stench of the alley, the aroma of rich leather upholstery filtered through the doorjamb. The third walked to the front of the car and stared at the two large head lamps recessed in their aluminum hoods. The Aston logo wings glittered up at him.

"Let's take it!" he whispered.

The two by the door looked at each other.

"I dunno, man . . . I mean, what the fuck is it doing here? *What* is this shit, anyway?"

"Who cares? We take it and ride."

"The fucking *gorillas* put it here, man! They're just aching for us to touch it. Fucker's probably wired . . ."

"You ever see a *gorilla* in one of these, asshole?"

Silence.

"Shit, I don't see no locks—"

"Candy ass! We take out this shitty little back window, play with the wires, and go pussy hunting. Oooh, yes, man, we going to score tonight!"

"What kind of asshole would bring a car like this here? Christ, if it's Letelier or his—"

"You got shit for brains? Letelier has a limo."

A soft click and a switchblade slid out from its recess in a bone handle. The sixteen-year-old stepped over to the wall of the building and squatted on his haunches. The mortar between the bricks had started to crumble years ago. Then the brick itself had splintered and chipped. It was an easy matter to scrape away the grayish powder and pry loose a whole brick.

"Gimme your coat!"

"What?"

"Your coat, cuntface! I gotta wrap it around the brick 'causa the noise."

The youngest stripped off his jacket, trying not to shiver as he stood there with only a T-shirt covering his chest. He watched as the brick disappeared into the folds of his jacket.

The boy stood back and, satisfied with his handiwork, cocked back his arm.

"Here come the good times!"

He never saw the animal. The first sensation his mind registered was a sudden breeze coming at him at head level. He discounted it as a gust of wind. There was nothing else in the alley, not in front of the car or behind it. Nothing else lived there except the rats, an occasional tomcat, and the slugs that feasted on the refuse.

The brick should have sailed through the air and smashed into the small rear window. Instead it seemed to hang in the air for an instant, then fall with a dull thud to the ground. The boy looked up in terror, but his hand was no longer there. All he was looking at was a stump, a fountain of flesh from which his life's blood gushed forth. A

110

scream began to work its way through his paralyzed throat.

The others were more fortunate. The dogs, all shepherds, silently launched themselves from the other side of the car. The boys did not move. They could not believe what was flying through the air at them. They had walked around the car. No dogs had been there! Yet the fangs that buried themselves in their throats were real, the crushing jaws tearing at the soft bone and cartilage, mangling the arteries. The youths almost died in unison, the last picture of their lives one of horror, their own death.

The third boy, who had dropped to his knees, was turning away when the animal came at him. He tried to crawl on his one hand, but then suddenly his back arched in agony as he lost his balance and the raw stump ground into the filthy asphalt. The pain unleashed his only scream, but in the next instant the dog had buried its teeth in the back of his neck.

One street away, in another alley, Leopold Ulric heard the scream. He did not break stride but only smiled and continued his brisk pace. He had visited the city on a number of other occasions, but never would New York remember him as it would after this one.

He walked almost soundlessly in the alley until he came to the rear door of the Casa Mendoza. The steel-sheathed fire door groaned as he pulled it away from its frame. The smell of old drink and marijuana hung in the fetid air of the corridor. From the bar there drifted the raucous music of a jukebox broken by the intermittent electronic sounds of a video game. Leopold Ulric stood very still. He was not afraid of the bodega or of anyone who was in here. He had no qualms about walking through dark streets and even darker alleys. He had traversed such ugly terrain many times. He was its master.

The staircase directly before him led to the upstairs room where the cousins Santiago and Roncaron were waiting. Earlier in the day Leopold Ulric had had a man meet him for a drink at the Plaza's Oyster Bar. Ulric had spoken the name of a dealer in San Francisco and given the man a number and a phrase. The contact had made the call from one of the hotel's pay phones. Ten minutes later money had changed hands. Ulric was told the material he had requested, a half pound of 70 percent pure cocaine, would be delivered wherever he wished. The virtuoso demurred. He would pick the drug up personally. Such quantity at such a price demanded a test prior to purchase. The contact had shrugged. Ulric had been cleared by the West Coast dealer. The contact would make the call to the cousins. The gringo would be given the address and time. After that the stupid son of a bitch was on his own. The cousins could do with him as they wished. The contact, appearing to all the world a prosperous stockbroker, even paid for their drinks —out of his cash commission.

Leopold Ulric smiled in the darkness. He took a deep breath of the dank air, and his head swam. Yes, he was expected. But by the front door. Undoubtedly the cousins had left word with the bartender to signal them when a gringo came asking for them. No one would expect him to go through the back door, which ordinarily could only be opened from the inside. Leopold Ulric started up the stairs.

The room was bare save for a splintered table dragged up from downstairs and several wooden chairs. There was no need for curtains over the only window since it faced a brick wall only four feet away. The linoleum floor was beyond hope.

Santiago was sitting facing the door, his chair leaned against the wall at a precarious angle, the front legs off the floor. His cousin was using the bathroom. The instant the toilet flushed, Leopold Ulric swung open the door.

Even if he had been prepared, Santiago could not have saved himself. His first reaction, however—lowering his chair so he could stand—made it very easy for Ulric. Four strides was all it took to reach him. Ulric's right arm swung up, his hand contorted into a claw. It caught Santiago under the jaw and around the neck. Ulric squeezed and slowly lifted the Colombian off his feet, the body wriggling, legs kicking out feebly.

The toilet was flushed a second time.

"Hey, you think this dude is gonna show—"

Roncaron opened the door to see his cousin dangling in the air before him. Santiago's face was blotched a hideous purple-red, his tongue hanging out, only the whites of his

112

eyes showing. Roncaron had time to groan once before Ulric's left hand shot out and seized him. The sound in his throat ended abruptly as his feet too left the floor.

Slowly Ulric turned into the room, the cousins rotating in his grasp like sides of beef. He thrust his arms out full length and forced every ounce of strength into his fingers. He tossed his head back and opened his mouth in a silent scream.

Ulric never knew how long he held them like that. It was not for lack of strength that he lowered the still warm bodies. He brought both into the bathroom and then released his grip on Roncaron. Slowly he lowered Santiago and caught him by the back of the neck, maneuvering the still breathing body until the head hung over the rim of the toilet bowl. Ulric hesitated a moment, fascinated, intoxicated by the act he was about to commit. Almost without his being aware of it his finger pressed Santiago's head deep into the bowl. When he depressed the handle, water ran over the head, the bowl filling rapidly until the hair floated. The corpus twitched, emitting the last desperate sign of life. Ulric flushed again. And six times after that.

When he was satisfied, he brought Santiago's head up, glanced at it, then carelessly threw the body aside. He reached for Roncaron and repeated his motions. The only difference was that upon finishing, Ulric adjusted the cousin's knees, plugged the drain with a wad of toilet paper, lowered the head into the bowl, and left it there.

There had been no haste in his killing. There never was. Had someone interrupted his pleasure, he would have savaged him. But all was calm. He dried his hands with his handkerchief and left the room, walking quickly downstairs. No one had noticed the broken rear door. As he stepped into the night he felt eminently satisfied.

Leopold Ulric walked down the alley and turned left on the small side street. He walked a block north and stepped into the alley, approaching his car from the same direction as had the Tribe gang members. Midway down the alley he saw a pair of legs sticking out over some soggy cartons. His hand brushed one of the boots, and the legs toppled into the garbage. If there was a torso attached, he did not see it. Ulric walked around the car to make sure there was nothing under the wheels. Carefully he stepped over a leather jacket that was still partially wrapped around a brick and unlocked the door. He did not turn on the head lamps until the nose of the Aston poked out onto the street.

Leopold Ulric headed uptown. There was a lull in the traffic, and he made good time, pushing the car aggressively, running lights, using the Aston's superior acceleration to weave through the flow. He turned off at West Fifty-fourth, guided the car through the inching traffic, and with a roar of exhaust that startled even the city's jaded pedestrians, shot across the sidewalk and onto the ramp that led to the underground parking lot located at the rear of the Metropolitan Tower. He was home.

The penthouse duplex on the fifty-first floor was one of four residences Ulric had around the world. There was an apartment in Paris, a villa in Grand Cayman, and a suite in the condominium tower adjoining the Peninsula Hotel in Hong Kong. He had been skeptical when his American agent, Sidney Nathan, had suggested a New York residence—in a building that hadn't yet been completed. Nevertheless he had been pleased with the end result. The suite dominated the southwest corner. Its floor to ceiling windows opened up the city to him yet placed him above the din. The rooftop terrace on the apartment's second floor was accessible from both the bedroom and the music room. In spring Ulric drew back the sliding doors and played to the dusk. He could almost see the notes of his compositions gliding over the city and could not believe that the whole of this turbulent humanity did not pause, at least for an instant, to be touched.

Leopold Ulric mounted the spiral brass-banistered staircase which led to a small sitting room adjacent to the music room. He crossed to the other side and entered the bedroom, unbuttoning his coat as he walked and dropping it along with his scarf on the bed. Quickly he stripped, letting his clothing fall in a heap at his feet.

"My Lord, you have made me sinfully ugly!" Ulric exclaimed as he appraised himself in the full-length mirror. Naked, his skin appeared even paler against the black, oily sheen of his hair. The eyebrows, arched and unusually long, added to the effect. Yet beneath the almost translucent skin pure muscle showed. It was the physique of a swimmer with its quivering pectoral muscles and vented latissimi dorsi. A single flex of the fist and the deltoids and trapezia sprang into position, the sternocleidomastoids of the neck bulging. Nature had ravaged his face, but in return, to maintain the balance, it had endowed him with a strength that was uncommon.

Leopold Ulric's thin bluish lips twisted into a sneer. He had had strength ever since he could remember, yet he did nothing to preserve it. He found athletics a bore. His hand dipped to his crotch. He also had this, a blood-swollen penis, long and thick, which was another monstrosity. But this too fascinated and repelled, and he so enjoyed the erotic terror it produced in women. Exultant over his kill, Leopold Ulric walked into the bathroom, past the sunken tub, and into the shower in the corner of the marble-walled room, a small mausoleum. He was not thinking of his kill because its juices still flowed through him. He was not fearful. He had killed before. He was protected in his deeds, always had been.

Leopold Ulric believed himself to be very much a product of his time. He had been born in the fourth decade of the twentieth century, at the time of the greatest cataclysm the world had yet inflicted upon itself. The retinas of his eyes were a storehouse of brutal, inhuman images, of fire storms and devastation, of walking corpses and human ash. Yet the images did not bother him; on the contrary, he feasted upon them. It was as though they were the same in quality and texture as those he remembered from a different time, a long-ago past in which other such memories had been formed. There was that place somewhere in the recesses of the brain which refused to forget, which delighted in adding to the catalog of horror. He was a child of eight before he consciously understood why this was so.

His mother was a simple Swabian peasant woman, his father a tenant farmer who preferred gambling and whoring in the neighboring village of Emmaus to steady work. At the advanced age of twenty-seven Theresa Ulric had at

115

last become pregnant. When her time came, the village midwife arrived to attend to the birth.

While the mother was transported into a painful, semi-conscious euphoria the midwife eased the child from her womb and held it to the light—and then she screamed. What she was holding in her arms was a perfectly formed human infant . . . yet instead of a face it had a white gauzy substance around its head. The midwife carried the child to a table and, laying it down quickly, started brushing the cawl away. The weblike substance fell away, revealing the face. Although the lips were very thin and tinged with blue, and the nose quite long, the features were regular. Except for the eyes, which were still closed. The midwife used a swab to wipe the lids. The child's eyes opened.

The old woman would never forget that moment when the infant boy stared at her. He did not cry or utter a single sound but gazed up at her with those black, fathomless eyes, flecked with red. The midwife almost gagged. The face suddenly appeared very old, ancient, as though it had been forming for years, generations, in the womb of Theresa Ulric. The infant opened its mouth and snarled, slowing raising an arm at her. She knew what it wanted. It was hungry and it wanted to eat. It wanted to feed. . . .

Several years later another incident occurred.

At the age of four, for no apparent reason, the boy Leopold fell into a cataleptic state. He passed twelve hours in coma before being pronounced dead. Because the attending physician could not identify the boy's malady, a rumor about an unknown virus began to circulate through Emmaus. The doctor advised Heinz Ulric to bury the boy as soon as possible. A priest was summoned and the burial arranged for the same day.

When the midwife heard of the tragedy, she could not help herself. She went immediately to the Ulrics' home. There, looking down upon a child she had painstakingly avoided for four years, she felt a past terror creeping up around her. Not even the presence of Theresa Ulric could comfort her. With good reason . . .

The incident that occurred prior to the priest's arrival was subject to various interpretations. According to The-

116

resa her child returned to life, spared because of her prayers. While waiting for the priest Theresa had knelt by the infant's bed and prayed to the same angel who had appeared before her the instant her son had entered this world. What the midwife had taken to be delirium caused by giving birth, Theresa fervently believed to be a holy vision. The angel had asked her what single wish she wanted for the infant. Theresa had asked that Leopold Ulric become the greatest musician the world had ever beheld.

Theresa could not believe that an angel would lie. When she finished her prayers, she waited for deliverance. It came to her as a movement within the burial shroud. To the midwife's frozen astonishment the eager mother unwrapped the white cloth in which her child was bundled. Then both women heard him cry, and the midwife shrank back as the child Leopold stared at her, his blue lips parting in a malignant grin.

At that instant the priest came into the room. Even before he laid eyes upon the child, his fingers were making the sign of the cross before him.

"He died!" the midwife whispered to him hoarsely. "I swear by Almighty God he was dead. It isn't possible for him to have survived the sickness!"

The priest remained silent, his gaze held by the iron eyes of the child. Then the small arms stretched out, clutching at them. The midwife saw the crucifix trembling in the priest's grasp, so tight was his grip upon it. And before both of them was the mother, once again on her knees by the bed, praying, prostrated like some heathen before a graven image she adored yet could not possibly look upon.

It was not an angel who visited you, the midwife thought fearfully. *God would not have permitted such a thing to come to pass. But something else did. Even in your mother's womb something rotten infected you. And then it came forth to look upon its creation. You have been so ill and will always suffer sickness because you are foul inside. You do not belong to life but to death. It would be better for you to die, but whoever's progeny you are will not permit that. Not until your purpose, God help us, is fulfilled. I should have*

117

murdered you at birth, strangled you with the cord that instead I cut to set you free.

Leopold Ulric finished with the dryer and gave his hair a final brush. The memory of the midwife was never too far from his consciousness. Her fear was the starkest he had ever seen in a human being. That was why he had spared her. Because she had glimpsed the truth. Even after he had become world renowned, he would return to Emmaus and call on her, now an old woman, and watch as a few more hours of her life were stripped away by the terror in which she beheld him.

Ulric crossed into the bedroom and quickly dressed in his white tie and tails. A few minutes later, as he adjusted the knot in his tie, the telephone sounded. Security informed him that his car had arrived. Ulric checked his watch, went into the music room, and took up the violin case. He opened it, smiling at the almost ethereal glow of the instrument. It was Otto Morell's greatest creation, and tonight its sounds would soar as no others. Ulric reached down and picked it up. He brought it to his chin and, holding it there, closed his eyes. The incredible fury of his kill sang through his veins, and his head throbbed with the passion that had passed from the lives of others into his own.

Chapter Eight

Sabina remained on the roof of the George Brown Polytechnic Institute until the crowd had dwindled to nothing. Her gaze was fixed on the emptying street below, but the images in her mind's eye were those of people who were no longer there: her Aunt Augusta, Abner Levine, Andreas Marcovici. Their accusations had paralyzed her, made her feel weak and somehow unclean. They also stirred an uneasiness within her, a fear.

When she at last felt the bitter chill of the wind, Sabina crossed the roof, making her way down and out of the building. She crossed the street to find the station house in bedlam. Unit patrols that should have been on the street forty-five minutes ago were being hounded out the door by the duty sergeant. The switchboard operators were going crazy with the incoming calls. Those that were logged were instantly passed to the dispatch desk, which in turn was backed up because units hadn't yet hit the streets. Through the glass enclosure of the captain's office she saw Antonopulous huddling with Jacobson of the Emergency Task Force Unit while Keshkorian, the community relations officer, was screaming into two telephones simultaneously. The final straw was the presence of a WABC news team that charged in behind her, cameras rolling. Sabina fled, ignoring Antonopulous's frantic gestures.

In the relative peace of the women's locker room Sabina changed into a black suit. The pounding on the floor above receded from her consciousness. She was dressing mechanically, without really being aware of what she was doing. Sabina was still afraid. Afraid to go to the church and face

119

the same people who had confronted her on the street. Jesus, what could she say to them!

Tears that had been held back at last spilled over. For a few minutes she sat on the bench in front of her locker, her long fingers pressed hard against her face. It wasn't the community's grief she had to deal with, or their loss. It was her own guilt for having allowed Otto Morell to be killed.

Sabina rose and gave one final appraisal in the round mirror hanging on the locker. The makeup hid her pale, drawn face, but it did nothing for her eyes, where nervousness and despair seemed so clearly reflected. For an instant she almost gave it all up, but instead she quickly grabbed her coat and ran up the back stairs.

The great hall of St. Bartholomew's was packed up to the front doors with mourners. Sabina squeezed inside, shouldering her way over to the table where candles had been set out. She dropped a few coins into the cardboard box and selected a taper. For an instant she felt giddy, the sweet incense clouding her thoughts, the voices of the choir, low and throbbing, overwhelming her. She glanced up at the arches that soared over the center of the cathedral and the glittering light that streamed forth from its three massive chandeliers. A shudder worked its way through her body. She felt as though she were ridding herself of some alien creature that had managed to infest her. There was nothing to fear here. She was among friends, people she knew, people who would help her. Someone touched her arm, another whispered soft condolences. Sabina felt grateful for this small comfort. She moved forward toward the aisle and saw her aunt standing in the front row. Beside her was Richard. She couldn't see Toby but knew he had to be there.

Something—someone—was out of place. Ulric. He had led Augusta Morell away from the station. He must have come here . . . Sabina glanced down at her watch, which gave her the answer: Ulric must have paid his respects and left for Lincoln Center to prepare for the memorial concert. Just as well. At this moment she didn't want strangers around her.

Sabina began to weave her way to the front of the

church, her thoughts following the priest's droning liturgy, when her beeper went off.

Oh, my God, no! She looked wildly around. On either side, startled then accusatory expressions met her confused search. The beeper was still sounding. People were hissing at her. Dropping the candle, Sabina fumbled with her jacket, her fingers desperately searching for and finding the communicator clipped to her belt.

For a few seconds she stood motionless, eyes squeezed shut. The scent and masses of people had suddenly become oppressive. Sabina whirled around and elbowed her way through the throngs, making for the nearest exit. She flung the door open and staggered onto a small metal landing, clutching the cold railing. The communicator sounded again. As quickly as she dared, Sabina clattered down the steps and ran across the half-frozen lawn toward her car.

She punched the buttons on the door frame at the base of the window and heard the click. Thane Sheridan's vehicles came equipped with computer-controlled locks. She slipped inside and reached for the second radio, set on a single frequency, at the same time firing up the engine.

"This is Orion Two," she said breathlessly, feeling the blood pounding in her temples.

"Orion Two, Orion One."

She identified the voice in the midst of background noise.

"Sabina, I'm coming in by chopper from La Guardia to Clarence Square. Meet me there."

"Thane . . . Thane, what's happening?"

"Mr. Bill contacted me on the plane from DC. Three bodies were found, still warm—"

"Children!"

"Not what you're thinking. Get down there. The area is cleared. No one except us and the medical team will get in. Mr. Bill says the Emergency Task Force has cordoned off three blocks. We'll be first in . . ."

The helicopter roar drowned out his next words.

". . . are you now?"

"About six minutes away. See you at Clarence."

Sabina replaced the microphone and automatically

121

strapped herself into the seat. In the rearview mirror she saw the spires of St. Bartholomew's.

"Forgive me, *Onkel,*" she murmured. "I'm so very, very sorry!"

Then she flipped on the siren, lights, and high beams and left rubber on the cement lot.

Not what you're thinking . . . That's what Sheridan had said. But he knew she was thinking only of the children, and he hadn't allayed that fear. Sabina swerved onto Hudson, taking the emergency center lane, the car at once fishtailing and shuddering as the suspension jolted across the ancient brick embedded between smooth trolley car rails that had never been removed.

She was moving fast. Desbrosses, Vestry, Laight, and Hubert streets flashed by. At Clarence Square, the only piece of greenery between the river warehouses and the tractor trailer depots, she swung hard to the right, coming to a stop at the unofficial boundary of Steuben Town. The scene here was no less alien to the character of the town, no less terrifying than the one she had witnessed at the station house.

Emergency Task Force trucks, large ten-ton vans, were positioned on three sides of the square. On their roofs were parade-ground lights, illuminating the pathetic naked-ness of an urban park. The beams were trained primarily on that area where, in summer, the city installed slides, swings, and monkey bars for children. That ground was now barren, converted into a makeshift pad for Sheridan's aircraft.

On the far side of the square, the ETF unit was posi-tioning itself at the foot of the streets that ran into the park. From the reflection of other lights Sabina guessed that the operation extended between West Street and Hud-son.

What in Christ's name has happened? And when?

"Ma'am, I'll have to ask you to move your car out of here."

The ETF officer was dressed in full gear: black flak jacket, heavy dark uniform, shin-high boots. Sabina no-ticed that the M-16 he carried was set for auto fire and the safety was off.

122

She flipped open her ID. "I'm waiting for Inspector Sheridan."

The officer checked her photo against her face and let her pass. Silently he escorted her to the command post vehicle.

"We estimate the inspector's ETA—" he started to say when the sky above them thundered. The pilot, obviously a vet, had swung his machine in from the north, staying high until the last possible moment, then dropping straight into the lights.

Sheridan jumped out. He seemed to stumble, but his ungainly motion could have been the result of the rotor wash. He looked directly at her, his face painfully white, hair askew, coat flapping, a refugee from another hostile land. *He looks so tired,* was Sabina's first thought.

He gestured at the car, and together they ran toward it. As soon as Sheridan slammed the door, he slumped back in the seat, head thrown back, eyes closed.

"We've gotta stop . . . meeting like this," he whispered, a crooked grin on his face. He noticed the pant suit beneath her coat. "Interrupted your evening?"

"I was at a memorial Mass for my uncle."

He shook his head. "God, I'm sorry. I didn't realize—"

"Thane, where to?"

"The corner of Harrison, the alley between it and Franklin. Go."

"The ETF?"

He rummaged in his coat pocket and handed her a folded envelope.

"Give it to perimeter security."

As Sabina swung the car around, nosing past the ETF trucks, Sheridan continued to speak. He was like a man who had just run a great distance, bearing an important message which had to be told before he could regain his second wind. Or sixth.

"Apparently you've had some trouble here at the precinct station house."

Sabina nodded but did not interrupt.

"You'll fill me in later. What I got from Mr. Bill is this: A car from the eleventh saw something in the alley. They investigated and came up with three bodies—or enough pieces to make three bodies."

"Thane!"

"Members of a local gang, the Tribe. The unit radioed their station. The captain, as soon as he heard the details, got hold of Rodgers. Mr. Bill hauled out the ETF and slapped a quarantine on a three-block area."

"Quarantine!" cried Sabina.

"Full force. The only thing that's been in the territory is an armored megaphone truck telling the people to stay inside their homes."

"On what pretext? Rodgers is leaving himself, the police, not to say anything about the city, wide open to a class action suit! The ACLU will hang him out to dry."

"The emergency is justified."

"How?"

Sheridan straightened up as the car approached the cordon.

"You'll see in a minute." He got out of the car and spoke briefly with Karl Jacobson, ETF commander. The rugged Minnesotan listened intently, then waved to his men to move the barrier while he began issuing instructions over the radio.

"Take us to that alley," Sheridan said.

"Thane, what happened in Langley?" Sabina asked quietly, nosing the vehicle into the empty street.

"We may have gotten lucky, very, very lucky."

The streets were empty, but Sabina could feel eyes upon her, staring down from tenement windows, the darkened doorways, the flat rooftops. A tin can bounced off the car roof, clattering in the darkness. It had been months since she had had to work this area, a place where she had once played, near a school she had attended. All lost . . .

"Christ, this must be what the Berlin Wall looks and feels like."

"The Wall is better. It has well-defined rules."

There were two vehicles parked at either end of the alley: a forensic examiner's station wagon and an ETF van. Two men in civilian dress were standing close to the van, smoking, talking, hand gestures punctuating rapid-fire words. The officers were in a classic square formation: in

124

pairs on both sides of the street, a unit covering each direction: north, south, east, and west, with the square secure between them.

"Don't get out yet."

Sabina glanced at Sheridan. She could feel him summoning what had to have been the final reserve of his energy. The face muscles tightened, the slack expression disappeared, the eyes widened. He undid his trench coat, and she saw the handle of the Venus.

"Don't have to reach too far for your gun," he said softly. "If you see, *feel* something coming at you, take it down."

Sheridan stepped from the vehicle and shouldered his way against the wind toward the two civilians. "Sorry to have dragged you out on a night like this."

Sabina edged forward, and Sheridan took her elbow.

"Gentlemen, this is Detective Sergeant Morell," said Sheridan. "Sabina, meet Drs. Arliss and Weingert, pathologists." He turned back to them. "Have you been briefed as to what to expect?"

"Generally, yes." Arliss nodded. He was the older one, and Sabina knew him by reputation. He was the best the borough had. And *he* was nervous.

"We'll need more light. Someone to . . . look out for us."

"That's why we're here." Sheridan tapped on the van, and instantly the alley was flooded with light. Both physicians donned two pairs of gloves, the kind used in contamination wards.

"I'll lead them in," Sheridan told Sabina. "You take the rear." He brought out the Venus and started to walk.

Thane Sheridan stayed close to the wall, keeping clear of the center of the alley. The high-intensity light clearly showed traces of footprints in the layer of dirt that covered the asphalt. These probably belonged to the patrolmen first on the scene. But there were other markings, firmly depressed, that looked like tire treads. Sheridan gave them a wide berth, at the same time giving thanks that the sleet hadn't worked the print away. He came around to the other side of the alley, where the refuse was stacked up. He flashed his light over the rotting cartons and overturned cans, penetrating the horror that lay there.

"What we're looking for is over here," he called back to

the physicians. "Put your tarp down. As soon as you're ready, we'll call up the morgue wagon."

Sabina heard the forensic experts move quickly toward Sheridan. She kept all her senses trained on her section of the alley. Her revolver was out, moving slowly from side to side, following her eyes as they coursed over every square foot. No feedback. The alley was dead.

Arliss and Weingert carefully unfolded a heavy vinyl sheet, all thirty-five square feet of it, and laid that over the ground. Sheridan pushed and kicked some cartons out of the way so that the forensic experts could get at the bodies. When Sabina, who had followed them, looked around, she understood what Sheridan had meant: The first thing Arliss and Weingert carried over to the tarp was a torso, legs attached, the thorax shorn away. A moment later they found the upper half of the corpse. Next they returned with a complete body. The third corpse had also been dismembered. It took five full minutes to find the head.

The team arranged the bodies on the sheet and under a cluster of flood lamps began examining each piece. Sheridan watched impassively as Arliss delicately lifted the flaps of skin where the torso had been severed, peering intently at the crushed veins and arteries, shredded internal organs, and splintered bone. All the while he spoke softly in the direction of the tape recorder Weingert had placed between the corpses. The younger physician was performing the equivalent examination on the severed head and right hand. Sheridan did not take his eyes off them. He realized that he had to give them as much time as they needed, yet every minute that elapsed put more distance between him and the killer. Or killers, human or inhuman. Sheridan focused his entire concentration on the bodies. The scent of the Rambler was weak. He could not understand why this was so. The place screamed of blood.

Arliss and Weingert were conferring, speaking in low tones, nodding as they correlated points of their examination.

"Inspector?" Arliss straightened up and began to advance toward Sheridan.

"Don't step on that!"

Sheridan saw the wrapped-up jacket at the last instant.

A ray of light had glinted off one of the studs. He stepped over and with one edge of the tarp carefully covered the jacket—and the protruding brick.

Sheridan glanced back at the doctors. "What's the consensus?"

"Get the morgue wagon down here," Arliss continued, unruffled. "I want the bodies in the labs as quickly as possible. We have to test for rabies."

"Rabies?"

"They were taken by dogs, Thane," Weingert said softly.

"Dogs did this?" demanded Sheridan, incredulous.

"I don't subscribe to the theory of huge alligators populating Manhattan sewers or rats growing to the size of cats," Arliss said. "But in this instance it would be preferable if I did. Thane, I've *never* seen bite marks like that. Whatever you have out there is monstrous."

"But you're certain it's canine?" Sheridan persisted.

"We've both seen this kind of bite, though not of this *size,* hundreds of times." Arliss shook his head. "Listen, we would like to be wrong, but I'm afraid we're not."

"How could an animal bite an adolescent in half?" demanded Sheridan.

"In this case it was several bites," Weingert said, pointing to the eldest youth. "The dog took his hand first, then came back for the rest. The other two died quickly enough. There's almost nothing left of their throats."

"How big?"

"Minimum two hundred pounds, twice the size of a St. Bernard, a big one."

"Breed?"

"Can't say."

"There can't be very many that size!"

Arliss looked at him carefully. "Until tonight I wasn't aware there were *any.*"

Sheridan escorted the physicians back to the ETF van, from where they called Thompson Street. He himself radioed Jacobson, telling the commander that the sanitized zone was to be searched, thoroughly, for dogs, probably a pack, large and vicious. No attempt was to be made to capture them. By the tone of his reply Jacobson sounded bored. Sheridan suggested he come over to have a look at the bodies. Above all, the zone was to remain in quarantine, nothing in, nothing out, until the search had been completed.

"What about bloodhounds?" Sabina suggested.

He hadn't heard her come up behind him.

"Jesus, I'm not thinking!" He relayed the order to Jacobson.

"Can you identify the kids?" he asked Sabina.

"Punks," she said, the voice dead. "Vicious, mindless punks who preyed on grocery store owners and old ladies coming home from church bingo. But even they didn't deserve this." She looked up at him. "Dogs?"

"Arliss and Weingert wouldn't confirm it unless they were sure."

"So a human being couldn't have carried out that butchery?"

"No."

"In some awful way I'm glad you said that," Sabina murmured

"So am I," Sheridan said. "But I can't understand what happened here tonight. Arliss figures the time of death less than two hours ago. But there hasn't been one report out from this area about anything unusual. And what took these kids down could hardly be missed."

"It's a tight-lipped neighborhood, Thane," Sabina reminded him. "Look at it another way: The bodies weren't found by locals. Given the weather, maybe there weren't too many people around. Even if someone had glimpsed the dogs, they probably wouldn't have reported anything. Not because of dogs."

"You don't believe Arliss." It was a statement, not a question.

"I saw the bodies," she flared. "It's just . . . just hard to comprehend something so vicious that isn't human. I mean, animals, unless they're rabid or maddened, don't dismember their victims."

Sheridan looked at her curiously. Then abruptly he nodded and hammered on the door of the ETF van with an open palm. He asked for a plastic bag, then went over and

128

carefully lifted the wound-up jacket by inserting a stick into a hole in the brick. He gave the bag to Arliss.

"Pass that to Morty, will you? Tell him there may be fingerprints and a tire marking."

"Are you going to sweep the area?"

"Inside and out. Before we're finished, the media will be salivating for our excuse. You're ready to stand by the canine story?"

"It's not a story!" Weingert snapped. "And yes, we do stand by it. Tests will—"

"Michael, it's all right," Arliss interrupted gently. "He meant no offense." He turned to Sheridan. "We'll run the tests at Thompson Street, then get them over to the midtown pathologist's office and handle the media from there."

"The best," Sheridan said. "And Sam, I'm sorry if I was sharp."

"De nada." Arliss looked out of the one-way armored glass. "Looks like the troops are moving in."

Sheridan stepped back into the night. Across Harrison Street ETF teams moved in flank formation, units of two peeling off to investigate alleys, apartment building foyers, and cul-de-sacs. The static of two-way radios crackled in the silence.

"Think they'll find anything?" Sabina asked him.

Sheridan's reply was lost in a staccato hammering of gunfire.

"Next street over!" Sabina yelled. She was off and running even before Sheridan had a chance to react.

He started off after her, footsteps pounding on the cold dry cement, one hand wrenching his weapon free. He caught up with her, and they circled into the adjoining alley together.

"Freeze!"

"It's Sheridan!"

The ETF officer ran up, M-16 ready.

"Excuse me, sir."

"What happened?"

"Those two came running out of that door. We gave verbal warning, then fired over their heads."

Sheridan swept past him to where another officer had

two South Americans lined up against the wall, fingers splayed across the brick, feet well apart.

"Armed?"

"Just knives, sir," the officer said, never taking his eyes off the two.

"What is this place?" he asked Sabina, gesturing at the fire door.

"The rear entrance of the Casa Mendoza."

That was when he smelled it.

"Keep them here. Support is on the way." The last sentence became redundant as the sirens closed in. Sheridan unhitched his radio.

"Clear out the front end of the bodega and secure, make sure that everyone knows Morell and I are going upstairs."

"Upstairs?" Sabina asked.

"They're fixating on something."

Then Sabina saw it as well: The two South Americans, probably Colombians, had their heads up, both looking in the same direction. At the upstairs window that overlooked the alley from the second floor of the Casa Mendoza. It was a look of stark terror.

"Let's go," Sheridan said softly.

He kicked back the door and entered the foul-smelling hallway. From up front he heard angry shouts and epithets as the bodega's patrons were herded outside.

Sheridan moved quickly up the stairs, conscious of Sabina behind him. He did not expect to meet anything or anyone—not alive. The two downstairs had seen something that had turned their bowels to jelly. If it had been alive and wanted them, it would have taken them.

Sheridan reached the second-story landing, pausing before the door that opened up on the back room. He recoiled at the stench that billowed out at him, not only that of human sweat and excrement but of something else, the residue of evil, of a force that had pervaded this area, carried out its butchery, then departed as freely as it had come. He knew a killing had occurred here, and it was mocking him.

He pushed the door open all the way, leading with the barrels of the Venus. There were no closets, no recesses. The room was empty. He slipped inside and moved along

130

the wall to the next door and pushed it open. A thin stream of water lay along the scarred floorboards, glistening under naked light bulbs. He looked across at Sabina, who was on the opposite side of the doorway. Then he nodded.

Roncaron and Santiago did not see the pair of weapons trained on them. They remained now as Ulric had left them, one kneeling over the toilet, his head immersed in the brimming bowl, the other sprawled across the filthy tiles. Sheridan holstered his gun, stepped over the puddle, and grasping Roncaron's head by the hair, pulled him out.

"Son of a bitch!"

He lowered the corpse to the floor and squatted, taking Roncaron's head between both hands. He tilted it back. There was a complete circle of ugly bruises around the neck, the bluish tinge punctuated by searing welts where the fingers had dug into the flesh.

"Strangulation?" asked Sabina.

Sheridan nodded. "Someone very strong . . ."

Quickly he examined the rest of the body. "No apparent wounds, no contusions around the skull, which means no one hit him."

"He was taken while conscious?" Sabina asked, incredulous.

"Had to have been. Unless an autopsy reveals they were both drugged. But I can't see that."

Sheridan straightened up.

"What happened at the precinct station house this afternoon?"

After Sabina recounted the details of the demonstration, Sheridan asked: *"Everyone* went to the Mass at St. Bartholomew's?"

"I'm sure of it," Sabina said firmly. Suddenly she realized where he was heading.

"No, Thane, they couldn't have done it! *No* one in the neighborhood could have done this!"

"What would *you* think?" Sheridan asked her. "A little girl is kidnapped and murdered. A community elder is killed a few days later. Today the neighborhood ties up an entire precinct station . . . and now three bodies in an alley, two up here. These two the killers of Otto Morell. What would *you* conclude, Sabina?"

She was about to loose her anger at his callous reasoning when suddenly she remembered.

"But that's not all of it, is it?" she whispered. "There was my little number downstairs, that fine display of cool and calm when *I* was ready to take out the cousins."

She looked up at him. "The South American enclave will want my head, Thane. They're going to remember Casa Mendoza as soon as we bring these two down. Then they'll link the killing here with the three kids in the alley. No one will remember what sort of animals they were. All the press will play up is that a cop threatened two suspects who then turned up dead, while a block away mothers of those kids will be screaming that their sons were also killed by that same cop. That's the way it's going to work."

He turned her away from the sight of the bathroom, feeling her shudder.

"Someone had to have seen something," he said. "We'll begin with the two downstairs. But it's the kids in the alley who are the best bet. They must have parents somewhere. Someone will come forward. They *have* to!"

Sabina shook her head and started for the door. She knew the police would have no cooperation. It was not the police who were law here. At that instant she felt sorry for Sheridan. He had probably never come up against the full power of silence.

Leopold Ulric timed his arrival at Lincoln Center meticulously, going through the performers' entrance at precisely five minutes to curtain. He smiled at the security with whom he deposited his instrument, asking that it be delivered to his dressing room, and proceeded directly to the service elevator. A moment later he was standing in front of the long carved gallery which serves as the lighting and acoustics terminal for the center. Oblivious to the startled glances from technicians, Leopold Ulric stepped inside and beheld a sight which never failed to thrill him.

The Metropolitan Opera House was the only hall in New York Ulric deigned to play in. Because the house was continuously booked by opera companies, almost no orchestra performances were held here. Leopold Ulric was one of the handful of exceptions. He had made it very clear to his

132

agent that he preferred the acoustics here. The African rosewood paneling was the very best music conductor. More, it was the sheer size of the hall that he appreciated, thirty-eight hundred seats with two hundred numbered standing positions.

Across the vast domed expanse he saw the magnificent chandeliers, set on tracks, each one thirty feet in diameter, the most incredible creations of crystal ever made. Below, on four balconies, three dozen loges, and the magnificent orchestra plateau, his audience waited. He leaned close to the glass that enveloped the gallery, staring greedily at the swarming humanity below. They were his people, these men in evening dress and women bedecked in European finery and flash-fire jewels. He did not strain to pick out individuals but looked out upon them as faceless subjects, the rich, the powerful, the influential who had come to pay him homage. He squeezed his eyes shut, feeling the blood raging in his temples.

Abruptly Leopold Ulric pulled himself away from the spectacle and returned to the first level. The corridors were empty. The orchestra had taken its place. The concertmaster and conductor were waiting in the wings. As he closed the door to his dressing room Ulric heard the ovation which accompanied the raising of the curtain and introductions. He ignored the flowers which converted the dressing room into a funeral parlor and snapped open the case. He detested the scent of flowers, but not even they could destroy the odor of his instrument. Ulric turned the violin over in his hands, inhaling deeply of the resin and varnish smell. He slid the bow out, already dusted, and delicately ran it across the strings. The resonance and pitch were perfect.

Leopold Ulric walked down the corridor past the other dressing rooms and up a flight of concrete stairs to stage level. He moved smoothly over the floor, littered with ropes and equipment, and stood in the shadow of the curtain. The national anthem had been played, the great hall was silent except for the faint rustle of people settling into seats. He glanced at his watch. Like his time on the balcony this, the one-minute interval before his appearance, was his trademark. Leopold Ulric squinted, his eyes adjusting to the lighting, then glided onto the stage.

The ovation was overwhelming. He hadn't even reached his position to the left of the conductor when the audience rose as one. Ulric appeared not to notice them. He moved swiftly, taking up his appointed position. He threw his head back and assumed the stance that distinguished him from all other performers: He pulled his left leg back and, placing all his weight on it, thrust the right one forward. It was a grotesque posture, ungainly and contorted. Ulric thrust the violin under his chin and held his bow high, the signal that he was ready.

For five minutes he did not open his eyes. From the first thundering chords of the opening movement to the beginning of his solo, he remained poised, a scarecrow in the spotlight hewn out of blackness, with even the face, with its deathly pallor, a parody of life. Yet when bow met strings and the melody poured out over the hall, the inanimate came into its own. Ulric's gestures became almost chaotic, the arm swinging wildly to and fro yet guiding the bow with unerring precision. The fingers, those thick powerful fingers, leaped and danced over the neck, sometimes scarcely touching the string, other times pressing it hard against the wood.

Only when he was halfway through the solo did Ulric look out onto the audience, his exceptional vision unaffected by the line of spot lamps. They were his. He could see the rapture and enthrallment, the mesmerization and, in the open mouths and flaring nostrils of some women, the lust.

At that instant he threw his head back. His blood sang with the memory of the kill, but that wasn't what had taken hold of him.

Sheridan! his heart screamed out in ecstasy.

Sheridan, you have found my hollow carcasses!

Oh, my friend, I knew you would not be far behind!

It was agreed by audience and critics alike that the Sibelius Concerto had never been played as brilliantly as it was that night by Leopold Ulric. It was not music. It transcended definition.

134

Chapter Nine

Somewhere in the early hours of the next day the clock ran out on Thane Sheridan. Forty-eight hours had elapsed since the morning of February 11. Some as yet anonymous child began living on borrowed time.

The bodies of the three Tribe members were the first to be taken away. Arliss radioed for Thompson Street to send another "black wagon," then he and Weingert followed Sabina Morell over to the room above the Casa Mendoza.

"It's a toss-up," Arliss said after a brief examination. "Either strangulation or drowning. We'll have to open them up to be sure. Might be difficult to determine just how alive they were when their heads went into the bowl."

"This whole area is going fucking insane!" Weingert hissed through his teeth.

Sheridan, who had been standing in the corner, regarded the young pathologist sympathetically. The tall, slightly stooped, prematurely gray physician had married recently and a baby was on the way. Small comfort that he lived in Queens. The Rosenbergs were Brooklyn residents.

"You might as well get back to the labs," he said. "I'll need the initial reports ASAP. These two will be forwarded directly."

Arliss pinched the bridge of his nose. "How soon is ASAP?"

"Before you take them to midtown." He paused. "Oh, and Sam? As far as the kids are concerned, the animals *are* rabid. Regardless of what tissue and blood samples show. Later on, if we have to, we'll plead an error. But right now I need an excuse to keep the area sealed."

"I hear you," Arliss murmured. His professional conscience didn't even flinch. At least people understood what rabies was; inexplicable monstrous dogs would only fuel the imagination.

"We'll give you whatever support you need, Thane," Arliss said. "But remember: There's something very real out there."

Sheridan posted an ETF officer in the room, then slowly went downstairs. Arliss and Weingert were riding shotgun in the wagon taking the three bodies back to Thompson Street. The second pathology vehicle had just pulled up. Sheridan looked out over the harshly illuminated street. Even through the crackle of radios, pounding feet, and barked commands he sensed an ominous silence over the street. It was as though an alien amoeba had invaded a piece of tissue. The corpus was silent, absorbing the intruder, waiting for it to spend its strength before closing in and destroying it. He looked up at the window at the rear of the bodega and was once again overcome by the stink of the Rambler. He had killed sooner than Sheridan had expected, in an area he could not have foreseen, taking victims Sheridan would never have anticipated as targets. The pattern seemed to be breaking. Did that mean the children were safe? Sheridan desperately wished he could believe so. But he couldn't.

He looked for Sabina and saw her by their car, the two suspects facing her, their hands in bracelets. She was going at them in staccato Spanish, but the words were bouncing right off their impassive faces.

"Anything?"

He saw the hatred in their dark eyes, the mixture of fear and contempt. Sabina finished, waited for an instant, then turned away.

"They won't say a damn thing without their lawyer," she said in disgust.

"What do you think—do they know anything?"

"They're scared shitless. You should have seen their faces when the body bags were carried downstairs." She looked at Sheridan. "We won't get anything out of them. The ETF hasn't found anything to connect them to either

136

killing. Letelier's lawyer will have them out on the street by noon."

"Take me home," Sheridan said quietly. "There's nothing more for us here."

He acknowledged his own weariness and sensed her frustration, which was becoming a nervous frenzy. They had to get out of the field, at least for a few hours.

Sabina drove them to Thompson Street in record time.

"You go on ahead, take a shower or something," she said. "I'll check with the labs."

When she returned to the apartment, she found Sheridan already in bed, his chest rising and falling as he breathed steadily, deeply. For the first time in as long as she could remember, she saw his face relaxed. Sabina hesitated, then went back downstairs. When she returned, she closed the door firmly and locked it.

She took a long, luxuriously hot shower, then padded across the room naked. She looked down at Sheridan's sleeping form and brushed the hair from his eyes. Sabina drew back the sheets and slid in beside him, reaching for his warmth. He rolled toward her and put an arm around her. For an instant his eyes opened and he smiled, but she knew he was still asleep and wouldn't remember anything.

"I don't remember a damn thing . . . I'm sorry."

She pressed a finger to his lips. His head slid across her shoulder and onto her breast, lips seeking the nipple. She uttered a soft cry as his hands gently stroked her thighs into parting and his tongue traveled lower, across the taut belly and into the musky dampness.

A few minutes later the sunlight spilled across the bed through the one-way plate glass.

She left him after a cup of coffee, taken in silence, her departure sealed with a light kiss on the lips. They had worked out the day's itinerary: Sabina wanted to meet with her aunt before Augusta left for the scheduled community meeting. Sheridan would peruse the overnight reports from the pathology labs. They agreed to meet at noon, at which time Sheridan would bring her up to date

137

on what he had gleaned from Langley. When she left him at the door, Sabina realized, from his expression, that neither one of them understood or had come to terms with what had happened between them last night. In a way this vagueness was disconcerting, yet the unfinished also held out promise. . . .

Augusta Morell lived in a small townhouse that her husband had purchased in the 1920s. Three years ago they had had the limestone facade sandblasted, the beginning of a revitalization period which swept down Horatio Street. Sabina parked directly before the gleaming black lacquer door with its brass lion's head knocker and ran up the three brick-lined steps. She unlocked the door and moved quickly through the center hall into the kitchen overlooking the back garden. A large pot of coffee rested on the gas burner; the sugar and cream were out on the table, the silver samovar and china cups gone. She retraced her steps, went through the dining room into the sunken front parlor.

As was her custom Augusta Morell was in the wing chair to the left of the black marble fireplace. Two other people were sitting opposite her, but neither had taken the chair next to her. That had been Otto Morell's favorite. Sabina knew no one would ever occupy it again.

"Good morning, *Tante.*"

As Augusta Morell looked up at her niece, Andreas Marcovici and Abner Levine got to their feet. The short slim barber smiled shyly at her while Levine patted her shoulder and nodded his head sympathetically.

"I'm sorry about last night—for leaving the Mass, *Tante,*" said Sabina. "Believe me, if there had been any choice—"

"We all listened to the radio," Augusta Morell said, her voice dry. The Viennese accent still clung to her words and made them curt and brittle. Those who did not know Augusta Morell might have thought her a cold woman. Nothing could have been further from the truth.

"What did you hear?" asked Sabina.

"That three young people had been senselessly murdered."

138

"There were more," Sabina said in a low voice. "Two more, in fact."

"We know that," Abner Levine broke in, speaking ponderously as though measuring each word. "That was on the news too."

"You think we had something to do with that?" Andreas Marcovici spoke up. His head could have been the model for a Roman bust, with its full, slightly wavy hair, flaring nose, and thick sensuous lips. His words were underlined with accusation.

"I didn't say or even imply that!" Sabina rebuked him. She turned to her aunt. "I came to apologize . . . and to see if there was anything I could do."

"I know you loved Otto as he loved you," Augusta said gently. "In the last few years there were times when our relationships were strained: We, this community, were beset by a malignancy, and you, the police, could do nothing to stop it. But above all we remained, and still do, family. You must never forget this, Sabina."

Augusta rose and from the samovar poured her niece coffee.

"But I also believe Andreas is right: Otto's killers have been murdered. Our demonstration outside the precinct house has been seen by the entire city as an expression of our anger. We understand that logically suspicion will fall on us. After all, who else would have had a better motive?"

"But you must understand, Sabina, that we didn't kill anyone," said Abner Levine. "Even the hardiest of us—and besides Andreas there aren't many—could not have strangled either one of those . . . those men. We wouldn't dare venture into that part of Steuben Town, even though it belongs to us as much as our own homes and shops do."

"If nothing else," Marcovici said bitterly, "the police should know *everyone* was at the memorial Mass. You can ask your own commissioner of police."

"No one is going to accuse you—any of you—of killing Santiago or Roncaron," Sabina said firmly. She hesitated. "There's evidence as to how they were murdered. It would have taken an extraordinarily powerful person, perhaps even two.

Sabina looked at her aunt. "But I must know, *Tante,*

what it is you're planning to do at this meeting later today. The incident at the precinct house, while ill-conceived, was at least understandable. But after last night the police are nervous. No one wants an overreaction. No one wants to see people hurt . . ." Her words trailed off on the stream of cigarette smoke.

"God help me but I wish I wasn't a cop!" she whispered. "It's a rotten time to be on the other side of the fence."

"You're a *policewoman*," Augusta corrected her sharply. "And a very good one. It takes a certain strength of character to face what you do every day. I'm only sorry that it's become impossible for the ordinary citizen to communicate with the police. The bureaucratic procedure has dehumanized them and us."

A silence fell over the four people. Each one recognized that the most painful part of the meeting was over. Yet it had to have come out.

"Madame Morell . . ."

Andreas Marcovici always addressed her thus, not only because he was the youngest of those present, scarcely thirty, but because he owed the Morells a moral debt. When Marcovici had first arrived in New York from southern Italy, it had been Otto Morell who had taken the young barber in. He had seen to it that Marcovici's hard-earned stake was not squandered by speculators or con men. He had found premises for the shop and cosigned the bank note, allowing Marcovici to bring over his wife much sooner than he had expected. Not a day passed in which the young barber did not in some way show his gratitude. Above all he was fiercely loyal to and now protective of Augusta Morell.

"Andreas?"

"Our meeting starts in less than two hours," Marcovici said punctiliously.

Augusta Morell smiled. Andreas would say nothing more lest he stray into committing lese majesty.

"You're right, as usual. Abner, would you show Sabina the proposal we've drafted?"

Abner Levine reached down and drew out a buff manila file from a worn briefcase. On the cover sheet Sabina saw the names of the people to whom the copy would be sent:

140

the police commissioner, the mayor, the governor of New York, and finally the President of the United States. She had no doubt that each of the men would read the document. Otto Morell's name was familiar to all of them. As for the President, Morell had presented his daughter with one of his violins. The chief executive tended to remember details like that.

For the next thirty minutes Sabina read in silence, smoking cigarette after cigarette, jabbing each butt into the ashtray. The three other people in the room did not stir. When she was finished, Sabina said, "You're really going to push them, aren't you?"

"It is a matter of survival," said Augusta Morell. "One can continue to ignore people, turn a blind eye on their welfare for only so long. You read history, Sabina. Very often events occur because people feel they *must* act. There is no longer the luxury of choice."

"There is another consideration," Abner Levine said slowly. "Too often we permit complexities to govern us. We have grown used to—some of us, that is—to dealing with a world in which certain steps and procedures must be followed, without which nothing else may happen. We have, to our folly, abandoned common sense. That is all this paper is, Sabina—a plea for common sense, sanity. Perhaps that is why you find it so striking, so . . . so revolutionary, if I dare to use the term. But you must remember, a lot of us who live here have *endured* revolutions. We have seen what happens, on the one hand, to people who do *not* rise to speak for themselves and, on the other, to rulers who are not responsive to needs."

"The term *revolution,* as I understand it, carries with it the connotation of progress," Sabina said softly. "What you're advocating in this paper is the basis for tyranny. You're asking, in fact, that the Miranda ruling be rescinded, that the police be given wide discretionary powers of arrest." She flipped through the pages. "That even though a person may not be physically or emotionally hurt by another's behavior, that same behavior could be construed as illegal. Christ, do you *realize* what you're saying?"

"I think a good many members in your own Police

141

Brotherhood would agree with us," Marcovici said. "You should ask them sometime."

Sabina had no answer, for she knew the barber was right.

"There is another consideration," said Augusta Morell. "And that is that simply because a direction has been followed for a length of time, it is thus legitimate for *all* time and *all* circumstances. Sometimes we follow tangents, not the real path. It is conceivable that we have erred in our direction, that while we wanted to leave something behind, evolve, as you would say, what we perceived and aimed for and where we eventually arrived were two different things.

"Forty years ago, even thirty, the policeman was a watchman, not someone fighting crime. He walked the streets. He knew the people. More often than not he protected the people he lived *among*. He was, Sabina, a community spokesman. Whenever necessary he was also an enforcer of its law, at times brutally so. But we believed then that the *community* was what was important. *Its* rights had to be protected.

"Yet over the years Abner and I and many others have seen things change. Policemen seldom walk the streets. They ride in cars. More convenient, you might say, more mobile, quicker, more effective. But have you noticed? No one *approaches* the police anymore. No one, except in an emergency, walks out to a patrol car or waves at one. The officers wouldn't know what to think. I have seen a cruiser pull up to a street corner where young hoodlums were gathered. The officer got out. He asked one of the boys some questions, the boy answered each one with a sneer. The patrolman shrugged, got back into his car, and drove off. Did the police learn anything at all from the encounter? Did they get answers to their questions? Of course not. And the hoodlums? From their point of view they had successfully humiliated a public authority. What more is needed to swell the ego to the point where one believes that *no one* will stand in his way, no matter what he wants to do?"

Augusta Morell paused and looked pleadingly at her
142

niece, her gray eyes reaching out to her, asking desperately that she understand.

"Abner has coined a nice phrase for what has been happening to us . . ."

The delicatessen owner bowed his head shyly, large fingers intertwining. He took a deep breath and looked up.

"I call it the story of the broken windows," he said softly. "There was a time, Sabina, before your own, I'm afraid, when families and individuals worked to preserve a neighborhood. People didn't move as quickly or easily as they do today. They strove to create the proverbial greener pastures right where they lived, not over the next hill. That was why broken windows were always repaired. . . .

"I remember walking in that part of Steuben Town which is no longer ours. I remember seeing those elegant apartment buildings standing empty. They appeared to me so very sad. Then the next week I would walk by again and see a broken window. The next week two or three more. After a while *all* the windows were broken. The garbage began to pile up in the courtyard. The front door had been broken down.

"This was a sign of neglect, Sabina. It showed that no one cared enough about one broken window to repair it, so two more were broken. That is how the process of decay sets in, because no one cares. It is also the beginning of the second stage. The building I'm thinking of belonged to old Herschel Kaplan, God rest his soul. He had a five and dime there. The kids who were breaking the windows began to hang around the store. When he asked them to move on, they laughed."

Abner Levine paused.

"They laughed, then after a while, when they saw the police couldn't or wouldn't charge them, they began to pilfer candy. When Kaplan tried to stop that, they beat him.

"So Kaplan, who had been beaten in the streets of Hitler's Germany, left. He had no fight in him anymore. He had been abused enough. That left another vacancy, and soon the bums moved in. They drank in the streets and slept on the front steps. During the day they became beggars. The decay spread from store to store, home to home like rot going from tooth to tooth.

"The rest you can see for yourself. The graffiti, stripped cars, the prostitutes . . . and the drugs, above all, the drugs. For those of us who were pushed out of our neighborhood the decay was as evident as the nose on your face. But not so to your police. They had rules and procedures to follow. The young officers had no stake in the neighborhood. They were on rotation. The older ones had already moved away. So what did they care? They could not feel the pain of decay. Our pleas had no meaning for them. You see, the police could not understand the concept of *prevention.* For them a situation was not real until it existed. To foresee a tragedy or even to be able to discern one already in the making was beyond them.

"So in the end a part of our community was permitted to die. The older ones among us had no physical recourse. The lawyers told us that the rights of the individual were sacred. And all the while our lives, everything we had worked so hard to maintain, preserve, and improve, died. *Where was the right of the community, Sabina?* Why didn't anyone help us speak up for that right?"

"It all comes down to a simple fact," Augusta Morell said. "Arresting one drunk or one adolescent for breaking a window seems harsh, even unjust. *But failing to do anything about it is to begin the process by which an entire neighborhood is corrupted.* I would not wish to infringe on the rights of a single human being, but neither can I permit his actions to destroy me."

"Another thing," Marcovici said quickly, before Sabina had a chance to answer. "Your own reports will tell you that it is no longer the older people who are being attacked. They have learned to cope. They cross a street to avoid the punks. They don't go out as often, or they wait until there is a group of four or five of them. It's ugly, Sabina, for our people to have to huddle like that so that they can walk their own streets. But I tell you here and now that I *won't* let those bastards dictate where I walk or when. They won't dictate to me or my wife or my child! The younger people who have a stake here will not be pushed around. We intend to maintain the kind of stake that's been left to us. And no one, especially not a snake like Letelier, is going to take it away from us!"

Sabina shook her head. She had heard the litany many times over. She was not blind to what was happening. People like Marcovici, who had his barber shop and home here, would *not* leave. He and others like him had been pushed too far. They believed they had nothing to lose by fighting.

"I'm surprised Jim and George aren't here," she said suddenly.

She hadn't noticed before, but the nucleus of the community was two members short.

"They're on a job," Marcovici said. "But they'll be at the meeting."

She nodded and lit another cigarette. "I wish I could tell you you're wrong about what you say. But you're not."

"Then support us!" Marcovici interrupted, excited. "Work with us the way Richard has been."

The ghost of her ex-husband. Sabina's anger flared. She wanted to tell Marcovici, all of them, that Richard's pious pronouncements in the press and at town meetings were just a smokescreen. A vote-gathering device. A fund-raising gimmick. Richard had always been smart enough to know just what kind of wave was coming in and how long he could ride it.

"Sabina?"

She evaded Augusta's gentle insistence on a direct reply.

"I support your aims. The whole department does. But I can't condone what is in that statement."

Her eyes flitted to Marcovici and Abner Levine, who averted their gaze.

"And you can't talk to me as though I'm an outsider. I was *raised* in this neighborhood, and I still live in it."

"You have a gun and the badge to use it," Marcovici said bitterly. "The punks have guns, and no one cares. What about us?"

"What has happened to *part* of Steuben Town happened over a period of time," Sabina said desperately. "I grant you there was ignorance, shortsightedness, and just plain stupidity. But it will take time to correct this—"

"We have waited, Sabina," Abner Levine said, slowly getting to his feet. "We have petitioned and pleaded. We

145

have been listened to but ignored. What happens is no longer in our hands."

The words shot through Sabina, chilling her to the bone. "What do you mean by that?" she whispered.

"Only that Otto's dream of cleansing this community, *our neighborhood*, was not murdered with him," Augusta Morell said calmly. "The presentation will be made. The people demand it."

"The people!" cried Sabina. "Please, let's be honest about this: You three people plus Jim and George are the moving force of the community. Kazan may be mayor, but in Steuben Town it's you five who make up the real government."

She turned to Augusta Morell. "And you, *Tante*, are now the elder. *Onkel*'s moral authority has passed into your hands. You can stop this paper. You must, because you don't know what kind of steamroller you'll be setting in motion if you don't. I know as well as you that there are hundreds of thousands, probably millions of people who would support such a petition. It would be more popular than Proposition Thirteen. And you know the good it would accomplish. But can't you understand how open to *abuse* your proposal is?"

"There is room for abuse in any human undertaking, no matter how noble or correct the motives," Augusta Morell agreed. "But if one thinks only of abuse, one becomes paralyzed, as we have. No, we must take that chance. I believe that *given the chance*, decency will prevail. In any case it is always easier to deal with the excesses of a few than with the corruption of many. A corruption that only continues to grow."

Sabina picked up her purse and rose. She walked over to the curio cabinet and stared through the glass at her aunt's collection of porcelain figurines. Gaily painted Meissen shepherds and shepherdesses smiled shyly at her.

"What about the evidence you mentioned?" she said, speaking to her aunt's reflection. "What and how much was *Onkel* able to dig up on Letelier's connections with Albany—and here in the city?"

"Otto was very secretive about that work," Augusta said. "He didn't tell me anything until a few days before
146

he died." Her voice faded. "You see, he didn't want me to worry."

"You should give it to me—or see that it gets to the Favereau Commission," Sabina said, turning around. "It could be important evidence . . . seeing that it was strong enough to kill him."

"I'm going through Otto's papers now," Augusta Morell said. "As soon as I—and all of us—understand what he left us with, we will make the necessary decisions. Until then it's no concern of the police. They have more than enough to do."

Her aunt's expression softened, the words losing their brittleness.

"Support us, Sabina," Augusta Morell said softly. "Don't fight us on this."

Sabina turned around, her eyes shining with tears.

"I don't know," she whispered. "I don't know if I can . . . what I'm supposed to do."

In one motion she stepped across and hugged her aunt. Then without another word she broke away and ran to the front door. The tears spilled even before she reached the street.

Chapter Ten

The sunlight had crept around the corner of the duplex apartment. A laser-thin ray moved across the pillows, warmed the girl's forehead, then settled directly on her right eye. She moaned. Her legs thrashed weakly for several seconds, then quivered and were drawn up against her belly. Instead of rolling over she brought her head down, her angel blond hair acting as a prism for the light.

Leopold Ulric stood at the foot of the huge water bed, a little island unto itself in the room. He watched intently as the girl's figure bobbed gently to and fro, then subsided. There was the rustle of silk as he drew back the sheet.

You can do anything you want, but don't mark me.

That was what she had said to him last night. Ulric stared at the trail of fingernail scratches along her smooth alabaster-white back. Eventually they would disappear. He lifted the sheet a little more and saw the jagged brownish stains of blood. His cock stirred against the diamond-patterned lining of his robe. This girl, a child of fourteen grown so old so quickly, wouldn't go near a man for a while. The little star-fucker had had her insides rearranged.

Leopold Ulric stood transfixed by the sight of the vaginal blood. The hint of down between her legs. His thoughts crossed from the sexual to feeding. He wondered how she would look if he just reached out and clamped his hands around her throat. He would crush the soft bones as easily as he would a small bird in one fist. The girl grunted, and the spell was broken. Abruptly Ulric turned away. He had never, *never* fed on those he bedded. Little did they know how truly fortunate they were. . . .

He entered the dressing area adjacent to the bedroom. It was finished in gold-green marble. Loosening the sash, he shrugged off his robe, letting it crumple at his feet. Swiftly he began applying various creams and lotions to his body.

Leopold Ulric's dermatological needs were catered to by the world's leading experts, Fromm Brothers of Lausanne, Switzerland. He used herbal and homeopathic creams daily to repress his normal, unusually strong and noxious body odor. Sometimes Ulric wondered what he would smell like if his skin were to be pierced by a cut. He could not imagine what lay under that frail tissue.

His father had been like that. A bastard in every sense of the word. The stench of death had permeated his very soul. During the war Heinz Ulric had been in charge of fertilizer distribution for the northern district—the district that included Belsen and Buchenwald. The fertilizer consisted of crushed human bone and ground human ash.

But even though Heinz Ulric's work exempted him from both military service, of which he was truly frightened, and real farming, against which his sloth rebelled, he was not satisfied with his lot. The war would end. There would be many less Jews certainly, but for all that, his lot in life would not have improved. There was also the Allies' revenge to consider. Heinz Ulric needed security in the future. His son was to be that security.

On the boy's seventh birthday he announced that from then on Leopold would be expected to pay for his room and board. When the wife objected, Heinz beat her. When the boy spat on him, he beat her again. The meaning was clear; he would not lay a finger on the boy. His hands and fingers were too valuable. It would be his mother who would suffer if Ulric refused to do the old man's bidding.

At the age of eight, in the midst of terror from the sky, Leopold Ulric played for the commandant of Bergen-Belsen, accompanied by the camp orchestra musicians. The commandant, Schrader, was so taken by the boy's performance that he gave Heinz Ulric forty pieces of gold, newly struck that morning. The old man knelt and tearfully kissed Schrader's hand.

By 1946 Heinz Ulric had not only secreted away a modest amount of bullion, he had become a virulent anti-Nazi.

When de-Nazification investigators arrived at the farm, they saw fields overgrown and choked, a young woman grown old far ahead of her time, a silent, bewildered farmer who stood protectively by his child, who always had a violin in his hand. The picture reeked of sincerity. The old man was invited to the British commander's office. A week later Leopold Ulric gave the first of many performances for yet another group of officers. There was no gold this time, but the Ulrics never went hungry either.

By the time the Nuremberg Trials started, the name of Leopold Ulric was known throughout the social centers of the Occupation Forces. After a command performance before the Allied general staff in Berlin the proud father was given a new passport for himself and his son. One of Europe's foremost violinists, the legendary Rolla of Florence, was waiting to instruct the boy. That night, as his father grunted away with his whore, Leopold Ulric murdered him. The following morning the father was found dead of multiple stab wounds. The hotel concierge remembered the whore, who shrieked her innocence. But the dagger used had her fingerprints on it. At her trial Ulric testified he had watched through a crack in the door as she stabbed his father. All the while he spoke his eyes never left the woman's face, and the sneer on his lips so taunted her that she tried to fling herself at him. Clearly the woman was not only guilty but also insane.

Leopold Ulric adjusted the Windsor knot of his blood red tie. The custom-made Dior blazer hung perfectly on his gaunt frame. Marc Bohan was the only designer who could dress him without making him look the scarecrow. He arranged the blood red handkerchief in the breast pocket and regarded himself in the mirror.

The memory of that first sacrifice never failed to stir him. His father had been a fitting victim—the vain, petty tyrant who could fawn as easily as abuse. And the killing had been so well done. He had come into his father's room and with the dagger cleanly sliced open the chest. His father's eyes had snapped open and his arms had started to come up. Smiling, the ten-year-old boy had slowly twisted the knife into the paternal heart. The arms fell back, the incredulous expression frozen on the dying face. And all the time the whore did not stir.

Leopold Ulric had drained some blood and capped it in a vial. When he had returned to the farm, he had offered this blood to the demon that walked with him. The demon was well pleased with the homage. It showed that the Winged One had not erred. The boy was a true corrupter of men. Not only had he offered up the blood of his blood. He had also given up the whore, an innocent, who would in due course die for an act she had never committed.

Leopold Ulric swept into his bedroom. His whore was still asleep. He hoped she would be here when he returned. Sometimes it was difficult to find the right sacrifice. That was when frenzy set upon him. God pity the warm and young and sweet who were within his reach at such a moment.

New York City's premier automobile repair shop was housed in a singularly unattractive two-story brick building in Lowther Mews off Canal Street. Throughout Vantage Motor Works' twenty-two-year existence at this address its upstairs tenants had ranged from a sweatshop garment operation in the early sixties to the current fencing and foil school. Punctually at half past four in the afternoon the rust-laden girders would sprinkle their metal flakes as students and instructors began their thrusts and parries.

The interior was utilitarian in design. Immediately past the black foyer door, which slammed rather than drew to a close, was the lounge. In the past one vehicle, on sale by consignment, would have rested on the pale green linoleum floor. But the display window, wired for alarm, had also been barred with a metal skirt. There was a Formica coffee table and several vinyl lounge chairs. Instead of a vehicle bookcases with locked glass fronts dominated the room. On the shelves was a pictorial history of the automobile as comprehensive and diverse as any in the country.

The office was partitioned off from the lounge: to the left a cubbyhole for filing cabinets and records; in the center a counter, an ancient swivel chair, and displays of Classic Car Finish, WD-40, and Armor All. Several framed cartoons bordered the doorway into the garage proper, the heart of VMW.

Sixty feet long, forty wide, in a fat L shape, with a grease- and oil-stained concrete floor, the garage was the operating room for some of the continent's finest vehicles. Behind two roll-down steel shutter doors, beneath fluorescent lamps, and bordered by compressors, air hoses, work tables, oxyacetylene equipment, and Hi-boy tool stands were the cars. Today a black Jaguar 3.8 rested next to a 1972 Aston-Martin on blocks. The Ferrari Daytona was flanked by a Maserati Quatroporte. Two Rolls-Royces, a little Silver Dawn, and a bulkier Wraith, were parked one behind the other. Along the east wall, between newly sprayed cam covers and oiled pistons, was an A. C. Cobra —in carefully labeled pieces.

"We're going to be late for the reverend's car, Jim."

George Percy, one hundred twenty pounds on a five five frame, leaned over the counter and snatched a Bic lighter. The Virginia tobacco in the Canadian cigarettes he favored obscured his face for an instant before the hacking cough dispelled the vapors. He ran a mechanic's hand— chipped fingernails with oil undercoating, grease lining the fingerprint whorls—through long wispy gray hair. The blue eyes watered behind round steel-frame glasses.

"What do you say, old son?" he said.

Jim Hansen looked up to see George's bulbous nose, pitted and veined, challenging him. He meticulously printed the total at the bottom of an invoice and tossed the Flexboard onto the makeshift desk.

"Fucking parson's going to keel over."

Percy stood on tiptoe, thrust his body forward, and looked at the bill.

"Sheet!" The intonation was pure South London.

Hansen rose off the antique swivel chair. He was the archetypal slow-moving, slow-talking big man. At five eleven he weighed in at two hundred and forty pounds, twice Percy's weight, and he was a little more than half Percy's age at thirty-two. His face was curiously smooth, like a baby's, still undefined. Small brown eyes regarded the world with utter calm. The light brown hair was neatly

153

trimmed by Marcovici once a week. The nails, ears, and nose were fastidiously clean.

"What'd you say, George?" he asked suddenly, as though he had just heard the profanity.

Percy shifted his hands deep into the pockets of his faded blue mechanic's smock. He shook his head, and cigarette ash spilled across his chest.

"Let's get going. Christ—"

The chugging of the compressor drowned out his next words. Hansen swept around him majestically and surveyed the work force of three other mechanics.

"Back in an hour," he yelled.

As George Percy followed him out he patted his twin Dobermans, which rested beneath one of the bookcases.

"I hope old Augusta doesn't listen to that niece," George muttered, easing the cigarette out the window crack of the hurtling Volkswagen Karmann-Ghia.

Hansen was driving, his belt on, working the brakes and accelerator with separate feet, his shifting deft and smooth. He stroked the gearbox like a professional, swerving onto Sixth Avenue and heading for midtown.

"I wouldn't sweat it, George," Hansen said, skirting into a sudden opening. "Things have gone too far for *anyone* to stop them."

"Sheet, I hope you're right. . . ."

Hansen looked across at his partner. George was getting old. Until last year he had been able to literally pull his weight in the shop; now he only directed the young mechanics. At fifty-eight, after forty years in the trade, his strength was fading; Hansen understood that George's sharp tongue and curmudgeon personality were only a mask for his fear.

In many ways George reminded him of Abner Levine. They were both tired men, their strength drained by a lifetime of honorable physical labor. George chose to come to the States after the war rather than return to an England that had been bled white. Within ten years he had earned the title of master craftsman and was a senior mechanic on the U.S. Grand Prix teams. Using his reputation as collateral, he had formed a partnership with Howard Davis, the industrialist, who was also an avid car collector. Vantage

Motor Works had been his creation, funded by Davis's money. But George was not an astute businessman. Davis maneuvered him out of the partnership when VMW obtained Manhattan's exclusive Ferrari dealership.

It had taken George Percy another ten years to rebuild. In that time he lost one wife to another man and gained another, who kept him on a short leash. But the new VMW prospered, and realizing his limitations, Percy asked Jim Hansen to come in and look after the business side.

"I know what you're thinking," George said at once.

Hansen didn't doubt it. Percy had a Cockney's sixth sense.

"I don't want to lose everything a second time, Jim. For me there won't be another chance. Christ, I remember the days when we didn't need the alarms in the glass or the grill across the window. One Dobie did the trick. Now those bastards walk around with poisoned meat and nerve gas. Fucking dogs don't stand a chance!"

"Nothing's going to happen, George," Hansen said smoothly. He turned east on Fortieth Street and headed for First Avenue.

"Before the month is over, we'll have the neighborhood back."

Hansen believed this unfalteringly. If George and Abner were the same age and shared common fears, he was closer to Marcovici. He not only had all his capital tied up in VMW but also realized that if the shop closed down even for a week, it would lose customers. Generally the people who owned exotics were halfway knowledgeable about their vehicles. The issue was not the justifiably exorbitant rates VMW charged but rather the length of time they kept a car. The work was not repair but craftsmanship. While owners appreciated this, they were also sufficiently possessive about their charges to want to drive them. They wanted to enjoy them, even to flaunt them. Hansen had built up the clientele on the quality of the shop's workmanship, but he knew if he closed, the majority of his customers wouldn't wait. They'd find service elsewhere and then stay there.

He swept by Tudor City and at Fifty-sixth Street turned toward Sutton Place. The Ghia bounced across the potholes, then shuddered as the suspension tried to cope with the cobblestones. When Hansen had set the hand brake, George clambered out and with his hands on his kidneys thrust his torso forward.

"Getting too old for this sort of sheet," he muttered.

He looked around at the four-story townhouses with gleaming black doors and curled iron-wrought trellises that came halfway up the windows. Even though it was midday, the roar of the Manhattan traffic was muted here. In the gray pallor the houses seemed to be closer together, as though huddling for protection. Farther up the street a Mercedes limousine drew to a halt. A bodyguard alighted first, then the wife of the UN Secretary-General.

A majordomo greeted the two men at the side entrance to one of the townhouses. He had both the keys to the car and the garage in hand. Hansen gave him the prepared receipt.

"Fucking eunuch!" George muttered darkly. Most of his clients didn't put on airs, but their staff was another matter.

He followed Hansen around to the back and into the lane where the garage stood.

"Hi, Mr. Percy!"

George looked up, and a smile creased his face.

"Hello, Hunter, how are you, then?"

He was a freckle-face boy of eleven, dressed in gray slacks, school tie, and blazer with a yachting club crest. He had stepped out of the enclosed greenhouse on the patio next door.

"Getting ready for class, are you, now?" George called out.

"Yes, sir. Are you here for Daddy's car?"

"Not this time, old son."

A few feet away George heard the lock pop open. Jim was pulling the garage doors apart.

"Robert is driving me down, but I'd much rather go with you."

"Jim, think we can drop the lad off at the NSDM?"

Hansen looked up, waved, and nodded.

"Go ask your mother there, Hunter."

The boy threw up his hands and disappeared inside.

Shaking his head, George walked over to where the gleaming 1937 P3 Rolls-Royce was parked. He ran a hand along the two-tone flank much as he would stroke a horse and slipped into the small but comfortable chauffeur's seat.

"Okay, bring her out," Jim called.

Slowly the mammoth car left its berth and turned into the lane.

"Turning over nicely," commented George as he stepped out.

The two men stood beside the car, listening to the engine.

"Timing," Jim murmured. "Carburetor need adjusting. . . ."

"Neat car!"

Hunter Mackenzie, violin case in hand, Burberry trench coat neatly buttoned, ran up to them, followed by the family driver, who nodded at the two men.

"Mrs. Mackenzie's compliments," the driver said formally. He turned to the boy. "I shall be down to pick you up at half past five."

"I will be waiting," Hunter Mackenzie said solemnly. Then he screamed as the driver's knees buckled and he sank to the ground.

The speed of the attack was unbelievable. Jim Hansen's eyes barely registered the dart sticking out of the driver's back before he felt a stabbing pain at the base of his throat. For an instant he choked, then reached for his throat. His arm was leaden, moving in slow motion. He clawed at the dart, and his fingers came away bloody. George was moving toward him as a third projectile hit him in the shoulder. Because of his thick mechanic's smock and fisherman's sweater its tip was only loosely imbedded in his flesh. Still enough poison seeped in to make him fall.

The man stepped out from behind the stone wall and walked toward Hunter Mackenzie. The boy backed away, then whirled around, dropping his violin. There was a good distance between him and the man, yet he had taken only three steps before he felt cold fingers seize him by the scruff of the neck and haul him off the ground. Before he had a chance to cry out again, a thumb pressed hard on his carotid artery, spinning him into oblivion.

The man picked up the boy in both arms and continued down the lane toward the river. At the water's edge he turned right and disappeared. He never saw George Percy crawling after him, struggling to remain conscious.

Percy heard the slamming of a car door, an engine firing up. "Son of a bitch!" he whispered, dragging his helpless body along. The sky was spinning, and beneath him the cobblestones seemed to quake as though the earth were trembling. Just before he succumbed, George Percy heard the engine roar again. His cheek sank to the cold brick, but there was a smile on his lips. A master mechanic for four decades, he recognized the distinctive rumble of that engine block.

Chapter Eleven

Wilder Nicholson III, director of the NSDM, was seated behind his desk, his gaze fixed on the ormolu clock on the mantelpiece of the Stuart fireplace. Green wood, for which he personally had paid a king's ransom, smoked disconsolately, its gray wisps of smoke matching both the weather and Nicholson's mood. The minute hand moved to noon, and the hour chimes sounded. It was eleven o'clock and—

"Mr. Nicholson?"

"Yes, what is it?" he snapped without bothering to look away.

When there was no answer, he turned and saw Leopold Ulric standing in the doorway, flanked by Nicholson's secretary.

"Mr. Ulric . . . maestro!"

Leopold Ulric glided into the room and took the director's proffered sweaty hand. He detested the men behind such hands. Weak, subservient, fawning.

"Mr. Ulric. I left specific instructions to be informed the moment you arrived—" Nicholson threw a dark look at his secretary, who shrugged helplessly.

"I asked *not* to be announced," Ulric stated.

"I see," Nicholson said, although it was clear he did not. He tried to cover up his confusion. "Well, perhaps I can introduce you to the members of the faculty—"

"Ah, my dear Nicholson, I believe I stated explicitly that my first concern is with my pupils. The staff can wait."

"Of course." Nicholson was almost oblivious to the insult.

"Good." Ulric cut him off. "Then perhaps you would be good enough to show me to the classroom."

"As you wish, maestro," Nicholson said deferentially. Damn the man! He had promised the staff a meeting. Still Ulric had a point: One of the conditions of his brief tenure was that he would not have to be involved with the staff in any way. Not that this surprised Nicholson. Ulric's demand for privacy—and anonymity when possible—was in character. He was scathing with performers and instructors whom he considered his inferiors—which was to say, just about everyone.

"I suggest we take the elevator. The room is on the fourth level."

"You may," Ulric said curtly. "I prefer to walk."

Before he knew what was happening, Nicholson found himself behind Ulric. The virtuoso had already reached the first landing before Nicholson had taken three steps. Humiliated by this man four years his senior, he plodded up.

"I trust you encountered no difficulties with our security people?" Nicholson wheezed.

"On the contrary. I left my vehicle out front."

Nicholson started. "Perhaps one of our people might take it into the lot for you. Leaving any car on the street—"

"I'm sure it is quite safe," Ulric said, and quickly mounted the last steps.

"Tell me, Director, are all my students accounted for?"

"Of course! It's a tremendous privilege for them—and an honor for the school—to have you here."

"I see. Then why wasn't I given the curriculum vitae of the student who is taking the place of Rachel Rosenberg?"

The agate eyes bored into Nicholson, making him more red-faced than he already was. He fumbled in his jacket pocket for the asthma inhalator.

"Forgive me, maestro . . ." The director hastily capped his medicine. "There has been no replacement for Rachel Rosenberg," he continued under his breath. "There were no runners-up to the students selected because no one thought there would be any need for them. And even if another student was being considered, no final selection would have been made without your approval."

Nicholson hesitated. "Mr. Ulric, I beg of you, don't mention Rachel to the other children. I can't tell you the effect her . . . her death has had upon them. On the entire school, in fact."

"A tragedy," Ulric stated. "But I tell you now, Director, that I will expect every pupil to give me his or her utmost attention. I will not tolerate absentmindedness for *any* reason."

"Believe me, you shall have it, maestro," Nicholson said fervently. "I'm pleased to say the entire class was at last night's performance, as well as the staff. A superlative rendition—"

Ulric slipped between Nicholson and the door of the classroom.

"I prefer to meet them alone," he said, and with that disappeared inside.

Leopold entered the room so swiftly that he caught some of the students looking out the window.

"Places!" he barked, and moved up to the standard schoolroom instructor's desk. He leaned on the stack of case files describing the students that he had requested and scrutinized his charges. He saw that three of the seven were from upper-class families. Their dress reeked of money. Two were neatly attired, though it was obvious the jackets and trousers were hand-me-downs. One was somewhere in between.

"We're missing someone, aren't we?" Ulric suggested.

The boys looked uneasily at one another, their glances cutting through the music stands before their chairs. One of the girls smiled to herself.

"If memory serves me correctly, it is one Hunter Mackenzie who seems to have misplaced himself."

The girl's smile gave way to a giggle.

"Very well. I will take your silence to mean I am correct," Ulric continued. "Such loyalty is, I suppose, commendable. However, let us be clear on one issue: My classes start on time. I expect you all here and ready before I walk through the door. No—repeat, no—excuses will be tolerated." He paused. "As Master Hunter will learn for himself if he arrives after the last person introduces him or herself."

Ulric came out from behind the desk and walked to the blond girl in pigtails, who had been smiling.

"What is your name, my dear?"

The girl rose. "Joanna Robinson, sir."

Ulric smiled, his eyes feasting upon this child. Not that she would be aware of his appetite. The eyes would never give him away. Without her being aware he raked her body with them.

Leopold Ulric moved from child to child, watching each carefully as he or she spoke. They were all nervous, as was only proper, but there was also a determined self-confidence about each of them. They were very good, undoubtedly some of the best in the country for their or any age. He knew that his being here was the proof of their achievement.

"You're Otto Morell's grandnephew."

The boy, with long curly brown hair, the straight almost severe nose of his father, and full cheeks inherited from Sabina Morell, glanced up at Ulric. The virtuoso saw the pain his question had caused the boy.

"Yes, sir," Toby Dwyer answered, his voice trembling.

"Show me your instrument."

He accepted the boy's violin and even before he held it up, realized it wasn't one of Otto Morell's creations. Ulric was pleased. It would have been an insult to Ulric had the old craftsman lavished one of his pieces on the boy.

"Your granduncle was an incredible man," he said softly. "Before he died, he made me an instrument which I shall use all the rest of my days. Did you attend the concert last night?"

"Yes, sir."

"And what was your opinion?"

"You were great, sir," Toby Dwyer answered sincerely.

"Was I now?" Ulric said weakly.

He longed to reach out and touch the boy's pale cheek, to run his fingers through the angel-soft hair, to feel the hard pulse of his blood in the instant just before he began to feed upon him.

"You too can play as I do," Ulric said recklessly. "If you were to let me teach you—"

Suddenly he stopped himself. The boy would be his, he vowed to himself. Not now. Perhaps not for a time, but before he left this city, he would have touched Toby Dwyer.

"Then you will be worthy of an instrument bearing the Morell name."

He walked quickly to the head of the class.

"I see that Hunter Mackenzie has not seen fit to arrive," he stated. "We shall begin without him. I have heard tapes of your playing. Now I must listen in person. You have each selected a piece. I have approved all. Joanna, would you begin? Three minutes, no more, no less. Stop even if you're in the middle of a run. Understood?"

The girl rose on long ungainly legs that in a few short years would mature to create havoc. Ulric sat back in the highly uncomfortable chair and closed his eyes, letting the notes wash over him. He already knew what other children he would take, but of all of them Toby Dwyer-Morell was the one whose face tantalized him from behind the veil.

Toby was playing when the interruption occurred. He was halfway through a Paganini Caprice when the door to the classroom was wrenched open.

Ulric's eyes snapped open at once.

Sabina Morell stormed inside, leaving a fuming but for some reason unprotesting Nicholson in her wake.

"Madame!"

Sabina ignored Ulric's cry. She came to her son and put a protective arm about his shoulder. Toby reddened and squirmed.

"Mom . . ." he protested. "Mom, what are you doing?"

Sabina did not answer him but stared transfixed at the seat that Hunter Mackenzie should have occupied. Leopold Ulric realized why she was here.

"Please, Ms. Morell . . ." the director pleaded.

"Toby, are you all right?" The voice was wooden, the gaze still riveted on the empty chair.

"Mom, I'm fine!" Toby cried. He was very close to tears, as much from embarrassment as confusion.

"And the rest of you?" Sabina's head snapped around to take in the nervous nodding.

"Mrs. Dwyer, I presume," Leopold Ulric said coldly.

"Detective Sergeant Morell," she said tonelessly, and as an automatic gesture flipped out her ID.

Ulric looked past her, his withering gaze on Nicholson.

"What is the meaning of this, Director?"

"Mr. Ulric, may I see you outside the room for a moment?"

As the virtuoso passed her son he said, "That was very good, Toby. The rondo was a little too fast but otherwise very good."

Nicholson beckoned them into an empty classroom and shut the door. Ulric saw the reflection of a flashing red light weave its way around the room. He went to the window and saw three police cruisers in front of the school.

"What the devil is going on here?" he hissed, addressing Nicholson.

"Maestro," the director started to say when Sabina cut him off.

"Your missing student!"

"There is no need to raise your voice to me!" Ulric turned on her. The full force of his gaze fell upon her, and Sabina shrank back. Ulric's hideously contorted features seemed to swim before her eyes, then dissolve into a luminous death's head, made all the more revolting by the long greasy hair that framed it. She was repelled by this man . . . and for some reason terrified.

"Hunter Mackenzie," she said at last. "He was kidnapped this morning . . . only a couple of hours ago."

She was watching Ulric closely, ready to record every impression of his reaction. But there wasn't one. The man had no soul.

"Kidnapped?"

"Three other men were injured."

"I fail to see what this unfortunate incident has to do with creating chaos in my class."

"Mackenzie was a student of yours—"

"Wrong, Sergeant." Ulric silenced her. "I have never even met the boy. Today was to be his first class—as it was for all the others."

"Detective Morell realized that Hunter was a student here," Nicholson added lamely. "She was concerned for the welfare of the other students—as well as her child."

"Couldn't a simple telephone call have set her mind at rest?" demanded Ulric. "Or was it absolutely necessary to turn this class into a three-ring circus?"

"I can't believe I heard that!" Sabina whispered.

"You certainly did, Sergeant," Ulric said viciously. "I am distressed by what you've said about the Mackenzie boy. But I suggest you would be more effective out there"—he jabbed at the window—"than in here creating panic. Here, I can assure you, everything is—or was—under control!"

Ulric turned to Nicholson.

"You will dismiss my pupils and inform them that tomorrow's class will take place as scheduled. Now you will excuse me."

Sabina caught up with Ulric at the staircase landing.

"We may want to ask the other students some questions," she said, matching him stride for stride. "Perhaps—"

"You may ask them anything you wish, Sergeant," Ulric said without breaking stride. "But if another one of my lectures is subject to such high-handedness, I will cancel my contract with the school. I suggest you take *that* up with the Board of Governors. If I leave, the students, including your son, will suffer! A tremendous learning opportunity will have been lost."

"We shall do our best to accommodate you," Sabina retorted sarcastically.

"Do that!" Ulric snapped.

The rest of the staff, milling about in the antechamber, looked up as they came down. Ulric didn't give them a second glance but moved right through them, Sabina in his wake.

"Mr. Ulric . . . Mr. Ulric!"

Sabina recognized the voice even before she saw the WABC news wagon. Reporter Tabby Kirsch, a braying blonde with a Rod Stewart hairdo and black leather trousers, elbowed her way through the throng of curiosity seekers. She managed to shove a microphone directly at Ulric's mouth.

"Mr. Ulric, would you comment on the kidnapping of one of your students, Hunter Mackenzie?"

Up ahead Sabina saw that the cameras were rolling, catching her and Ulric together.

"No comment!" Ulric snapped, and pushed her away.

165

Kirsch staggered back but came after him again. Sabina saw Ulric's agent, Sidney Nathan, waving at him from beside a black car.

"Mr. Ulric, this is the second student from the NSDM to be taken by the psychopath—"

"There is no evidence of foul play!" Sabina said sharply, and immediately regretted it. Kirsch turned on her.

"Detective Sergeant Morell—"

Before she could go any further, Ulric reached for her arm and steered her to one side. With his other hand he covered the microphone.

"Listen, you cocksucking little bitch," he said, smiling pleasantly, his breath hot in her ear. "You come near me again and and I'll stuff that microphone up your cunt!"

Sabina saw Kirsch twist away, her eyes wide with terror. Ulric smiled at her and disappeared into the crowd. An instant later Sidney Nathan was closing the door behind him.

"Do you know what that bastard said to me!" shrieked Kirsch.

"Sister, I don't care *what* he said to you," Nathan spat at her. "And you should watch what you call people in public. Leave him alone!"

The reporter backed away, bumping into Sabina. The microphone hung limply in her hand.

"He's sick!" she whispered, and Sabina realized Kirsch was trembling. "Whatever else he is, he's one sick mother!"

Sabina Morell registered the words. As she watched the heavy sports car pull away into traffic something deep within her echoed the newscaster's sentiments.

Sabina returned to Thompson Street. When she entered the apartment above the lab, she saw Thane Sheridan hunched over the desk, both elbows on the worn green leather blotter, a red phone receiver cradled against his ear. Langley.

"Yeah, Al, listen, the lab managed to lift a print off that tire tread. Partial but they tell me the definition is good. Your hardware shouldn't have any problems coming up with an I.D. . . . . Yeah, it's en route now. The jet should have left La Guardia twenty minutes ago.

"And Al, for Christ's sake, get the results back to me as soon as you can. The son of a bitch has taken another one. A boy of ten. . . . No, no body. It's the same pattern. He'll be taking them to his nest."

Sheridan paused then finished. "Right, Al, thanks."

He rose and ran his fingers through his hair.

"Hi."

She crossed over and kissed him lightly on the cheek.

"Hi."

"Anything more from the site?"

"Not a damn thing. No one saw or heard anything. He must have gotten into Sutton Place sometime during the night and waited."

"I can't buy that." Sheridan shook his head. "The area's too heavily patrolled. He had to have had transport, and an unfamiliar car would have drawn attention."

"Unfamiliar?"

"Chevy, Dodge, or some other ordinary sedan. Something that would stand out in that neighborhood."

"What if it *wasn't* an ordinary car?" Sabina said quietly. "What if it was the kind a patrol car wouldn't look twice at? Expensive, foreign . . . blending in with the neighborhood?"

"I suppose you're already checking the Rolls dealerships and specialized leasing companies?"

"You betcha."

"Hirsh will call as soon as his toys run the print. Maybe we'll be able to narrow down the choices." He hesitated. "How's your boy?"

"He's all right."

"Then what's wrong?" he asked softly.

"Goddamn Ulric!" Sabina cried. "He made me feel like such an idiot." She described the virtuoso's reaction after she had broken up his class.

"I suppose his reaction was justified," Sabina continued. "But Christ, there wasn't an ounce of understanding in that man. He had no idea of what had happened. He didn't seem to care at all about the Mackenzie boy—only his precious class. Then there was something else."

167

She told him about Ulric's encounter with Tabby Kirsch from WABC.

"I've run into her on several occasions, and I can't once remember getting the better of her. Nor has anyone else I know. But Ulric floored her. Whatever it was he whispered to her made Kirsch lose her cool."

"A creative tantrum," Sheridan said. "I suppose when you're catered to as he is, you think you can do anything you like. The important thing is that Toby is all right. And the other kids."

"I don't know what to do, Thane," Sabina said. "First the Rosenberg girl, now Hunter Mackenzie. I think the Rambler has targeted the NSDM. And I'm scared. I want to get Toby out of there until we catch up with the monster."

Sheridan brought his arms around her and held her close. He didn't say anything. She was a professional, and she would come to accept what both of them already understood: The Rambler *had* targeted the school. Sheridan wasn't about to deny it. But even though they knew this, even though if enough pressure was put on the school trustees they would close classes, that wasn't the answer. The NSDM had to remain open. The Rambler could not be frightened off now. If the school closed, he might start up elsewhere. Killing out of fury and vengeance. No, something in the killer drew him to the NSDM. He had struck once inside the premises and once outside. The children had to stay. They were the bait that could not be removed. Such thinking sickened Sheridan, but he knew, as did Sabina, that there was no alternative. The Rambler was circling around the school like a vulture, his diameter becoming smaller and smaller. Twice he had swooped down, twice he had escaped. But next time he would have to go a little lower, maybe take a little longer to execute the kidnapping. Sheridan was waiting for him . . . somewhere behind the children.

Sheridan cupped Sabina's face in both hands. The fear and uncertainty in her eyes cut him to the marrow. She was suffering, and the terror would not abate until the Rambler died. Sheridan damned his helplessness.

168

"What about the flechettes?" asked Sabina. She pulled away and poured herself some coffee.

"Stonefish venom. Very rare, very exotic, requiring someone knowledgeable to handle it. The lab said that the doses must have been calculated to coincide with the body weight of the victims. Too much and we'd have three corpses on our hands."

She whirled around. "Christ, you know what that means? He *was* waiting. He *knew* Percy and Hansen would be coming for the car."

"Maybe," Sheridan cautioned her. "But we won't be able to run with that until we speak to them and the chauffeur."

"When will that be?"

"This evening at the earliest."

"That long!"

"I got an update from the hospital twenty minutes ago," said Sheridan. "Even though we told them what they were dealing with, the doctors didn't have any antidote on hand. Hansen and the driver regained consciousness briefly, then went into convulsions. Percy is still out."

"Can they do anything for them?"

"Center for Communicable Diseases in Atlanta has sent up the serum. Percy, because of his age and physical condition, is the questionable one. The other two will pull through."

"Where could he have gotten his hands on it, Thane? I mean, how common *is* stonefish venom?"

He knew what she was really asking: Was the poison a clue?

"Not very," Sheridan said slowly. "Langley experimented with it in the sixties—which is why Atlanta could make up an antidote. It was used in covert operations for about two years before it was decided that the substance was *too* toxic, too volatile to be used in the field. In a lot of cases incapacitation turned out to be lethal. Those administering the drug found out that even correct doses tended to kill the person, who, say, was going to be moved across a border."

"What else?" asked Sabina. "There's more."

""The other people who like to use it are diabolists,"

Sheridan said. "In Haiti the stonefish is prized by priests, who used it on human sacrifices. I've read accounts of similar uses in Indonesia, Malaysia, and parts of Brazil."

"That's the tie-in, isn't it?" Sabina said weakly. "That's our link to the Rambler. There hasn't been any mention of stonefish in your other reports, but there've been other references to the occult."

"He's never had to snatch a child that way," Sheridan said, thinking aloud. "Goddamn it, but he's on some kind of misbegotten schedule himself! He has to be—otherwise why risk taking on three men? George Percy might have been easy to handle but not Hansen—not with his weight and strength. And the chauffeur was trained in antiterrorist maneuvers. Yet in spite of this the Rambler decided to take them all out. He didn't want to wait until the boy arrived at school. Or any other more opportune time. It's as though he needed him *now!*"

"But for what purpose?" cried Sabina. "If he doesn't kill his victims immediately, then why take the risks?"

The ringing telephone spared him the admission of ignorance. Sheridan answered, listened for a minute, then turned to Sabina.

"The television!"

She switched it on just in time to see the mayor's press secretary walk into the City Hall communications room. The man, a former White House staffer, was uncharacteristically grim, ignoring members of the media to whom he usually smiled or waved.

"This is a prepared statement briefing, a copy of which will be circulated among you. There will be no question period."

The shouts of protest started up immediately, the City Hall reporters being less decorous than their White House counterparts. The secretary ignored them.

"At eleven-fifteen this morning Hunter Mackenzie of 4 Sutton Place was abducted by person or persons unknown while outside his residence. Three other people were also injured in the attack.

"As of this time no ransom demand has been received, nor have the abductors made any attempt to communicate with the boy's parents.

"Alistair Mackenzie has asked this office to inform members of the media that neither he, members of his family, nor anyone associated with the Mackenzie Industries Group will be available for comment. The media is asked to refrain from seeking contact with any of the above mentioned so as not to jeopardize or hinder the investigation.

"In reference to the investigation the FBI has been alerted to the possibility that the perpetrator or perpetrators may have crossed the state line in commission of the felony.

"The following is a photograph and particulars of the victim. Anyone seeing or having seen Hunter Mackenzie is asked to call the special emergency number 555-1700. If the sighting should occur outside the boundaries of New York State, the FBI number is 555-1000.

"No one should attempt to approach either the victim or anyone accompanying him. The perpetrator or perpetrators are considered armed and dangerous."

The spokesman gathered up his notes and turned on his heel, oblivious to the cries that erupted from the fourth estate. The pandemonium in the communications room was replaced by a picture of Hunter Mackenzie grinning lopsidedly. Beside that were the vital statistics and across the bottom the two phone numbers.

"How smoothly old Colin lied," Sabina commented, unable to keep the disgust from her voice. "I'm sure I detected Mr. Bill's deft touch behind the orchestration. That was him on the phone?"

Sheridan nodded. "He had no choice. He had to try to keep the press from connecting the killing of Rachel Rosenberg and the Mackenzie kidnapping." He paused. "Not that it will do much good."

He noticed her perplexed expression and nodded at the television.

"Rodgers was forewarned about what your aunt would say. He's had his shot at the disclaimer. Now it's her turn. And I think she'll stand him on his ear."

Sabina watched as the *Eyewitness News* camera panned the hall in the basement of St. Bartholomew's Cathedral. Every available seat was taken. People were squeezed up against the walls and the low podium that separated the

171

small stage from the floor area. Behind a long, banquet-style table sat Augusta Morell, flanked by Abner Levine and Andreas Marcovici. A technician came up and deftly pinned a lapel microphone on Augusta's jacket. She smiled up at him, and he gave her the okay signal. The camera switched to the commentator, who did a forty-second lead-in, tying this conference to the one that had just ended at City Hall, then introduced Augusta Morell.

Thane Sheridan had been right: Her aunt did not back down. She spoke not only confidently but sincerely, her eyes dropping to the prepared text only three times.

"She hasn't changed a word," Sabina murmured. "It's what she told me this morning—verbatim."

But she was wrong. Augusta finished with the presentation and paused for the standing ovation. Then she held up her hands and continued.

"This morning, only a few hours ago, another child was taken. His family does not live in Steuben Town, but Hunter Mackenzie was known to us. He was a student at the New School of Drama and Music. He spent a great deal of time among us. We considered him one of our own." Augusta Morell paused. "As we did Rachel Rosenberg.

"Yet the police refuse to make any connection between the two tragedies, even though it is clear they are related. I ask the mayor and his commissioner: *Why is this so?* What are you hiding from us? If you are saying nothing because there is nothing to tell us, then be good enough to admit this. But do not lie to us or the people of this entire city!"

The widow leaned forward slightly, gazing directly at the unblinking lens.

"And last night even more tragedy occurred. Three young people and two men were viciously murdered on the outskirts of our community. The police organized a massive search operation for what they described as a pack of rabid dogs." A faint ironic smile. "But this morning we hear nothing more about such animals. The bodies have been removed, the police have withdrawn. What was the purpose of bringing in the Emergency Task Force? What, if anything, did its investigation reveal? What, in God's name, is happening to us all?

"I would be lying if I said I grieve for the passing of Santiago and Roncaron Hernandez. They were evil men, and their lives will not be missed. They exemplified the worst type of malignancy that has infected Steuben Town. Their kind must leave or else they too shall perish.

"But to the mothers of the murdered children I offer my heartfelt sympathies. I beg of you: Join with us, all of us, in making this community safe and decent for all our children. Don't allow yourselves to be duped or terrified into living with the horror that has invaded our homes. Reject it once and for all! I promise you, you and your families have nothing to fear from us. Step away from the evil which the likes of Letelier bind you by. Because I promise you: They shall not have us suffer any longer. . . ."

"Quite the lady." Sheridan pressed the remote, and the picture disappeared. "I'd hate to have her mad at me."

Sabina remained motionless.

"There's something wrong," she said slowly. "There's something she's not saying." She looked up at Sheridan. "It's as though she's saying one thing but meaning something else."

"I'm sorry, I'm not following."

"She's threatening Letelier, but at the same time she makes it sound as though she *knows* her appeal won't change anything. Letelier will continue, and so will whatever else she's set in motion."

"I think you might be reading a bit much into her words," Sheridan suggested gently.

"No!" Sabina said stubbornly. "There's something just beneath the words. I can almost reach out and touch it!"

"All right," he said carefully. "Think about it, but easily. Let the answer come at you instead of going after it. Because in the meantime we've got one hell of a lot of work to do this afternoon."

He crossed back to the desk and picked up a single sheet of computer printouts.

"The horsehair?"

Sheridan nodded. "Al's hardware came through with a complete analysis."

"And it's not a needle in the haystack?"

"We lucked out," Sheridan said softly. "That particular

173

horsehair was part of a shipment that came in from Xian Province in China."

"Now I'm not following."

"Most of the material has been shipped from the *south* part of the country. Xian is in the *north*. Apparently that's where the best horsehair is found—something about the way it's treated at the source makes it unique."

"And . . ." she whispered.

"There's only one distributor for it in the whole country," Sheridan finished. "About twenty minutes' drive from here."

"If it's that unique . . ." Sabina started to say. "Christ, let's go!"

Chapter Twelve

The three mothers were not old women—the eldest was only in her early forties. But their lives had been menial, filled with constant struggle against an alien and uncertain environment. They had come to a promised land because of their husbands, but while the males were hard, resilient, the women had never been able to adapt. So they had set out together to leave their mark on the few narrow streets that were now their home. They did not mix with other women and were secretly glad when other families had been driven away. They sent their children to be educated in a foreign tongue but understood nothing of how or what they learned. The male children were allowed to roam, answering only to their fathers. The females were taken into the factories or, if they were pretty, given over to Letelier for education. The mothers knew but never referred to what their daughters became—drug and money couriers. They only knew that Emil Letelier was their benefactor and protector. Just as in the towns and villages of their native Colombia, here, too, a single man dominated the social life, set and enforced the rules all lived by.

The room the three women were in was large, with very high ceilings. Once it had been the top floor of a garment factory. The architect had replaced warped floorboards with colored marble, erected twin Corinthean columns along the sides to give a coliseum effect, and had had the walls paneled. The interior designer had selected the Gobelin tapestries, objets d'art, and the ornate, fragile Louis XVI desk which rested square in the center beneath a gently turning overhead fan.

"We have come to petition before Letelier."

175

The statement reflected the fundamental relationship between the South American immigrants and Emil Letelier: Anyone of the blood, no matter how lowly, could come to these august quarters and petition. In return for being heard total fealty was rendered to Letelier. The women had watched silently from their windows as the police invaded their streets, but they had offered the intruders nothing. They had watched and listened as the older white woman had appealed to them from the television. They did not understand many of the words she had used, but her sentiments and meaning were clear. Still they ignored her. Their loyalty was to Letelier. To him and him alone they would come demanding justice for the killings of their children. Each knew that the contract would be honored. They had no need of the white man's law or a white woman's pleas.

The man behind the Louis XVI desk regarded them impassively.

"Please, sit down," he answered them in their native Spanish, indicating a row of six frail antique chairs lined up before the desk. The women obeyed silently.

"What is your petition?" he asked formally, although he already knew the reply.

"We have come on behalf of our sons," one woman said. "We do not believe what the Anglos say about dogs. We have come seeking Letelier's protection for ourselves and vengeance for the killings of our sons."

"Letelier has instructed me to say that he shares your grief," the man said impassively. "He will see to it that your children are buried and that suitable compensation is made. More, he has instructed me to do whatever is necessary to extract vengeance." The man paused. "I myself swear to do that and to bring you evidence when my oath has been completed."

The women were silent; then in unison they rose. One of them said: "We know you have the trust of Letelier. We are satisfied."

The mothers departed as silently as they had come. The man behind the desk looked after them, tapping a silver stiletto letter opener on the blotter. He threw the knife down with a clatter and reached for the twin aluminum

176

crutches. He slipped his arms through the loops and, gripping the handles, manuevered himself out of the chair.

He was short and slim, of indeterminate age because the slicked-back black hair and creaseless features revealed nothing. He walked across the marble floor to the couch in quick jerky motions, the tremendous strength of his upper body literally propelling him forward, as though it wished to be free of the burdensome trunk. His legs had been paralyzed by polio since boyhood. Withered and useless, they were a constant affront to him. They were also the reason he was never known by his true name but, instead, by the sobriquet Letelier had bestowed upon him: Aleijadinho, the Little Cripple.

Aleijadinho twisted his torso around and, removing his crutches, sat down on the couch. He leaned forward and extracted a cigarette from the ivory box, lighting it with a gold lighter. He drew the smoke deep into his lungs, but still the tobacco failed to calm him. There was something very wrong with the way things were going.

Aleijadinho had been with Emil Letelier for over twenty years, since the days when Letelier had made his first contacts among the Indians of Bolivia and Peru to procure the coca leaves. A coffee grower's son, his condition had made it impossible to work with his father. But while his parents ignored him, Letelier recognized his quick mind. Aleijadinho had a magical touch with numbers. His memory was equally prodigious, sparing Letelier the need to keep damning evidence of his operations on paper.

When Letelier started his processing factories in Lima, it was the Little Cripple who looked after the day-to-day organization. Graduating from bookkeeper to full-fledged accountant, he became Letelier's investment counselor, finding safe and profitable havens for the millions of dollars Letelier was receiving from North American drug wholesalers. In time Letelier came to realize that the Little Cripple had become indispensable to him. Yet Aleijadinho never attempted to cheat his master as other lieutenants did. His fealty was in part due to his infirmity. Aleijadinho could never run away from Letelier.

In the last years Aleijadinho had asked for and received authority to deal in one more area of Letelier's endeavors:

punishment by execution of those who crossed his master's path. After his first arrangement for a killing he discovered he enjoyed drawing up executions. It gave him great pleasure to meticulously draft the demise of one who had offended Letelier, plan the killing from start to finish, intricately, lovingly. Most of all he enjoyed interviewing the assassins.

But there was something wrong. Two matters, in fact—

"I trust you *will* be able to keep my promise to them."

The voice floated high over the room, coming from the gallery that ran the length of the room. Its glass sheath was in reality a one-way mirror behind which Emil Letelier had one of his many offices. There was also a private entrance from the street, so Aleijadinho never knew when his master might be up there, working, observing.

Aleijadinho twisted around but did not rise. Such formality had been dispensed with many years ago. He watched as the tall, exceptionally long-legged Letelier moved swiftly down the spiral staircase. Attired in a designer three-piece suit, his silver-gray hair swept back along the temples, the sharp angular features of the face—a predator's face—glowing with a tan, Emil Letelier could easily have passed for a diplomat or merchant banker. Both of which, in a sense, he was. Aleijadinho marveled at the seemingly inexhaustible well of energy this man drew on.

"Will you be able to keep my promise?" Letelier repeated. It was known throughout the community that Aleijadinho spoke freely on his master's behalf.

"I will," the Little Cripple answered.

"You realize what is at stake here," Letelier said, sitting on the cushioned armrest of the sofa. "It has never, *never* happened that any of my people have been killed in our neighborhood."

He cares nothing for the cousins, Aleijadinho thought. *They were dispensable foot soldiers. As for the punks, they had more machismo than brains. Nevertheless since they were part of the community, their deaths have to be investigated, justice meted out. It is the dread of vulnerability which he fears. The not knowing.*

178

"I ask you to believe me, Letelier, when I say that Santiago and Roncaron were not murdered by any of your rivals," the Little Cripple said firmly. "I have spoken to *all* my people—in Harlem, Queens, the Bronx, Little Italy. Even Chinatown. No one has moved against you. There is one constant reaction: surprise. And some fear because the renegades responsible have yet to be identified. If you appear vulnerable, so do the others."

"Could it have been the police?"

"Again, no. You are secure in both midtown and Albany."

"Yet the police invaded us last night," Letelier hissed, his eyes glittering like freshly minted silver pieces.

"That was not because of the cousins," the Little Cripple assured him. "They were found quite by accident. As for the three children, I have seen the coroner's photos. They *were* attacked by dogs."

"Let me grant you the theory of mad dogs," Letelier said harshly. "But why the Emergency Task Force? Why a quarantine with all the legal risks?"

"I cannot answer that," Aleijadinho replied. "Not yet."

"But you do have a hypothesis?"

Aleijadinho inclined his head. "I think the police action, the attack on the kids, and the killings of the cousins can all be traced back to a single cause: the death of Otto Morell."

At the mention of the old man's name Letelier sucked in a breath through his teeth. Oblivious to his anger, the Little Cripple continued, "Otto Morell was, at the beginning, a hindrance. When he did not desist from his investigation of your relationship with the police, he became a threat. As such he was dealt with in the only possible way.

"We anticipated an adverse reaction because Morell was not only a community elder, he was a renowned man in his own right. Yet all his accusations failed to bring any concrete action against you. Midtown and Albany were holding fast, respecting their part of the bargain made with you.

"But then people remembered the child was taken, later found dead. Suddenly the two killings are fused. There is a clamor for action. But against whom? You, of course. You

179

are the leading suspect in the Morell murder, even though nothing can be proven. On that springboard other suspicions are launched"—the Little Cripple paused—"which will be fueled by the kidnapping of Hunter Mackenzie."

"I do not murder or abduct children!" Letelier said contemptuously.

"I believe that is well understood where it needs to be known," Aleijadinho said placatingly. "However, I am suggesting that two things happened simultaneously: The community of Steuben Town decided to move against you, and the police, realizing this, took advantage of the situation to show their colors, as it were."

"The latter we can deal with," Letelier said coldly. "And the former?"

"As I mentioned, dogs are what destroyed the three kids. There is only one person in Steuben Town who has such animals—they are Dobermans, kept in the Vantage Motor Works garage to protect against intruders, and they are the property of George Percy."

Emil Letelier made a steeple with his fingers.

"So they have decided to fight," he murmured, a smile creasing his lips. "I think I like that . . ."

"I also believe the attack on the Tribe members was coordinated with that upon the cousins," Aleijadinho continued. "As yet I don't know who could have carried it out. Quite possibly Percy's partner, Hansen. He's a big man, not one to be intimidated."

"Even he would have needed help against the cousins," Letelier stated flatly.

"In time we will know," the Little Cripple answered calmly.

Emil Letelier rose to walk off the sleep that numbed his left leg.

"They are a stupid people," he said, shaking his head as much in sadness as in disbelief.

"They are desperate," Aleijadinho corrected him. "And that makes them dangerous."

"Your recommendation?"

"I would suggest that you do not employ your own people to deal with the situation," Aleijadinho said concisely. "Any action against the community could easily be seen as
180

coming from you. It is imperative that it not be traced back to you. To this end I have taken the liberty of making inquiries about independent contractors—specialists in assassinations and demolitions."

Emil Letelier smiled. "And a name?" he asked softly.

"One of the best happens to have returned to the country only last week," the Little Cripple said. "He comes very highly recommended and would be the perfect instrument to execute the plan I have drafted."

Aleijadinho paused, savoring the moment.

"He is known only as Nevada."

Thane Sheridan had been right: The sole importer of horsehair from Xian Province in China had his offices twenty minutes away from the lab on Thompson Street. But both Sheridan and Sabina had to wait over two hours before Lee Hong Kew of Kew Imports, Inc. returned from his dim-sum luncheon. Not even the sight of their badges induced Kew's octogenarian Cantonese secretary to divulge the name of the restaurant where her employer habitually dined.

"If he doesn't show up in five minutes, I'm going to book her for obstruction!" vowed Sabina.

The leatherette fabric of the chair she had been sitting on clung tenaciously to her pant suit. Even though the temperature outside had suddenly dropped to below freezing, moisture covered the filthy windows. The office, divided in half by a rickety picket railing, was jammed with desks. Each one had a young Chinese woman glued to a telephone. The high-shrilled cries and shouting never subsided as orders were screamed into mouthpieces and questions directed at intercoms. In the midst of this bedlam sat Kew's elderly despotic secretary, surveying the work of her charges with the help of a bamboo ruler with which she alternately cuffed the backs of heads and slammed desk tops.

Sabina glanced at Sheridan, who appeared oblivious to the chaos.

"You're crazy!" she muttered darkly, and got to her feet. Behind her the jacket pulled free from the leatherette with a sickening ripping sound.

"Hold on." Sheridan caught her by the arm. "I think that's our man."

Lee Hong Kew, exceptionally tall, his bald pate a glittering golden dome, entered the office, his arms working like a windmill. He snatched memos off one desk, glanced at them, and in a voice no louder than a whisper issued instructions. He seized telephones, scribbled on memoranda, and in a matter of seconds covered each of the ten desks in the room. When he came before his secretary, the octogenarian furiously waved her bamboo stick in the direction of Sheridan and Sabina. Kew's soft caramel eyes settled on them; then without a word he opened the door to his office and bowed to them.

"You must forgive my aunt," he said in clipped British English. "She has ruled with that cane since when *I* worked behind one of those desks."

Sheridan began to introduce Sabina and himself, but Kew waved away the formalities.

"My father's sister reads English as well as you." He smiled. "And she can discern between real and phony identification. Please, sit down. I am at your disposal and very curious indeed as to why the Homicide Division should come to me."

"Mr. Kew, do you import washed and treated horsehair from the Xian Province?" Sabina led off.

"Correct, Sergeant." Kew crisscrossed his fingers and leaned forward. "But the firm my father founded imports a great many things. From mainland China and Hong Kong. As well as from across Southeast Asia. I would be hard pressed to say what percentage of our business is concerned with horsehair, but it is approximately a fraction of a fraction of one percent."

The gold of his ring glittered as it caught the lamp.

"Why Xian, Mr. Kew?" asked Sheridan.

"It was my grandfather who opened the channels for trade back in the twenties. He was something of a musician. In addition to his other endeavors he brought over what was considered the finest horsehair to be used in the making of bows for stringed instruments."

"The very best?"

"Without exception, Inspector Sheridan. Out of rever-

182

ence I have continued his tradition. Unfortunately I was not blessed with his musical talents."

"We understand that Xian horsehair is sought after only by certain craftsmen," Sabina said. "Since you are the exclusive importer, would you give us their names."

"There are only a handful," Kew said. "But they are such unique individuals I can tell you their names from memory."

He waited until Sabina had her pad out.

"There is Gerussi of Boston, the largest customer possibly because he makes bows exclusively. Handel in Philadelphia. Maarten in Connecticut, although he hasn't ordered, I don't believe, for over a year. And finally, Sergeant Morell, your great-uncle."

Sabina's head jerked up, but Kew's smile was disarming.

"Forgive me. It is not a matter of one-upsmanship—your not telling why you need this information and in return my saying nothing about knowing who you are. I grieve with you, Sergeant. I enjoyed not only Otto Morell's business but his friendship also."

"I'm sorry," Sabina stammered. "I didn't know." She looked down at the list. "Only four."

Kew shrugged. "A handful, as I said."

"I imagine there is an equally exclusive Xian agent for Europe," Sheridan said.

"Certainly, Inspector. But he is my cousin. You have only to ask for any information and it will be here on Telex within hours."

Kew paused. "I hazard to guess that your inquiry has to do with Otto Morell's tragedy. Only because of my respect for him—and so for yourselves—have I desisted from asking. Know that my door is open to you at any hour. My resources are your own. But please, for all our sakes, let justice be done."

Sheridan got to his feet. "It will, Mr. Kew. And thanks in no small part to you."

"This is my card with my home telephone number. Please avail yourselves of it whenever necessary."

If there was such a thing as rush hour in Chinatown, Sabina Morell and Thane Sheridan stepped right into it. Sheridan took one look at the frenzy in the street and drew Sabina into an all but empty tea parlor. A stainless steel pot of "flower water" was immediately placed on their table along with two porcelain cups and the bill.

"What's wrong?" asked Sheridan as he poured. Sabina was staring into her cup, watching the bits of leaves swirl in concentric circles.

"Suddenly I feel the Rambler is very close to us," she said, looking up at him. "It's as though I've passed him on the street, even bumped into him without realizing who he really is."

"What are you saying?"

"That the Rambler could be someone within the NSDM. An instructor."

"You were handling the background checks on the staff," Sheridan reminded her. "Anything?"

Sabina shook her head. "But I want another run, this time through FBI, Langley, and Interpol computers."

"I'll set it up."

"Nothing on the truck—the white panel?"

"*Nada.* Mr. Bill still has an APB out on it, but he thinks it has probably been through the chop shop by now."

Sabina ground her cigarette out savagely. There were hundreds of chop shops—garages that specialized in the cutting and repainting of stolen vehicles—in Manhattan, Queens, and the Bronx. Even more across the river in Jersey. There wasn't the manpower or the time to hit them all. Even if the resources could be marshaled, a car never stayed more than six hours in the shop before it was ready to be moved out.

"I can't believe that no one saw or heard anything down in Sutton Place," Sabina murmured. "Nothing about a perpetrator, a vehicle . . . nothing!"

"Let's concentrate on what we *do* have," Sheridan advised her. "A list of names. How do you suggest we split them up?"

Sabina flipped open her pad and glanced at the names.

"I guess Gerussi in Boston is the man to start with," she said. "He's the most prolific of the three. If anyone has

184

made custom-order bows in the last while, it would be he." She paused. "He and *Onkel* were very old friends."

"Call him."

"Now?"

"Why not. If he's there, you could take the seven o'clock Eastern shuttle, talk to him, and get back first thing in the morning." Sheridan looked at her. "If Gerussi will speak openly to anyone, it's you. This way we don't have to waste time setting up liaison niceties with the Boston PD."

"Have you any spare change?" she asked, and Sheridan dug into his pockets.

She returned from the rear of the tea parlor ten minutes later.

"Did you get hold of him?"

She nodded. "He's going to pick me up at Logan. I'll take the seven o'clock shuttle out of La Guardia."

Sheridan glanced at his watch. "We'd better move. Even with the siren and flashers . . ."

She told him to forget the tunnels and try for the Fifty-ninth Street Bridge. Oftentimes when the other routes out of Manhattan were jammed, this relic still moved traffic.

"You called it," Sheridan grunted as he held the wheel loosely, the car skating over the wire mesh.

"Are you going to check on Hansen et al, Thane?"

"As soon as I drop you off."

"Call me as soon as you're through?"

"Better yet, you call me at midnight. That way we'll both have enough time if need be."

Sheridan took the airport cutoff and steered for the Eastern shuttle ramp.

"Not even enough time for you to change, pack an overnight bag," he murmured, slipping an arm about her shoulders.

Sabina pressed herself against him, her lips hungry for his.

"I'll make do—for now," she answered, her voice husky. "But I expect compensation when I get back."

"Lady," Sheridan said, "that's one hell of an understatement."

The Beekman Memorial had one of the best emergency

rooms in the city. At any given time over a dozen specialists were on call. The fact that a toxicologist was present at Beekman when Percy, Hansen, and the Mackenzie chauffeur were brought in, plus the instant hook-up with the Center for Communicable Diseases in Atlanta, saved the lives of the three men.

"Stonefish venom." Harry Siegal shook his head. "What the hell will they think of next? Reminds me of the time some turkeys in their town got together and cooked up a batch of polluted strychnine. Fed it into tourists' drinks through an eyedropper. The stuff was odorless, tasteless but potent. Shit! The victims would pass out either in the room or on the street, then start frothing at the mouth. All the symptoms of a bad peyote trip—and they would last four to six hours. The lucky ones were only robbed or raped. Three committed suicide while under the influence."

The young toxicologist turned the corner smartly and threaded his way through the emergency station corridor. Sheridan followed right behind, his eyes flickering off the people who crowded the hard, narrow benches or lay face up, groaning, on stretchers while paramedics and ambulance attendants filled out report sheets.

"Slow evening, so far," Siegal said over his shoulder. "Business picks up around midnight and peaks at four. That's when you see what *really* lives out there."

With an unnerving sixth sense the toxicologist suddenly darted to the last elevator in a bank of four, jamming his shoulder between the doors.

"Hustle!"

Sheridan sweated the interminable crawl to the sixth floor.

"Yeah, I can't figure it anymore," Siegal told him, disconcertingly intruding on Sheridan's thoughts. "Here it is the middle of February. Usually I *live* at the Beekman because it's the warmest place in the city. But the way that wind is blowing around outside . . ."

Sheridan said nothing but followed Siegal into the isolation ward. In the lockers both men stripped and donned a pair of light protective suits, including hoods with visors. The three victims in the unit were constantly monitored for signs of contagion. Although all signs had thus far been negative, Siegal wasn't about to take any chances. Both he and Sheridan passed through the "burn" cubicle in which ultraviolet waves incinerated whatever foreign bacteria they carried.

The isolation chamber was twice the size of a normal semiprivate room. The three beds were lined up against one wall, placed so that the patients faced the glass partition beyond which was the monitoring station. A series of wires ran about the beds, their terminals dipping down like thin octopus arms, fixed to the patients' limbs and chests. As Sheridan padded across the sheer lino in static-proof slippers he was repelled by what he saw.

"Swelling of the joints and muscle tissue is a characteristic effect of the venom," Siegal told him. "There's nothing we can do except keep feeding them the antidote and hope to hell their constitutions will hold."

The Mackenzie chauffeur was lying on his side with one arm outside the covers. Sheridan guessed it had swelled to twice its usual size, with ugly bumps straining a skin already stretched close to bursting. Sheridan walked around the bed and suddenly stepped back.

"He took the dart in the back," murmured Siegal. "That's why it looks as though someone stuck in an air hose and began to pump."

But James Hansen was worse. Already a big man, he had taken the flechette in the throat. As a result his neck, upper chest, and face had swelled horribly, the flesh literally trying to break out of the skin's stranglehold. Sheridan figured that only the respirator, which forced air into Hansen's overtaxed lungs, in effect breathing for him, was keeping the man alive.

"I told you not to expect anything," Siegal reminded Sheridan as he saw the despair in his face. "They've another twelve hours of fighting before the venom begins to break down. They can't hear or see you. As for talking . . ." He shook his head.

"Percy doesn't look too bad," Sheridan countered, stepping over to the frail English mechanic.

Percy's left arm was outside the covers, bloated from the tips of his weathered fingers straight up to the shoulder. It was as though his head and torso belonged to a pygmy while a giant's arm had been grafted on for some perverse reason.

"The tip of the dart barely scratched the skin," Siegal said. "He was wearing tight-knit mechanic's overalls and underneath them a heavy sweater. Even so, you can see the damage. He wouldn't have had a chance if the flechette had penetrated with full impact."

"Any way of inducing him to speak?"

"You mean a little amphetamine? Not a chance. His constitution is holding its own. We're ahead of the game with him. Nothing he has to say can be that important."

"Don't make such presumptions!" Sheridan turned on him savagely. He wondered if Siegal was married, had kids.

"Jesus Christ, can't you give a dying man a bit of peace. You're worse than a pair of fucking fishwives . . ."

The outburst trailed off from the lips of George Percy. Siegal reacted instantly, pressing the readout button on the computer beside the bed. Percy grinned up weakly at Sheridan.

"Nervous sort, ain't he?"

"Mr. Percy . . . George."

"Don't talk to him," Siegal snapped.

"Stuff it, sonny," Percy whispered and broke into a fit of coughing. "You another like him?" he asked Sheridan.

"Police. I work with Sabina Morell."

"Ah, little Sabina, eh? Where is she, then? How come she hasn't come round to visit old George?"

Sheridan realized that Percy would not hold out for long against the tranquilizers that were still coursing through his system. Siegal was no doubt furious that the dose he had administered hadn't been sufficient to keep the old man out. Sheridan had to work fast.

"George, the man who shot you . . ."

Percy squinted up at him.

"Christ, Sheridan, give it up, will you!" Siegal exploded.

"Not until you put him under!"

Siegal almost ran from the chamber in search of the hypodermic.

"George, did you see *anything*? Anything at all? George, the Mackenzie boy is gone!"

"Know that," Percy answered, words slurring. "Saw him being carted off."

"Who, George—who carted him off!"

"Couldn't see that, too fast. . . . But know something better." He grinned elfishly. "Know what he was driving. . . . Tell Sabina that George knows."

"I'll tell her, George, I promise. Go ahead, what was he driving?"

"It was the engine, you see. The engine gave it all away. . . ."

By the time Siegal returned with the Demerol, George Percy had lost consciousness and Thane Sheridan had the look of a man who has just broken the bank at Monte Carlo.

Chapter Thirteen

The evening of the following day

Leopold Ulric was coating his naked body with scent, working the delicate oils into his skin to achieve a brilliant sheen. He was alone in his duplex penthouse. Tonight he did not need to be serviced prior to his performance. He would take a tidbit on the way to Lincoln Center.

Ulric hummed to himself as his fingers kneaded the hard bony flesh. The piece was Tartini's "The Devil's Trill," with which he would conclude this evening's performance. The choice would be much more fitting than the concertmaster could have imagined when he had agreed on the selection.

Leopold Ulric was calm now, his concentration slowly blocking out everything except the coming performance. Occasionally, however, the virtuoso dipped into his memory. The humiliation of having yesterday's class interrupted still burned within him. However, this morning he had been somewhat mollified when a grim Sidney Nathan accompanied him to the NSDM. In the presence of all seven members of the Board of Directors the agent had made it patently clear that if another such incident should befall Ulric, the contract would be summarily broken. There would be no more chances; no excuses would be tolerated. The board members fell over one another in their assurances that the maestro would not be hampered or inconvenienced in any way. Ulric accepted the appeasement with his customary frigidity. Little did the fools know that he *reveled* in the presence of these children, that he wouldn't have parted from them for *any* reason.

His wonderful, precious children . . . They were all that mattered to him in this world. He existed in it only because of them, through them, their blood and innocence, which he rendered up . . .

Leopold Ulric felt the soft, distant thunder of his blood. His palms suddenly became moist from anticipation, and he hurried to dress. Within minutes he was in the private elevator descending to the garage. There would be no limousine this evening. He could not permit others to be where he would go now. Bootheels snapped off concrete as Ulric walked swiftly to the Aston-Martin. When the engine roared to life, the virtuoso straightened out his arms against the wheel, pure joy coursing through him.

Leopold Ulric understood that one part of his fascination with children stemmed from the fact that they, above all other creatures, possessed an innocence which made them his kin. Children had within them the whole of Eden. They were living testaments to the existence of Paradise. Not until they had lived on this earth for a time did this aura diminish and intuitive knowledge come to be replaced with the crass commodity that passed for wisdom or experience.

Ulric believed that he too was an innocent. Not like ordinary children. He had never been that. But in his own inverted universe, which was ruled by different lords, had a different history, was governed by harsher, bloodier laws, he was pristine. When he thought back to his early childhood, Ulric marveled at how the demon had guided him. He could see himself lying in the crib in the middle of the night, eyes wide open. In the same room, a few feet away, his father was lying with his mother, snoring like the sated pig he was. And beside the crib sat the demon, stroking the baby with its horny taloned hands, gazing down upon it with the most hideous green-yellow eyes, its mouth open as the words came forth on a wind of rot and stench. The baby did not fear the demon. He neither screamed nor wailed but lay there quietly, his mind open to the true history being told to him.

The knowledge imparted by the demon made Leopold Ulric an ancient man even before he was done with childhood. He carried in his mind the knowledge of what had happened, was happening, and was about to happen. His mind soaked up the images the demon presented to him, and to this day he could call back any particular vision he wished: the most primeval times, when mankind lived on the earth with the race of Lucifer's children, the terror of the nights in caves and swamps when humans were food for demonkind, the eventual decline of the rule of monster and the ascent of man.

Unlike other children Leopold Ulric had no fear of the night. It was his element. He was silent and had no sense of wonder, because to him all things were known. The demon had recounted to Leopold how long ago his father had pledged allegiance to and been granted membership in the Thule Society. Devoted to the study of the occult and the ancient Germanic alphabet which would open the doors to the netherworld, the society had demanded that Heinz Ulric seal his compact in a perversion of the Abraham sacrifice. And unlike the Hebrew patriarch, Ulric, through sorcery, had bartered his firstborn's soul even before the child was conceived. Therefore, although he was of human parentage, the child Leopold belonged to other, greater ancestors.

As he drove, Ulric marveled at how unswervingly he had been guided. The instrument of which he was a master seemed to have been fashioned only for his use. The killing of his father had been the most natural of acts, something which had been predetermined. And with that killing he had stepped across the threshold into a conscious awareness of his past and his destiny. The demon had returned to him then and, seeing that his hands were bloodied, was pleased. It meant that he was ready to serve, to bring upon the earth through his demonically instilled genius a profound and utter corruption. So it was that Leopold Ulric had become the next in line of the Pied Pipers, the devil's progeny whose destiny it was to lure the children of the Lord away from the Light.

Traffic thinned out as Ulric reached the periphery of Steuben Town. Leopold Ulric carefully avoided the main thoroughfares, staying in the maze of streets that ran along the waterfront. He turned off at the Cunard Container Terminal yards and slowly guided the car in between the rows of silent tractor trailers. The same place where, not two weeks ago, Otto Morell had met with his fiery death.

Ulric parked the Aston next to the depot office, on the other side of the compound from the night watchman's hut. On a night like this one, cold with the threat of rain, he doubted anyone would be stirring. Quickly he walked east to Broome Street, disappearing into the recess of a converted doorway. The heavy-duty lock yielded to the magnetic key, and he was inside, gliding up the dirt-laden stairs, the odor of ancient brick and mortar sweet in his nostrils. At the landing he opened still another lock, and on the door at the end of the corridor, yet a third. Sometimes he wished that some poor fool would try the locks. The first, in the street, would yield. But once inside, the intruder would become the pleasure of the dogs.

Ulric pushed open this last door and stepped into the room, turning on the light, which illuminated only a rough circle of weathered floorboards. There were five cots lined up side by side. Each had a thick white pillow at the head and four had the blankets neatly tucked down. Beside each one was a hospital issue IV drip stand as well as an automatic enema dispenser, which drained the waste from the series of tubes. On the fifth bed lay Hunter Mackenzie. Both his arms were tucked inside the blankets, his head cradled in the pillow. Leopold Ulric stepped over and pinched the IV whose needle disappeared into the boy's forearm. The flow was steady, the measure in the bag indicating the boy was receiving the proper amount of liquid vitamins and protein per hour. Ulric dropped to his haunches and made sure the catheters were also working as they should, removing the bodily wastes, which, after passing through the automatic system, were incinerated.

Leopold Ulric smiled to himself and stepped over to the temperature-humidity controls. He thought the air a little chilly and so adjusted the thermostat. Then he came over and sat down on the cot beside the unconscious boy. From his evening jacket pocket Ulric brought out a leather carrier, akin to a traveling manicure set. He unzipped it, extracted a syringe and a vial of 30 percent solution Valium. Tossing back his long oily hair, he held the syringe to the light while drawing back the plunger, then leaned forward. The needle disappeared into Hunter Mackenzie's forearm, the Valium coursed into his veins; sleep would now continue.

"Forever," Leopold Ulric whispered, stroking the boy's fair hair. "Soon you will have other playmates beside you. You will not be alone. It is always difficult to be the first, but you have been very patient, and I love you for that. . . ."

Ulric's eyelids fluttered, then closed, images of the abduction moving slowly across his mind. It had all been so ridiculously easy. The thought of the suffering of the men pleased him more than death. He had used stonefish venom before, never in America but in Europe. It was a potion he enjoyed employing because it had no other purpose or effect than to cause pain. He had been careful to anoint the flechette tips with precisely the right amount of venom, load and fire in a precise order so that each projectile reached the victim for which it had been specially intended. The gasps and convulsions that followed echoed sweetly in his ears as he reached for the boy. . . .

Leopold Ulric opened his eyes and stroked the fine hairs on the boy's forearm.

"You will be the first to be rendered up to the demon. I will serve all of you in quick succession and watch as he feeds upon you. I wish I could have you for a little while longer, but my master is hungry. The last time . . . ah, the last time I was almost too late in the feeding. I could have been destroyed, do you realize that? I could have been taken because the demon remained unfed. So you will have your playmates soon, I promise you that. And you shall all sleep together until it is time. . . ."

Leopold Ulric carefully stored the used syringe in its case and slipped that back into his jacket. He rose and took a final look at Hunter Mackenzie. There was no compassion or love in his eyes. No pity or the faintest glimmer of charity. All that the black opaque orbs reflected was a bottomless lust and hunger.

Ulric reached up and took hold of the lampshade, swinging it slowly around to illuminate the few feet beyond the cots. Where the circle with its four inverted crosses had been made by him, the circumference consisting of the ashes of human bones and organs. Rachel Rosenberg's bones and heart. He moved the light all the way around until he was certain the circle was still intact. That meant that the demon had not penetrated it. It might have come sooner, hungry for Hunter Mackenzie, its appetite unappeased by the Rosenberg girl. But the circle protected Ulric's offering. Carefully he stepped over the ash and took a final look at the sleeping boy.

"Tonight I will play for you!" he whispered, and with that was gone.

One aspect of New York life which continually fascinated Sheridan was the discrepancy between the outward appearance of apartment buildings and the suite interiors. West Twenty-eighth Street had not, for the most part, undergone the exterior face-lift of the adjoining streets. The brickwork was dirty, some of it with the remains of thirty-year-old gray paint clinging to it. But the interior was a different world.

The ground-level apartment was at the end of a short corridor, a cord of firewood stacked to the side of the front door. The entry opened to the kitchen to the left, a small living room with a fireplace to the right. Beyond the living room was a dining room-cum-study. The huge bedroom took up the entire front section of the apartment. As soon as he stepped inside Sheridan felt at home. The honey-colored pine planks of the floor, the comfortable old chairs by the fireplace, and the soft pastel prints hanging on the exposed brick walls all produced an intimacy he eagerly accepted. It was the reflection of the woman who lived here.

"You're early."

Sabina greeted him at the door, a kimono-style housecoat clinging to her figure. She swung her arms around his neck and drew him to her.

"That scent is fantastic," he murmured.

"Thank you."

She led him inside and said, "Why don't you make us drinks while I finish dressing?"

Sheridan struggled out of his coat and went over to the bar.

"I realize that even lowly cops have to take time off, Thane," Sabina called from the bedroom. "But a Lincoln Center concert."

"I'm a music freak."

"Uh, huh . . ."

When she reappeared, Sabina was wearing a white evening suit trimmed with golden thread. Her throat was bare except for a choker of tiny diamonds. Her raven hair was swept back across one shoulder. Across the other she trailed a black mink cape.

"Jesus, I don't know if I can afford this," Sheridan said, his throat suddenly dry.

"You'd better, buster. I'm out for blood tonight."

They laughed easily, one gaze dancing off the other. Sheridan handed her a Manhattan, and they walked over to the grate. He poked at the logs that were burning down, inhaling deeply of the sweet air, her perfume, and the pungent odor of the wood.

"So, Inspector Sheridan, *wie geht's?*"

"Tell me about Boston first," he suggested.

"Actually I managed to kill several birds with one stone," Sabina said, sipping her cocktail. "First off, Gerussi *has* made about a dozen bows in the last four to five months. But they were all for overseas customers. He showed me the list. None of the musicians has been in the States in the last ninety days. That eliminates them.

"The reason I was late coming back is that Gerussi called up the two other makers. I thought it would be better for him to make enquiries rather than us. He knows all the others, has dealt with them for years."

"And?"

"Handel in Philadelphia works almost exclusively for the Philadelphia Philharmonic. They're going on tour next week, so everything he's done in the last few months has been for them."

"None of the musicians happened to play in New York during this time?"

"No, Handel was certain of that. In fact the orchestra will open in San Francisco and work its way back. There's a recording session scheduled in New York at the end of April."

"That gets them out of the way," Sheridan said.

"The same goes for Maarten in Connecticut," Sabina told him. She leaned forward to allow Sheridan to light her cigarette. "Maarten told Gerussi he's taken very few orders in the past year, almost all from clients he's been dealing with for years. Apparently Maarten's health is poor—the rheumatism in his hands is quite severe."

"And none of *his* customers has any connection with the NSDM."

Sabina shook her head. "None."

"That leaves your uncle," Sheridan said quietly.

"If I had gotten back in time, I would have gone to see Augusta. *Onkel* kept meticulous records. They're still probably in his Broome Street workshop."

"We can get to that tomorrow," Sheridan told her.

"Now what about you?" Sabina asked impatiently. "You really sound as though something has happened."

"First off," Sheridan said, sitting back, poking at the cherry in his drink, "your run on exotics turned up dry. The Rolls dealerships reported no loaner out. The leasing companies accounted for all their vehicles."

"Damn!" Sabina bit her lip.

Sheridan held up his hand. "However, Al came through with a positive ID off that tire print on the jacket. It's a Michelin XWX radial."

"Great. But Michelins are fairly common these days," Sabina countered.

"The XWX was the forerunner of the TRX. Both are used on high-performance machines. When it was introduced, the XWX went primarily on sports exotics—the Ferraris, Porsches, that sort of thing."

"That still leaves a lot of iron out there."

"It would except for one factor: George Percy is positive he identified the engine of the car the kidnapper used."

Sabina sat up quickly. "You've spoken to him?"

"Last night. Hansen and the Mackenzie driver were still out of it, but the flechette barely broke Percy's skin. He was able to give me a little . . . enough."

"But they'll all recover?" Sabina asked anxiously. "God, I feel so callous for not having asked before!"

"They'll be fine," Sheridan assured her.

"All right, what about the car!"

"Percy swears it's an Aston-Martin. According to him, a late model, V-8 engine, well tuned."

"Jesus, is he certain?"

"He says he is. You know him better than I: Is it *possible* for someone to be sure of something like that?"

Sabina thought for a moment. "It is," she said slowly. "George is a master mechanic. He's worked on exotics all his life. I've seen him put his hand on the cam covers of a running engine and diagnose a problem. I know I would take his word for it." She hesitated. "Assuming that was the kidnapper's car."

"An Aston would fit into that neighborhood," Sheridan pointed out.

"I don't know, Thane, it's tenuous." She frowned. "On the other hand there can't be more than a handful of such vehicles in the city."

"There aren't. I got a complete list from Aston-Martin Lagonda, the major East Coast dealer, in New Rochelle."

He passed her the paper.

"As well as a DMV printout." He handed her the Department of Motor Vehicles computer sheet.

"The two lists tally, Sabina," he said, the excitement straining his voice. "Aston owners are a tight lot. They have their own club, service the cars religiously."

"What are the red marks?"

"I managed to check out those owners. They were either out of town and the cars accounted for or else had the car where it was seen by other witnesses."

"That leaves twelve," Sabina murmured. "Between the two of us we should be able to run this down by tomorrow, the day after at the latest."

"We also have one other thing going for us," Sheridan said. "According to the Aston dealership the owners of most of the older models have replaced the XWX tire with the TRX. We're looking for one of two things: either a V-8 still running on XWX's or one which has been to the shop very recently."

Sabina stared at him. "As recently as the killings in Steuben Town," she whispered.

Sheridan nodded and rose. "One more thing. Did you happen to notice the last name?"

Sabina scanned the list, and when she looked up at him, Sheridan was smiling grimly.

"Perhaps after the concert we can ask Leopold Ulric how his car is performing these days. . . ."

Aleijadinho always arrived at the last minute for a performance, timing his ungainly entry with the dimming of the house lights. He did so because he did not care to jostle his way through the crowds in the foyers or keep moving his legs back for others to pass before his seat to theirs. The Little Cripple always reserved the first three seats on the aisle in the first row in the mezzanine. He was always escorted by two very young whores, procured for him by a midtown connection.

Aleijadinho twisted his body from side to side, taking care to plant his crutches firmly on each step. The girls, a pair of long-legged twins, blond and made up to look older than their sixteen years, preceded him, taking their places, leaving him his seat on the aisle. Both whores had been thoroughly briefed by their pimp as to what had to be done for their client. As soon as Aleijadinho sat down, one girl took the aluminum crutches away from him.

The curtain rose, and Aleijadinho sighed contentedly. He loved the symphony even more than the ballet or theater. He was a season subscriber to Lincoln Center and had his own box at Carnegie Hall. Music, dance, and drama were the worlds he escaped into in order to rejuvenate himself, completely clear his mind and let his soul float on the beauty around him. He loved the smell and dress of the crowds, the rich beauty of the women, and the calm assurance of their escorts. This too he devoured hungrily, because it was a world he could never belong to. Although he was well aware that those who saw his companions envied him, Aleijadinho knew too well that his physical deformity would make him the eternal spectator, never one who belonged. Having people stare at him, demanding that they acknowledge him by their curiosity about a crippled dwarf with such lovely companions was his only revenge.

Aleijadinho settled back in his seat and let the first strains of Schumann's Violin Concerto wash over him. For the next half hour as he followed the shifting of the melody, waiting for the crescendo which would signal the start of Leopold Ulric's solo, his mind turned from time to time to the thought of the assassin. This morning the Little Cripple had spoken to the man known only as Nevada. Although he had dialed the San Francisco area code, Aleijadinho was certain the killer was actually elsewhere. A series of clicks and pauses confirmed that a switching machine was transferring the call. Nevada had been informed of the Little Cripple's interest in his services. Aleijadinho and his principal had both been vouched for. As soon as Nevada confirmed a bank deposit of 50 percent of his fee, he would come to New York. That afternoon Aleijadinho had had forty thousand dollars transferred from one of Emil Letelier's Geneva accounts into a secret number at the Grande Banque de Bâle.

The Little Cripple savored the moment. Emil Letelier had given him the responsibility of eradicating all opposition in Steuben Town. This charge had meant moving against Otto Morell. Aleijadinho knew Morell had been trying to unravel the twisted skein that was Letelier's relationship with the powers of the city and Albany. He had thought that the old craftsman's search was a waste of the little time he had left on this earth. Aleijadinho himself had arranged those relationships and was certain the puzzle was impenetrable. Still, Letelier had spoken, and Morell had been stopped.

As the second movement came to an end Aleijadinho leaned forward, straining for a glimpse of the virtuoso. His eyes scanned the right-hand side of the stage, in the area of the concertmaster, where the soloist generally stood. He saw nothing but blackness. The final chords of the piece were flying high into the vaulted cupolas, fast disappearing. If Ulric didn't make his appearance immediately, the integrity of the composition would be lost. All around him Aleijadinho saw the audience straining in anticipation.

Suddenly the music exploded. It would have been impossible not to see Ulric standing where he now appeared had he been there earlier. Yet the gasps from the audience told Aleijadinho that everyone had missed the virtuoso's entrance. The Little Cripple leaned even farther forward, both hands clutching the low railing that ran along the top of the mezzanine. He was fascinated by Ulric, who stood in a single spotlight. His stance, as usual, was grotesque, one leg thrust out, the rest of his body leaning back on the other leg, the arm holding the violin high, the bow skipping and dancing along the strings with scarcely a touch of his hand.

For the next forty minutes the Met audience was spellbound, unable to take its collective eyes off the musician. His music was seducing them, penetrating their very souls. Aleijadinho felt himself drawn to this man, who was as ugly and misshapen as himself and yet had complete and utter control over people. The Little Cripple threw his head back and squeezed his eyes shut. He wanted nothing more than to reach out and touch this genius, speak to him, tell him how much he loved what was happening to him.

There was no more than a minute left in Ulric's solo when Aleijadinho's mind snapped. Ulric's face seemed to swim up at him from the stage, beckon him forth. The music, now demonic and grotesque, was a hellish symphony from which he could not escape. Ulric's grinning expression paralyzed him; the seesawing motion of the violin seemed to want to draw him toward it, across the vast expanse of air straight onto the stage.

"No!" Aleijadinho whispered. Desperately he turned to his girls and recoiled. They were both staring at him, their teeth bared in hideous smiles, like two inhuman creatures about to feast on their prey.

"Help me!" he begged them. "Don't let him take me!"

The whore beside him hissed savagely, a rattlesnake about to strike.

"Go to him," she said, eyes burning into his. "He commands it. Go!"

The Little Cripple opened his mouth, but the words would not come forth. Both girls were staring at him, their lips moving quickly, silently, as though in some ancient incantation. Aleijadinho felt himself move forward in his

202

seat. His fingers were still curled around the railing, and he straightened out his arms, trying to hold himself back.

"He demands you!" the whores hissed at him. One of them reached out and raked the side of Aleijadinho's face, tearing open four jagged strips of flesh. But in his last instant of consciousness Aleijadinho did not yield to the pain. His fingers, bleeding now as its edges cut into them, remained curled around the railing. It was the music that overwhelmed him. The final thundering chords of the orchestra joining the soloist literally lifted the Little Cripple off his feet. He was catapulted out of his seat and flung over the railing. For an instant he hung on; then his arms snapped out of their sockets, and he began falling toward the orchestra seats. His last thought was that he would land on the heads of those below, that somehow this would break his fall. But that was not the case.

The body of Aleijadinho, the man so in love with death, sailed over the edge and struck one of the glittering chandeliers. A rain of glass exploded over the audience as the Little Cripple's contorted form was impaled on the crystal spikes. The chandelier shuddered, some plaster falling from the moorings. But it held. Even the jerking, kicking motion of a dying man could not wrench it free.

Thane Sheridan had been watching Aleijadinho throughout the performance. Now he was on his feet as the last notes echoed away and the hall was reduced to the stark silence of terror. He glanced at Leopold Ulric, who was looking at the cripple, then followed his gaze across to one of the loges. There, flanked by Andreas Marcovici, Abner Levine, and his wife, sat Augusta Morell. She too was looking at the swaying corpse. Sheridan was certain he saw a light smile appear on her lips. Then Augusta Morell rose, and she and her party began to leave the loge.

From somewhere in the orchestra a woman screamed. The spell was broken, and pandemonium erupted.

Chapter Fourteen

"Get downstairs and coordinate security! When a squad arrives, get the body to Thompson Street!"

Thane Sheridan was moving even before the words left his mouth.

"Where are you going?" cried Sabina.

"After Ulric!"

Sabina's head snapped back in the direction of the stage. The orchestra members were on their feet, staring up at the grotesque spectacle before them. But the spot where Leopold Ulric had been standing was vacant. The virtuoso had disappeared.

"Sabina, come on!"

She followed him out of the loge, conscious of stepping on and tripping over feet. She wedged in behind him, letting his bulk clear a path for them to the door.

"Police!" Sheridan roared as soon as he snapped back the door that opened up on the mezzanine proper. "Police! Get out of the way!"

Thane Sheridan didn't care who was in front of him. Gripping Sabina's hand, he pushed and elbowed his way into the throng streaming toward the wide red-carpeted steps that led to the exits on the ground floor. Men cursed him as he bumped them aside. The women uttered short, shrill cries like startled birds.

When they reached the main floor, Sheridan spotted a Lincoln Center security team vainly trying to get through the main doors at orchestra level.

"Over here!"

He held his badge high, and an instant later the four of them formed a flying wedge which pierced the remainder of the mob. Thane Sheridan was the first to break through. He grabbed one of the security men.

"The performers' dressing room. Let's go."

The young agent staggered as Sheridan pushed him forward but to his credit didn't even turn around. They ran in tandem down the slight incline, past the pit where the orchestra sat during ballets and operas and around to the door which led to the corridors under the stage proper. As soon as they were through it, Sheridan collided with the concertmaster.

"Where's Ulric?"

Bewildered, the elderly musician blinked back.

"Where's Ulric!" Sheridan repeated, gripping the man's shoulder.

"I . . . I don't know," the concertmaster stammered.

"The dressing rooms are this way," the young security agent volunteered, coming to the concertmaster's rescue.

Weaving to and fro along the narrow, concrete floor corridor, bumping into musicians or their instrument cases, the two men raced around to the back of the hall.

"Not there! That's for the locals," the security agent shouted as Sheridan started down another hall. "The superstars are upstairs."

They pounded up the metal steps to the second level and burst through the fire door. The security agent went first, pausing a fraction of a second before each door.

"Okay, it's this one!"

The security agent was about to knock when Sheridan shouldered him aside and flung open the door.

"Jesus Christ!"

Sheridan recoiled at the overwhelming odor. Ulric's room was filled with flowers—dozens of roses, carnations, tiger lilies, violets, and varieties Sheridan could not identify were bunched in glass vases on the counters and coffee tables.

"It's a goddamn funeral parlor," the agent said, disgust underlying his words.

Sheridan passed through the main area into the dressing room. He checked the walk-in closets and the bathroom.

"No coat, no instrument," he said grimly. "If he was driving, which way would he go?"

"A guy like Ulric would have a limo," the security agent said. "In fact I remember his having one the other night."

"All right, where would *that* be waiting for him?"

The security agent led the way out to the back of the Lincoln Center complex. Beside the stage doors and ramps which were used to load and unload the stage equipment were half a dozen limousines, the engines idling. But all the drivers had gotten into a single vehicle. Sheridan tapped on the glass and flashed his badge.

"Who's driving Leopold Ulric?"

"No one, mister. He didn't want a car tonight."

"Have you seen him?"

The driver looked over his shoulder at his buddies and repeated the question.

"Frank saw his car parked around the other side, closer to the main hall," one of them volunteered.

The security guard shook his head. "Not possible. That's for the garbage containers. No way any size car would fit in there."

"What *kind* of car?" Sheridan asked impatiently.

"Black sports coupe . . . an English job."

One of the other drivers piped up: "An Aston-Martin. Mean-looking set of wheels."

"Obliged," Sheridan said and moved off, running across the asphalt, the soles of his boots cracking the thin sheet of ice that covered the puddles.

"I'm telling you there's no way he could park a car in there," the security agent shouted after him. "If he's not in the lot—"

Sheridan turned the corner and was suddenly faced with what appeared to be a dead-end alley.

"I told you—" the agent started to say when Sheridan motioned him to stay silent.

Carefully he looked into the alley. Along one side, next to the cyclone fence, were the garbage bins, huge wheeled containers whose white paint was streaked with dirt and rust. There was a space no more than four feet across between these and the solid brick wall on the right.

"I know I heard something," Sheridan muttered. He

strained to see right through to the end of the alley, but there was no light, no reflections.

At that instant a heavy engine shrieked to life. Twin high beam lights snapped on, blinding both men. The unmistakable sound of squealing tires whined across the brick.

Sheridan flung himself at the security guard, his body hurtling the young man toward the space behind the last garbage cart. The car was almost on top of them, its engine deafening, the oversized tires impossibly close to the carts. With one final shove Sheridan sent the security guard sprawling. At the same time he himself was rolling, coat flapping as he tried to reach his gun. That was his mistake. The tip of the gleaming chrome fender caught the edge of the coat. In a split second Sheridan was jerked alongside the vehicle, his face only centimeters from the spinning tires. He could not hear himself screaming but knew that he was. The entire left side of his body was being flayed. The fabric of his coat, jacket, and trousers was shredded, the asphalt burning his skin. If he couldn't get loose, it would only be a matter of seconds before a change in direction would fling him under the car and into the path of the onrushing rear wheels.

Sheridan reached up and clutched at the coat fabric. He gave two vicious tugs, then a third. Looking up, he saw the chrome tip cutting into the material. Desperately he thrust his body to the right while at the same time yanking on the coat end with his remaining strength. The fabric finally gave way just as the car swerved left. Even though he was clear of it, the vehicle's momentum carried him so close to the wheels that the edge of the rear tire grazed his cheek. As the car roared past, Sheridan rolled and lifted his head, trying to get a glimpse of the rear plate. But the lights which would have illuminated the numbers were dead. Only when he tried to stand did the full impact of the pain hit him. His whole left side was on fire; his knees buckled and he pitched forward, his entire body shaking uncontrollably.

"What in God's name happened to you?"

Sabina Morell broke away from the ring of firemen who

208

were setting up rigging to hoist down Aleijadinho's body and ran down the aisle. She stopped cold when she saw Sheridan's bloodied left side. Instinctively she reached out and touched his face. Her palm came away bloody from the cut the tire had slashed into his cheek.

"Paramedic!"

The security agent who had been propping Sheridan up from the other side led him to where a stretcher had been pulled out.

"It wasn't possible," he kept repeating. "Just not fucking possible!"

"What are you saying?" Sabina demanded.

"Shut him up!" Sheridan whispered hoarsely. "Get Mr. Bill down here to read him the riot act."

Sabina stared at him, but Sheridan said nothing more as the paramedic eased him down on the stretcher and cut away what was left of his jacket and trousers to get at the wounds.

"Christ Almighty," Sabina breathed.

"Looks a lot worse than it really is," the paramedic reassured her. "All the wounds are superficial, just deep enough to have broken blood vessels." He began to apply antiseptic lotion. "It'll sting like hell for a while. Then the aches will set in, but nothing's broken." He looked at Sheridan. "You're one lucky dude."

"Thane, who did this?" Sabina demanded. He saw the concern, the anger in her face but shook his head.

"Get Mr. Bill," he repeated. "And make sure the security guard doesn't talk to anyone. Please . . . it's important."

"Thane!"

"Sabina, *please* . . ."

She backed away, fighting against the instinct to stay by his side.

"Come on!" she said savagely to the security guard.

The young man, his gray blazer filthy from the fall in the alley, hands and face caked with greasy dirt where he had rolled next to the trash bin, stumbled after her. The adrenaline had stopped flowing. He was back in a familiar place, seeing recognizable faces. Shock was setting in.

"I'm telling you, it wasn't possible!"

Sabina gripped him by the elbow, leading him away from the others toward two uniformed patrolmen who were at the entry doors.

"What wasn't possible?" she asked softly.

"There's no way that car could have been in the alley." The security guard shook his head like a drunk. "It was too large."

"What car?"

"The one that tried to run us down. Kill us. Christ, if it hadn't been for that cop, I'd be all over the road."

"Can you describe the car?" Sabina asked urgently.

"No . . . the lights. It was coming right for us."

"The driver?"

The security guard shook his head. "The cop pushed me out of the way. I don't know why he did it, jumping in front of the car like that. Christ, he came that close to being killed."

"But you said the vehicle came at you out of the alley," Sabina persisted.

"It did, but it couldn't have! There's no way *any* car could have fit in that lane, much less a monster like that."

Sabina felt her flesh crawl. The same sense of evil, the presence she had encountered after she and Sheridan had spoken with the importer Kew, crawled over her.

"Wait here," she told the security guard.

Sabina gestured to one of the patrolmen, who stepped over to him. Quickly she explained to him that she wanted the security guard held incommunicado until William Rodgers arrived. Then she stepped out into the orchestra lobby and called Rodgers's special number. The call was relayed instantly to Mr. Bill's residence. He promised to be at Lincoln Center within thirty minutes.

Sabina returned to the grand salon. She looked over and saw that the paramedic was still working on Thane Sheridan. She pushed aside the desire to go over to him. There was one matter she had to look after now, before someone else got there accidentally.

Drawing her Blackgama cape around her, Sabina quickly made for one of the exits. The wind had picked up, and it carried her along to the east side of the building, toward the parking lot. Only two limousines remained, the

210

drivers chatting in the car. She slipped by them, heading for the alley.

Sabina stopped dead a few feet away from the first bin. She couldn't see a damn thing because of the darkness. Quickly she ran across to the limousines and opened the driver's door of the first.

"Put your high beams on and get over by that alley," she ordered the driver, the gold detective shield glinting in the vanity light.

"Lady—"

"Move it! This is official business."

She slammed the door on him and ran back the way she had come. Behind her the stretch car began to move, bathing the area ahead of her in dazzling white light. Sabina ran up to the garbage bin and turned around.

"Come on, move it up some more!" she shouted, waving her arms.

The limousine inched forward. The driver lowered his window and stuck his head outside.

"A little more!"

"No way, lady! I can't get this heap in there. This is as far as she goes!"

Sabina stared down the alley. Black asphalt with broken puddles of water. The crushed gravel in the blacktop glittered like diamond edges. She squatted down, running her hand along the ground. No one would be able to lift a print off this. If a print existed.

Sabina turned around. The limo driver was right: His vehicle was much too wide to enter the area between the bins and brick. And Sabina could see that no ordinary vehicle, not even a subcompact, could have been parked here. As the security guard had said, there was no fucking way. Yet something had almost killed him and Thane Sheridan. Something that had been in this alley. She had to speak to Thane—right away. The hair on the back of her neck was rising—and not because of the cold.

Sabina twisted around the front end of the limo and ran back inside.

"You sure you don't want some painkiller?"

The paramedic held up a Syrette of Demerol, and Thane

211

Sheridan was tempted. His entire left side felt as though it had been brushed with fire coral.

"Forget it. Just clean me up and give me something to ease the burning."

The paramedic shrugged. "We're going to get you to a hospital. You're going to need stitches for your cheek anyway." He squeezed Sheridan's hand. "I'll get an ambulance for you. We don't have to wait for this guy."

The paramedic looked up. "Did you see what happened?"

Sheridan nodded. "Yeah . . . I saw it all."

The firemen had removed a square of seats and erected ladders and a rigging at the base of the chandelier. Two of them had climbed up and were now extricating the body of Aleijadinho from the jagged spikes. Whenever they moved the body, slivers of crystal cascaded to the floor below, falling as delicately as icicles. Sheridan watched as a hoist secured by guy wires to a metal tripod was maneuvered into position. When the lower part of the body was strapped in, the firemen lifted the torso off the spikes, taking care not to place any more strain on the wires securing the mooring to the ceiling. Slowly Aleijadinho's corpse was lowered, in the manner of a mountain climber who had perished on the face of a cliff.

Thane Sheridan looked away. The smell of the blood still gagged him, although he realized it was irrational. But the presence of evil was overwhelming. He could feel its residue around him. He knew he had been wrong in going after Ulric—yet he had done so instinctively, obeying the primeval reaction of a hunter to his quarry. And Ulric had almost killed him. Sheridan was certain that that had been his car and that Leopold Ulric had been behind the wheel.

Why?

And the death—no, the murder—of Emil Letelier's most trusted lieutenant . . .

And the presence of the two whores, who had done nothing to stop the Little Cripple from flinging himself over the railing . . .

And the presence of Augusta Morell with her friends,

watching coldly as the body was impaled on the spikes, smiling with grim satisfaction as Aleijadinho died . . .

Factors, all of them relevant, yet he couldn't put them together into an intelligible whole. Not yet.

"Thane?"

He twisted around to see Sabina Morell standing beside him. He saw that the toes of her boots were wet and the cuffs of the pant suit soiled.

"Where have you been playing?"

"Out by the garbage bins."

"Anything?"

She shook her head. "Thane, I don't know how a car—"

He held up his hand. "Later. Right now I want you to track down the two ladies of the evening who were with Aleijadinho."

"Shouldn't be much of a problem. I have a fair idea of where he gets his young fluff."

"What about Mr. Bill?"

"The cavalry's arrived."

Sabina looked around to see William Rodgers standing beside her, resplendent in evening dress.

"Looks like we were all stepping out tonight. Sergeant, I must say you look very fetching."

Sabina blushed.

"As for you, Thane, you look as though you've been hit by a truck."

"I'll get an APB out on the car," Sabina said at once.

"No, not yet," Sheridan said. "Bill, that security guard over there . . . he was with me in the alley. I want him to disappear for a little while."

"How long?"

"A week, ten days."

Mr. Bill stroked his clean-shaven jaw. "I'll think of something. What did he see?"

"Something he can't believe. And if he starts talking about it to the press, we've had it."

"I understand Puerto Rico is nice this time of year," Mr. Bill mused. "Maybe we can arrange something through the witness protection program."

He paused. "Who did this to you, Thane?"

"Not here."

"All right. We'll get you into a private clinic and clean you up. After that I want the whole story. All of it, Thane, I mean that."

Sheridan nodded. "Before you do anything else, get a list of all the students at the NSDM for me."

"Thane!" Sabina cried weakly.

He looked up at her. "I'm sorry. But he's going to take another one down."

"How do you know that?" Rodgers demanded.

"Believe me, Bill, I know. I think I've finally penetrated the son of a bitch. I think I've gotten into his mind. . . ."

Chapter Fifteen

The final casualty count for the evening was mercifully low: Aside from the single fatality only eight people were injured in the evening dress stampede. All but one had simple sprains or twisted ankles. An elderly women suffered a broken collar bone when she tripped over the hem of her gown and fell against a Henry Moore sculpture.

"All told, we got off lucky," Mr. Bill commented.

He and Sabina were seated in his limousine, which was wending its way to West Twenty-eighth Street. Twenty minutes earlier they had watched a Schaffer Clinic physician administer liquid Valium to a protesting Thane Sheridan. But Rodgers had been adamant: his inspector would spend the night under medical observation. Tomorrow, if the wounds had at least begun to heal, he could be discharged.

"I wish he'd take it easy for a few days," Sabina said suddenly.

"So does he, I'm sure," Mr. Bill grunted. "But he can't. He's too close."

"Too close to what?" demanded Sabina. "He's pushing to get himself killed!"

Mr. Bill shrugged. "I've seen it happen before with Thane. Somehow he can see things before anyone else can. It comes from thinking in a particular way. Take math, for example. Not everyone can conceptualize equations, relate to them as we do words. But there are those who can "read" a page of symbols as easily as we would a page of Vonnegut."

"I have problems with Vonnegut," Sabina muttered.

Mr. Bill refrained from comment.

"It's going down on the books as suicide, isn't it?" she added a moment later. "What happened to Aleijadinho?"

"What else can we call it? When you start rounding up the witnesses tomorrow, they'll all tell you the same thing: The Little Cripple flung himself over the railing. That's what Thane saw. And that means *no* one saw anything different."

"It didn't happen that way," Sabina said softly. "He knows that."

"Maybe it didn't," Rodgers conceded. "But unless we have proof to the contrary . . ."

"I'm going to track down the two whores," said Sabina. "They'll talk to me or else I'm going to make them accomplices."

"Ease up, Sergeant," Mr. Bill cautioned her as the limo pulled over to the curb. "It's been a rough evening for everyone. Pour yourself a stiff one and get some sleep. We'll pick up the remaining pieces tomorrow."

"Good night, Mr. Bill."

William C. Rodgers cocked one eye at her.

"Good night, Sergeant," he said dryly.

One o'clock had come and gone by the time Sabina stripped, showered, and gulped down the whiskey Mr. Bill had advised. She fell asleep almost immediately, and it seemed to her that the alarm went off just as quickly. Sabina put on a pair of dark jeans and a black turtleneck and threw on a battered sheepskin jacket to wear outside. At half past three she had gotten her Triumph 8 out of the all-night garage on Ninth Avenue and was headed uptown. Unbeknownst to Mr. Bill, she had, while he was with Sheridan, called the Metropolitan Tower security administrator and obtained a list of all early-morning deliveries. The first consignment, from Handee Landree, arrived punctually at four o'clock at the Fifty-fourth Street entrance. While the truck waited for security to clear it Sabina slipped out of the shadows of a doorway and hopped onto the rear bumper, gripping the twin door handles. The truck started slowly down the ramp. As soon as it was inside, she jumped away, crouching and rolling out of sight of the television monitors. From there it was only a short walk to the doors which opened to the staircase leading to the residents' parking spaces.

The price of Leopold Ulric's duplex penthouse had included three parking spaces. The single bay was at the far end of the garage, bordered by two solid concrete walls. The Aston-Martin was parked on a diagonal, taking up a piece of all three spots.

Sabina went up to the car and squatted on her haunches, her fingers exploring the tread pattern on the vehicle's right front tire. The rubber was cold, but it was also fresh. Along the sides tiny rubber pricks still protruded from the main body. Usually these were worn off in the first five hundred miles of a tire's life, probably less on a high performance machine such as the Aston.

Sabina checked all four tires. Each was a Michelin TRX, each brand-new. She toyed with the idea of jimmying open the trunk but thought better of it. She was trespassing. Forced entry into Ulric's car would constitute an unauthorized invasion of his privacy. She didn't want the slightest legal complication where the virtuoso was concerned.

Sabina came back to the front of the car by the right side of the chrome bumper. Carefully she ran her fingers around the sharp rim, then lay flat on her back and pulled herself under. A few seconds later she felt something besides cold metal. With one twist she brought out a jagged piece of cloth.

"Jackpot!" she murmured.

The cloth belonged to Thane Sheridan's coat. Quickly Sabina deposited it in a plastic bag and stuffed that deep inside her jacket. She was tempted to put the cloth back so that in the subsequent investigation it would be found on the vehicle, but she figured that forensic would get enough metal slivers off the cloth to match them with the composition of the bumper. Also there were threads still caught in the metal. Unless Ulric was to make a point of changing the entire bumper, the evidence would remain. Not even the most conscientious cleaning would get rid of every particle of evidence.

And, Sabina thought, if Ulric had been concerned about

evidence, he never would have delayed cleaning the car. The job would have been done that night.

A few minutes later Sabina stepped through the elevators into the plush foyer of the Metropolitan Tower. She walked briskly across the marble expanse, flashing a smile at the concierge, who was raising his hand to his cap. Suddenly he stopped and stared after her. But by the time he had gotten up from behind the console desk and shouted at her, she was out the door.

By six o'clock Sabina's Triumph had borne her across the Triborough Bridge and was humming along Route 278 toward New Rochelle. She drove at a moderate speed and at Pelham Manor pulled off the New England Thruway for breakfast. Forty-five minutes later she was back on the road again, sipping coffee and watching the dawn struggle against the grayness of the night, reluctant to depart. She left the I-95 at North Avenue and headed northwest toward the Wykagyl Country Club. Turning off Cameron, she made for Overlook Road and arrived at the East Coast Aston-Martin dealership just as the doors were being unlocked.

"May I be of service, madam?"

John Coxwell could have stepped out of a British gin advertisement: tall, swept-back silver hair, gray trousers, blazer, and club tie. Sabina looked wistfully into the showroom with its Volante, Aston coupe, and the newest model, the futuristic Lagonda, and shook her head.

"Not as far as cars are concerned, I'm afraid." She flashed her ID. "But, yes, I believe you can give me some information."

The general manager donned his best skeptical expression.

"Perhaps if I might inquire as to the nature of your visit . . ."

"Do you have a client by the name of Leopold Ulric? He's the musician. Very well known."

Coxwell led her over to the lounge area and rolled over a trolley with silver service and chafing dish.

"Croissant?"

"Coffee'll be fine."

Coxwell poured for both of them, then settled beside her.

"Yes, Mr. Ulric is a client," he said carefully. "But before we go any further, Detective Sergeant, I must ask you if you have jurisdiction to pursue an inquiry here in New Rochelle."

"This is an informal visit," Sabina said crisply. "Mr. Ulric's vehicle may have been involved in an accident. We would like to be sure before troubling him unduly."

"Yes, of course, that's very considerate of you." Coxwell beamed.

"Has his Aston been in for service recently, say, within the last two weeks?"

"It has."

"You're certain?"

"Detective Sergeant, we are not a large organization, as you can see. Therefore we have a close rapport with all our clients. Mr. Ulric's car was brought here from the city precisely ten days ago."

"For a complete change of tires, Michelin XWX's replaced by the TRX's."

Coxwell was momentarily flustered but hid the surprise well.

"Just so."

Sabina took a deep pull on her cigarette and looked away. She focused on the low-slung front end of the Lagonda, and the image of Thane Sheridan being dragged along by Ulric's car flashed through her mind.

"May I have a photostat of the work order and final bill, please?" she asked tonelessly.

"Detective Sergeant, we do not, as a rule, offer such information without good reason."

"If I didn't have good reason, Mr. Coxwell, I wouldn't have schlepped out here this morning," Sabina said, her voice dangerously low. "You can give me a copy now, or else I can come back in two hours with a warrant, in the company of the New Rochelle police. If there happen to be newspeople in the area, I could include you and your company in a homicide investigation."

She ground out the butt and looked at him.

"So which way is it to be?"

Coxwell drew himself up. "I quite understand your position," he said stiffly. "If you would be so good as to wait a few minutes . . ."

Sabina nodded absently. Her stomach had gone cold and empty, a sure signal that she had finally settled on the right suspect, found the true direction of the investigation. But Leopold Ulric . . . how could it be?

The family resemblance was striking: the same high cheekbones, taut chin, and full, sensuous lips. Even the demeanor was the same: Augusta held her head high, the posture accenting her long, still smooth neck. Her back was straight, her hands folded delicately in her lap.

"Yes, Inspector, Sabina could have been my daughter. In a way I suppose she is."

The statement caught him off guard.

"I'm sorry, I didn't mean to stare."

"That's quite all right." Augusta Morell laughed. "It's flattering. You see, Sabina came to live with me and my late husband when she was ten years old. Her mother, my sister, made a poor choice in terms of a husband. Horace Kunckle was Farnham's only attorney. He was also an alcoholic, abuser, and lecher. My sister stood by him stubbornly, determined to reform him. Instead she worked and worried her way to an early grave. When she passed away, we brought Sabina down to live with us."

"And she took your name?"

"Yes. It was only natural."

To Sheridan that much was evident. He shifted slightly in the wing chair to keep the weight off his left side. The rest in the hospital had helped, as much, he thought, as the salve he had applied to the raw skin. The doctors estimated five days before the nerve ends had a chance to heal. But at least the pain was reduced to a dull ache, and he could move around.

He wasn't sure exactly why he had come, alone, to see Augusta Morell while Sabina was away. Perhaps he wanted to form an opinion of this woman without her niece there. An objective opinion, not clouded by a relative's presence. He could also ask certain questions which otherwise might have gone unspoken.

"More coffee, Inspector?"

220

"Thank you."

Sheridan had arrived at nine o'clock. Even as he rang the doorbell he felt somewhat guilty. Given what had happened last night, it somehow wasn't right to disturb Augusta Morell.

The first surprise was the immediate opening of the door. The second was that Augusta Morell appeared fresh, dressed in an almost formal blouse, skirt, and jacket ensemble, as though she were expecting someone. Yet she assured him that wasn't the case.

"Isn't it tragic what happened last night?" Augusta Morell said softly.

"You were there?" Sheridan asked.

"Of course I was, Inspector." The eyes gazed at him frostily. "You saw me."

"Yes, I did."

"I knew of Aleijadinho," Augusta Morell went on. "He was Emil Letelier's henchman. An evil, vicious man."

"But his death was a tragedy nevertheless?"

"Oh, no, Inspector, I would not pretend to grieve for scum like him. I was referring to the interruption of such an exquisite performance, the effect of the suicide upon the audience. Shocking, really. I understand a number of people were injured."

Sheridan couldn't believe the cool, matter-of-fact tone. There was something very strong, merciless in this woman. It was something based on a profound hate.

"Do my sentiments—or lack of them—concerning the deceased shock you, Inspector?"

"Yes, they do," Sheridan admitted quietly.

"I hope you believe me when I say it grieves me to have lost so much compassion," Augusta Morell said. "But it is not possible for a person to keep on giving endlessly, without having something come back. In the better days we worked for the community, building it, molding it, enjoying what we had created, hoping to pass the fruits of our work down to others who would follow. Follow, preserve, and add. Not destroy, Inspector.

"I can't tell you how terrible the last few years have been. How deadly it's been for all of us to watch Steuben Town decay and break apart. Sadder still to have to pay in

221

fear and finally in blood for the privilege of living here. Decency, fair play, compassion, all these tend to disappear so quickly as the tragedy is compounded. Such qualities are not easy to replace. Perhaps, for the time being, it's best not to even think of them. . . ."

"You're convinced Emil Letelier's the one who's destroying Steuben Town?" asked Sheridan.

"That is a self-evident truth, Inspector."

"Mrs. Morell, why was your husband killed?" he demanded suddenly. But if the widow took offense at his question, she didn't show it.

"Because Otto was coming too close to linking Emil Letelier with certain elected officials here in the city as well as in Albany. Men who were protecting Letelier's drug enterprises."

"The Favereau Commission hasn't managed to come up with any connection," Sheridan reminded her.

"Otto's investigation led him to the commission, Inspector. In particular, two outstanding public servants who had been—what is the current expression?—very tight with Letelier."

"Did your husband gather any evidence of malfeasance?"

"Only circumstantial, Inspector. Surely you know how convoluted relationships between organized crime and government are. Otto spent the better part of two years trying to work his way to the truth."

"He must have gotten close if someone felt the need to murder him."

Augusta Morell's reply was noncommittal. "He did . . . very close."

"And all the while he worked at gathering proof during those two years, Letelier's people ate up more and more of Steuben Town."

"They want it all, Inspector," Augusta Morell said fiercely. "But we're not going to give it to them. It is not a matter of race or creed. We can coexist, work with anyone. But *no* one is going to destroy us."

"Just how do you propose to protect yourselves?"

Augusta Morell smiled. "The way you saw: mass demonstrations, propositions, political support of candidates who will espouse our cause. All legal, nonviolent means accorded us by the Constitution."

Thane Sheridan said nothing. There was a piece missing, and he couldn't quite grasp it.

"Inspector, may I ask why you called on me this morning?"

"My apologies." Sheridan smiled. "I didn't mean to get sidetracked."

Augusta Morell inclined her head but said nothing.

"Gerussi of Boston had told me that your husband made some bows to accompany instruments on order. I would like your permission to go to his shop and check the record books. To see whom the final orders were for."

"I see. What does this have to do with, Inspector?"

"The murder of Rachel Rosenberg."

The gray eyes sharpened in pain.

"I'm afraid I still don't understand . . ."

Quickly Sheridan explained about the horsehair found at the NSDM, its subsequent identification, and the names of those craftsmen who used it.

"Yes, Otto bought from Kew for many years, and his father before him," Augusta Morell said softly. "It's quite amazing how you've managed to deduce all this from a single hair. Still . . . Of course I have no objection to showing you my husband's business records. I'm afraid, though, that you'll not find very much. It's simply not possible that any of Otto's clients could have had anything to do with poor Rachel's death. You're talking about some of the world's leading virtuosos, Inspector."

"I know. But no matter how tentative the lead, it must be checked."

"Yes, I can appreciate that, under the circumstances."

"Then you have no objection to opening up your husband's workshop."

"That won't be necessary, Inspector. After Otto's death I brought all the accounts and business records here. His shop is sealed. I will not open it again ever. Let whoever buys it do what he will with it. As for myself, I cannot set foot there again!"

* * *

"I still don't understand why you don't want to go after Ulric now!"

Exasperated, Sabina Morell rose and began to pace back and forth between the fireplace and Sheridan's working area. The time was half past ten. Even the triple laminated windows couldn't keep out all the noise coming from the delivery trucks that crawled up and down Thompson Street.

"I also don't know why you went to see Augusta without me! You could have waited until I got back."

Sheridan looked across at her. "One thing at a time, okay?" he said. "That piece of cloth you retrieved from Ulric's car is part of my coat. But as evidence it would be inadmissible. You didn't have a warrant to go after his personal property."

"I keep telling you, there's more fabric there! I didn't remove all of it. And if we get a warrant now, we could sweep his apartment as well."

Sheridan inclined his head. "Granted. But I don't want Ulric picked up right now."

"Christ Almighty, he tried to run you down! You and that security guard. If nothing else, we can pick him up on reckless driving."

"And then what? Where do we go from there?"

Sabina took a deep breath and ran her fingers through her thick hair.

"All right, we know Ulric came after you last night. We have evidence on that. From my uncle's records we also know that Otto had just finished building a violin and bow for him—"

"Now hold it right there. Your uncle built the violin, but when was it delivered?"

Sabina stopped dead, puzzled. "I don't know."

"Another point: When did Ulric enter the country? Before the killings or after?"

"Immigration would be able to tell us that. Ulric's probably on a sixty-day entry pass—even longer if he's going to tour."

"That's step one." Sheridan nodded. "If he arrived before the killing of Rachel Rosenberg, then we check out when he picked up the instrument. There was only a four-day span between her death and your uncle's murder. Unless the instrument was delivered to him later on, the pickup had to have been made sometime within those forty-eight hours."

"There's a problem though." Sabina frowned. "Assuming Ulric had the violin and bow and he did kidnap Rachel Rosenberg, why did no one recognize him at the NSDM? His face is too well known, especially in musical circles."

"I never said this would be easy," Sheridan said grimly. "We would also have to place him at the scene of the Mackenzie disappearance."

Sabina came over and sat before him on the ottoman.

"Thane, do you think Ulric is the one? Is he the Rambler?"

He didn't answer for what seemed a long time.

"I don't know," he said at last. "I wish I could be sure, but I can't get a bearing on the man. On the one hand, it seems inconceivable that someone of his stature could be responsible for taking children off the street . . ."

"But then again, something made you run after him last night," Sabina said softly. "You zeroed in on him, no one else. The second you saw Aleijadinho go over the railing . . ."

Sheridan rose and came over to the coffee maker. He poured himself another cup and stood with his back to her.

"There's something wrong in all of this," he murmured. He turned to face her. "We've established that only a small number of violinists use bows with Xian horsehair. Of all of them only Leopold Ulric is in the city, has been to the NSDM, and could have inadvertently dropped such a hair. Who knows? It could have been clinging to his jacket or something and been brushed away when he went after Mrs. Rosenberg.

"Leopold Ulric also tried to kill me. Even though I didn't see him behind the wheel or get his plate number. We also know he had his tires changed."

"Which also ties him into the South American killings," Sabina broke in.

"Another anomaly. Is Ulric taking the children *and* committing slum murders at the same time?"

"Jesus!" Sabina breathed. "If he is . . ."

"Then we have to get to him," Sheridan said urgently. "Because he's on a psychotic binge. The blood lust is driving him into a frenzy."

"I'll take Immigration," Sabina said. "But I'm willing to bet that he arrived in the country a week or so before he was due to start his concerts and NSDM classes."

"Sabina." He reached out and touched her arm. "Why were you upset that I went to see Augusta alone?"

She smiled, embarrassed. "I guess I'm just protective about her. I don't want her going through any more than she has to."

Quickly she changed the subject. "What about yourself?"

"I'm going after the two whores who were with Aleijadinho last night. I want to know what they saw."

What Sheridan didn't mention was that there would also be another visit paid to Augusta Morell. Thane Sheridan could not understand how such a meticulous record keeper as Otto Morell could have failed to note the exact date of that final meeting he must have had with Leopold Ulric to pass him the violin.

Chapter Sixteen

For the next two days Leopold Ulric did not venture out of his duplex penthouse at the Metropolitan Tower. After returning from the concert he had immediately telephoned Sidney Nathan, who was watching the midnight newscast. After repeated assurances that he was all right Ulric instructed Nathan to cancel his next performance, scheduled for this evening, as well as postpone the remainder of his classes at the NSDM indefinitely. This unleashed another barrage of concern, which Ulric cut short by demanding that Nathan keep the media away from him. The phone he was speaking on now would be disconnected at the end of this conversation. Ulric gave Nathan another, unlisted number, to use in case of an emergency. After he had had time to absorb the shock of that evening, Ulric would call and a new performance schedule would be drafted.

As he padded silently back upstairs to the bedroom Leopold Ulric smiled to himself. The killing of the Little Cripple had been a magnificent act, consummated solely by the ferocity with which he had imbued his music. It had been an exhilarating experience to watch as the music literally reached out to Aleijadinho, embraced him, wove its invisible threads around him until . . . with a sudden jerk, a fierce projection of will, he was jerked over the side. To die like some speared, squirming fish. Aleijadinho's death had not been quick, and this too pleased the virtuoso.

If only the next incident of the evening had been so successful, Ulric mused. But Thane Sheridan had refused to die. Ulric had been aware of Sheridan in the audience, and of his purpose: to watch both himself and Aleijadinho. Nor was he surprised that Sheridan had chased him. He was

227

unique among men, this big police inspector. He alone had gone off the beaten path, abandoned usual procedure, and set out after the killer of his son in his own fashion. Or rather in the fashion he believed the killer was using. Sheridan had studied the other killings very carefully. He had learned much from them. In Chicago his patience and study had almost been rewarded. But in the last instant Ulric had slipped away.

Leopold Ulric admitted to himself that he would have been disappointed if he had been able to kill Sheridan so easily. Eventually, of course, the inspector would have to die. There was no choice in the matter because his kind did not give up. Thirst for vengeance was one of the strongest motivating factors in the human constellation. And Sheridan had an endless supply of hate to fuel his own.

How close can I bring you to me? Ulric asked silently. *In some strange way, Sheridan, I have grown to love you. You have become like no other adversary—worthy. Ever since I took your son, caused your wife to destroy herself, you have followed me, from city to city, body to body. . . . You aren't aware of this, but several times I doubled back and watched from a distance as you strove to catch me. If you only knew how sometimes I wanted to help you, give you a hint, turn you in the right direction. But instead I watched . . . watched as you were driven by your pain, your hate, your singleminded purpose. And I longed to tell you that it was a purpose I could never allow you to fulfill, for if you succeeded, then I perforce would have to be destroyed. That same purpose always kept you from truly understanding what I am, and without that understanding you could never hope to know all of me. If we were to come together, it would not be to act and kill together. No, we would be like two scorpions in a jar, and one of us—you—would have to die. . . .*

A thought stirred deep within Ulric. He had had Sheridan at his mercy. At any time he could have turned the wheel a fraction and sent him beneath the rear wheels. But Sheridan had fought hard for his life. He deserved to live. To live to try one more time.

That was it, Ulric decided. He would permit Sheridan one more chance. After he failed, he would reach out for him and take him in his grasp. Ulric's eyes gleamed in anticipation. There on the bed were his two playmates. Perhaps before he offered Sheridan to his demon, he would show him what it was the beast ate . . . how very delicious his little boy had been. . . .

The rain and sleet storm that was battering Manhattan had reserved its full fury for the exposed areas of Long Island. Many of the coastal roads beyond East Hampton were awash; the major highways were passable, but state police were warning motorists to avoid road travel when possible. Visibility was less than a hundred feet, and the constantly fluctuating temperature was causing instant ice sheets to form across the main arteries.

From behind the safety of the triple-plated floor-to-ceiling glass that served as one entire wall of his living room Emil Letelier watched the storm churn out its fury. He had no fear of the storm and in fact smiled when he heard the creaking and booming that came from the neighbors' houses farther along Dune Road. Those who built here, next to this exposed stretch of beach, did so in the resigned knowledge that once every five or six years a storm like this would erupt and cripple their houses. As far as Letelier was concerned, such surrender to the inevitable was asinine. But then again, what could one expect from morons who paid more attention to external aesthetics than to the nature of the land and sea around them?

Emil Letelier's home was constructed on concrete piles one foot in diameter. The design had not been made by a geometrically inclined Moishe Safdie or an orientalist like Erikson. Condor's Nest had been drafted by a naval architect, to stand like a ship out of water, its bow thrust out *toward* the ocean, the sweeping side lines designed to split and deflect the winds. The hewn redwood beams had been cut to precise specifications in California, and the roof was literally bolted to the superstructure. The architect had assured Letelier that even gale-force winds would do little more than rattle some shutters.

Emil Letelier turned away from the window and faced the mammoth fireplace that was visible from any point in the octagonal living room. The man standing in front of it, a cognac snifter held delicately between thick, powerful fingers, was still staring at him. Letelier was certain that this man, with the incongruous name of Nevada, had never taken his eyes off him.

"How did you get here?" Letelier asked abruptly.

"You mean, how did I arrive at your front door unannounced?" Nevada asked.

"Whichever way you wish," Letelier snapped irritably.

"Your heat and motion sensors are utterly ineffectual during this kind of storm," Nevada recited. He ran one hand over a bald shining pate, then brushed his long mustache. It was a gesture Letelier had noticed before.

"The fog and sleet pretty much obscured the video cameras . . ."

The shoulders, torso, and thighs were massive, evidence of constant workouts with weights or a Nautilus. The face was done in clean-cut lines, sharp, angular, as though it were only a rough draft. Nevada lost nothing because he wasn't tall. He moved like a cat, smoothly, silently.

"As for the dogs, the wind and water confused their scent to begin with. A few pieces of treated meat did the rest."

"They are trained not to go after meat given by anyone except the handler!"

"Then your man doesn't feed them properly." Nevada shrugged. "They were hungry."

"Was all this subterfuge necessary? After all, you were coming as my guest."

"Correction," Nevada said softly. "My arrangement was with Aleijadinho, not you."

Letelier could not quite place the man's nationality. There was some Spanish or Portuguese in him, he was certain. Or Arab.

"Aleijadinho was in my service," Letelier said.

"Granted. But that scarcely means he wanted my services on *your* behalf."

The implication was clear: This killer made no assumptions. The issue could easily have been one of a servant hiring the means by which to dispose of his master.

"It was also quite disconcerting to read that the man I was *supposed* to meet had decided to fly off into the void. Who knows the reasons for such a twist in fate?"

230

Nevada smiled. A single gold tooth glinted at Letelier.

"Aleijadinho was a loyal associate," Emil Letelier said tonelessly. "He contacted you on *my* behalf. The degree of trust I placed in him is reflected in the fact that I never intended to deal with you myself."

Letelier paused. "But under the circumstances I must. What specific details did Aleijadinho pass on to you?"

"None," Nevada stated. "However, before we proceed, let me tell you what I *do* know. You control the cocaine and amphetamine market for greater New York. Thus far your organization has been protected by various officials, municipal and state. But the citizens of Steuben Town have taken a dim view of what has been happening to their community. One Otto Morell took the initiative to move against you. When he did so, you had him murdered.

"However, you did not expect community retaliation. Otto Morell's killers were subsequently murdered. You still do not know by whom. Moreover, there have been other killings among your own people. Now your chief lieutenant is said to have committed suicide.

"All of this means you are losing face and stature among your rivals. They see you as vulnerable. You want to hire me to correct that impression."

"You're well informed," Letelier noted.

"I read a lot." Nevada smiled. "It's not hard to fill in the gaps."

Emil Letelier pursed his lips. "Aleijadinho never committed very much to paper. He had an excellent memory. However, we discussed the project briefly, enough so that I can reconstruct his plan."

His eyes bored into Nevada's.

"What I wish is a swift, short reign of terror," he said softly. "You are to go for selected targets at the same time, so that by the next dawn Steuben Town is shattered, stunned by what happened. I want an example made of those who dared to move against me."

"And who are 'they'?" Nevada asked softly.

Emil Letelier settled himself in a thronelike chair before the fireplace.

"James Hansen," he said coldly. "Coowner of Vantage Motor Works. Destroy that precious garage of his and everything in it. Make certain he suffers, but do not kill him.

"George Percy, his partner. He keeps two dogs on the premises. Destroy them and dump them on his doorstep.

"Abner Levine, delicatessen owner. Perhaps fryers would explode in his face.

"And finally, dear Augusta Morell." Letelier's eyes glittered. "I want her to die by that which she tried to stop."

He fished in his jacket pocket and tossed a small plastic packet of white substance to Nevada.

"Eighty percent pure cocaine. Treated with strychnine. Inject it into her. In all likelihood she'll rush out into traffic and kill herself. If the strychnine doesn't do the job first, the cocaine will burst her heart."

Nevada had caught the packet in his gloved palm and in one motion slipped it into his own pocket. In the heat of his desire for vengeance Emil Letelier had made a cardinal error. The heavy plastic retained fingerprints beautifully.

"And you want all this done in the space of a single evening?" Nevada queried, irony tingeing his words.

"There is a fifty percent bonus if everything happens within a specified time period."

Once again Nevada ran his palm over his bald pate, then stroked his mustache.

"I need a minimum of three days to study the movements of these people," he said. "Another two to round up the supplies. I assume they aren't to be away from the neighborhood. No sudden trips, things like that?"

"I doubt it."

"And the order in which you mentioned them, that's the way you want them taken down?"

"Exactly."

The gold tooth glittered. "I think I can accommodate you." Nevada smiled.

"I don't expect to see or hear from you again," Letelier said. "Fifty percent of the bonus will be deposited in your account tomorrow. After that I want only to read about the results in the newspapers."

"Oh, you shall," Nevada assured him. "Believe me, you shall."

Nevada declined Emil Letelier's offer to drive him to

where his vehicle was parked. Instead he shouldered his way across the half mile of muddied expanse, buffeted by the winds, to the point where he had left the Bronco four-wheel-drive truck. The vehicle fired up at once, and Nevada made his way along Dune Road to Route 27, which would take him the length of Long Island back to New York. He drove slowly, as much out of respect for the storm around him as to allow Letelier's surveillance to keep up with him. There was almost no traffic on the route, and he did not see headlights in the rearview mirror. But he knew they were there. And if they were that far back, it meant Letelier's people had found the truck and planted a locating device on it, probably a microtransmitter as well. Nevada began to hum "The Battle Hymn of the Republic" so as not to disappoint his audience.

He crossed the Fifty-ninth Street Bridge and headed downtown, always driving at a leisurely pace, stopping on yellow lights. Manhattan was deserted. Nothing, not even a gypsy cab, was out tonight. He parked on Chambers Street next to City Hall Park, let the engine idle until he saw the lights behind him, then got out and began to walk into the park. Fifty feet later Nevada turned around quickly. Letelier's people were behaving true to form. They had gotten out of their car, were crossing the street about a dozen yards behind the Bronco. The assassin reached inside his coat pocket and brought out a transmitter.

The explosion that destroyed the Bronco hurtled flaming steel across the street. The gas tank erupted seconds later, leveling whatever was left of the chassis. By the time Letelier's men had raised themselves off the street, their quarry was nowhere to be seen.

Sabina Morell spent the better part of half a day at Immigration headquarters at Duane and Worth streets. After her police ID got her into the building, the stonewalling began. First a clerk, then her supervisor, explained that all information on entrants was confidential unless written release was Telexed in from Washington. It took Mr. Bill four hours to clear Ulric's file with D.C. When the contents were finally reproduced on the clattering machine, Sabina realized the first piece of the case against the violinist was in place: Leopold Ulric had been cleared at Immigration JFK Airport three days before Rachel Rosenberg had been kidnapped, then murdered.

When she telephoned Sheridan with the news, she was disappointed by his low-key reaction.

"Can you take over for me in looking for those hookers?" he asked.

"Sure, but—"

"Look, I think I'm on to something down here, but I have to keep at it."

Her initial reaction was to want to ask for details, but Sabina quashed her curiosity. Sheridan had closeted himself in Thompson Street. She hadn't asked what he was working on, nor did he volunteer any information.

"Call me as soon as you've picked them up."

Sabina went to Manhattan North Public Morals. By calling in favors she got the files on all the young high-class hookers who had been collared in the last three months. On the strength of her Special Investigations ID she removed a duplicate of the documentation, committed it to microfiche, and headed for Margot Bell's desk.

"Sabina Morell, as Ah live 'n breathe!"

The soft Carolina drawl made Sabina laugh out loud. Margot had lived in Manhattan for the past ten years, but her accent hadn't diminished one iota. The tall, coltish girl with swirling strawberry blond hair and a face that had brought her dozens of modeling offers rose from behind her desk and embraced Sabina.

"Lord, chile, it's *good* to see you!" Margot Bell squealed. "It's been *months!*"

Sabina glanced around at the rest of the pit. The other officers looked on, their eyes hungry and resigned at the same time.

"Still a heartbreaker, eh, kid?" she whispered.

Margot tossed her hair back. "Oh, them? You mustn't pay *any* attention," she said, loud enough for everyone to hear. "They're just a bunch of good lusty guys. Isn't that right, fellas?"

Those officers who didn't wince, blushed.

"Come on, honey, let's get us some coffee and talk girl talk."

Sabina Morell imagined Strauss's "Thus Spake Zarathustra" thundering in the minds of the men as her friend walked out of the squad. She followed, shaking her head.

"You have them wrapped around your little finger," she said once they were in the battered coffee lounge.

"And sometimes between my little ole legs!"

"Gevald!" Sabina muttered.

She and Margot Bell had met up in the FBI Academy. They had done their rookie year together and roomed at Quantico during the FBI course in firearms, unarmed combat, and surveillance. Margot Bell had walked away with the sharpshooter's trophy that year. She had also bedded and broken the hearts of enough males to create a collective depression when she left.

"Scuttlebutt has it you're working for the Gray Man?" Margot said, eyes just over the rim of her cup.

"Say again?"

"Mistah William C. Rodgers."

"True enough," Sabina said quietly. "That's also why I'm here."

"Anything you need, honey." The banter was gone, replaced by a hard professional tone.

Sabina slipped the microfiche out of her purse.

"Hookers. Top of the line. Fifteen, sixteen years old at most. I'm looking for a pair that serviced Aleijadinho, Letelier's lieutenant. Have you heard of him?"

"Oh, yes." Margot nodded.

"He was a cripple who liked young fluff. Because of his handicap he may well have had a select few whom he always called for. I'm gambling that that was the case."

Margot tapped the microfiche with an elegantly sculptured fingernail.

"And this?"

"A three-month sheet out of midtown. I'm hoping you'll recognize some names."

"The memory's pretty good. Follow me, chile," Margot said.

"Are you desk-bound now or still working under cover?"

Sabina asked as they took the elevator to the fourth floor morgue with its audio and film equipment.

"Honey, Ah'm *always* under cover!"

Sabina winced.

"But Ah tell you, this has got to be the plushest job Ah've ever landed. Lots of diplomats and such uptown. Foreigners who want the Minnesota blondies right off the bus. But all very discreet. Ah work the clubs and bars where these dudes roam, or rather their drivers and assistants. When the pick-up is made, Ah follow them home and bust them on the doorstep. The kid goes to Morals, the driver and principal generally walk. Diplomatic immunity, you know . . ."

Suddenly her voice became hard.

"But I tell you, honey, one day some fucking Arab or Frenchie is going to lay a hand on me, and I'm going to break his dick in half. Their immunity don't mean jack shit to me. Not when they use it to corrupt children."

Margot flashed a smile at the elder officer behind the counter and signed in. She led Sabina straight to the back, moving between high metal cabinets crammed with yellowing files. Facing the grime-laden windows were three microfiche machines. Sabina pulled up a chair as Margot slipped in the plastic, switched on the unit, and began to scan.

"This have anything to do with that psycho who's been taking our babies?" Margot asked softly, her eyes dead on the screen before her.

"Everything."

"When you find him, take him down hard, honey. His kind *never* get any better."

Although Margot Bell had a tender social conscience and devoted a good deal of her free time to the Shelter the Homeless program, she had no mercy for anyone who hurt children. That was why she stuck to Public Morals instead of any of the dozen other more exotic assignments she could have drawn.

"Okay, this one looks familiar."

Margot froze the frame, and Sabina jotted down the file number.

"Yes, remember her *well*," Margot said softly, staring at

the face, which, even in black and white, was too young, too vulnerable to be anywhere but in a high school yearbook.

A few minutes later she picked out three more. By the time the microfiche ran out, Sabina had noted five file numbers.

"All but one of them are run by a pimp called Ludwig," Margot said, getting to her feet. "Rumor has it his daddy was a Hun."

"Know where to find him?"

Margot glanced at her watch.

"Half past four . . . Hell, Ludwig ought to be getting out of bed just about now. Let me make a call and see which hole he crawled into for his beauty rest."

They made it to West End Avenue and Eighty-first Street in fifteen minutes.

"The last time I was here, there was a church on this corner." Sabina looked at Margot. "Wasn't there?"

"Oh, yes, honey, there surely was," Margot said, getting out of the car. She looked up at the gray concrete and brown brick high-rise that had gone up during the summer and fall. "I guess God believes in co-ops. Land values being what they are . . ."

She looked back at the car. "That's one hot set of wheels. Rodgers is doin' right by you."

Sabina recognized the opening gambit but let it pass. Margot was too good a cop to press and would wait for her to volunteer information. There was nothing Sabina could tell her. Not right now.

"How many places does this Ludwig have?" she asked.

"Four. Scattered all 'round town. I know what you're thinking, but this snitch is golden. If she says L. is here, that's where we'll find him."

The Puerto Rican elevator boy clicked his teeth in appreciation as the two women entered the lobby of a prewar building.

"Hit it, sonny, and keep your eyes on the road," Margot snapped at him.

"Arriba, arriba, ándale, ándale!"

They were in the twelfth-floor corridor when Margot slowed and took out a .357 Magnum from her purse. Without breaking stride she screwed a custom-designed silencer on to the barrel.

"It's going to be like that?" Sabina murmured.

Margot shrugged. "You never know."

Sabina positioned herself on the left side of the door, withdrew her own weapon as Margot rapped twice. After a few seconds a young girl's voice, low, trembling.

"Who is it?"

"Police. Open it up."

The footsteps retreated quickly, just as she expected. Without hesitation Margot pumped two bullets into the doorframe, one just above the knob, the other four inches higher, where in all probability there was a chain. The door swung open on its own momentum, the thick steel chain dangling, splintered.

"Ludwig, it's Morals."

Somewhere in the recesses of the apartment a toilet gurgled.

"Stupid son of a bitch," Margot breathed. "Two grand worth of coke shot for nothing."

She raised her voice. "Come on out, Ludwig, honey. Nice and easy, arms on the head."

The corridor ran the length of the apartment. The walls had been done in rough plaster and smelled fresh. The dark floorboards shone beneath the overhead track lighting.

"Is that you, Margot?" a male voice called out, followed by another flushing.

"Yes, it's me. Come on out, Ludwig. This is no time to be shy. I've brought a friend. We're here to talk, not to take you down."

The black who appeared in the corridor was tall, with exceptionally long bare legs. He wore only a tank top and shorts, and his hands were fumbling with the zipper. Gold coins on a loop set off a glistening ebony chest.

"Gotta let a man answer nature's call," Ludwig said, breaking into a smile. Very slowly he moved his hands away, fingers splayed. "Now, you just take one good look at me, momma. You *know* I ain't armed. Except for this." He patted the bulge around his crotch.

"Fuck off," Margot told him, matching his smile. "Where can we talk?"

"Why, right here." Ludwig's arm swept to the right. "But we don't have nothin' talk about 'cept that shot-up door. And your warrant."

In five quick steps Margot reached him, the silencer against Ludwig's kidneys.

"How much fluff you got in here?" she asked coldly. "And talk to me straight, honey, I'm in one shitty mood."

"Hey, no problem. Only three out-of-town visitors."

"Where?"

"They're restin' right now."

"Okay, Ludwig, let's retire to your study."

Margot pushed him into a room done up in Italian modern. The design was perfect down to the gold-flake wallpaper.

"You've redecorated, Ludwig."

The pimp shrugged. "You know how it is, a man's got to keep up with the times."

"Sit down there on that thing that resembles a chair."

Ludwig squatted down on the mobile cushion, elbows on knees, hands between his legs.

"Who's your friend?" he asked, grinning up at Sabina.

"We want to know where a couple of your girls are," Margot told him, fishing out a pair of photos. Her gun was lowered, but from Ludwig's expression she knew Sabina had hers trained, probably on his genitals.

Ludwig's eyes flickered across the photos.

"Can't really say—" he began.

"Cut the shit, Ludwig!" Margot hissed. "I'm not here to tromp all over you, although it's high time I did—just to keep you honest. Give me what I need, without the crap, and we'll be on our way."

"I say, momma—"

"Otherwise we bust hard, Ludwig. And I don't need any fucking warrant when I have suspicion of a felony. Now you've gone and flushed some vitamin C down the chute. You're going to need all the money your fluff in there can pull in. And when you put them out on the street, I'll be there. I'll ram that pimp-mobile of yours and in the course of arrest burn your wardrobe. *Then* where will you be?"

"Let me see the pictures!" Ludwig said, voice low, dangerous.

"Did you send any of these girls to Aleijadinho two nights ago?"

"Yeah, those two."

"Where are they now?"

The black bit his lip. Margot had never seen him so worried.

"Come on, Ludwig," she coaxed.

"Listen, you gotta know, after what happened at the Met—"

"Like what?"

"You know, the cripple becoming a flyer."

"So?"

"Well, the ladies were strung out."

"And being the sugar daddy you are, you thought the best way to make them forget was to get them right back into action," Margot snarled.

"You gotta understand, they was requested!"

"What do you mean?" Sabina broke in sharply.

"They didn't show up after that," Ludwig said.

"Ludwig, I'm tired of pulling teeth. Let's move it, shall we."

"What I mean is, a dude called me."

"Who and how did he get the number."

"Said one of the ladies gave it to him."

"He took the girls?" Sabina demanded.

"Yeah, said he was going to party with them."

"Shit, Ludwig, you don't expect us to buy that!"

"Then buy this, bitch!" Ludwig's head snapped up, eyes seething with hate. "The fucker came by in a limo and paid up front for three days. Double rate."

"Who was he?" Sabina asked, voice flat.

"Don't know. Kinda short, with curly hair, mid-forties maybe older. Looked like a promoter, record executive, somethin' like that."

"And the plate number, Ludwig," Margot said. "You'd never let your stable off the leash."

The numbers on the license meant nothing to Sabina, but the description did. She was willing to bet her pension that one name connected the two.

Chapter Seventeen

River Towers was a massive affair of stone blocks which loomed over Eightieth Street and the East River. Located on Eightieth, its front portals with their elegant grillwork faced East End, dominating the street much as a monarch, seated at the head of the table, towered over his knights.

Built in the mid-twenties, River Towers, with its turrets, crenels, and merlons, exuded personality. Abner Levine thought it expressed a lofty disdain. The other co-ops and condominiums along Eightieth might be modern, taller, and provide more contemporary amenities, but they had no soul. Their exteriors were singularly unappealing. The interiors couldn't compete with River Towers' twelve-foot ceilings, foot-thick walls, beveled windows, and fireplaces of green and black Italian marble.

Abner Levine was standing by the concierge's desk in the magnificent domed lobby. He looked fondly around him, noting appreciatively the trappings of style, the Deladier chandelier, the paneled walls with oils under soft accent lights, the high gloss leather couches, and the carefully placed vases of fresh flowers.

"Thank the Lord some things don't change," he said softly.

"Here life will never change," Bleeker said. "Because if it does, it will mean the end of River Towers."

Levine looked up at the aging porter. Bleeker had been in this building for as long as anyone could remember. Levine had first met him a scant nine years ago, when he had first catered for the Grafsteins.

241

"Gently with that trolley!" he called out to the teenaged black wheeling a cart into the elevators.

Bleeker looked askance at Levine.

"A community project," Levine said. "Someone's got to give the kids a chance."

"You're a good man, sir."

"And amen to that." Levine smiled.

He turned around and waved to his wife. She was leading two other teenagers, who were also pushing large aluminum carts. Esther Levine rolled her eyes theatrically. Her husband shrugged. He did not feel comfortable bringing catering through the main lobby either, but River Tower security had insisted. All deliveries now came through here. The servants' and delivery entrances had been sealed after a kidnap team had penetrated the Tower and almost made it to the seventh floor, the whole of which belonged to a former secretary of state. The private security firm hired to overhaul the system had also recommended Bleeker's dismissal, noting that he was an anachronism. The net result of that recommendation was the outraged owners' threat to cancel the firm's contract. But the firm backed off quickly, and now Bleeker coexisted with a team of eight agents who monitored the activity of the building from what had once been the superintendent's quarters.

"That's the last of it, then," Levine said. "Got to be getting up there."

Bleeker, resplendent in navy blazer and gray trousers, straightened his back a fraction. It had taken him a long time to break the habit of touching his cap.

"We shall see you on the way out, sir."

Levine waved his hand and stepped into the elevator. He gazed up at the camera lens nestled in the upper left corner and snorted. It was a different world now, even here.

The Grafsteins' apartment had three entrances: the central one with two double doors, another to the storage room, and a third, which opened directly to the pantry. Levine chose this one and walked inside.

The pantry was the size of an ordinary bedroom. Even with the cupboards and shelves there was more than enough room for Esther to do the final preparations. Two of the boys were lifting out trays of finger sandwiches, each one made by Levine's cooks under Esther's guidance. The food leaned toward the tastes of a Jewish palate. Among the delicacies prepared for the buffet were a dozen varieties of smoked fish, chopped liver as the centerpiece of the meats, freshly made cole slaw, sweet pimiento peppers, sours in brine, onion rolls, still warm, a dozen loaves of caraway seed rye, and trays and dishes of other temptingly exotic specialties.

"Abner, Esther, you've gone and outdone yourselves again!"

Mordecai Grafstein, short, slim, with a Dali mustache that dominated his face, poked his head around the corner.

"Sours!" he said dreamily and snatched a pickle from the tray.

"Mr. Grafstein, there is more than enough for everyone. If you want, ask!"

The senior senator from New York winked and chomped. His beautiful wife, Amanda, appeared, three maids in tow.

"Are we ready? The children will be here any moment."

"Boys!" Esther Levine commanded, and the trays were passed.

"So, Abner, let's go into the kitchen and get out of the way."

The kitchen, done in white tile with a slate floor, was twice the size of the pantry. Mordecai Grafstein was a gourmand who delighted in gadgetry. Levine hated to think what his electricity bill for this room alone was.

In spite of his protestations Grafstein poured the delicatessen owner a Beck's and a whiskey for himself.

"L'chaim, Abner!"

"L'chaim, Mordecai!"

The two men sipped their drinks, sitting back, at ease with each other.

"How goes it in the neighborhood, Abner?" asked Grafstein.

"Not well . . . not well at all." Levine looked at him over the rim of his glass. "Nothing will be well until we get rid of Letelier."

Grafstein said nothing. He knew as well as anyone, maybe better, what Steuben Town was going through. He

243

made it a point to be informed. The community had always supported him, and he also had many friends there, of whom Levine was the closest. He looked upon the deli owner as a spokesman.

"To tell you we're doing what we can, *as fast* as we can, is poor comfort," Grafstein said heavily. "But I give you my word, Abner: Letelier will be put away."

"Of that I have no doubt," Levine said. It sounded to Grafstein like a categorical statement.

"I want you to believe me, Abner," Grafstein said, leaning forward on the table. "I'm speaking to you as a friend, an old friend."

"And I accept what you say in that light," Levine answered. "But with all the killing, the violence of the South Americans . . ."

"If we can shut down Letelier, close his drug operation, the neighborhood will be different!" Grafstein said vehemently. "The Colombians, Ecuadorians, Dominicans, they're not bad people, Abner! But most of them are like you or my father were: scared, poor, huddling together in the only form of community they know. You can't break something like that overnight."

"I know, Mordecai, I know. I have no quarrel with you on that point. But you people in Albany must move, and quickly. Otherwise there will be nothing left to save."

His eyes darted to his left. "I think we're being watched!" he said conspiratorially.

Mordecai Grafstein turned around. "Got you now. Come on!"

The twins bounded into the room.

Hannah and Ruth Grafstein. Nine years of exuberant, dark-haired energy, punctuated by their father's flashing green eyes, softened by the peaches and cream complexion inherited from their mother.

"Uncle Abe!" they squealed delightedly, flinging their arms around his neck, planting wet kisses on his grizzled cheeks. Abner Levine hugged the girls, rumpling their hair.

"Oh, Uncle, you shouldn't have!"

In unison they stood back and smoothed out their curly locks.

244

Children, Abner Levine thought. What a joyful yet terrible way to measure time.

He had known Hannah and Ruth when they were in swaddling clothes. The celebration of their birth, when they were two days old, was the occasion of his first catering for Mordecai Grafstein. Since then, he had been here every year on their birthday. The first few years he had provided his finest delicacies for the adult gatherings the Grafsteins held in honor of the births; then, when the twins were old enough to have their own parties, he had included a special selection for their friends. In the course of time a gentle love had grown between Abner and the twins. It was more precious to him than he dared to admit. Looking upon them now, seeing how they had grown, he realized that he must have aged twice as fast. How many more occasions like this one were left to him?

The twins oohed and ahed at the trays of food still being carried from the pantry. They clustered around Esther, badgering her about the cake. This too was ritual. The girls knew they wouldn't get a glimpse of it until the right moment, when it would be wheeled in, eighteen candles glowing, nine for each sister.

"You and Esther will be staying," Mordecai Grafstein said, draining his glass.

That too was part of tradition: Although those who attended the twins' birthday party, bringing their own children, were the wealthy and powerful, Grafstein always insisted that his friend stay.

And as always Abner Levine said, "Thank you, for a little while."

At half past five the first guests began arriving. For the most part they were younger than the Grafsteins, who had had their children late in life, when Mordecai was forty-five, his wife thirty-nine. The mix, leavened with a sprinkling of Mordecai's associates, was perfect. Legal minds took on the arts, bankers bantered with publishers, and media celebrities huddled with conglomerate directors.

While in the other wing of the apartment the children held their own party. . . .

Julian Foster had noticed the twins' absence when he helped one of the maids roll in the gaily painted wagon which resembled one of the thousand hot-dog wagons on Manhattan street corners. Under the pink-and-white umbrella were steam trays of weiners, buns, fries, and other delights that fueled puberty. There were fourteen children in the room, most of them already seated at the long catering-style table, nudging one another in the ribs, pointing at the wagon.

Where were the twins?

Julian Foster whispered to the maid to take the orders while he slipped out into the kitchen. Foster was British, a companion who tutored the twins in music and art history. He had been chosen by Mordecai Grafstein after a long and thorough search. The senior senator from New York demanded a man who could also protect his offspring. Julian Foster, who had served on the London Metropolitan Police Force and had functioned as bodyguard to the young Prince Andrew, was such a man.

Foster moved through the kitchen quickly, his eyes missing nothing. He opened the door to the pantry. The twins were ingenious in finding ways to get what they wanted—from a peek at their cake to a new pony.

The cake trolley was there, the linen cloth draped over the handles, the cake beneath it ready. No trace of finger smears on the icing.

Foster moved quickly. He glided unobtrusively through the cocktail party in the living room, checked the sunroom, the conservatory, Mordecai Grafstein's private den, and the twin balconies. He took the stairs to the second floor two at a time and made a thorough search of the entire floor—all five bedrooms, the guest quarters, his own room and the maid's, the bathrooms and sauna.

Nothing.

Returning downstairs to the party, he saw the maid cheerfully lining the children up for hot dogs. Still no sign of the twins. Julian Foster moved quickly to the tiny cubicle off the main doors, next to the hall closets. Locking himself in, he activated the cameras. The six screens on the console gave him a view of both corridors of River Towers, the elevators, the lobby, and the garage.

Nothing.

Had he been a less experienced man, Julian Foster

might have hesitated. Perhaps he would have conducted another search of the apartment. But he felt his heart moving fast, adrenaline pumping saliva into his mouth. Every instinct about protection, survival, danger that had been honed during his years of training was screaming. He picked up the phone and within a few seconds was speaking to River Towers security. Even as he was detailing the situation men were moving throughout the building, covering all conceivable exits, checking the gardens and garage.

Five sweat-filled minutes later security called him back: no sign of either Ruth or Hannah Grafstein. The Nineteenth Precinct of the NYPD had been notified, cars were on the way.

"I'm already running late, Sergeant. I'd appreciate it if you'd keep it brief and to the point."

Sidney Nathan slipped some buff files into an inordinately expensive Ian Mankin briefcase, snapped the locks, and glanced up at Sabina Morell.

She was standing before his desk, thinking that the briefcase was a fair reflection of the agent's taste: subdued and very expensive.

"Are you the registered owner of a 1983 Cadillac Pullman limousine, license PVR-733?" she asked without preamble.

"That's my car. Why? Has it been in an accident?"

"On the night of February 14 were you in your car around 1 A.M.?"

Three distinct stress lines appeared on the agent's forehead. "Yes . . ."

"And did you at that time go to an address on West End Avenue, to six seventy-two to be exact?"

She could tell by the eyes that he knew she knew.

"What's this all about, Sergeant?" Nathan asked softly.

Sabina's eyes bored into his. "According to my information you had two young girls, *underaged girls*, in your car. You drove to West End Avenue to pay their pimp for their services for three days."

"I don't have to listen to any more of this garbage!" Nathan said stonily. "Anything more you have to say can be said to my attorney."

"That's the hard way of doing it," Sabina said. "You can go that route." She paused. "But if I waste my time on you and there's another homicide, I'm going to haul you in as an accomplice. Obstruction at the very least. Count on it."

"What are you *talking* about?" Nathan whispered. "What homicide?"

"In case you haven't been reading the papers, we have kids being murdered or disappearing off the streets," Sabina said acidly.

"I know all about that—"

"What *I* want to know is who those two girls were for!"

Sidney Nathan drummed his perfectly manicured nails on his crystal-topped desk.

"Hookers," he muttered.

"That much I gathered," Sabina said acidly. "For yourself?"

"No!" Nathan realized what he had blurted out. "Oh, shit!"

"Shit is right. Now you'll go straight down the line, or else I'll charge you with procuring and corrupting minors."

"They weren't for me," Nathan repeated. He swung his chair around, and gazed out the window at the skyscraper.

"Were these the girls?" Sabina tossed two photographs on the desk.

The agent didn't even bother to pick them up.

"Yes."

"You collected them at the Met after their original client became a flyer."

"How did you know that?" Nathan asked, his gaze unwavering.

"Who told you to pick them up?" Sabina asked softly.

The agent swiveled his chair around.

"Detective Morell, in addition to being an intermediary and business manager, I am also licensed to practice law in the State of New York. That being the case, I must observe the confidentiality of an attorney-client relationship." He paused. "Do you understand what I'm telling you?"

Sabina understood well enough. He wanted to tell her

248

but not in so many words. Nathan was gambling that she would remember Leopold Ulric was his client.

"Where did you take the girls?"

"I dropped them off near the Metropolitan Tower on Fifty-fourth. I couldn't tell you where they went from there."

She looked at his impassive features. "You don't have to concern yourself with that," she said.

Just before she opened the door, she turned back to him.

"Your efforts on behalf of your clients are commendable," she said dryly. And walked out.

Thane Sheridan looked at the collection of files, Telexes, data printouts, the tire tread match-ups, a piece of his coat off the Aston fender, the Xian horsehair string off a violin bow, and finally the Customs log documenting Leopold Ulric's entry into the United States three days before Rachel Rosenberg's murder. He called this hard evidence. The courts would label it circumstantial.

Sheridan felt the cool air prickle the hairs on the back of his neck. He wished the windows of this apartment hadn't been hermetically sealed. Even though the air was recycled every hour, the odor of sweat and cigarettes somehow eluded the filters. He rose, paced, then returned to the desk and leaned forward on his arms, looking over the piles of data as a general would his troop placements.

He was right. He could smell it, taste it. He could almost *see* Ulric doing it. . . . Sheridan looked up at the large map of the U.S. he had tacked on the wall. A series of red lines linked the cities of San Francisco, Denver, Las Vegas, Tallahassee, St. Louis, and Chicago. Above each city was a slip of paper with two dates: when the bodies of the children had been found and the time when Leopold Ulric had been in that city. Without exception Leopold Ulric had arrived three days before the murder of the first child. He had left twenty-one or twenty-three days later, always within forty-eight hours after the bodies had been discovered.

Six cities . . . In four Leopold Ulric had performed a series of concerts as guest soloist with the local orchestra. There had been no performance in Las Vegas. Instead Ulric had had a recording session in the new RCA studio. According to Sheridan's information the facilities were experimental, unique. The Recording Company of America had enticed Ulric with more money than it had ever lavished on any one performer. But to Sheridan the reasoning was obvious: If a performer of Ulric's caliber and temperament was pleased with the equipment, RCA had its imprimatur. There wasn't a recording studio in the world that wouldn't sit up and take notice.

Tallahassee had been the odd city out. It had neither a world-class orchestra nor a university music department that could have enticed Ulric to lecture there. Nor had Ulric stayed in the city: There were no hotel records with his name in them. Sheridan had spent three hours trying to find the handle before an American Express car rental record came over the computer. Then another, then three more for a total of five. Five trips between New Orleans and Tallahassee. In each case the cars had been rented the day before another child had disappeared. The rentals had spanned a twenty-one-day period.

Sheridan's eyes followed the red lines.

Why? Why did you choose these cities, so different from one another? There's no connection between any of the victims. No relationship between their parents and you. So what made you kidnap and murder the children?

Motive. Sheridan realized his argument would be ripped open for lack of a motive. Under the guise of a routine spot check Customs and Immigration had had Interpol and the West German Ministry of the Interior run a check on Leopold Ulric. Interpol had come up with nothing. The Germans had reported back that the violinist didn't even have an outstanding parking ticket. In both cases, Sheridan was informed, queries had come back to Washington as to why a check was necessary on such a public figure. Sheridan had immediately closed down any further probes. He couldn't chance a leak on the other side of the Atlantic, a leak which would undoubtedly find its way back to Ulric's agent and finally to the musician himself. He didn't want to cause a ripple of suspicion.

Why did you kill them?

Sheridan had hated to pull back the probes because he

250

still did not know his man. He had had the FBI scanners unearth everything that had been printed on the musician, but without exception they had found absolutely nothing about his personal life. From *Time* to *Paris Match* and *Der Stern* the articles extolled Ulric's musical genius and his almost flagrantly ostentatious life-style in the fast lane. The gossip papers continually linked him to a dozen starlets and jet-setters. But there was absolutely nothing about the man, who he was, where he had come from. And Leopold Ulric guarded his privacy in a hard, brutal way. When a London journalist had announced he would undertake an unauthorized biography, the virtuoso had retaliated like a striking snake. The journalist's publisher was put on notice by Ulric's London lawyers that if the project went ahead, a lawsuit would be launched immediately. Sidney Nathan had informed the London Philharmonic that his client would cancel a series of concerts and recordings. The music powers huddled with the publisher who then worked their way out of the contract. The journalist had written two outraged articles about the matter for a tabloid, but nothing more had come of it.

What are you hiding?

Thane Sheridan knew Ulric was a particular kind of killer, the most elusive because he had enough control over his madness—at least until now—not to kill where he lived. Although Ulric traveled a great deal, his spiritual home was Europe, West Germany. There were no reports from there of children being kidnapped and murdered. Nor from France, Italy, England, or Spain. Not anywhere Ulric "lived."

Leopold Ulric could calm the bloody passions which aroused him until he was traveling. He had made a number of sojourns to the United States during the last two years. That was when he had begun killing, well away from his home, on alien territory he could safely leave when the lust had been satisfied.

Yet there was something else. The pattern Sheridan could not understand. The undeniable ritual that lay under the seemingly haphazard choice of victims and locales.

What are you answering to?

Somewhere within Ulric was a twisted need to feed powers which he believed he had to satisfy. Powers only he could see or feel, which were invisible, inaudible to anyone else. These demanded sacrifice, a kind of sacrifice that could only be accomplished through ritual. Hence the killing of the first child, to open the door to the beast. Then the abductions and the mass slaughter when all the victims were assembled.

Maybe you're breaking, Sheridan thought. *Perhaps the time has come when you can't control the passion any longer. In San Francisco, Denver, Chicago, and all the other cities you killed children who had no connection with one another. But now you're taking them from one specific area: the New School of Drama and Music. That doesn't make sense! I know you realize this. So why do you continue to do it?*

Not because Leopold Ulric wanted to be caught. Psychopaths of his sort did not retain that shred of conscience which eventually wormed its way into a killer's methodology and made him careless. If they had ever possessed a conscience, it had been stolen a very long time ago. Sheridan knew that if he could ever unravel Ulric's mind, he would discover a history of killings. Somewhere in the years gone by there were countless bodies. Perhaps the first had been dogs and cats, chickens and other farm creatures. A series of animal slayings that stopped as abruptly as it had begun. A few months or a year later a hobo or derelict would have been found with his throat slashed, an incident almost impossible to trace back, unless the craving for blood had driven Ulric to murder several helpless men. And from the helpless he would have proceeded to others, maybe even the very young.

If I dig long and deep enough, I'll find the bones. If nothing else, there will be the bones. . . .

But now I have to take you. Somehow I must take you before you kill again. Even if I break your pattern, that might be enough. Because if I have to release you and you are ravaged by craving, you will make that one mistake. . . .

The blue phone sounded. Even before Sheridan had the receiver by his ear, Sabina was speaking.

"The Grafstein twins, daughters of the senator—they

were taken from a birthday party in their home. Thane, they also attend classes at NSDM . . ."

"Get over to the Metropolitan Tower! I'll meet you there. We're going to take him now."

Chapter Eighteen

"Mr. Ulric is not at home."

Thane Sheridan stared down the impassive expression of the Metropolitan Tower concierge. The man's eyes flickered once more to the gold shield lying on the cold marble counter.

"How do you know that?" Sheridan asked tonelessly.

"The alarms in the suite activate as soon as the front door key bolts the lock," the concierge said. "I know for a fact that no one but Mr. Ulric has a key to his suite. Except the building manager, who carries a master."

"Couldn't he have locked himself in from the inside?" Sabina demanded.

The concierge shook his head. "There are two locks on each door. One is used to secure the suite from the inside; the other needs the key and closes the door from the outside."

"Get the manager," Sheridan snapped. He touched Sabina on the shoulder, and they moved into the center of the lobby.

"What happened at the Grafsteins'?" he said in a low voice. They had arrived at the Metropolitan Tower literally within seconds of each other. There hadn't been time for her to tell him anything.

Sabina quickly ran down the details of the Grafstein party, the discovery of the twins' absence by their companion, Julian Foster, and the subsequent alarm.

"River Towers security has nothing on any of their surveillance tapes for this afternoon," she said. "I did a fast scan on them. The ones from this morning and yesterday will be delivered to Securitex headquarters within the hour. We can pick them up there."

"You're thinking someone tunneled his way in a day ago and waited?"

"Even that doesn't sit right with me," Sabina said. "River Towers security is considered to be the best. If someone got past it, he, she, or they are top-of-the-line professionals."

She paused. "Thane, as much as I can't believe it, there's no other explanation. The guest list at the cocktail party reads like a Who's Who of New York. We're checking the junior partners at Grafstein's firm, those who brought their kids, bit I doubt we'll turn up anything. They've been vetted a dozen times over."

"What about servants?"

"They're the obvious suspects, but Grafstein vouches for each and every one of them."

"Anyone else leave the premises before the alarms went off?"

"One catering truck, belonging to Abner Levine's delicatessen. It's traditional for Levine to do the food for the party. He and Grafstein are old friends."

She anticipated his next question. "We have the truck, the driver, and three boys who were helping Levine. First reports indicate they couldn't have had anything to do with it."

"How so?"

"Levine left his cousin, Saul, in charge of the store. The truck arrived at the store within twenty-five minutes of leaving Grafstein's residence. There's no way it could have made a detour."

"One stop, a few seconds to transfer the kids . . . that's all it would take," Sheridan said tensely.

"Forensic's going over the vehicle, but don't get your hopes up."

She touched his arm. "Thane, is Ulric the one? Are you absolutely sure?"

He read the desperation in her voice and wanted so much to say yes.

"He is. We don't have enough to put him away, but all

the pieces fit. I can make him nervous, get him to make a mistake . . . if I can find him!"

When Sheridan strode back to the desk, another man, slim, short, and dapper, was waiting for him.

"Inspector Sheridan?"

"The same. We'd like to see Ulric's suite."

"Have you a warrant?"

"I have cause to believe that Mr. Ulric is the victim of an extortion conspiracy."

The manager paled. "But I don't understand—"

"Despite our instructions Ulric is probably in the course of carrying out the ransom demand. If we move quickly, perhaps we can forestall what will otherwise turn out to be a tragedy." Sheridan paused. "Even a fatality."

The manager looked hard at Sheridan, trying to read the truth or the lie in his eyes. Sheridan knew the manager would believe him. The urgency and desperation that underlined his words were not false. Only they were there not for Ulric but for the children.

"If you would follow me . . ." the manager said.

Thane Sheridan expected to find nothing of consequence in Ulric's duplex, and that was exactly the case. Of all the rooms in the suite only the library and bedroom on the second level felt lived in. The rest could have been a theatrical set.

"His violin is here, but look at this."

He passed an official-looking receipt to Sabina. It was a sales slip from Tiffany's.

"A hundred grand," Sheridan whispered, loud enough for the manager to overhear. "Paid in cash."

Abruptly he turned to the manager.

"Nothing you've heard must go beyond these wall," he said urgently. "Until we find Mr. Ulric . . ."

He let the implication sink in.

"You have my word," the manager said firmly. "If there's anything else I can do—"

"Just make sure the concierge understands."

The manager held a finger to the side of his nose.

Just before the elevator doors opened to the lobby, he said, "Good luck, Inspector. I sincerely hope you find him."

"Bet your tight little ass, I'll find him!" Sheridan said through his teeth once they were outside.

"Now what?" asked Sabina.

"Let's get out of this rain and into my car."

She lit cigarettes for both of them as Sheridan moved the vehicle half a block away from any prying eyes at the Metropolitan Tower lobby.

"What did you find, Thane?" Sabina asked quietly.

The story came out in a rush of words, fueled by adrenaline, frustration, and guilt . . . guilt at not having put the pieces together sooner. Much sooner.

"But as you say, there's nothing we can take to court."

"The son of a bitch will never see the inside of a courtroom!" Sheridan said savagely. Suddenly he dropped his head back against the headrest and closed his eyes.

"Which way to go on this?" he whispered. "Put out an APB . . ."

"If you're sure, if you mean to take him down, then an all points bulletin works against you," Sabina said.

"But if it's only two of us after him—"

"He might take another child—or kill—before we get to him."

"Would Nathan know where he is? Could we lean on him?"

Sabina shook her head. "Ulric's canceled his NSDM classes indefinitely. His next concert appearance isn't until Tuesday, four days from now. Apparently Nathan is used to Ulric's disappearing between concerts unless there are other things—gala dinners, openings—which have been specifically included in his schedule."

"If he runs now, out of the country, we won't get him back," Sheridan said. "There's no way extradition proceedings will work against someone like him. Not with the kind of evidence we have."

"And if he leaves, then the children he's already taken will die," Sabina said dully. "We'll never find them in time." She paused. "He may even kill them before he leaves. He could be doing that right now."

Sheridan reached for the radio-telephone.

"The airports have to be covered. All along the East Coast. The Metroliners out of Grand Central to Boston,

258

Washington, Montreal, and Toronto. We'll alert Canadian border patrols."

"Only to report contact or to intercept?" Sabina queried.

"To report contact only." He looked up at her. "I don't think he's going to run. He's going to stay here until whatever he's begun is finished. We might not get wind of him for twenty-four, maybe forty-eight hours, but he'll still be here."

Just before the connection was made to Mr. Bill's office, Sheridan said, "There's also Nevada to send after him."

The events that followed dovetailed perfectly with Thane Sheridan's plans. The New York papers kept the Grafstein twins' kidnapping on the front page for two days straight. AP and UPI picked up the story and went national with it, supplementing the coast-to-coast coverage provided by the networks.

That Saturday a long piece appeared in the *Times* in which an enterprising reporter outlined the common elements in the Rachel Rosenberg murder and the subsequent abductions. The primary one was the fact that all the victims had been students at the NSDM.

Which led the Fourth Estate to Leopold Ulric. Nathan's office was inundated with so many calls concerning the violinist's whereabouts that the agent relented and gave a full-scale press conference. On the Saturday night news Sheridan watched the agent try to convince reporters that he had no idea where Ulric was. The virtuoso had been so upset by the first kidnapping that he had canceled his NSDM classes indefinitely. There was no telling when these would resume. As for the Tuesday concert Nathan assured the press that Ulric would play. His client was, the agent declared, a consummate professional who had never in his entire career disappointed an audience. As an artiste Ulric had the right to privacy and contemplation, especially in view of the disconcerting circumstances.

Smooth as snot, Sheridan thought, disgusted, and switched off the set.

But if the press relented from persecuting Sidney Nathan, they released the full force of their righteous queries upon the police. The commissioner's press office was inun-

259

dated with demands for a special task force. Rumors concerning off-duty vigilante officers patrolling certain areas of the city were rampant. The ranks of private security agencies were depleted.

Yet the facts remained: The police had no suspects in either the Mackenzie or the Grafstein abduction. Nor anything more on the Rosenberg killing. Thane Sheridan thought of Abe Rosenberg, the man who refused to utter a sound until his daughter's killer was brought to justice. . . .

Still, the press had turned out to be an unwitting ally. Its members were on the lookout for Ulric. The stories had also made an impression on the border patrols, who, according to the deputy director of the northeast region, were paying closer attention to highway and rail travelers.

The two hookers, Sheridan thought. *If we can find them, we'll find Ulric.*

And Leopold Ulric was scheduled to perform at the Met on Tuesday. If Sheridan didn't get to him before then, Ulric would kill again. Sheridan had no doubt of this. Finally he had cracked the riddle of Ulric's pattern of lust.

The house on the North Shore of Long Island reigned over four acres of Brookville land. Set well in from the road, the mansion, a miniature duplicate of the Trianon, was shuttered for the winter. But the guest house, a three-bedroom cottage, had been opened and cleaned on the owner's instructions. The caretakers were not informed of the visitor's identity. He would have his own key and was not to be bothered. Leopold Ulric knew that the word of Lord Francis Grey, owner of England's largest movie production conglomerate, would be obeyed to the letter.

Beyond the French windows the surf was boiling along the sand, creeping up quickly on the beach, driven by wind which would not spend itself. Even though it was only half past three, the gray in the sky was quickly giving way to black. On the horizon Ulric saw the greenish tinge of the thunder line.

He turned around. "It is time. Get dressed."

The two child whores were stretched out before the fireplace, a mink rug between their bodies and the carpet.

They were naked, fingers trailing over each other's bodies, the lazy prelude to passion.

"Now!" Ulric spoke softly.

The girls rose in one motion and with a loving smile at him left the room. Ulric watched them go. They had been with him ever since the killing of the Little Cripple. And they would remain by him for as long as he decreed. The music had ground out their cores, turned them into hollow people, with no will other than his own.

Leopold Ulric walked over to the coffee table and picked up the photographs. He had had the girls for two days. During this time there wasn't anything they hadn't done for him, to him, or to each other. Yet not a flicker of emotion passed over his features as he flipped through the color Polaroids. Suddenly he laughed, a harsh, guttural sound. Perhaps he should leave them for Sir Francis. His fondness for the underaged of both sexes was legendary. But Leopold Ulric never left mementos of his visits. Carefully he fed the photos to the fire, fascinated by the orange, green, and blue flames as the heat worked on the chemicals. That was how he imagined the fires of hell to look, all different colors, blending, changing, always consuming. He thought of his demon, who dwelt in the furnace, the demon to whom he sacrificed, whose servant he was on this earth.

How long shall I walk among men? Ulric asked silently. *How long will I continue to despoil and corrupt?*

Forever! Because in all the centuries he had walked the lands of the earth he had not witnessed the slightest change in man's basic desire. It was this desire he catered to, promising death, vengeance, unspeakable horror. And men had flocked to him, offering anything if only he would serve them.

Ulric accepted. He did so because what men offered him he then placed upon the plate of the demon . . . who in turn replenished his powers.

So it was that the circle was complete. Evil being served by evil to perpetuate evil.

When the child whores came back in, they were, like him, dressed in heavy black trousers, dark parkas, and waterproof boots. Without a word Ulric led them out the front door and across the crushed gravel to the garage. A moment later the thundering purr of the Aston engine sounded.

The drive to Dune Road took less than twenty minutes. As he turned off the highway Ulric doused the headlights. He did not need them to see into the night. Occasionally he glanced to his left, at the houses that had collapsed or were being held up by dozens of jerry-rigged supports. He chuckled to himself at the inane vanity of those who dwelt here, like ants, always aware that the destruction would come but that their stubborness would hold and the rebuilding process would begin again.

He was pleased that Emil Letelier stood apart from such pitiable specimens. As terrible as the storm had been, Letelier's home remained untouched. Even now the great cathedrallike prow faced the wind head-on, secure, inviolate. Somewhere in the darkness Ulric heard the barking of dogs, but that did not concern him. Nothing Emil Letelier would try to do concerned him.

Ulric brought the car around to the front of the house. Even before the engine was shut off, one bodyguard appeared by the driver's door. Without a word Ulric opened the door and in a motion that was too quick for the eye slammed his open palm against the man's nose. The cartilage snapped, the momentum of the blow driving splinters into the brain. After the two child whores had got out of the Aston, he sent them off into the night to deal with the others who prowled the grounds. He himself went up to the front door and opened it as though the electronic locks were nonexistent.

At half past four Emil Letelier was in his study, on the second floor of the house. The room was in the prow of the structure, its slanted windows looking straight out on the ocean. The bedroom, from which he had just come, was directly above, connected to the study by a spiral brass staircase.

Letelier was holding a shaker in one hand, stirring the martini mix with the other. He looked up briefly at the blonde sitting across the room, her legs stretched out on the leather sofa, soft white on agate. Like the late Aleijadinho, Letelier preferred his women blonde, older perhaps, but white, pale white.

He was pouring the drinks over ice-filled Old-Fashioned glasses when he heard the girl utter a short, weak cry. By the time he looked up, she was dead, her neck twisted, broken in Leopold Ulric's hands.

"Madre de Dios!"

The exclamation escaped his lips at the same time as his hand reached under the counter, fingers scrambling for the gun he kept there. It was a credit to Letelier's instincts that he didn't stop to think who the intruder was, how he had entered, or what had become of his bodyguards. Self-preservation was all he knew. Yet even that could not save him.

By the time Letelier brought the gun out, Leopold Ulric was within inches of him. It was child's play for him to knock the weapon out of the hand, embrace Letelier around the neck, and squeeze. The last image Emil Letelier had was of a grinning death's head suspended above him, its monstrous visage slowly descending upon him, mouth open, saliva dripping over teeth that belonged to no creature he knew.

Nevada had had the Letelier house under surveillance for almost forty-eight hours, ever since he had made contact with Sheridan. He had slipped onto Dune Road early the following morning, breaking into the house next to Letelier's, two hundred yards away. He had checked out the location thoroughly. The owners were in St. Vincent; the caretaker had come out earlier to supervise the shuttering of windows broken by the storm and the subsequent interior cleaning. Nevada had set himself up in one of the top-floor bedrooms of the geodesic structure. The vantage point offered an unimpeded view of Letelier's house; the windows could be opened fractionally to permit the protruding acoustical gun to focus on the building. High-speed cameras with a telephoto lens kept a photographic log of activity around the house. Infrared film denied Letelier the cover of darkness. As far as Nevada was concerned, it had been a choice stakeout: safe, dry, and warm.

Until now.

As soon as Nevada had identified the Aston-Martin plates through the night-scope, he had punched in the numbers to the emergency circuits which would sound Sheridan's communicator. He waited long enough to identify Ulric and witness the killing of the bodyguard before slipping out of the house. Now he was running, hard and low, staying close to the water's edge. When he saw Ulric emerge from the house carrying a body in his arms, Nevada threw himself on the sand. Despite his experience in Nam and the jungles of South America he still could not believe what he was seeing.

Leopold Ulric carried the body of Emil Letelier as though it were weightless. Between the crashes of the surf he heard the Colombian moan and gurgle. Ulric was pleased that Letelier was still alive. He wanted him to die slowly, as was right.

He came around underneath the house and waded into the surf. The water level at the post closest to the beach was waist high. With one hand Ulric held the body up against the concrete pillar. With the other he swung a thick rope around Letelier's chest and waist. Looping it twice around the man and the post, he came around to face Letelier. The dealer's head sagged forward. Ulric pried his mouth open and shoved the rope into it, adding another coil to the post. Then he knotted the ends twice.

Nevada watched as Ulric stepped out of the water, apparently impervious to the pull of the surf. He went under the house and came out onto the drive, one hand on the roof of the car, looking around him, his head tilted upward slightly, as though he was scenting the wind.

Nevada eased the .44 Magnum out of its holster and began crawling on elbows and knees. He concentrated on Ulric, but in the back of his mind questions churned: What had happened to the dogs? And the outside bodyguards? The two girls Ulric had brought with him had disappeared into the night. They couldn't have taken out the guards. Yet no one had stopped Ulric.

Where were they?

At thirty yards he threw the safety. Ulric remained motionless, his chest clearly visible above the car. Nevada continued to inch forward. Sheridan had been specific:

Take the man down, any way you can, at the first opportunity. Don't wait for me, don't try for a collar.

After what he had seen Ulric do, Nevada thought the advice gratuitous.

At twenty-five yards he cocked the hammer and stopped dead. Nevada allowed three seconds to elapse as he tensed his leg muscles, then in one motion rose out of the sand. Even before he was fully standing, the gun was trained on Ulric, the sight moving up his chest. When it reached the heart, Nevada fired.

Nothing.

Ulric turned his head toward Nevada very, very slowly. In the light streaming from the house Nevada saw a smile on the thin lips. Without hesitating he fired again.

A neck shot.

A head shot.

"Oh, sweet Jesus!"

But they were upon him before he could react. One blade drove into his back between the buttock and the kidneys. Nevada screamed, arching his back, his arm shooting up, the final spasm pulling back the trigger for the last time. Out of the corner of his eye he saw another blade swing down, burying its tip in the bone of his forearm.

The two child whores brought the body down as wolves would a stag. Instantly they began stabbing indiscriminately . . . the legs, arms, groin.

"Enough!"

They whirled around, teeth bared, to see Ulric standing over them. The virtuoso squatted down and pulled up Nevada's head by the hair.

"How I do wish you had been Sheridan," he murmured. "Did you know I've sent him a Father's Day card ever since San Francisco?"

He waited as though believing Nevada could answer him.

"No, of course you don't. Thane doesn't mention the cards, but just the same, he dies a little bit more whenever one arrives."

Ulric released Nevada's hair, the head falling into the sand. The whores had done well. Nevada was dying. He

265

would be dead before Sheridan arrived. But he would live long enough for his suffering to please the demon.

"Take him to another post."

The water was up to their breasts, and the child whores had difficulty strapping Nevada's body to another pillar. But they managed, and when they were through, Ulric was already in the car. He snapped on the high beams to look at the night's handiwork. He thought it very good. The contract he had come to perform was one corpse closer to being fulfilled.

Thane Sheridan was at Thompson Street when the communicator went off. Even though he knew Nevada was on the stakeout, he had not expected the call. The surveillance was a long shot. He had put no stock in it.

Sheridan opened the line to Mr. Bill at home.

"I need a Huey evacuation chopper, with floodlights, on Trade Center Tower stat."

Mr. Bill didn't ask why. "The National Guard will provide. What's your destination?"

"Dune Road, Long Island."

"I'll see to it no traffic strays in your flight path." There was a pause. "Good hunting, Thane."

The next call went out to Sabina, who was at home. She was to meet him at Center Tower 2 whether or not her hair was dry. Sheridan strapped the Venus into its casing and left. As he drove through the deserted financial district he prayed Nevada had followed orders—for once in his life.

"What's happening?" Sabina shouted at him as he stepped out of the fire door. The rotor wash snapped her words away, flinging them into the night.

"Ulric . . . he's out on Long Island."

He grabbed her hand, and together they ran to the open hatch. The copilot helped them inside, and the machine lifted off as soon as the hatch was secure. Sheridan gave the copilot the destination, then turned to Sabina. Her hair *was* wet beneath the woolen seaman's cap.

"Your timing stinks."

"Yeah, so it would seem." He was holding her close without realizing it.

266

"Nevada?" she whispered.

Sheridan nodded. "I hope to Christ we're in time."

He unbuttoned his coat and slipped the Venus out.

"Can you handle one of these?" He cocked his head at the fifty-caliber machine gun.

"It's been awhile, but sure."

"You stay put and give me cover if I need it. If Ulric makes a move for his vehicle, total it."

The giant craft thundered out over Long Island, moving low and fast, the pilot using VHF and parabolic radar to guide him. From the radio came a continuous chatter of air controllers at Kennedy and La Guardia diverting flights from the area.

The helicopter swung over in a wide arc, coming in low over the waters.

"Drop me on the beach, gun facing the house!" Sheridan yelled. The copilot gave him the thumbs up and spoke into his microphone. The pilot threw the switches, and floodlights for landing came on.

As Sabina moved into position behind the gun, Sheridan pushed back the hatch doors. The Huey was still five feet from touchdown when he jumped, tumbling, getting his feet and running toward the house. The barrels of the Venus weaved from right to left. Sheridan heard nothing over the engine clatter. He had to rely on his eyes and instincts alone. But they were more than he needed.

He saw the bodyguard first. From the angle of the neck, Sheridan knew he was dead. Crouching, he ran toward the house, then suddenly turned to his left. Ropes around the pillars. A head lolling to one side. Holding the gun high, Sheridan plunged into the water, moving his body from side to side against the surf. He reached Emil Letelier first. Too late. The water had slackened the ropes, and the body had sagged a few centimeters. That was all that was needed for the sea to pour into the dealer's mouth.

Sheridan moved around him to Nevada. The salt had cauterized the wounds, but the ropes were stained red. Gently Sheridan lifted his head.

"Never could follow orders . . ."

Blood erupted with the words, spilling over Sheridan's fingers.

"Easy . . . We'll get you out of here."

"I saw him . . . Ulric . . . the two . . . two girls."

"Ulric!" Sheridan whispered.

"The two cut me . . . He killed Letelier."

"Don't talk anymore!" Sheridan said fiercely. "I'll be back for you."

"Just like old times . . ." Nevada managed a ghost of a smile.

"Yeah, like old times!"

Sheridan waded back onto the beach and ran to the helicopter.

"Get Mr. Bill on the line," he said hoarsely. "We can go public now. I want a warrant out for Ulric. Murder one!"

Chapter Nineteen

Sabina had never seen such conflicting emotions in a man as she did in Thane Sheridan that night on the beach.

When she finally reached him, he was hacking away at the ropes which bound Nevada to the concrete pillar. Sheridan was screaming, howling with every thrust of the knife, his neck tendons bulging, eyes squeezing shut. When the last of the ropes snapped, he lifted Nevada's bleeding body in his arms. His lips curled back over his teeth, a warning to anyone who might reach out to help him. Yet all the while he walked along the beach Sabina could hear him whispering to the dying man. She didn't catch many of the words, but their meaning was unmistakable: He was asking for forgiveness.

The helicopter lifted off as soon as Sheridan had strapped Nevada into a cot. He spoke only a dozen words, asking Sabina to radio the state police to come for the other bodies. Then he told the pilot where to fly.

"I *can't* land at Mount Sinai! Sure, they have a heliport, but not for a rig this size."

"Set it down!"

Sabina saw the pilot recoil, and she knew he must have caught the ruby-red spark of madness dancing in Sheridan's eyes.

Sheridan ministered to Nevada during the twenty-minute flight. He gave him morphine to stop the weak convulsions and thrashing and set up a plasma IV. The cuts were cleaned as thoroughly as possible, antiseptic pressure bandages applied to the worst wounds. By the time Sheridan was finished, his arms were blood-streaked to the elbows, and the floor around him was littered with cot-

269

ton swabs, used Syrettes, and pieces of Nevada's torn clothing.

Sabina, who stood away from all this, was relieved to see the trauma unit waiting on the helipad. The pilot never fully touched down but through sheer skill kept his machine within inches of the ground so that the wounded man could be moved. The orderlies removed the entire cot, sliding it out and onto a gurney. The first physicians were leaning over Nevada even before the helicopter doors closed. Sabina ducked as the machine lifted off, but Sheridan stood there, the blasts from the rotor wash rocking him. When she rose, she found he was shivering uncontrollably, the wet clothes clinging to him like a second skin.

"Call Mr. Bill," Sheridan said, the words coming out slowly. "Get an APB out on Ulric. His car. Surveillance at his apartment."

"Thane, please, let's get inside! You're going to freeze!"

For a second he looked at her quizzically, his beard and mustache coated with frozen brine, his hair askew. The madness erupted briefly in his eyes, then faded.

"Oh, Christ, what have I allowed to happen!"

His knees buckled, and he crumpled to the pad.

Sabina stayed with Sheridan the whole night, sleeping on a cot in his room at Mount Sinai. He awoke only once but to her surprise drifted off again without protest. When she awoke the next morning, Sheridan was out of bed, dressed, and ready with her breakfast tray.

"Nevada?"

"Holding his own," Sheridan said. "Barely, but he's holding. He was under the knife for six hours."

She struggled out of the cot, caught her reflection in the mirror, and grimaced.

"Give me five minutes."

When she returned, they shared a breakfast of juice and coffee.

"Are you all right, Thane?" she asked softly, reaching for his hand.

He nodded and managed a tiny smile.

"Everything's going to be fine. We're almost at the end now." His words trailed off. "Almost there."

"I don't understand."

He reached out and switched on the television by the bed. *Good Morning America* had broken off to allow local affiliates to present the news. The lead story for the New York station was the killing of Emil Letelier and the others and the manhunt for Leopold Ulric.

"We'll flush him out," Sabina said, her gaze focused on the picture of the virtuoso that filled the screen. "There's nowhere for him to hide. One unit will take him down."

Sheridan shook his head. "I spoke with Mr. Bill. There is to be no contact when he's spotted. The patrol will maintain surveillance and radio in. I don't want anyone touching him but me."

"But if he spots surveillance, he may grab someone off the street, present us with a hostage situation," Sabina objected. "He should be taken at the first opportunity."

"Ulric won't play it that way," Sheridan said. "You see, I know him now. I know exactly what he'll do. Right now he's somewhere on Long Island—a friend's house, something like that. He won't move out today. But tomorrow, Tuesday, he has a performance. Like Nathan told you, Ulric's a professional. He won't miss the concert. Which means that sometime tomorrow he'll head back to the city. He'll be driving the Aston. He'll be spotted before he gets off the expressway. If he notices the surveillance, he won't care. He'll drive straight into town, to the Metropolitan Tower."

Sheridan paused. "That's where we'll take him."

"You honestly believe he'll allow himself to be taken—just like that?" Sabina asked, incredulous.

"Just like that," Sheridan echoed. "He'll feel absolutely safe. The wind and rain obliterated any evidence outside Letelier's house. I doubt the state police will find anything on the inside that could be linked to Ulric."

"But—"

Sheridan held up his hand. "I know what you're thinking. But an hour ago the hospital issued a statement to the effect that a police officer working under cover at Dune Road died. He did not survive surgery."

Sabina stared at him. "And so Ulric thinks the only witness . . ."

"Is dead," Sheridan finished for her. "That's why he'll come home. Because he thinks it's safe."

From the City Housing Authority archives Thane Sheridan managed to pull copies of the original blueprints for the Morell house. The entire street had gone up in the spring of 1932. As far as he could tell, there had been no major architectual renovations. Sheridan paid two dollars for copies of the blueprints and went to another department.

The files at the Department of Sanitation confirmed what he had suspected: There were no alterations to the foundations of any of the houses on Horatio Street. If any excavation had been done, it would have had to be cleared by the city because of the underground pipe system.

Sheridan's final stop was the local Con Ed office. Their records went back only twenty years, but that was enough to give him the answer he wanted: The Morell residence had never used more than the normal amount of electricity needed to run a house that size.

By the time Sheridan returned to Thompson Street, he was all but certain that Otto Morell had not built a cache in the basement of his home . . . which meant that what Sheridan was looking for would be found in the house proper. Augusta Morell would have stored it in a safe, very likely innocuous place. But still he would not have to dig for it. Using two cups for weights at either end, Sheridan spread the blueprint copies on the coffee table. He did not move until every detail had been unerringly committed to memory.

A few minutes after midnight Sheridan slipped off the sidewalk into the narrow passageway that separated the Morell house from its neighbor. His surveillance had lasted ninety minutes, sixty of which had been spent watching darkened windows after Augusta Morell had turned out the lights and gone to bed.

Sheridan walked around to the back garden, taking care to stay on the strip of grass that ran right under the windows. He could not take the chance on the stone walk, where the ice might crack under his weight. It took him fifteen seconds to jimmy the locks on the double French doors and let himself in.

From his first visit Sheridan knew that the Morell home was not wired for alarms, actual or silent. Nevertheless he stood absolutely still for a minute, listening to the faint pulse of the house, letting his eyes become accustomed to the semidarkness. He was lucky: The light from the street-lamp was so strong it bathed the parlor and living room in a pale blue hue. Sheridan unbuttoned his coat, shrugged it off. He removed his short after-ski boots, replacing these with rubber slippers. The tight leather gloves were still on his hands when he set to work. This was not an oversight.

Using a pencil light, Sheridan tackled the most obvious places first: the two floor-to-ceiling bookcases on either side of the fireplace, the revolving book stand beside Otto Morell's favorite chair, the glassed-in bookcase in the dining room where first and special editions, bound in leather, were lined up, the gold-embossed lettering sparkling.

He moved swiftly across the hall into the tiny room which had been the craftsman's study. Most of the space was taken up by an ornate parson's desk. Ignoring the other bookcases, Sheridan slipped in behind the desk, drawn by the neat piles of papers and files arranged on the worn oak. He thumbed through the lot, coming across everything from invoices to old ledgers. He realized Augusta Morell had indeed cleaned out the contents of Morell's workshop. Not that he had expected Morell to keep the book in his workshop, but his widow's thoroughness now saved Sheridan a trip to the workshop.

He examined the parson's desk carefully, pulling out each of the tiny drawers above the writing space, running his fingers underneath the wood, feeling for a spring-loaded catch. There were none. He tested the drawer beneath the writing board, then pushed the chair back and got down on his knees. The big drawers on the left opened easily and were filled with receipts and income tax forms. The drawers on the right refused to budge. Yet there was no telltale brass lock.

Whoever had designed the desk had been a craftsman of unquestionable skill. It took Sheridan ten minutes to find the first spring catch. But maneuvering the catch was not enough. There must be a secondary mechanism which activated this one. A quarter hour passed before he located the second device, which had been built into the front leg, its panel almost invisible against the grain of the wood.

The triple drawer rolled out silently. It was over a foot deep, yet it contained only a single volume, the size of a family Bible, the ancient leather of the cover soft as doeskin, with the cracks and creases of ancient skin. The gold had faded from the lettering, but as Sheridan held the tome to the light he could make out the Gothic German script: THE OLD WAYS.

"Lord in heaven!" Sheridan whispered. His grip tightened on the volume as though his fingers were frozen to it. There was no author's name beneath the title, but Sheridan did not need it. The book was a compendium, the collected works of many writers. Its existence had only been rumored, never verified. Of its authors it was said that they had all been great men, endowed with unique psychic and spiritual powers. They had all been magicians, conjurors of spirits . . . and of demons. They could travel through light . . . or through darkness. Thane Sheridan now knew which road Otto Morell had chosen.

Leopold Ulric left the guest house on the Brookville estate at one o'clock on Tuesday afternoon. He had sent the two child whores back to the city early that morning and so made the drive back alone. At the Southampton turnoff on the expressway he spotted the state patrol car weaving through traffic and settling directly behind the Aston. Ulric, who had been careful to stay within the fifty-five-mile-per-hour speed limit, gave the car its head. The speedometer edged to eighty as the Aston flexed its muscles, but although the patrol car kept up with him, it made no attempt to overtake and pull him over. Satisfied, Ulric throttled down to sixty. Thane Sheridan knew he was going home.

For the last two days Leopold Ulric had been monitoring the noon and evening news carefully. At first he had chuckled on seeing himself so prominently displayed on the screen, but he quickly became bored with the repetition. Sheridan, he thought, was playing this one very reports stated that Leopold Ulric was being sought as a material witness in the slaying of Emil Letelier, his bodyguard, and an unidentified woman. Nothing was said that connected Ulric to the now dead undercover police officer. Nothing even intimated that Ulric might in any way be involved in the disappearance of the children. Sheridan wanted to flush him out. To flush him out, then follow him. Ulric knew Sheridan did not expect him to go to his nest. But he did want to take Ulric by himself, probably alone or with that bitch of a detective. Ulric's hands tightened on the wheel, the great muscles in his arms bulging. One day he would like to meet Sabina Morell on intimate terms, show her his true face. He would let her live for a while to regret that.

Ulric crossed into Manhattan on the Triborough Bridge, headed down FDR Drive to the Sixty-third Street cutoff. On Second Avenue an unmarked Dodge sedan replaced the state police vehicle. Ulric pushed the Aston through the midafternoon traffic, entered the garage of the Metropolitan Tower, and parked, as he always did, diagonally across the three bays. Fifteen minutes later he was stretched out on a rattan recliner in the Florida room, looking out at the mists that wove around the skyscrapers, a glass of orange juice in one hand, the telephone receiver in the other.

Sidney Nathan had been frantic. He spieled off a dozen questions before Ulric managed to cut him off and told him precisely what he wanted done. To his credit Nathan listened without interruption. When Ulric finished, the agent was laughing. Ulric hung up, finished his orange juice, and went into the bathroom. He took a long, very hot shower, oiled and scented his body, and donned a dove-gray three-piece suit. His timing was flawless. He had just finished knotting his tie when the front door chimes sounded.

Thane Sheridan heard the peal of chimes and stepped back across the hall, moving slightly to his left. If bullets came, neither he nor Sabina were in the line of fire, whereas the Venus covered 90 percent of the doorway. Sheridan thought the possibility of Ulric shooting at them remote. But he almost wished the virtuoso would try.

"Yes?"

Sheridan stepped forward, the gun barrel moving to cover Ulric, who was standing in the doorway, an ironic smile creasing his bloodless lips.

"Ah, Inspector Sheridan."

The black eyes glittered, the triumph went undisguised. For an instant Sheridan believed he could not restrain himself. The hunt was over. Two years of torture were done with. But the memories which had made those months hell flooded his senses. He had vowed to kill the man who had murdered his son and destroyed his wife. He had sworn to do so on their memory. Yet he could not squeeze the trigger. Not because of fear or loathing or guilt. He was beyond that. But only Ulric knew where the children were. Sheridan had to know where the nest was before he destroyed this creature.

"Keep your hands away from your body and move back," Sheridan said softly.

Ulric obeyed, but his eyes, mockery and arrogance streaming from them, never left Sheridan's.

"Give him Miranda."

Sabina moved in, closing the door behind her, and quickly rattled off the requisite phrases.

"Move over against the wall."

She patted Ulric down and cuffed him.

"Inspector, I suggest you tell me exactly what is going on here."

"You're charged with the murder of Emil Letelier, another man, and a woman, as well as assaulting a police officer with intent to cause bodily harm."

"I see. And the warrant?"

Sabina drew out the document from her purse.

"What kind of charade is this?" Ulric hissed suddenly. "I don't know any Emil Letelier. I've never heard the name before—"

"Where are the hookers?" Sheridan demanded.

Ulric threw his head back and laughed, his slick greasy hair falling across his face.

"Hookers, Inspector?"

"The two children Sidney Nathan procured for you after your last performance," Sabina said harshly.

"Oh, you mean my admirers, who chose to become my

companions," Ulric chortled. "My goodness, Sergeant Morell, they are long gone. And who knows where?"

"Ulric!" Sheridan called out softly, suddenly. "Where are the children?"

If there was any positive reaction to Sheridan's gambit, Sabina missed it. The musician merely raised his eyebrows in question.

"Now it's children, Inspector. What the devil are you talking about?"

"You let us find Rachel Rosenberg," Sheridan said, his voice hoarse, almost a whisper. "After you tortured and mutilated her, you gave her back. But where are the Mackenzie boy and the Grafstein twins?"

Sheridan approached Ulric and stood very close to him, his lips curled back in disgust at the stench oozing out of this man.

"Where are they, Ulric? I know they're alive. Give them back to me. We can work something out."

"I repeat, Inspector: I don't know what you're talking about. The names you speak of are familiar to me only because they belong to students who attend my NSDM classes." Ulric paused. "Classes which, I'm sure you're aware, have been canceled."

"Ulric, there's something you're not aware of," Sheridan retorted. "We *know* you killed Letelier and his guards—"

"Yes, Inspector, and I am also supposed to have killed a police officer." Ulric laughed.

"I didn't say that."

Ulric fell silent. For the first time Sabina felt the musician was uncertain.

"The warrant doesn't state you're wanted for the *murder* of an officer," Sheridan said softly. "For Letelier and his people, yes. But I said 'assault a police officer *with intent* to cause bodily harm.'"

He paused. "Nevada is alive, Ulric. You and your teenie zombies didn't finish it."

Leopold Ulric said nothing, and Sheridan took advantage of his silence. He had struck home and he knew it.

"Deal with me, Ulric!" he said urgently. "When we find the girls, we'll break them, and they will turn state's evi-

277

dence. You'll be taking the walk alone. But you can talk to me, Ulric. You can tell me where the children are. If we find that they're safe . . ."

It seemed to Sabina that Ulric was on the brink of collapse. His whole body was trembling, as though he were dressed in cold, wet clothes.

He's done it, she thought. *Thane will crack him open.*

Leopold Ulric threw his head back and laughed, the high, shrill chortle inhumanly loud. "You have nothing, Inspector!" he gasped. "And I assure you, you have made a grievous error in coming here."

"Son of a bitch!"

Thane Sheridan almost lost it all right there. Something within him snapped. Or perhaps it was the realization that he would never get Ulric the right way, legally, by the book. At that instant he accepted what he had understood all along: He would have to become a killer in order to stop the killing.

"What's going on here?"

The voice froze him. Sabina whirled around, gun sliding out of the belly holster.

"There is no need for melodrama, Detective," Sidney Nathan said icily. He stepped inside, followed by half a dozen reporters.

"My question still stands: What is going on here?"

"Ulric's under arrest for suspicion of murder," Sheridan said, and grabbed the chain between the handcuffs, jerking Ulric's arms up.

The photo flashes erupted. Later, when the pictures were published in the morning edition, they would show the grimace of pain on Ulric's face, the unnatural angle of his arms, the open contempt of Sheridan's expression.

"Inspector, I must protest the treatment—" Nathan was shouting.

"Shove it!" Sheridan muttered. He pushed Ulric directly into the pile of reporters, who were shouting questions, using Ulric to pry an opening in their ranks.

"What was that, Inspector?" Nathan demanded quickly.

"Which murder?" a reporter shouted.

"Sabina, get the elevator and keep them out of it!" Sheridan yelled.

With one hand on Ulric's collar and the other on the cuffs Sheridan steered the musician through the mass of bodies, the barrage of questions.

"Where are you taking him?" another reporter demanded.

Sabina slipped outside the elevator while Sheridan maneuvered Ulric inside. She spread her arms out, her gun visible, straining to keep the mass back, then jumped in as the doors were closing.

"Christ, they're animals!" she breathed.

"Still think you'll hold me, Inspector?" Ulric demanded. "That was just a taste of what is to come."

Sheridan ignored him. He slipped out his radio and adjusted the scanners to an open frequency.

"All units, vicinity of Fifty-fourth and Fifth. Code Three, repeat Code Three."

Officer needs assistance.

"You've run out of magic," Sheridan whispered. "No one's going to get you out now."

But they almost did. When the elevator doors opened, the hot blaze of television lights caught the three of them. Sheridan responded at once. He gripped Ulric with both hands and savagely propelled him into the crowd. Cries of anger and pain filled the lobby as a cameraman staggered back, his equipment crashing to the marble floor. Sheridan kept pushing, oblivious to the questions and epithets being hurled at him. Then he heard the sirens.

"Get to the doors!" he screamed at Sabina.

Sabina broke away from the crowd and raced for the doors. Two patrol cars had just screeched to a halt, the officers spilling out, guns pulled.

"Get these bastards away from us!"

The patrolmen waded into the crowd, pushing and shoving. A black patrolman bodily picked up a reporter and set him down on the concierge's desk. Slowly a corridor was formed, and Sheridan was able to propel Ulric through it and out the doors. He half-dragged, half-walked the musician to his car and heaved him into the backseat. Sabina ran around to the other side, barely managing to slam the door shut before Sheridan shot the vehicle into the traffic.

"Beautiful orchestration!" he said furiously, shooting a red light at Seventh Avenue.

"They'll crucify you, Sheridan," Ulric cackled in the backseat. "I would have preferred to do as much myself, but now the wolves will have you."

The insane laughter made Sheridan tremble. He had the evil contained, at least for now. But he still had to kill it.

Three hours after formally booking Leopold Ulric on three counts of murder and one of attempted, Sheridan returned to 1 Police Plaza from Mount Sinai Hospital. He went directly to William Rodgers's office, where the director and Sabina Morell were waiting for him.

Sheridan deposited his dripping coat in the closet, passed by the strategy board, noting that the Battle of Yorktown had been replaced by Waterloo, and headed for the bar. He glanced at Mr. Bill, seated behind his desk, and Sabina, sitting on the edge of the couch.

"Anything for anybody?"

Both shook their heads, so he poured himself a stiff whiskey, neat.

"Nevada's slipped into a coma," he said softly, taking a sip. "The doctors won't predict recovery."

"We know," Mr. Bill said. "I called the hospital a few minutes ago."

The comment was lost on Sheridan.

"They were so sure," he murmured. "Sure that they'd reached him in time, that they could stabilize him . . ."

He sat down heavily in the old green leather club chair before the desk.

"I honestly don't know how we're going to work this," he said heavily. "One witness and right now he's no good to us. But we can keep Ulric—"

"We *can't* keep him," Mr. Bill said.

Sheridan looked at him over the rim of the glass, slowly drained the whiskey, and put the glass aside.

"What do you mean?" he demanded softly.

"Sidney Nathan got hold of Jack Chertoff," Mr. Bill said. "You know Chertoff—one of the best, if not *the* best criminal mind in the country. It took him two hours to review the situation. Then he placed a call to the PC, who called me. The release order's being signed." Mr. Bill glanced at his watch. "Just about now Mr. Ulric should be a free man."

Sheridan remained very still. "You can't let that happen," he said, his voice low. "You don't know what you're doing. We have a cop's testimony—"

"We have *nothing!*" Mr. Bill interrupted harshly. "Only you heard what Nevada managed to say. There are no witnesses, no tapes. And at the moment Nevada can't help us."

"He's a fucking killer!" Sheridan whispered. "For Christ's sake, don't you understand—"

"I understand that you went after Ulric because you believed he was the Rambler—"

"He *is* the Rambler!"

"You have no proof of that," Mr. Bill snapped. "A lot of circumstantial evidence but nothing you can give to the DA. Until a few hours ago you did have him on a triple murder count. But not anymore."

"We can't let him go," Sheridan repeated, speaking as though Mr. Bill hadn't said a word. "I'll give everything to the DA. We can still build a case . . . break Ulric and find those children . . ."

Sabina rose and came up behind him, placing her hands on his shoulders.

"We can't, Thane," she whispered through her tears.

She bade him stand and led him over to the tall windows. Below Sheridan saw another crowd of reporters. He recognized the criminal lawyer, Chertoff, and Sidney Nathan. They were flanking a triumphant Leopold Ulric, who, in spite of the icy rain, was stopping to comment to reporters.

"My darling," Sabina whispered. "I'm so very sorry. We don't have anything anymore. Another child was taken. The call came in an hour ago. He was taken while Ulric was still downstairs, in the detention cells . . ."

Part III

Chapter Twenty

The spectacle at once disgusted her and made her remember. The Claus von Bulow trial.

For two weeks Sabina had been an observer at the Newport, Rhode Island, trial. Ultimately what had come to fascinate her wasn't the sparring between the prosecution and the defense, or the testimony of the various witnesses, saturated with personal opinions and prejudices. It was the reaction of the spectators—the famous and infamous, the leisurely rich, for whom Newport was a stepping stone on their yearly pilgrimage around the world, the locals, who observed the comings and goings with a keen, sardonic eye. The trial had polarized Newport and New York opinions as to Von Bulow's guilt. It was talked about as far west as Fiji. In Europe it fueled the Riviera gossip mills for two solid months. This in itself had not surprised Sabina. Given the cast of characters, the attendant publicity was to be expected. What outraged her was the righteous passion of those who, in the face of evidence and common sense, championed von Bulow's innocence. Stenciled on everything from T-shirts to tote bags to bumper stickers were the almost hysterical renderings: "Claus is innocent!" and "Free C. von B.!"

The adulation became fiercer after the Newport jury handed down the guilty verdict. Swayed by the bleatings of celebrity authors, the trial groupies marched and shouted, wrote letters to the *Times* and their congressmen for a new trial. Or failing that, the launching of an immediate appeal. The indignant conviction that justice had been miscarried gave a sanctimonious edge to the preachings of the faithful in their efforts to convert the disbelievers. And sanctimony soon gave way to violence, whether verbal or physical. The supporters of C. von B. were ready to martyr themselves for their fallen idol.

Such a mass reaction—Sabina ventured to label it mass hysteria—was being repeated at the Met tonight, at the second to last performance Leopold Ulric would give. The preconcert chatter in the lobbies and lounges dealt exclusively with the hideous treatment the virtuoso had received at the hands of the police. To have arrested such a remarkable man—a veritable genius—was calumny. The police force, personified by a certain Inspector Sheridan, was roundly and enthusiastically condemned. Chertoff, Ulric's lawyer, instantly became the toast of the black tie set, while Sidney Nathan regaled dinner party guests with accounts of how he and Ulric had orchestrated the media presence at Ulric's arrest.

Cheers, laughter, backslapping. No one commented on the conspicuous absence of the Mackenzies and Grafsteins. And as of last night the Binghams, whose son, Greg, was a diabetic who had no chance of surviving more than forty-eight hours without his medication. The name of Emil Letelier went unmentioned. Multiple killings and the disappearance of children were considered a wet blanket. The smart set would not permit such unfinished business to tarnish its glee at one of their own winning out over the system.

The ovation which greeted Ulric when he came on stage was thunderous. It lasted a full five minutes. The obeisance was repeated before the intermission and again at the beginning of the second half of the program, when it became glaringly embarrassing. Yet Sabina had to admit that Ulric's performance that evening merited the four curtain calls his audience demanded of him. With each bar he played he repaid all the words of praise that had been heaped upon him. The scarecrow figure with the grotesque posture transformed what seemed like a hideous misuse of his instrument into the sweetest, most savage rendition she had ever heard. Through his music Leopold Ulric vindicated himself. His execution destroyed the vaguest shadow of doubt as to his innocence and replaced it with a single outraged question: How could *anyone* have believed that a man so gifted, so completely dedicated to his music could be considered a party to murder?

Sabina slipped out of her seat after the second encore. At the door of the box she paused and looked back at the capacity-filled hall. Then she pushed it open and quickly made for the escalators.

Let Ulric bask in his glory. Let him think he had won, believe that applause made him invincible. Let him think that Sheridan was obeying the restraining order the court had slapped on him, that he no longer had to look over his shoulder. Let him make the one mistake she and Sheridan were waiting for.

Sabina ran quickly across the expanse of Lincoln Center to Columbus Avenue, where her car was parked. She unlocked the door and brought down the umbrella. After she had lit a cigarette, she picked up the red phone and dialed Sheridan.

Tuesday night had faded into Wednesday morning. Even though the mantelpiece clock had struck half past one, the assembled did not make any move to leave. Each of them had to get to work in less than six hours; the elderly would sorely miss the lost sleep.

Abner Levine rose from his chair, knee joints cracking like kindling, and came over to the fire. He rolled another log into the grate, then straightened.

"Can I get anyone some more coffee, tea?"

George Percy scrutinized the bed of leaves in his cup and shook his head. Unlike Hansen, whose robust metabolism had completely shaken off the aftereffects of the venom, Percy continued to suffer from cramps and nausea. In the last two days his diet had consisted solely of tea and dry toast. Nothing more would stay down.

"He promised he would come right after the performance," Andreas Marcovici said darkly. The stainless steel band of his chronometer caught the lamplight, its glare hitting Jim Hansen directly in the eye.

"He'll come," Hansen said, lips barely moving, eyes hooded. He folded his hands across his impressive belly and stretched his legs out a little closer to the fire. A sudden gust of wind flung icy rain against the parlor windows.

"I still say it's a mistake to bring him here," George Percy said querulously. "I never wanted to see any part of the bastard . . . so long as he done his job."

"But that's precisely the point, George," Augusta said patiently. "We have to keep up our end—yet suddenly we can't."

"As though what we've done hasn't been enough!" Percy whispered. "Christ, we've bought ourselves a life-time of bleedin' hell!"

"But George, it was you who brought this matter to our attention," Augusta reminded him.

The little English mechanic slumped into silence. Augusta drew a sigh of relief. Since they had assembled two hours ago it had been like this. First one voiced reservations or made veiled accusations, then another. It had taken all her patience and skill to prevent arguments from erupting into full-fledged battles. She could not have them fall apart now. Not when they were so close and Ulric himself was coming here.

"George, you're sure your information is correct?" asked Levine for the third time that evening.

Hansen spoke up quickly, knowing his partner had reached the end of his tether.

"There's no mistake," Hansen said, sitting up. "The Fairfax child is going away. Old man Fairfax told me that when he brought the car in yesterday."

"Jim's right," Augusta Morell said. "One of the instructors at the NSDM told me the same thing."

She considered the white lie expedient and harmless enough. In truth Augusta had met Morgan Fairfax, Stuart's mother, at the school. The woman had been so nervous and eager to get out of the building, she almost brushed by Augusta without recognizing her. But Augusta, sensing something was not right, called after her. The two women spoke—or rather Augusta listened for a few minutes as Morgan Fairfax breathlessly told of her and her husband's decision to remove Stuart from the school.

"I don't care what *anyone* thinks!" she had said. "All the children who have disappeared attended the NSDM. I don't know what it is about this place, but until someone

288

finds this maniac, I'm not letting Stuart set foot in here! And I'm not the only one. The Robinsons and the Steins have taken their children out too."

When Augusta pointed out that perhaps sending Stuart to Europe was an extreme measure, Morgan Fairfax retorted, "I should think the Grafsteins, Binghams, and Mackenzies would like to have the option!"

"No, there's no question that Stuart Fairfax has already left," Augusta murmured. "We have to find another child."

"I don't know if there's anyone in this room who's still capable of doing that," George Percy said quietly, looking up from his cup. "Christ, Augusta, we've all gone through hell for what we've done. To take another kid—"

They all heard the opening of the front door, the brushing of footsteps on the hall mat, the door closing.

I was the last to come in, Levine thought suddenly. *I locked the door behind me!*

The footsteps proceeded down the hall, then stopped. Leopold Ulric stood just inside the parlor. He was still dressed in white tie, his eyes glittering as he surveyed those who had gathered to wait for him.

"Still, a bargain is a bargain," he intoned, glaring at Percy. "I have almost fulfilled my part. You have one more child to deliver to me to satisfy your end."

Before Augusta had a chance to reply, Abner Levine burst out, "The contract is finished! You've come to do what we've asked. We've paid you. It's over!"

"Not yet," Leopold Ulric answered, his tone silken, as though he were savoring a fine wine. "You see, Emil Letelier's demise has created a vacuum, one which will be exploited very quickly by others of his ilk. You should know the mentality of these people, Levine: They are hyenas. When one falls, the others move in to feast on the carcass. In this case it is your community they shall feed on unless I warn them off."

Leopold Ulric stepped a little farther into the parlor.

"If you do not honor the bargain, then everything you have done so far will be meaningless," he said. "The vermin will be back. You will lose everything you have fought to keep."

He looked around at them. "Otto Morell called upon me to perform a service, one which neither he nor any of you could do. You called upon me, fervently, pledging anything I wished if I would kill in your name, rid you of the pestilence that was threatening to overwhelm you. And why did you do this? Because there was not one among you here who had the stomach or the strength to kill for yourself."

Ulric laughed softly. "Ironically it was Otto, the eldest and weakest of you all, who had the courage to face the vermin. More, he had the courage to summon me. I knew his strength, recognized and respected it when we first talked. The words of murder came easily off his lips because he understood that a few *had* to die so that many would survive. I believe that had he been a younger, stronger man, he himself would have accomplished the task."

Ulric paused. "But it was left to me." His arm flung out in an arc, the long bony finger pointing in turn at each person. "And each one of you was told the terms of the bargain. Each one of you *swore* to uphold them!"

"Haven't we?" Andreas Marcovici cried. "Haven't we done everything you wanted?"

"Not quite. There is still another child owed me."

"But there are no more children!"

"Ah, yes. I know of your predicament. The Fairfax boy has been taken away." Ulric smiled. "It would have been convenient to have taken him—as you did the others, leaving tantalizing clues for the police which would point to my involvement."

Silence.

"You haven't forgotten about *that*, have you?" Ulric continued. "That too was part of my bargain with Otto: that never, at any time, for any reason, would suspicion fall on any of you. You were to let the police follow me—if they could do such a thing. And one of them has. Fortunately for all of us Inspector Sheridan has met with something other than success."

"But we can't break with the pattern," Abner Levine pleaded. "The security at the NSDM is impossible to deal with. Your own classes have been canceled. There aren't any children left! If we were to take one off the street—no, we couldn't do that! We're finished! We'd make a mistake, and that would be the end of everything!"

"Ah, Abner, but you're so wrong." Ulric chuckled.

He looked at Augusta Morell.

"There is *one* student left, isn't there, my dear?"

It was almost three A.M. before Leopold Ulric opened the door of Augusta Morell's house. Across the street, on a roof several houses down, Thane Sheridan adjusted the lens on the Starlite scope. The musician's body shimmered, a phosphorescent green outline against a red backdrop. Sheridan squirmed beneath his poncho, the only cover he had had from the sleet during the three-hour surveillance. Ulric appeared at the doorway alone. The parlor lights were still blazing. No one else was leaving with him.

Leopold Ulric drew his fur cape around him and stepped onto the sidewalk. He floated rather than walked over the thin layer of snow. When he reached his car, his head began to turn in Sheridan's direction. Suddenly he seemed to think better of it, quickly opened the door of the Aston, and slipped behind the wheel. Sheridan watched the car's progress until it turned the corner of Greenwich Street, then refocused on the Morell residence. Still no one else had come out.

Sheridan could imagine what was being said in the parlor, the senseless, desperate arguments being flung back and forth. Perhaps Augusta Morell and the rest of the community still believed they could find a way out. Sheridan knew better. They could twist and turn every possibility a dozen ways. It would do no good. They would end up exactly where they had been when Ulric had left them: caught in the tendrils of a nightmare they had made for themselves, from which they could not awake until all the terms of the compact had been satisfied.

Sheridan wondered if by now any of them really wanted to wake up.

"I still have one hell of a hard time believing all this."

Thane Sheridan heard Sabina's comment while he toweled his hair. A double whiskey and a long hot shower had driven most of the chill from his bones. He wrapped the long terrycloth robe around him tightly and took the chair closest to the fire. Sabina, curled up on the love seat, looked at him skeptically.

"You don't *want* to believe it," Sheridan told her, reaching for his glass. He took a sip and lit a cigarette. "Neither did I, I guess. Otherwise I would have seen the pattern long before this."

He glanced at the files strewn across the coffee table, the printout sheets from police computers in San Francisco through Chicago. All the backtracking he had done while Sabina had been running after Ulric.

"There was a case in Missouri not too long ago," he said softly. "A small place—can't remember the name. Anyway, there was a town bully, a real mean son of a bitch, from all accounts. Used to threaten people with shotguns and revolvers. Even shot a few to make his point. The town went through three sheriffs. Each one resigned after he threatened to press charges against the guy. And so the situation went on. Until one day, at noon, the bully arrived in town. He was getting into his truck when someone unloaded two barrels of double-O buckshot into his chest.

"The funny thing about that was there were no witnesses. At least a dozen people saw the killing, but no one came forward. The state police investigated, the FBI was called in because the killer may have crossed a state line, but no one broke the silence. The grand jury concluded that Billy Bob Ryan or whoever the hell he was, was killed by person or persons unknown."

Sheridan held his whiskey to the light, pursed his lips, and sipped.

"A conspiracy of silence, CBS called it. Morley Safer interviewed some of the townspeople. Do you know what they told him? They said they knew who had done it, but they weren't talking. And why should they? Ryan had terrorized them, physically and mentally. The courts had done nothing, the police even less. So what recourse did they have? Nothing but a modern version of *High Noon.*

"The situation was pretty much the same in San Francisco as here," he continued. "A neighborhood victimized by punks and small-time hoods. There too no one listened, paid any attention to Abner Levine's 'broken windows.'

292

But instead of the community taking up arms itself, it imported an exterminator."

"Ulric?"

"Ulric."

"And a variation of the same story happened in every other city the Rambler stopped to visit?" Sabina's tone was incredulous.

"The printouts have it all," Sheridan said. "The pattern is seamless. Victimized people, a ritual murder, punk killings start, children begin to disappear. The last two dovetail."

"So the community in effect hires the Rambler, Ulric," Sabina said.

"Yes."

"And they pay him in children!"

"That's right. It's the old Pied Piper myth: the unknown musician who rids the town of Hamelin of its rats and is promised gold. When the town reneges, he takes the children. The only difference is that here the children were part of the bargain, right up front."

"Thane, that's crazy!" Sabina exploded. "What you're telling me is that normal, everyday people in half a dozen major cities are guilty of kidnapping and are accessories to murder!"

"Is it that crazy?" Sheridan asked quietly. "I don't think so. I think people will always protect what is dear to them, precious: their families, their neighborhood, everything that is, in essence, an extension of themselves. They protect their past and with it the continuity into the future. You're a mother. You know this is true."

"But to kill children—"

"Why does it seem so outrageous? Only a few hundred years ago some societies drowned female babies. In this century children were sent into coal mines and textile mills. They were sold off to pimps and whiteslavers to pay off debts or simply to get some cash."

"But today—"

"Today nothing has changed," Sheridan said sorrowfully. "Human nature doesn't change that quickly. We like to think it does, but no . . . Do you think Germany today is a nation of different people from those who permitted children to be led to the gas chambers? Not a chance. The German psyche didn't change on May 3, 1945, when Berlin was taken. No thunderbolt from the sky changed national characteristics that had been evolving for centuries.

"The same thing here: People had relied on the judicial and police systems to protect them and everything they had worked for. The system failed them. It stood by and did nothing to halt the decay. People realized that *they* would have to do something. Self-preservation. And if a few must die in order that many may live, well, that too could somehow be tolerated. Not without pain, not without grief or even madness. But survival had to win out. Regardless of the quality of the victory."

"Then you're saying that those people in San Francisco in fact killed your son!"

"Yes, they did. I will probably never find out who they are. But my son disappeared while Ulric was carrying on with his bloodbath on their account. When he finished, he took my son's life as part of his payment.

"Look at the readouts, Sabina. Leopold Ulric gave performances in every city at the exact time when killings and disappearances were occurring. They started a few days after he arrived and ended just before he left."

"That's why you brought Nevada in to get close to Letelier," she said dully. "You broke the pattern. Once Letelier's people started dying, you knew that if you got a man close to Letelier himself, he was bound to run into Ulric."

"And Nevada did," Sheridan said. "He'll never get out of that coma. After I take Ulric down, after he's burned, I'm going to pull the plug. Nevada lived too long, too hard, to be allowed to die like that."

"You realize what you're saying," Sabina murmured as though she hadn't heard the last words. "You're telling me that someone in the community has hired this madman." She looked up at him. "You're saying that my aunt and the people around her—Levine, Marcovici, Hansen, Percy—are all in collusion. That *they're* guilty of kidnapping the children, that they're responsible for the murder of Rachel Rosenberg."

"They're as guilty as sin," Sheridan said softly.

"They've made their pact and carried out their end of it. Just about. There's going to be one more killing, and I'm going to let Ulric carry that out. Then one more child will be taken, and I'll let that happen. Because when they take the child, I'm going to be right there. I'll break whoever carries this sickness through, and that way I'll get to Ulric's nest."

"I can't believe you," Sabina whispered, jumping out of the love seat and turning her back on him. She whirled around. "Christ Almighty, do you know what you're saying?"

"They hired him, Sabina. They made a contract as surely as if they were renting a house or a car. The neighborhood was going under. You knew that better than anyone. So they made a deal—"

"You're crazy!" she breathed, then caught herself and stared at him, head shaking slowly as though she didn't want to believe the realization dawning on her.

"You let me cover the kidnappings . . ." she said, voice quivering. "You let me do that because you were watching for the killings. Aleijadinho, Letelier. That's what you were following, the killings you knew—or thought you knew—Ulric was carrying out. . . ."

She looked at him in disbelief. "And you never told me, never shared that information with me. Yet you knew all along."

She rose and hugged her arms around her shoulders.

"Damn you for leading me on. And you're wrong, Thane! Wrong! Do you hear? It *can't* have happened that way!"

Sheridan rose and came to her, but she flinched at his touch.

Yes, it did happen like that, my love, he thought. *And it will happen one last time. Except now I know whose child will be taken. May God forgive me for not telling you!*

Chapter Twenty-one

Willie Taylor was three hundred and five pounds of pimp, dope importer, and sociopath compacted onto a five-foot-eight frame. Willie was built in three stages: trunklike legs, a gelatinous torso, a perfectly round head the size of a heavy bowling ball. At the Caribe Lounge on Lower Broadway he was known as Wee Willie. On the street he was the Snowman. Either sobriquet pleased Willie. He wore his fat like a badge of pride.

At half past three on Thursday morning, Wee Willie was seated at his table near the back of the Caribe Lounge, listening to the Breakers rumble on about the joys of Rastafarianism. Although Wee Willie wasn't one of the faithful, he had contributed generously to the Rasta war chest. He also owned a hefty piece of the club.

When the band took a break, Wee Willie ran a linen napkin over his shiny face. On cue the white hooker on his left dabbed his jowls with cologne. Willie squeezed her thigh, then gestured for her to get out of the booth. His lieutenants had stomped in. It was time to look after business.

The Snowman was particularly happy that morning. A major shipment straight out of a Peruvian "cleaning factory" had brought in sixty pounds of 85 percent pure cocaine. Street value: about a million two. What with all the busts along the Florida coast both New York and L.A. were feeling the pinch. Wee Willie was pleased when his number-one man, the negotiator, reported that the Coast had paid a premium for early delivery.

The Hatchet also brought good tidings. Emil Letelier's stranglehold on the cocaine trade was definitely at an end. Letelier and the Little Cripple had been the pillars of the organization. No one else in the organization was familiar with all the moving parts. The consensus was that the territory was up for grabs. A few discreet meetings with informers within the South American community confirmed fear and disarray. Letelier's influence had been so pervasive that his death affected almost everyone living in the conclave.

The Snowman basked in the glowing promise of such reports. But he knew he had to move quickly. The Sicilians and other black groups were also on the prowl. He had to be first in, with force. During the next hour, while the Breakers thundered on about Haile Selassie, the Snowman issued concise instructions to his men: Letelier's girls were to be picked up, one by one. Pimps from Harlem would be contacted to do the job. Letelier's shooters were to be visited, offered employment on the usual terms. If anyone refused, he was to be taken out then and there. All the storefronts which serviced drugs were to be called on. Again the same arrangement would be offered with similar consequences for refusal to play. The Snowman himself would look after Letelier's pipeline down south. It never hurt to have alternative sources of energy.

The war council broke up at five o'clock. The Snowman's white Rolls was brought around, an umbrella held over him as he walked the half dozen steps from the club to the car. His lieutenants showed their respect by waiting in the freezing sleet until the Rolls pulled away. As they went back into the Caribe Lounge they didn't have the faintest suspicion that they had just paid their last respects to the Snowman.

At six o'clock on Thursday morning Leopold Ulric made five telephone calls. He had returned to his suite not twenty minutes earlier and was dressed in a black turtleneck sweater and dark trousers. The only article of clothing he had removed from his person was a pair of fine kid gloves. These had been stuffed into a small plastic bag. As he dialed Ulric examined his hands. He couldn't detect a speck of blood—even though the gloves had been drenched with it. As he waited for Augusta Morell to answer the phone—his fifth and last call—he glanced at the

298

fire blazing in the hearth. Blood and flames, the aroma was intoxicating. . . .

Augusta Morell was a habitual early riser, even during the winter. But she had to have her five and a half hours. During the last two nights she had managed barely half that amount.

She answered the phone on the second ring. Even in her weary condition she recognized the voice. Leopold Ulric spoke slowly and precisely, but when he was through, he hung up immediately, leaving Augusta sitting up in the darkness, the receiver humming in her hand. She forced back the scream that was threatening to choke her and threw the receiver at the wall. Staggering to her feet, she managed to reach the bathroom as nausea overwhelmed her.

The terror robbed Augusta of ten precious minutes. When she had finally managed to dress and leave the house, she walked like an automaton, in long, jerky strides, seemingly oblivious to the driving sleet. She moved quickly into the warren of short streets which led her ultimately to Houston Street. She crossed Houston and slipped around the corner of the Swift's meat-packing plant.

"Dear God in heaven!" The wind drove the words away as soon as she uttered them. Augusta Morell stood stock still. Before her was the long, wide driveway which serviced the bays of two plants on either side. The big rigs, the Reos, White Stars, and Peterbilts, stood silently in two even ranks, their chrome piping gleaming from the overhead floodlights.

"This is what he saw," Augusta Morell muttered to herself. "This is what Otto saw before they killed him."

She moved ahead, weaving slightly as the winds slammed into her from all sides. Something was happening at the far end of the drive. . . .

Five cars were parked in a rough semicircle by the yard manager's shack. All were pimp-mobiles, highly customized Eldorados, Mark Lincolns, and Sevilles. The owners of the vehicles had each received a call from a man whose voice they didn't recognize, who didn't identify himself.

But what he had to say stunned them. The soft, horrible voice that could not have belonged to a human being had said that the Snowman was waiting for them. If they did not want to end up as he had, they should heed the warning he represented. A location was given, and the line went dead.

The chiefs of the city's rival organizations, each controlling a well-defined piece of territory, didn't hear Augusta Morell come up. When she bumped against one of them, he whirled around, hand reaching for his gun. But when he saw her, he hissed, like an animal recognizing and fending off danger, something evil. The chiefs backed away, letting her pass.

"Witch!"

Augusta Morell jerked her head toward the man who had whispered the epithet. The dealer backed away from this creature with sodden rattail hair, the white bony face with bluing lips and eyes that burned red. He knew her, they all knew her.

"No, it's not true," Augusta Morell whispered. "I didn't do anything—" Her voice broke when, directly opposite the manager's shack, dead in the center of the yard, she saw the tall metal spike that had been driven into the ground. Augusta approached it and ran her fingers along the cold metal, then knelt down. The asphalt in which the spike had been planted showed no evidence of having been dug up. Whoever had planted it had driven the shaft into the asphalt with unimaginable strength. Inhuman strength . . .

Augusta Morell rose and stepped back. She thrust her face up into the black dawn and saw what it was that Ulric had left for her: the head of the Snowman, cleanly severed at the neck and driven down onto the sharp end of the spike. The mouth was gaping in a scream that would last into eternity, while the eyelids had been pinned back so that the terror of death could not be hidden.

"Like Vlad the Impaler . . ."

Augusta Morell turned around, and immediately the men stepped back. The message was clear to them: This is the boundary of the witch's neighborhood. Heed the Snowman's warning and do not cross it.

Augusta Morell shook her head, words failing her. But they backed away from her as though she were Death itself.

Thirty yards away, in the relative comfort of a Reo cab, Thane Sheridan had been watching. He waited until the chiefs got back in their cars and slowly drove away before slipping out into the sleet storm. He jumped down and came around the front of the cab in time to see Augusta Morell disappear into the gloom of Washington Street. Sheridan headed in the opposite direction. He knew where she was going, where he could intercept her if he wanted to. He was one step ahead of Augusta Morell now, running even with Leopold Ulric.

Jim Hansen was invariably the first to arrive at Vantage Motor Works on any given morning. By seven o'clock the first pot of coffee had been brewed. Fifteen minutes later George Percy appeared for his cup; within half an hour the pot was empty as the mechanics wandered in. Punctually at eight the pneumatic drills started up.

Jim Hansen was going through invoices in the office cubbyhole when the Dobermans growled. Ponderously he shifted his bulk out of the chair and went to the counter. He had spoken about the dogs to George. At night they served a purpose, but during the day they tended to make customers uneasy. Hansen had never liked Dobermans, believing them to be too high-strung. The day would come when one of them would take a nip at a client.

The dogs had fallen silent. Hansen moved around the counter and stepped into the postage stamp showroom to see Augusta Morell scratching one of the beasts behind the ear. As the dog looked up so did Augusta Morell, who silently walked past Hansen and into the office. When he came in, she closed the door behind him.

"Augusta, what happened?"

She smiled faintly at him. "I look a mess, don't I?" She paused, and her eyes glazed over. "I haven't been sleeping well, Jim. I've been worried, very worried . . ."

"Let me get you some coffee."

Before he could move into the garage bays, her voice

301

froze him. "How could you do it, Jim? How could you give Toby to him?"

Slowly Hansen stepped back into the office and closed the door after himself.

"Why, Jim?" Augusta Morell whispered. "After Ulric left, we all agreed that we would find him another child. The last one he wanted. You were there. You remember. I said I would do it this time. George agreed, so did Andreas and Levine. So did you! That was the way we left it—that I would bring the last child to Ulric! What happened, Jim? Why did you betray me?"

"How do you know we betrayed you?" Hansen asked softly.

"Because Ulric has killed again!" Augusta Morell shrieked. "And he wouldn't have done so without being certain that the child would be brought to him today!" She clutched at his beefy forearm, the nails digging into his flesh. "What have you done?"

He gripped her wrist between thumb and forefinger and pressed. Augusta gasped as pain shot through her arm, and her fingers went limp.

"He wanted Toby," Hansen said softly. "He's *always* wanted him, since the time he first set eyes on the boy at the NSDM."

"And you promised Toby to him?" Augusta asked in disbelief. "After you all promised *me* he wouldn't be touched!"

"We had no choice," Hansen said viciously. "You knew we were lying to you! If you didn't, you're a fool!"

Augusta Morell threw her head back, and a guttural moan escaped her lips. She started to shake her head from side to side. "A fool . . ." she repeated. "I trusted you all, and I was the fool." She stared up at him, haggard, eyes burning. "When did you decide?"

"After we left your house that morning," Hansen said impassively. "We came here, discussed the matter, took a vote."

"And *everyone* agreed?"

"Everyone."

Hansen leaned forward. "You've got to try to understand. To remember! It was *Otto* who brought Ulric to us.

It was *you* who took up the slack when he was murdered. *You* kept us together, made us do . . . do everything that had to be done! How could you think we would stop now—when we had sacrificed so much to save ourselves?"

He held her by the shoulders.

"One more, Augusta. That's all he wants, and we'll be free of the Leteliers forever. That's what Otto wanted, why he conjured up this . . . this Pied Piper."

"Yes, Otto brought the Piper," she whispered. "Brought him because we had no choice. And when he was killed, I took Otto's place. But I can't let Ulric have my flesh and blood, Jim. Not Toby."

"You'll have to, Augusta. You haven't any choice in the matter. Not anymore."

Augusta looked past Hansen to see George Percy standing in the doorway to the office. She made a move to rise.

"Don't, Augusta, please." Percy gestured to Hansen. "Jim, get out of here."

Percy turned and gave a low whistle. Instantly one of the Dobermans was at his side.

"Apollo, sit! Watch!"

The Doberman took two steps and squatted on its haunches before Augusta Morell.

"It'll all be over within a couple of hours, Augusta," Percy said gently. "We're all murderers now, and since we've already damned ourselves, we'll go all the way."

He paused. "You know my dogs, Augusta. Please, please don't move. Don't cry out. Apollo will tear your throat out if you do."

He began to close the door on her.

"It would be so needless . . . . after everything. Just a couple of hours."

As he turned the lock George Percy heard a wretched sob grip the old woman.

Thane Sheridan had watched Augusta Morell enter Vantage Motor Works. He continued surveillance until eight fifteen. By then he was reasonably certain Sabina's aunt would not be coming out for some time. Perhaps never.

Sheridan started the motor and slipped his car into the

thickening morning traffic. A block away he hit the siren and flashers. The Upper East Side was at least a half-hour drive.

The jockey brought Richard Dwyer's Toronado under the portico. Dwyer slipped him a dollar, as he did every day, and sighed. He supposed on days like this, with even the portico canvas leaking from the weight of the sleet, he got his money's worth out of the sullen Puerto Rican.

"Come on, scout!" he called out to Toby, who was showing the doorman his new digital watch. Dwyer wondered sourly why Sabina couldn't at least go halfers on the electronic wizardry their son wanted. He made a mental note to review detectives' salaries when he got in today.

"Mr. Marcovici!"

Toby scampered away from the doorman toward Andreas Marcovici, who came under the portico, huddling from the onslaught.

"Want to see my new watch?"

"Christ!" Dwyer muttered under his breath. He came around and stood by his son.

"Andreas, how are you?"

"Wet, Mr. Dwyer. Very wet."

"We'll give you a lift, Mr. Marcovici," Toby said solemnly.

"What are you doing here, anyway?"

"Just stopped by to visit a friend." Marcovici laughed. He looked at Dwyer. "Don't worry, Mr. Dwyer. I can get back all right."

Toby gave his father a pointed look. Richard Dwyer inwardly cursed his son's habit of taking in strays, then felt ashamed of himself. "No problem," he said gruffly. "It's on the way."

Marcovici tousled the boy's hair. "Very kind of you, Mr. Dwyer. If you don't mind my saying so, I think Toby needs to have his hair cut." He tugged at the golden locks, and Toby squealed.

"I've been meaning to get him to you," Dwyer mumbled, head craned to see oncoming traffic.

"Look, I can do him before I open up for business," Marcovici said brightly. "A thank-you for the lift, eh? Would you like that, Toby?"

"Neat!"

"I don't know . . . We're running late as it is." Dwyer stepped on the gas and cut off a Checker cab.

"No problem, Mr. Dwyer. School's just around the corner. I walk him there myself, promise."

"Yeah, okay. That'll be just great," Dwyer said, surrendering. What the hell, it was six bucks in his pocket, a week's tips for the goddamn jockey. . . .

So intent was Richard Dwyer on negotiating the late-morning traffic crush that he never noticed the beige sedan that kept up with him, always staying a car or two behind.

Just as Thane Sheridan had expected, both Marcovici and the boy got out at Broome Street, in front of the Italian's barbershop. On the sidewalk Toby looked back, then scampered around to the driver's door. Richard Dwyer lowered the window, and his son leaned in to kiss him on the cheek. He ran back, and both he and Marcovici waved just as the barber opened the door.

Sheridan cruised down the street and parked half a block away. He went up Broome Street but didn't see any of the cars he was looking for. Then he started on the alleys on either side of Marcovici's building. In the one on the left-hand side he got lucky: A white panel truck was parked between rows of garbage bins and crates, its front end pointed at Delancey Street. The plate numbers were New York commercial. The owner, as Sheridan already knew, was Abner Levine.

Thane Sheridan ran all the way back to his car, wrenching open the door and slamming it hard once he was inside. His fingers curled around the steering wheel, knuckles bled dry.

He could take both of them out right now. He felt the pressure of the Venus barrel against his right side. He could go in and take them without injuring the child. Then he'd go back for Percy and Hansen . . . and Augusta Morell.

Yet he couldn't. Not yet. He had to allow Marcovici and

Levine to commit themselves. He had to let them take the boy, drug him, and haul him into the back of the van and take him . . .

"Dear Christ in heaven!" Sheridan whispered.

To save the boy he had to wait until Toby Dwyer, Sabina's son, was actually kidnapped. The felony had to take place. *He had to let it happen!*

"They won't hurt you, son," he whispered. "Just like at first they didn't hurt my boy. They'll put you to sleep, as gently as they can because they *can't* let anything happen to you, let you hurt yourself. But afterward . . ."

Sheridan slammed the car into gear.

"I'll be waiting for you, son. You won't know it, but I'll be there. He's not going to take you or any of the others, I swear it!"

Chapter Twenty-two

Sabina Morell had not been able to sleep the night Thane Sheridan had told her his conclusions about Ulric. After he had gone to bed, she stayed up, smoking, drinking tepid tea, running his words over and over in her mind. They were still tumbling in her consciousness when she lay down beside him. She watched him sleep, the heavy body completely relaxed but the face taut, a cold, bitter resolution etched into the lines. She knew then that nothing she could say or do would change his conclusions. He believed he had solved the riddle of Leopold Ulric. In so doing he condemned the family and friends she loved.

He was gone when she woke up four hours later, and she was grateful for his absence. She didn't want to say anything to him or hear any more of what he had to tell her. His words gnawed at her, challenged her to think as a professional and not as one involved. But that was impossible. The revelation was too fresh, its wounds too tender. She needed time. Time to be able to step back from the words and look at them critically, to examine the ramifications from every possible angle. The whole of that day, Wednesday, she spent alone, going over and over the material he had left, following the pattern, slowly, cautiously applying it to the killings in her city. She replaced the names of past victims with those of the present victims, the names of unknown conspirators who had brought in Ulric as the exterminator with those of people she had loved and lived with almost all of her life. She silently argued against Sheridan's reasoning and challenged every assumption he made, fighting all the time, fighting for the innocence she was so afraid of losing.

At half past seven on Thursday morning the phone jarred her from a weeping nightmare.

"The Cunard Container Terminal," Mr. Bill was saying. "Apparently Letelier wasn't enough. Someone's taken down the Snowman. Is Sheridan with you?"

"N-no," Sabina stammered.

"Then you better find him, because I haven't heard from the son of a bitch in over twenty-four hours!"

Sabina arrived at the terminal sixty seconds before the homicide squad. She pushed her way through a group of trucks being held back by a combination of blue-and-whites and patrolmen. The yard manager was screaming about having to roll the trucks, shaking his fist in the direction of the pike.

The pike . . . Sabina walked up to it slowly, unaware that she was bumping into officers who, like herself, were staring at the severed head, mesmerized. Like Augusta, she too looked at the base of the pike and saw that it had been driven cleanly into the ground . . . as though the asphalt had been warm, like pitch.

There's going to be one more killing. . . . Then one more child will be taken . . . .

Sheridan's words collided with and were refracted by the blue-and-white spinning lights.

"Christ Almighty!"

"Sergeant . . . Sergeant!"

She turned to the young patrolman beside her.

"Sergeant, what do you want us to do?"

She saw his mouth drop open as she smiled. *He thinks I'm crazy,* Sabina thought. Her voice sounded strange to her. "Keep everyone away," she said mechanically. "Homicide's on the way. Just keep everyone back."

Before the patrolman could say anything, Sabina whirled around and was running through the puddles to her car. It took her less than three minutes to get to Augusta Morell's house on Horatio Street.

Sabina didn't bother with the doorbell but used her own key. She swept into the house, shouting Augusta's name. Her own voice followed her up and down the staircase, through the kitchen and parlor. Finally she stopped running and leaned back against the door, breathing hard.

308

"One of three places," she said to herself. "The garage, the barbershop, Levine's delicatessen . . . Only three places!"

Sabina slammed the door behind her and raced to the car. Vantage Motor Works was closest. She'd start there.

The Doberman's head snapped up as she entered. The dog recognized Sabina's scent, knew her to be a friend. But the stink of fear and anger coming off her confused the dog. It rose and silently blocked her way.

"Sabina!"

George Percy poked his head around the corner, giving her a yellow-toothed grin. He clicked his teeth at the dog, which immediately retreated.

"What can I do fer ye, luv?" he asked, wiping his oily hands on an already sodden cloth.

"Is Augusta here?" The question sounded hard, callous to her. "Christ, I'm sorry, George. It's just that I have to find her. She's not at home—"

"Hey, Sabina, dear, settle down." He came toward her and gingerly took her elbow. "Come in the back here. We'll get you a cuppa and settle you. Come on, then."

"George, no . . . I have to find her."

Yet she allowed herself to be led through the tiny showroom and up to the counter. Jim Hansen was standing up, his expression one of concern. George was still guiding her gently. From the garage proper she heard the compressor start up.

Then the scream: "Sabina!"

She reacted as though branded. Her right arm shot out, the elbow catching George square in the mouth, snapping the front teeth. In the same motion Sabina dropped to a crouch, seizing the gun out of the belly holster. The first bullet from the snub-nosed .357 Magnum dropped the Doberman just as it had launched itself at her. The second blew away the lock on the door to the office.

The Doberman inside the cubbyhole had leapt at Augusta as soon as she screamed. By the time Sabina slammed the door back with her shoulder, it had torn away the right side of Augusta's neck, the blood spilling over its muzzle, driving it into a frenzy.

A third blast from the gun blew the dog halfway up the

opposite wall, instantly streaking the paint with gore. Sabina flung herself beside her aunt, kneeling in blood, Augusta's head on her lap. But the Magnum remained trained on the doorway, where Jim Hansen was standing. The pitiless expression in his eyes was the final vindication of what Sheridan had told her.

"Sabina . . ."

She couldn't afford to look down.

"Don't talk. I'm going to get us out of here."

She felt a weak grip on her wrist.

"No time . . ." Augusta Morell whispered, choking on the blood. "Andreas . . . Andreas has the boy."

Still she dared not look down.

"Who, Augusta? Who's the boy?"

The grip on her wrist tightened as nothing more than a gurgling sound escaped the dying woman's lips.

Sabina lowered her head, then finally her eyes. Augusta Morell had hardly the strength left to speak, but she mouthed the single word.

"Toby?" Sabina screamed.

The fourth bullet caught Jim Hansen high on the right shoulder, splintering the bone and shoulder socket. He dropped to his knees, mouth working furiously in pain and anger, then fell at her feet.

"It's too late!" he said with a grimace. "The bargain will be kept!"

Gently Sabina lowered her aunt's head into the pool of blood. The eyes were glazed, lifeless, the expression one of immeasurable sorrow, of someone who has been trapped by damnation. Sabina rose and carefully stepped around the bodies, her gun leveled at George. Behind him the mechanics clustered at the doorway to the garage.

"Sabina, don't," George said thickly. "He'll kill you too!"

Without a word she moved around him, the bookcases in the showroom, the dead Doberman, and toward the door.

"If you call Marcovici, I'm going to come back and kill you, George!" she whispered. "And if I don't find the children, *all the children,* I *will* come back for you!"

For thirty seconds Sabina sat mutely behind the wheel of her car. Her mind was screaming at her to turn the key in the ignition and get away from Vantage Motor Works and the horror that had erupted there. But she couldn't move. Her fingers were clamped around the steering wheel, body pressed hard against the seat.

"Help me . . . someone please help me and my baby!" she whispered.

The mother in her was in anguish, refusing to heed the pleas of the professional. She wanted someone to reach out and touch her, hold and comfort her. She wanted someone to save her baby . . . to save her.

"Thane!"

The scream erupted from her mouth, and then her entire body was racked by sobs. Tears were still flowing as her trembling fingers reached for the key.

It was half past nine, and Abner Levine was drunk. He knew that at his age and with his lack of tolerance it took only three or four shots of schnapps to put him over the edge. By the time he had returned to Marcovici's barbershop, he had consumed almost a pint of Old Mr. Boston.

"I couldn't help myself, you understand." Levine was babbling on, slumped in one of the plastic seats next to a magazine rack. "The way he looked at me when I gave him the boy . . . Toby. Andreas, I swear I thought he was going to kill me! The lust in his face, the thunder of that ugly car of his, me all alone in the garage . . . My God, it was hell!"

"Abner, please—"

"But I gave him Toby," Levine cried. "I kept our bargain. Then I ran back to my truck. I found the bottle and took a drink. I sat there looking at him as he stuffed Toby into the trunk, then drove away."

Abner Levine shuddered. "Forgive me, Andreas, but I couldn't help myself. Oh, Lord, what have we gone and done?"

"Shut up!" Marcovici screamed at him, snatching the almost empty bottle from Levine's shaking hand. He wondered how in God's name the old fool had managed to drive all the way back here. It was a miracle he hadn't piled up.

It would have been better if you had, Marcovici thought viciously. The young barber had no pity for Abner Levine. He truly believed that what Levine had suffered was nothing compared to the torment he himself was going through. Because it had been he, Andreas Marcovici, who had enticed the boy into his store, had him sit up in one of the chairs, and all this while Toby prattled on about one thing or another. As he had reached out with the chloroform-laden rag in his palm Marcovici had glimpsed the portrait of his wife and daughter hanging on the wall. Toby's struggle caught him by surprise because for an instant he had forgotten where he was and what he was doing. Marcovici had had to grab the boy by the throat and force his head back, feed him on the chloroform. He would never forget—*never!*—how Toby had looked up at him: Somewhere behind the terror lay disbelief that a man he trusted implicitly could be harming him.

"So what do you have to worry about?" Marcovici snarled aloud.

Levine started. He had drifted off into a stupor, but the barber's words quickly sobered him up.

"The same thing you do."

Marcovici pivoted in the direction of the voice, toward the front of the store. His mind registered someone familiar, Sabina Morell, and he tried to smile. Until his eyes saw the gun in her hand, the blood-encrusted skirt, the streaked and torn pantyhose.

"Sabina—"

"Back off! Move against the sink, hands on the mirror. You too, Abner!"

Sabina crossed the black-and-white tile floor, shoving Marcovici against the sink. He cried out as his groin hit the ceramic basin. With one hand Sabina hauled Levine over beside him and cuffed the older man.

"Where is he?" she hissed.

"Sabina, who—" Marcovici began.

She dug the gun barrel into his kidney.

"Don't fuck with me! My son! Where is Toby?"

"He's in school," Marcovici said quickly. "I gave him a haircut and took him to school."

She raked the gun barrel across the side of his face, caught him as he was falling, and hauled him to his feet.

"Try again, monster," she said through her teeth. "I called the school. Toby's not there."

312

"Then your . . . your husband— Oh, God, what are you doing to me?"

"Talk!"

"Your husband gave me . . . a lift here," Marcovici panted. "I gave Toby . . . gave him a haircut. Took him to school."

Sabina jammed the gun into the nape of Marcovici's neck, then reached around his waist with her left arm. Her fingers found the wall phone unit, punched the numbers for Richard Dwyer's private line. He was on the line instantly, sounding, as usual, irritable and harassed.

"Hello?"

"Richard, it's Sabina. Where's Toby?"

"Sabina? What the hell— What do you mean, where is he?"

"I called the school. He's not there. He never arrived."

"That's crazy. I dropped him off at Marcovici's place for a haircut. Andreas said he'd take him over to the school—"

Sabina hung up.

Where, Andreas? Where did you take my son?

"Nowhere, I swear it!" Marcovici sobbed. "Love of God, Sabina, *he* took him! Abner!"

"Abner?" Sabina breathed. "Christ, you too!"

"Sabina, we had to," Abner Levine started to babble. "I wanted you to know what we were doing. I insisted! But the others, they said you wouldn't understand."

"Understand what, Abner?"

"That we had to bring in Ulric. Your uncle was right. To save ourselves, our community from these hoodlums, we had to bring in someone who could deal with them."

Levine licked his lips, shaking his head nervously.

"Yes, we had no choice. I was sure you would understand."

"Where did you take Toby, Abner?"

"Don't tell her!" Marcovici screamed.

Sabina raised her gun and smashed it across Marcovici's neck.

"Is that what you will do to me?" Levine asked quietly. "You would do this to an old man?"

"No, Abner. Because you will tell me where you took Toby."

"To Ulric," Levine said defiantly. "I kept our word."

"And where is Ulric?"

"Sabina—"

"Where is he?"

Levine began to weep.

"I can't tell you . . . I can't break the covenant." He stared at her, pleading. "We would all be lost then."

"You were lost when you conceived this insanity!" She paused. "Abner, if there is any love left in you, any compassion for all the children you've taken, tell me where Ulric is. Tell me now!"

"Can't," Levine cried, the single word tearing his soul apart. "I could not do that to Otto."

And then she knew.

The first staircase rose from the street door to a landing twenty steps up. The second opened onto the workshop proper. Over the second landing, under the sloping ceiling, was a small loft which overlooked the entire work area. It was here that Otto Morell once kept pieces of wood left over from the making of his beautiful instruments. He seldom threw anything away, believing that one day he might find a use for a sliver of mahogany or rosewood. It was here too that Thane Sheridan was waiting, the back of his head touching the angled ceiling, his legs splayed out in front of him. In spite of the coolness in the workshop he was drenched in sweat. His elbows were pressed hard against his ribs to keep his hands from shaking. The fingers were curled around the butt and stock of the Venus so tightly that the gun and the man might have been one. Sheridan no longer knew how much time had passed since he had squirreled himself away in the loft. He knew only that he had to hold out until Ulric arrived with the last child, Sabina's son, Toby. Then he would keep his part of the bargain. In the meantime he just sat there, staring out with vacant eyes at the horror below.

The children were all there, four of them, lying on cots placed side by side. An antiseptic odor pervaded the workshop, or perhaps he only imagined this because of the hospital equipment: IV stands with plastic liter bags suspended from their hooks, the tubes snaking down, disappearing into pale forearms. Catheters protruded from the sides of the cots, emptying the waste into sealed aluminum jars. There were fresh towels, stainless steel bowls, and jars of disinfectant soap on the worktable, so he presumed Ulric returned here regularly to bathe the children. He saw no evidence of bedsores or rashes.

In spite of the attention they had received, the debilitation of the children was frightening. The Mackenzie boy, taken first, was in the worst condition. His thinness was almost skeletal. The muscles in his arms and legs had atrophied to the point where the skin was taking on a translucent quality.

The Grafstein twins, Ruth and Hannah, fared slightly better. The color had fled from their faces, and their nails were discolored, the pink replaced by a pale white. But Sheridan guessed that their metabolism was slower. In photographs they appeared chubby, as though still carrying baby fat. This was gone now, and he could see the blue veins beneath the skin.

Greg Bingham, the last victim, appeared almost normal. His fingers moved weakly as he slept, pawing at the fitted sheet. Sheridan remembered he was a diabetic. But the injection marks on the underside of the arm appeared fresh. Ulric knew.

Sheridan walked around each child, his mind placing his own son's face on each one. Then he came to the last cot, the still empty one, the one waiting for Toby. Sheridan turned away and climbed back into the loft.

Sheridan never heard the door to the street open and close. He almost missed the footsteps on the stairs. But when Leopold Ulric appeared, his back to the loft, carrying in his arms the inert body of Toby Dwyer, Sheridan was sitting up, hunched forward, the barrel steady on the virtuoso's back. He watched as Ulric gently deposited the body on the last cot, loosened the boy's collar, and took off his shoes. He brought an IV bag out of the cabinet-size refrigerator and hung that on the stand. From one of the cupboards he brought out a catheter tube and waste container, placing these beside the cot. Ulric leaned over Toby and was unbuttoning his shirt when suddenly his head snapped around, black greasy hair obscuring his face for an instant.

"Sheridan!"

The grin was feral, neither human nor animal, and madness danced in the agate eyes.

"Ah, Sheridan, so you've found me out, have you?" Ulric chortled. "You've come here to die!"

Sheridan said nothing. The Venus barrel was rock steady.

"You think that toy can harm me?" Ulric challenged him. "For shame! You must know who I am!"

"Who are you?" Sheridan said slowly, as though each word was an effort.

Ulric put his hands on his hips and thrust his bony torso forward.

"I am the Piper!" He laughed, the words booming. "I am the wrath upon the land! The scourge, the exterminator!"

Before Sheridan could blink, Ulric had whirled by the cots, flinging back the sheets covering the children.

"I will show you something, Sheridan," he cried. "Something no one else has ever seen. Yes, I shall show you!"

With unimaginable speed Ulric slipped the IV tubes out of the children's arms, then removed the catheters.

"My payment, Sheridan! They are my coin—for services rendered! Aren't they delicious, so young and innocent. They are the wellspring of my power!"

"How did Morell bring you here?" Sheridan asked. He thought his voice sounded tired, very far away.

"Ah, now, Otto was a magician." He cocked his head at Sheridan. "Or perhaps you didn't know that?"

"No."

"Yes, he was. A conjurer who had studied the Old Ways, who understood the concept of a continuum."

Ulric moved to the worktable and snapped open his violin case.

"His last creation," Ulric said proudly. "Made for me. Perhaps his most exquisite work. It was an offering I could scarcely refuse.

"So I came to him, Sheridan. Just as I had come to all those other cities you followed me through. You followed, you searched, but you did not know who to look for. What to look for. Perhaps you did not want to believe I existed. You demanded a rational explanation. Even after I took your son, you still clung to reason.

"You see, I have walked through the ages. I am immortal, like time itself. I was in the darkness when the first man-creatures squatted around their fires. I watched the Pyramids rise and the Temple of Jerusalem being destroyed. I drifted on the wind of the Black Death in Europe and watched as the crematoria consumed the children of Abraham.

"But those who knew of me, who would pay my fee, those were spared. And throughout the ages there has never been a lack of people who, for self-preservation, will practice the blackest arts, commit the most foul crimes, render up their most precious resources. As long as people will do evil to exist and perpetuate themselves, I shall live."

Ulric uttered a wicked laugh. "Which means, my dear Sheridan, that I *am* immortal, here for all time!"

Ulric snatched up the violin, placed it under his chin, and suddenly his fingers danced over the strings. The children stirred.

He played a little more, and one by one the children sat up, zombies.

"They are hungry, Sheridan, from their sleep," Ulric crooned. "They want to feed. Shall I give you to them?"

The laughter was inhuman. "Yes, I believe I shall!"

And as he played, the children got off the cots and slowly grouped themselves around the ladder leading up to the loft.

It was then that the echo of a slamming door traveled up the staircase, followed by the pounding of feet. Leopold Ulric stopped playing, the bow and violin held in one hand.

"Another curious one!" He laughed as Sabina appeared on the landing. "Sheridan, we have a guest!"

Sabina whirled around to see Sheridan sitting in the loft, the Venus pointed at Ulric. Then she saw Toby and made a move toward him.

"Sabina, destroy his violin!"

The command seemed slurred to him, a tape recording running at half-speed.

"Thane—"

"Destroy the instrument!"

Her gun was already out, and within the confines of the shop the explosion was deafening. But the aim was true, and the bullet hit the instrument squarely, shattering it to matchsticks.

"You believe that will stop me?" Ulric screamed. "Fools!"

"Thane, shoot! For God's sake kill him!"

He had a clear field of fire and could have mowed Ulric down with a single burst. Instead Sheridan moved the Venus aside. There was only one way to kill Ulric.

"Thane—"

When she saw him put the Venus aside, Sabina aimed at Ulric.

"Sabina, get the children out of here!"

The voice was horrible, grating, as though uttered by a serpent.

"The children, Sabina! Save the children!"

He was coming down the ladder, facing forward. Sabina screamed. There was nothing resembling a human face on Thane Sheridan.

"The children . . ." the thing whispered as it shambled past the children, some of whom were looking around themselves, their eyes sleepy but nonetheless open.

Sabina huddled them together and shepherded them to the landing.

"Go, go quickly."

"But I don't have clothes . . ." one of them whispered, and began to cry.

"Run, darlings, O dear God, run!"

Slowly, leaning up against the walls, they started to move down the staircase.

"Thane!"

But when she looked back, Sabina saw that he had disappeared . . . into something she could not describe, something that came to Leopold Ulric with its arms outstretched and seized him, crushing the virtuoso against its chest.

"No!" Ulric screamed. "I have paid! My demon has been given the sacrifice! Balavis, I call upon you . . . help me!"

318

In a voice that could only have been born in hell itself, the thing that had been Sheridan roared back its answer: "I am Asmodeus!"

It drew Ulric to itself and for an instant towered over him. Backing away down the stairs, Sabina heard Ulric's spine crack, then the ribs snap one by one.

"You are *mine!*"

The jaws of the beast opened, and a sheet of flame poured over Ulric, consuming him, then the creature. Sabina screamed once, then stumbled down the stairs, the inferno billowing out after her.

Chapter Twenty-three

Two days later

She remembered the events of that morning with an intense clarity. There were no shadows around the images. Not a single detail faded or was blurred. Later the doctor told her they had had to increase sedation to twice the dosage just to keep her unconscious.

But even that was no help. When Sabina at last opened her eyes, the images followed into the light.

She was standing in the street, facing the door which opened to the staircase. Except that the steps could no longer be seen. Beyond the door was a solid wall of fire.

The crying of the children broke through the incomprehensible horror which mesmerized her. She ran to the car, wrenched open the door, and quickly bundled the children inside. From the emergency kit in the trunk she brought out a blanket and covered their nakedness as best she could. Then she started the engine and threw the heater to maximum.

"Mom . . ."

She heard her son's voice, the shivering plea which at any other time she would have responded to instantly. But not now. The fire had burst through the roof, and flames were shooting into the gray morning. The steadily falling snow had no effect upon them.

"Thane . . ."

He was gone, lost to her forever, consumed by something she had seen but could not believe existed. This realization broke what was left of her strength. Sabina's head fell forward onto her hands, the fingers curled around the wheel, and she sobbed quietly, without shame, without pause. That was how the fire and rescue units found her a few minutes later.

"Are you feeling a little better?"

Mr. Bill was standing at the foot of the bed. The raised eyebrows formed two precise horizontal lines across his forehead.

"Yeah, I guess so . . . The children?" Sabina struggled to sit up, pushing the pillows against her back.

"They're in the next ward. The Mackenzie boy and two others have lost a lot of strength. They'll be kept here for a week or ten days. Something to do with physiotherapy, I'm told. The others can go home anytime."

"Do they remember anything?" Sabina asked.

"Not a thing." Mr. Bill shrugged. "I sat in on a hypnosis session with the Grafstein twins—nothing."

"Better that way," Sabina murmured. She bit her lip and looked away. She had to ask.

"Thane?"

Mr. Bill hesitated. "The workshop—hell, the entire building—burned right to the ground. There was nothing the fire department could do. We managed to identify Ulric by dental plates. As for Thane, there was nothing left. Absolutely nothing. The pathologist still can't believe that *everything* burned."

Sabina sensed that Mr. Bill was fishing. She changed the subject.

"What about the media?"

"No one's been able to get to the children," Mr. Bill said. "I've quarantined the entire floor. The parents tell me once the children come home, they'll be 'on vacation' for a few weeks, to let the hue and cry die down.

"As for what happened on Thompson Street, I've issued the following statement: Leopold Ulric, who had been a prime suspect in the Letelier killing, has been positively identified as the Rambler. The missing children were found in his presence. Two police officers, yourself and Thane, actually witnessed him bringing a child to the hideaway."

"And Augusta, she's dead—"

"A Doberman went berserk."

"The others—Abner, Jim, George, Andreas?"

"Hansen is in the hospital with a gunshot wound. George

322

Percy hit him accidentally while shooting at the dog. As for the others—" Mr. Bill shook his head. "What do we do with them, Sabina? We can't prosecute them on kidnapping charges, because we haven't the proof. As to their relationship to Ulric, he's dead and they're not talking. So there's not much to go on . . ."

The head of Special Investigations ran a hand over his silver-gray hair. Sabina had never seen indecision in Mr. Bill. He reached down and pulled out a padded courier envelope, the flaps sealed with red wax.

"Thane delivered this to me a couple of days ago," Mr. Bill said, staring at the packet as though willing to see through to its contents. "It's addressed to you. The seals are a nice touch." He hesitated. "You have my word that I haven't opened it."

He came forward and gently placed the package within her reach.

"As I say, there's not much to go on. Perhaps that's the best way to leave it. But you'll be the one to decide that. If you want to share what he left you, fine. If not . . ."

He let the words hang, watching as Sabina's fingers grazed the package, as though she were afraid it would burn her.

"Let me know," Mr. Bill said softly, and let himself out.

The letter was attached to the leather-bound volume by an elastic band. Sabina pulled it free and stared at the ancient tome, deciphering the German title. A shudder passed through her body, and suddenly she felt very cold. She pushed the volume away.

The letter had been typed on the old manual Sheridan had had on Thompson Street. She recognized the fat characters and telltale smudge marks. There was no date in the right-hand corner.

My dear Sabina,
    By now you must know that I am dead. I pray that you weren't at the workshop to witness what happened, but you must believe me when I say that in my death Ulric also died. He will never come back again, Sabina. He will never take any more children. I pray that your little boy and the others are all right. If God is merciful, they

323

won't remember anything of the nightmare forced upon them.

It is selfish of me to reach out to you like this, but no man wants to die alone, without someone knowing, caring. This, then, is how it all came about. . . .

I suspected a relationship between Augusta Morell and Ulric right from the beginning. You see, I had long ago abandoned the idea that I could deal with Ulric as with any other subject. Policemen are trained to work with reality, objective facts, concrete evidence. This could not be the case here. Your aunt was involved because of what happened to Otto Morell and Rachel Rosenberg.

In each city the kidnappings were preceded by a ritual murder. This killing was the opening of the door, the invitation for Ulric to come in, the first sacrifice to him. I don't know who it was who actually took Rachel from the NSDM that day. I suspect Levine. But it couldn't have been your uncle . . . not with the cast on his foot. Nevertheless, Rachel was delivered unto him, and he was the one to bring her to Ulric.

Now you must take a leap of faith, because what follows is beyond the rational scheme of things.

I knew that Ulric was not a human being as you or I. I knew he was the manifestation of a force. In the drawer of Otto Morell's parson's desk I discovered the key by which your uncle summoned Ulric.

The Book of Old Ways was only rumored to exist. In all my research into the occult I only came across references to it. The single thread of continuity throughout the ages was this: as in Jewish folklore, where there are the Just Men, who bear on their shoulders the ills of their world and who, through their goodness, keep evil at bay, so too there exist in all times men with special powers, magicians, conjurors, men versed in the arcane arts. Your uncle was such a man. And that he was the keeper of *The Book of Old Ways* means to me that he was the most powerful of all these men. It is possible that he was responsible for bringing Ulric to other cities, acting as the intermediary between this world and the one Ulric inhabited.

And what of Ulric? Before reading the *Book* I could only speculate, try to put pieces together from other, inadequate sources. The *Book* told me what I had to know to destroy him.

You see, Ulric is truly a servant of the demon whose name is Balavis. In the hierarchy of hell Balavis is a powerful fiend, charged with the corruption of souls. Ulric wasn't lying to me when he said he had walked this earth from time immemorial. Throughout the ages he has been known as many things. Various names have been ascribed to him—for example, the Pied Piper of Hamelin. He has carved out for himself a definite persona as the unearthly power which, in return for souls, will perform evil on behalf of those who sacrifice to him.

When I read the *Book,* I came to understand that Ulric could not be killed. Not by bullets or knives or bare hands. *The source of his power had to be murdered:* the demon Balavis. There was only one way to do this.

Sabina's eyes slid off the pages. She did not want to read further. She knew now how Sheridan had killed Ulric. All the same she continued.

Sabina, I believe in the power of evil as surely as I do in the power of goodness. I respect it because I've seen it work firsthand. To destroy Ulric—and he *has* to be destroyed—I knew I had to appeal to a demon more powerful than his own. As you read this I have already pledged myself to Asmodeus, the demon of destruction. I have given him my blood, and he is satisfied with me. When the time comes, he will be by my side. Ulric and Balavis will be destroyed in the same instant. . . .

I am very much afraid now, Sabina. I feel as though I've already passed away from this world. I feel dirty and polluted. Yet there is no other way. Ulric must be stopped. No harm can come to the children he's taken.

God, I can't go on! Sabina, may God bless you and look after you always! Know that I love you and . . . and I ask you to do one last thing for me . . .

Sabina reread Sheridan's letter. She cried as the words

burned into her memory, but she would not stop. When she finished, she reached for the telephone and dialed out. Sheridan's last wish was so easy to grant.

Sabina sat back in the bed, looking down at the *Book*, remembering the words of his postscript:

The *Book* is yours now. I suppose it was technically Otto's property, so it belongs to you. You must destroy the *Book*, Sabina. We have no need of it. People like Abner Levine, Jim Hansen, George Percy, Andreas Marcovici—they are all decent men. Frightened, bewildered, unable to understand what is happening to them. I don't believe we can condemn them because they succumbed to the temptation to take the easy way out. Who can say you or I wouldn't, at some point, have done the same? But there is no reason for the temptation to continue to exist. Destroy the *Book*, Sabina, and with it the keys to hell. . . .

At that moment the nurse entered to announce her visitors. Sabina asked her to tell them to wait and went into the bathroom to wash her face.

"Come in."

Rabbi Schecter entered first, his face mirroring concern and curiosity. Edna and Abraham Rosenberg followed.

"Please come closer."

When they were beside the bed, Sabina looked at Rosenberg and said, "Mr. Rosenberg, your daughter's murderer is dead. My partner, Thane Sheridan, died killing him. I beg you to believe this is true."

At first there was no reaction in the sad vacant eyes. Then slowly the tears formed and trickled down the ancient cheeks. The self-imposed silence was broken by two trembling words.

"Thank you!"

After they left, she gazed at the *Book* lying on the starched white sheets. Calmly she picked it up and, opening the closet, shoved it deep into her handbag. As Thane had said, the *Book* belonged to her now.

Epilogue

From the journal of the scholar Gotha, forty years later

I departed from Hamelin that same morning, the twenty-third day of June in the year of our Lord 1376. After leaving the mayor's council room I ran to my house and quickly packed whatever clothing was at hand. I did not know where I would travel or for how long. . . . No, that is incorrect. I would follow the Piper wherever he went, to discover what it was he intended to do with the children the mayor and corporation had rendered up to him. I understood that I could not challenge the Piper or interfere in any way. His power was beyond my comprehension and my ability to deflect it. I, who had seen it firsthand, had no illusions.

As it happened my journey lasted no more than three days. The Piper led the children up along the banks of the Weser to where it emptied into a lake whose name I was unfamiliar with. He skirted the edge of the shore, the children always in his wake, singing and dancing. It was a chilling sight to watch children frolic hour after hour, without pause, drawing an inhuman energy from that cursed instrument. It was only with the greatest difficulty that I managed to keep pace with them. As I think back on it perhaps I too had become possessed by the notes.

After a day and a half of travel the Piper came to the Redoubt, a formidable range that forms a natural barrier between Brunswick and her sister state. In truth I swore he could go no farther. I had learned so little. . . .

The Piper came to the face of the cliff and directed his music at the rock. Instantly the face of the mountain trembled, and a cave appeared where there had been nothing but stone. The Piper wove his instrument to and fro, guiding the children inside. No sooner had they disappeared than he too backed into the cave. I swear that as the rock moved to seal them in the Piper stared at me and laughed. . . .

Upon my return to Hamelin I was told that six children had disappeared, presumably drowned, in the course of Saint Simon's feast day. From all accounts the parents accepted such a verdict, their guilt for their drunken behavior, which had led them to ignore their children's actions, silencing any questions they might have had.

Nor, curiously enough, was there any mention of the Piper among the townspeople. No statue was erected in his honor, no holiday proclaimed in his name. It was as though people carefully walked around the fact of his existence, unwilling to admit to it yet by that very silence acknowledging it.

For my part I too made no mention of that obscene creature nor of the devilish bargain he had struck. But the image of the Piper did not leave me from that day on. Although Hamelin remained my home, for the next forty years I traveled far and wide, always seeking clues as to what might have happened to our children. I pursued every legend, every folktale, every romantic ballad. There is one more story left to explore, but I am too old now, tired and disappointed. Still, the fable intrigues me. . . . It seems that in the land of Transylvania a strange race of subterranean creatures has been observed. They speak in unknown tongues and dress in odd patchwork rags. It is also said that they venture out only at night, and that a haunting music accompanies them, paralyzing their human victims, upon whom they delight in feeding. . . .

JOHN SAUL

SUFFER THE CHILDREN

One hundred years ago in Port Arbello a pretty little girl began to scream. And struggle. And die. No one heard. No one saw. Just one man whose guilty heart burst in pain as he dashed himself to death in the sea . . .

Now something peculiar is happening in Port Arbello. The children are disappearing, one by one. An evil history is repeating itself. And one strange, terrified child has ended her silence with a scream that began a hundred years ago.

A Royal Mail service in association with the Book Marketing Council & The Booksellers Association.

Post·A·Book is a Post Office trademark.

ALSO AVAILABLE FROM CORONET

KEN EULO

☐	26668 6	The Brownstone	£1.50
☐	28069 7	The Bloodstone	£1.75
☐	33964 0	The Deathstone	£1.95

JOHN SAUL

☐	22687 0	Suffer The Children	£1.95
☐	25548 X	Cry For The Strangers	£1.95
☐	28107 3	When The Wind Blows	£1.95
☐	25864 0	Punish The Sinners	£1.95
☐	32058 3	Comes The Blind Fury	£1.95

All these books are available at your local bookshop or newsagent, or can be ordered direct from the publisher. Just tick the titles you want and fill in the form below.

Prices and availability subject to change without notice.

CORONET BOOKS, P.O. Box 11, Falmouth, Cornwall.

Please send cheque or postal order, and allow the following for postage and packing:

U.K.—50p for one book, plus 20p for the second book, and 14p for each additional book ordered up to a £1.63 maximum.

B.F.P.O. and EIRE—50p for the first book, plus 20p for the second book, and 14p per copy for the next 7 books, 8p per book thereafter.

OTHER OVERSEAS CUSTOMERS—75p for the first book, plus 21p per copy for each attitional book.

Name ....

Address...

....